Dear Reader:

How many secrets do you hope and pray will follow you to your grave? How many secrets do you wish would hurry up and come out so that you do not have to run from them any longer? There is always a thin line when it comes to secrets; some would be better off buried and others need to be set free. Mimi has a nineteen-year-old secret that threatens to destroy everyone around her, including herself. After making sacrifice after sacrifice to protect the feelings of others, there comes a point when Mimi has run out of options and everything comes to light.

Betrayed by Suzetta Perkins is a novel about broken promises, dysfunctional families, and strained friendships. It is amazing how fleeing mistakes can alter a lifetime. We all have those rare memories where we wish that we could turn back the clock and do things over again. Perkins does a remarkable job of making one think: *What if?* As always, Perkins storytelling is captivating, brilliant, and engrossing. She never disappoints when it comes to spinning realistic tales of life's greatest and most painful moments.

Thanks for supporting all of the Strebor Books authors. You can contact me directly at zane@ericanoir.com and find me on Twitter @planetzane, and on Facebook at www.facebook.com/AuthorZane.

Blessings,

Zane

Zane
Publisher
Strebor Books
www.simonandschuster.com

ZANE PRESENTS

BETRAYED

ZANE PRESENTS

BETRAYED

Suzetta Perkins

SBI

STREBOR BOOKS

NEW YORK LONDON TORONTO SYDNEY

Strebor Books
P.O. Box 6505
Largo, MD 20792
http://www.streborbooks.com

This book is a work of fiction. Names, characters, places and
incidents are products of the author's imagination or are used
fictitiously. Any resemblance to actual events or locales or
persons, living or dead, is entirely coincidental.

ISBN 978-1-59309-363-1
ISBN 978-1-4516-1837-2 (e-book)
LCCN 2011928044

First Strebor Books trade paperback edition September 2011

Cover design: www.mariondesigns.com
Cover photograph: © Keith Saunders/Marion Designs

10 9 8 7 6 5 4 3 2 1

Manufactured in the United States of America

For information regarding special discounts for bulk purchases,
please contact Simon & Schuster Special Sales at 1-866-506-1949
or business@simonandschuster.com

The Simon & Schuster Speakers Bureau can bring authors to your
live event. For more information or to book an event, contact the
Simon & Schuster Speakers Bureau at 1-866-248-3049 or visit our
website at www.simonspeakers.com.

To all Fayetteville State University Alums
For memories made
Some to forget and others to hold in our hearts for a lifetime.
Bronco Pride

represent my character, Angelica, to the wonderful discussion, lunch, and book signing, it was a perfect day. To my sistahs in Danville, Virginia, the Round Table Literary Club—LaSheera, Tora, Vanessa, Twozynn, Roxanne, Tonya, Katina, Hannah, Taffene, and JaShaun: what a time, what a time, what a time. I had a knockdown, drag-out wonderful good time, so much so I didn't want to go back to North Carolina. Each one of you are worth a book unto yourself. And to my sistahs in Jackson, Mississippi, All That Jazz and Circle of Color Book Clubs, you made me feel like a *Queen*. You embraced me, fed me, showered me with gifts, and chauffeured me all over the city and showed me what real love felt like. I'd like to give an extra shout-out to Barbara Williams, Margaret Bullocks-Matory, and Vanessa Wilson; you went over, above, and beyond anything I expected. A big hug to Emma, Yvonne, and Felisha. And to my sister-girl, Angela Moore, thank you for showing me Jackson by way of the side trip to the hood to get some finger-licking E & L barbeque ribs. Last, but not least, I thank Pat Mendinghall and the Sisters Unlimited Book Club in Fayetteville, North Carolina for loving me and saving a spot on their book club read list for me again. Your beautifully laid table, the unlimited glasses of wine, the great book discussion, and the good conversation was more than enough. However, surprising me with the presence of my dear friend, Sherry, who flew all the way from Detroit to be with us, was priceless.

A book can't exist without the publisher who invests time and money to give an author voice. Zane and Charmaine, I appreciate you, Strebor Books, from the bottom of my heart for your continued support of my work. My endeavor is to always give the reader a good story and you've allowed me to do so. It's a unique experience to be part of the great Strebor family.

To my agent, Maxine Thompson, you are a jewel. I appreciate you because not only are you a hustler, but you believe in me...my work and understand my passion. I promise to move on some of those promotion strategies we discussed.

I'd like to end with a salute to you, my readership. Writing is my passion, but you give my passion wings. Your email that encourages me to write "the sequel" is the best form of flattery. I have stories waiting to get out, although, as my dear friend, Juanita Pilgrim tells me, I'm not moving fast enough. But I will get them out. I appreciate the two-page list of things that should be in the next book, Saundra Shorter. Emily Dickens, I appreciate the candid conversations we had about the characters as if they were real people. First Lady, Nancy Anderson, thank you for your unwavering support. LaWanda Miller, thanks for the cheerleading chants, and Mary Farmer, thanks for being my friend. Karen Brown, congratulations in advance because your book is about to be born.

September 27, 2008

I don't believe in fairy tales or happily ever after. It's not possible because I have a deep dark secret concealed in the bowels of my being, threatening to explode and expose what I've taken pains to keep hidden for the last nineteen years. There's no need to try and figure it out since there's nothing about me... nothing that I've said or done over the years that would betray my secret. That's what I want to believe, but the truth is, there was always a chance I'd be exposed...that the truth would be revealed.

The only reason I'm saying anything at all is...I'm afraid. My days may be numbered...maybe weeks away from discovery. I'm afraid that all I hold dear will suddenly vanish from my grasp. Scorn me. Point an accusing finger at me. Look at me in disgust and write me completely out of the lives of those I love dearly.

In the event something happens to me, I want Raphael and Afrika Nicole to know that all I've done was to protect them. My thoughts are premature, but going back to a place where I have no desire to go frightens me. And if I have to, I'll fight the demons that may threaten to smear my good name.

My name? My friends call me Mimi, although it has nothing

to do with my real name, Setrina. Mimi was bestowed upon me by my best friend, Brenda. I like to sing and run up and down the scales like I'm Aretha or somebody. But the truth of the matter is I haven't sung many songs, despite attempts by big record companies to make me a star because they happened to be in the one place I decided to let my hair down. I turned them down; exposure would certainly put me in the limelight and attention is the last thing I want.

Wow, I haven't said Brenda's name in years. Reason being, she's part of the secret or should I say...one of the reasons I have a secret at all. Actually, I never expect to see her again.

Mimi Bailey

1

Mimi sat in the kitchen at the round glass table inset in black marble atop black wrought-iron legs and re-read the entry in her brand new journal. Satisfied, she closed the cover and pulled the book to her chest, reliving in her mind the conversation she'd had a few days ago with her daughter. For nineteen years she had managed to bury and keep a secret hidden and safe, and now the decision to return to Durham, North Carolina, against her better judgment, could possibly make her nightmare a reality.

Unpacked boxes littered the hallway of her new, two-story, two-bedroom condo positioned on a lake. The newness still hung in the air like a home that had been ravaged by fire; only it was the smell of freshly painted walls and new carpet instead of burnt wood.

Mimi sat up straight at the sound of voices at the front door. "Hey, Mommy," Afrika shouted. "I brought home my new friend that I was telling you about."

Looking for a place to hide the journal, Mimi jumped up from her seat and pulled out a drawer that she had unconsciously labeled junk, and threw the book in it.

She turned around and stared into the face of her daughter and another young lady who looked much like Afrika.

Mimi's eyes jutted from their sockets and lit up like lights on a Christmas tree as she gazed at what appeared to be a clone of her daughter. She held onto the kitchen counter with her hands for support, her back up against it, afraid to let go for fear that she'd faint.

Mimi closed her eyes for a second and, in her subconscious, saw the man who had torn away her clothes and violated her, leaving her humiliated and broken.

Afrika laughed and snapped her fingers. Mimi opened her eyes. "Mommy, what's wrong with you? You look like you've seen a ghost."

"Nothing. Nothing at all."

"Mommy, are you sure? Don't get all weird on me."

"Yeah, yeah!" Mimi couldn't take her eyes away from Afrika's friend.

"Well, this is Asia; the friend I've been telling you about."

"Asia?" Mimi mimicked. "Oh, my God."

"I know," Asia began. "People say that Nikki and I could pass for twins."

"Twins," Mimi said under her breath. Slapping her hands on her hips, Mimi leaned to one side and looked at Afrika. "So you're going by Nikki, now?"

Afrika always liked to be called by her first name. Prior to coming to Durham, all of her friends called her that.

"Your name is not Nikki?" Asia asked.

"Nikki is short for Nicole, but it's my middle name.

Now, Mommy, please. I want to be called by my nickname, if you don't mind. As Asia was saying, we're known as the freshmen twins."

Asia continued, "Everyone freaks out when we tell them that we only met a few weeks ago."

"You and Afri...ah, ah Nikki are twins, they say. I must apologize for staring. Ah, Nikki," Mimi looked at Afrika to confirm that she had chosen the right name, "told me about this wonderful person she had become friends with and had so much in common with. I just didn't know how 'in common.'"

"I'm a little darker than Asia, but our hair is about the same length and we wear it in a ponytail. We're about the same height, and we both love pizza," Afrika said all in one breath. "But, Mommy, you won't believe this. We both had a sixth finger that was taken off."

Mimi's tongue stuck to the roof of her mouth and refused to open.

"Mommy, what's up with you? Did you hear what I just said?"

"Afr...Nikki, I heard you. I'm shocked; that's all," Mimi said, not venturing to look at Asia. She wanted to run as fast as her legs would take her. It was a mistake, coming back to Durham. Her husband had begged her to go to Germany with him, but it was Afrika's desire to go a Historically Black College—North Carolina Central, to be exact. Mimi didn't want to hear anything else—nothing about what Afrika and Asia had in common and in particular, who Asia's parents were. She held her heart until she felt Afrika shaking her.

"Mommy, what's wrong? You're acting so strange. Should I call Daddy?"

"No," Mimi said, catching her breath and really taking a good look at Asia this time. "Ladies, forgive me. I'm a little stressed out with all the moving. I'm going to make an appointment soon to make sure I'm all right."

"I'm going to call Daddy," Afrika said, full of concern.

"No, no, that won't be necessary. All your father will do is worry."

"My dad is in the Army," Afrika explained to Asia. "It's his last tour of duty, and he wanted Mommy to go with him. But you know how mothers are. Mine followed me to Durham so that I would have someone close by, if I needed anything."

"Where did you come from?" Asia asked.

"Fort Riley, Kansas. My dad was stationed there, but I'm glad to be in a big city. We had to drive either to Topeka or Kansas City to experience the life of a big city."

"My parents, my brother, and I have lived in Durham all of my life," Asia explained. "But my grandfather was in the military, and he and my grandmother lived in Germany once."

"So did my grandparents," Afrika said. "Wow, another coincidence."

"It's a small world," Mimi finally said.

"I stopped by so Asia could meet you, Mommy. I was

hoping that you would be up to going out to lunch. I told Asia what a cool mom I had—that you were fun to hang out with, that you loved shopping, and that you were the life of a party and could sing your ass off. Oops...I mean, can sing your butt off."

Mimi smiled.

"Yeah, you're going to have to hang with us one Saturday, Mrs. Bailey," Asia said. "Maybe do some karaoke. And I want you to meet my parents."

Mimi fixed her face so the fear that seemed to encompass her body wouldn't show. She didn't know what it was, but it was more than a premonition. If anything, the cause of her fear was standing in front of her. No facts to prove anything, but it didn't seem to be a case of mistaken identity.

With a smile on her face, Mimi patted the two girls on their backs. "I'd love to hang out with the two of you one Saturday. Just give Mommy some advance notice, ah, Nikki."

"Great, Mommy."

"And don't forget; I want you to meet my parents," Asia said again.

"Okay, okay," Mimi said with less conviction as she wiped her brow with her fingers. "I'll do that."

She kissed Afrika and gave Asia a hug goodbye. *If your parents are whom I think they are*, Mimi thought to herself, *I have no plans to ever meet them.*

She watched as Afrika drove off. Then a terrible thought

lit up her mind like an unexpected lightning bolt that splintered the sky. What if Asia took Afrika to meet her parents? Would the same thoughts cross their minds that had crossed hers when they saw Afrika?

"My God, I have to warn Afrika," Mimi said out loud. But to warn her would require Mimi to give Afrika an explanation. What would she say?

The devil was definitely busy and conspiring to wreak havoc on her life; although she hadn't been in Durham a good month. At any cost, she was going to shield her child from the threat that might possibly expose her secret that had the potential to be a tabloid size story, even if it meant giving up the $300,000 condo she had yet to completely furnish. Mimi pulled her journal from its hiding place and began to write again. She ended with "Afrika must never find out." Signed Mimi Bailey.

2

"Your mom was real tense," Asia said to Afrika, as they drove down Fayetteville Street heading back to their dorm. "Maybe you should call your dad, in case something is really wrong with her."

"You're right," Afrika said. "I can't figure out why she was acting so strange, and I don't know what I'd do without Mommy, if something happened to her. She's devoted her entire life to me—to make sure I had the things I needed. Even when she protested my going to Central, she gave in with some reservations, and instead of going to Germany with Daddy, she came here so that she would be available to support me whenever I needed. My mom was once offered a recording contract by Clive Davis of Arista Records."

"You mean the guy who made Whitney Houston a household icon?"

"Yep, one and the same."

"Oh, my God, Nikki! That's so exciting. Why didn't your mother sign?"

"I was seven at the time, but according to my grandma, Mommy said she couldn't subject her daughter to the life of a recording artist and she was obligated to be there for her husband and his military career."

"No offense, Nikki, but that sounds like a cop out. Maybe your mother was scared. Did she live a sheltered life?"

"No, my grandparents were and are still very outgoing. They lived for my mom. In fact, they encouraged my mother to sign the contract so she could live her dream."

"What about your dad?"

"I don't think he was as excited about it, according to my grandma. At the time, my dad was a young Army officer barely starting his career, and he understood what the recording industry was like since one of his close cousins was a rapper. But Grandma said Daddy would've let my mom sign, if she really wanted to. So I chalk it up to her being afraid. Maybe it was even out of her comfort zone. But at church, if someone asked Mommy to sing for a big event, girlfriend, she would throw down. I wonder if she regrets not signing that contract."

"Maybe we can get your mom to sing at a campus function."

"That's not a bad idea."

"If you don't mind, Nikki, let's stop by my house so I can introduce you to my parents. I'd love to see their faces when they see you; although, I've told them all about you."

"I guess seeing is believing."

"They're going to do a double take like your mother. You may have already seen my father."

"How so?"

"He works in the Admissions Office on campus. In fact, he's the director. You couldn't miss him. He's kinda handsome, if I do say so myself. I hear what some of those wild bitches say about him."

"Well, I haven't seen any fine, sexy man on campus, let alone at the Admissions Office. Call and see if your parents are at home."

Asia pulled her cell phone out of her purse and dialed her parents' number. Just when she was about to hang up, someone answered on the fourth ring. "Trevor, that you?"

"Hey, Asia; what's up, sis? How's college? Momma's going to give me your room."

"Hold up, Trevor. Stop talking crazy and telling lies on Momma. Ain't no way you and your stanky gym shoes smelling self is going to find a way into my room. Not even in your dreams, boy."

"Ask Momma. Get out of here!!" Trevor suddenly screamed.

"What's up with you, Trevor?"

"Meow."

"Beyonce pounced on my bed. I would've killed that cat a long time ago if Momma wasn't going to kill me afterwards. Who names a stupid cat Beyonce?"

"Whatever. Put Momma on the phone so she can tell me what a liar you are."

"Hmph, you're gonna have to wait because Momma is at the beauty shop getting her hair done and Dad's on campus."

"A'ight. Don't let me come home and find your crusty butt in my room. I don't want to have to do a Chris Brown on you."

"That's wrong, Asia. Chris didn't mean to hit Rihanna."

"Whatever. I'm out." *Click.* Asia put her cell phone away. The girls laughed.

"I can't wait to meet your brother," Afrika said.

"He's a trip but we're closer than close. Remind me to pick up a present for him. His birthday is next Friday. He graduates from high school next year, and I'm sure he's going to come to Central since both my parents are alums."

"Really? My mother also went to Central, but she left after her first year. I don't know why. She transferred to Hampton University, which is where she met my dad before he joined the Army as a Lieutenant. Asia, our lives have so many parallels."

"It's scary, isn't it?"

"Since we're about the same age, maybe our parents' paths crossed. When is your birthday?"

"December sixteenth," Afrika said proudly.

"Nikki, you won't believe this."

"Don't tell me your birthday is on the same day as mine. If it is, I'd have to wonder whether or not one of us was adopted. Because that would truly mean we are twins."

"No," Asia started. "How about ten days younger than you? I was born the day after Christmas. That means our mothers were pregnant at the same time."

Afrika remained quiet as she sat at the stoplight. She reflected on her mother's reaction when she saw Asia earlier. For some unknown reason, seeing Asia was like a trigger...a reminder of something her mother wanted to forget. The way she acted, someone would've thought she was on the verge of having a nervous breakdown. Or was it all an act?

"Earth to Nikki."

"Sorry, girl. I was in another world."

"Obviously."

"You were saying that your birthday was..."

"Ten days after yours."

"Well, that proves that we were meant to be best friends; sisters."

"I don't know about you, Nikki, but my freshman year is going to be on. I've got a great new best friend, we're both on the cheerleading squad, and all that's left is to find the man of my dreams like my mom did her freshman year."

"I'm going to concentrate on my studies. I'm going to be a stock broker on Wall Street."

"Sister CEO. Finally, there's something we don't have in common," Asia said. "I say go for yours. My mother didn't get her degree right away because she was pregnant with me, and at first aspired to do nothing but be a mom and nurture me. But she did go back to school after a year off and studied hard. She's a psychologist, analyzing everything that doesn't make sense to her. My mom is also a life coach. It's big business, and she has a high-profile clientele. It wasn't until later in her life that she found her real niche."

"What is that?"

"She's a genealogy specialist and loves getting families together. You have to attend one of our family reunions. They're big events; especially since my mom found relatives we didn't know we had from every corner of the globe. She's like a bird picking worms out of the ground after a good rain."

"I definitely want to meet your mom."

"I'll check to see when she gets home. Maybe we can run over there later."

"Just let me know."

3

Mimi unpacked a few boxes that contained her porcelain figurines. She gently unwrapped the packing material from around each piece and carefully sat them on the built-in shelf in her living room. Opening another box, she pulled out a family picture of her, Raphael, and Afrika when she was five years old.

They were an attractive family—Afrika, in her long, curly pigtails and candy apple ribbon that matched her taffeta dress, Raphael, in his Army dress blues, and her, in her favorite Jones New York suit. They were the perfect family and their lives were full and prosperous. Mimi's husband made full bird, Colonel, two years ago and the other love of her life was now in college.

She remembered the day she met Raphael. It was blazing hot, and she had only been in Hampton a few days. With a baby growing inside her womb, Mimi decided to go to summer school so that she wouldn't get behind when the baby came.

She strolled onto Hampton's campus to register, and coming out of the cashier's office was the most handsome man that she'd ever seen. Mimi could tell he lifted weights;

he had muscles that not only popped from underneath his cotton shirt but the rest of his body as well. He was tall, but not too tall that she couldn't reach up and put her arms around his neck and swap kisses with him in her dreams. He had a thick head of cold, wavy, black hair. She didn't want him to catch her looking at him, but when she came out of the admissions office, he was standing off to the side like he was waiting for somebody. What she didn't know was that he was waiting on her— maybe to make her acquaintance or get a sandwich and a cold drink at the student lounge. Mimi looked at the picture again. She smiled. Besides the sandwich and cold drink, she gave herself to Raphael on the first day they met. In her heart of hearts, she knew he was going to be her husband.

On the marble mantle above the fireplace that separated the living area from the ultra modern kitchen with its black and white decor, Mimi sat the picture. Before taking her hand away, she glanced back at the picture, brushing Afrika's face as if it were flesh, then focused on her eyes, imagining that there were two of them. Someone once said that each person had a twin in the world, but the likeness of Asia to her own daughter was too uncanny.

Mimi dismissed her thoughts and finished unpacking. She stacked the empty cartons out back in the storage area in a corner. She glanced around, measuring with her eyes to see if she'd have enough space to place a few more things she wanted to store. In doing so, she saw a red book that occupied a corner all by itself. Mimi picked up the telephone book and thumbed through the pages, finally deciding to take it inside the house.

With the book in her hand, Mimi plopped down on the suede couch, one of the few things she had bought for the house, and put her feet up under her. She lifted the cover and fingered the first few pages, finally getting up enough courage to flip to the white pages. She looked at it and allowed her eyes to slowly scan the page as her fingers did a slow crawl, serving as a guide. When she neared the "Ch's," she abruptly pulled her finger out of the book and slammed it shut.

Mimi threw the phone book down and ran up the stairs to her bedroom and closed the door. No one could calm her nerves like Raphael. She reached for the phone and dialed the country code for Germany but set the phone down after thinking better of it.

Mimi laid across her four-poster white bed in a fetal position. The peach-colored walls with white trim soothed the tension she felt. Moments later, Mimi's eyelids were limp and sleep overtook her.

Instead of blacking out, she was consumed by a dream that had manifested itself many times before over the last nineteen years. Her eyelids fluttered as she imagined a medium brown, medium height woman emerge from a shadow and knock on a door. She was dressed in a white, loose-fitting cotton blouse with a red camisole underneath and blue leggings. A man opened the door, dressed in only a pair of sweatpants, his chest bare, and pulled the woman inside, closing the door behind him. She tried to leave, but the man blocked the door.

His breath smelled like a refinery; he was obviously drunk. There was small talk and then an argument ensued. There was lots of yelling, shouting, and pointing fingers. And as if the man had superhero strength, he picked up the woman and threw her on the sofa. He tore away her clothes like a savage beast and pulled down his pants and...

Huffing and puffing, Mimi jerked up, swinging her arms wildly with sweat covering her face before finally stopping to stare at nothing in particular. She grabbed her heart, crossed her arms over her chest, finally lifting her legs over the side of the bed in attempt to keep from shaking.

Mimi eased off the bed, stood up, and walked slowly to the bathroom like she was a mummy or high on drugs. She gasped at the sight of herself.

"Okay, Mimi," she said out loud, rinsing her face and blotting it with a cold cloth. "Pull yourself together, girl. You're making more out of this than there is. You're imagining things. Afrika is going...is going..."

Mimi rushed from the bathroom, ran downstairs, and grabbed her BlackBerry. "I'll send her a text. Yeah, that's what I'll do."

A, this is Mommy. I really like Asia; she seems like a very nice girl. I'm not trying to alarm you, but be careful about getting too involved with her and her family. Take some time to meet other kids instead of having one exclusive friend. Love you. Mommy.

Looking over the message one more time, Mimi nodded her head in approval and pressed SEND.

It was almost as if Afrika had been sitting at the other end waiting for Mimi's text. In under a minute, Mimi received a reply from Afrika.

What's up with you, Mommy? You're acting weird. I really like Asia. You have nothing to worry about. Love, A.

Maybe it was the quiet in the room that sent chills down Mimi's spine, but Afrika's diss in her text message made her shiver. "Afrika," Mimi said out loud, "Mommy knows best." She needed proof, but in the meantime, Mimi had to protect Afrika at all costs. Mimi typed another message, looked at it, and hit the CANCEL button.

4

"Hey, Asia. Where are you?" Afrika asked as she let her back-pack drop from her shoulders to the floor of her dorm room, while she held onto her cell phone.

"Hey, girl, I'm at the dining hall. I was famished and came straight from class with some of the other girls on the squad. Hurry up; I'll wait for you."

"Okay. I'll be right over after I pee."

The dorm suite was home to eight girls. There were two persons to a room, and they all shared a kitchenette that housed a refrigerator, a small stove, and a three-seater sofa and one chair. Afrika and Asia lived in separate suites but down the hall. Afrika liked her roommate, but she and Asia had more in common.

Afrika packed her books for her remaining classes. She took one last look in the mirror, smoothed down the edges of her hair, swished her ponytail, sucked her teeth, and winked at herself. Glancing around the room, she seemed satisfied that she had all she needed.

The sun was high overhead. Students strolled across campus, eager to get a bite to eat or head to their next class. Even though school had been in session for a month,

Afrika was enjoying her freshman experience so far. She walked proudly as she made her way across campus.

"Asia," a male voice called. "Asia, Asia," the voice called out again when Afrika didn't stop. "Asia."

Afrika turned around, her ponytail slapping her in the face. A couple of feet away stood a handsome, middle-aged man, with thick black sideburns, closed-cropped brownish-black hair, wearing a red linen jacket, a red and white striped shirt accented by a white collar and cuffs, and black Hugo Boss slacks. Afrika smiled and then looked him up and down. She came to her senses when she realized the man was staring straight at her—through her.

Squinting, the gentleman pulled back his head, unsure that the young lady who stared back at him was who he thought. "Asia?"

"No, my name is Nikki."

"I'm sorry…I've mistaken you for my daughter. She resembles you a little."

"You mean, Asia?"

"Yes, do you know her?"

Afrika walked over to where the man stood. She had to agree with the talk on the yard that Asia's father was definitely fine. "Yes, I know Asia. We're on the cheerleading squad together. Everyone says we could pass for twins."

"Well, they say that everyone has a twin in the world. Excuse my manners. I'm Mr. Victor Christianson."

"Nice to meet you, Mr. Christianson. My mother says the same thing about having a double somewhere out there in the world."

"Is your mother from around here?" Victor asked, as he watched Afrika with renewed interest.

"We came here from Kansas. My dad is a Colonel in the Army and he just left for Germany. My mom moved to Durham to be close to me."

"Oh, I see. Well, it was nice meeting you, Nikki. If we can assist you in the Admissions Office, don't hesitate to stop by."

"Thank you, Mr. Christianson." Afrika waved goodbye.

Victor turned and walked in the opposite direction, but stopped, turned, and watched as Nikki walked away.

THE CROWD HAD DWINDLED IN THE CAFETERIA BY THE TIME Afrika reached it. She got a tray and headed for the pizza station. Her mother said she was going to turn into a tub of cheese if she didn't leave the pizza alone and start eating some vegetables. When it came to pizza, she wasn't discriminating—Domino's, Papa John's, Pizza Hut—you name it.

"Nikki," Asia called from across the room, waving her hand.

Afrika headed straight to the table and joined the group. "Asia, I met your dad a few minutes ago. I was on my way to the cafe when he called your name, thinking

I was you. You should have seen his face when I finally turned around."

"I bet he had the same look on his face that your mother had when she saw me."

"Shoot, he looked like he was having an out-of-body experience, the way he kept staring at me."

"It would be something if you were really sisters," Erika, the head cheerleader, said.

"I'm not adopted," Afrika said before Asia had a chance to speak.

"Neither am I," Asia added, looking at the group that now stared back at her. "It's a coincidence that we sort of have some of the same features. We're not twins, not sisters, and we're not adopted. So cool it."

Afrika nibbled on her pizza and allowed the others to continue with their conversation. This was the first time that she'd seen Asia become upset over the comparison between the two of them. She knew who she was...she was the daughter of Setrina and Raphael, and that was it.

Lost in her thoughts, Afrika put the pizza down and recalled the text her mother sent her. She pulled out her cell phone and looked at the message again. There was no rhyme or reason to the message. She shut the phone, picked up her pizza, and began to nibble on it again.

"Earth to Nikki," Asia said, now standing over her with tray in hand. "Girl, you aren't tripping about all that crazy talk about us being adopted, are you?"

"Hell no," Afrika said. "I know who I am and who my

parents are. After awhile, they'll be saying that the whole cheerleading squad is sisters since we wear the same makeup and the same hairstyle at all our games."

"You're right. After cheer practice, why don't we go to my house? My brother's birthday is today and I'm going to drop his gift off. My mom will probably have cake and ice cream. I'd go tomorrow, but since we have a football game and the Ques are giving the party of the year, Trevor won't see me tomorrow."

"I can't believe a week's gone by already since we went to my mom's house. I was supposed to remind you to get the present. Sorry, I forgot."

"Don't worry about it. My handy-dandy BlackBerry reminded me. So, are you up to going with me?"

"I don't know. I have a lot of homework to do, Asia."

"Nikki, this is Friday night. You have all day Sunday to do your homework."

"Well…

"What's there to think about? After practice?"

"Okay," Afrika relented, her mother's warning sounding an alarm in the pit of her stomach. "Okay."

5

"Hey, hey, hey. Do it Eagles. Do it Eagles. Do it Eagles. Eagles Do it. Hey, hey, hey. Heeeeey! Go Eagles!!"

"Good practice," the cheerleading coach announced. The squad that was fifteen strong kicked their legs and clapped their hands. "You all are dismissed."

Afrika and Asia picked up their gym bags and headed toward Asia's car. "Nikki, why are you dragging your feet?"

"I'm not sure I'm ready to meet your family."

"Look, Nikki. We are down to earth. We live life to the fullest and love to have fun."

"It's awfully late," Afrika said, offering another excuse.

"You wouldn't be saying that if we were going to one of those frat parties. Look, I'll drive extra slow, if that would make you feel better. I know how you feel about my driving. We have to go to Chapel Hill; so let's go."

"We're not going to a frat party, Asia. Meeting the parents is a whole different matter, but I'll go."

"I don't know what the big deal is; I just want to give Trevor his birthday present."

"Well, let's go."

Asia maneuvered her baby blue Toyota Camry down

Fayetteville Street and onto Interstate 40. Several exits later, Asia took the Chapel Hill off-ramp and headed toward the University of North Carolina at Chapel Hill.

Darkness made it hard to totally assess the neighborhood Asia had driven into, but from the little Afrika could see, she could tell that it was upscale with manicured lawns. Asia drove up into a long, circular driveway that ran parallel to the wrap-around porch with Boston ferns still hanging from their baskets, although it was mid-September. Light from the interior lit the house from the inside and motion sensor lights flooded the outside.

"We're here," Asia announced, jumping out of the car. "Come on, Nikki. Let's go say 'Happy Birthday' to Trevor."

Afrika slid out of the car and exhaled. Flashbacks of Asia's father staring at her like she'd been reincarnated and her mother's messages to be careful of getting too close to Asia's family made her feel ill-at-ease. She looked at the large, massive house and sighed.

"Come on, Nikki. What's taking you so long?"

"You forgot Trevor's gift in the back seat. I'll get it for you."

Afrika grabbed Trevor's gift, closed the car door, and walked to the front of the car where Asia stood. Asia put her arm through Afrika's. "Okay, girl, let's meet the folks."

For most of Afrika's life, she had lived in one military housing area or another. Although their quarters were befitting the officer that her father was, nothing had prepped her for the gorgeous, upscale dwelling that Asia and her family resided in. And according to Asia, her mother, Dr. Brenda Christianson, was doing quite well for herself and was often asked to provide retrospective insight on some subject related to her profession and some current economic crisis on a local news show.

The house was tri-level with wall-to-wall hardwood flooring covered with expensive Chinese rugs. The rooms were painted in light pastels to give it an airy feeling. The living room opened up to a cathedral ceiling with a balcony that connected some of the second-story rooms to the other. A large, spacious kitchen tiled in black and white sat in the center of the house and contained modern stainless steel appliances to include a state of the art industrial oven, a huge pantry, and more cabinet space than one could imagine. A long black and white granite counter that could serve as a table ran the length of the kitchen. The dining room mirrored the colors in the kitchen, with a table that sat ten and a china cabinet finished in highly polished black lacquer. A long hallway led from one side of the kitchen to a cabana that contained a large stainless steel grill and miniature fridge, and swank patio furniture in colors of orange and yellow that connected to a hot tub with stairs that dropped down to the swimming pool. On the lower level of the house was a large game room that housed a professional size pool table, jukebox, and popcorn machine that sat right outside of the theater room that housed thirteen velvet high-back seats and a large retractable screen and a projector.

Afrika's lip was still on the ground after her tour. The uneasiness she first felt had long since vanished; she felt right at home. And Trevor was just as crazy as Asia said he was; especially after he recovered from seeing his sister in double. Even the cat—Afrika hated cats—didn't understand what the fuss was all about and retreated to an undisclosed portion of the house.

"Where are Mom and Dad?" Asia asked Trevor. "I'm sure Mom baked a cake for your seventeenth birthday."

"Asia, please. I'm too old for birthday cake and ice cream. But I'll gladly accept that package over there that looks like my birthday present." Trevor walked to the table where Afrika had dropped his present and picked it up. He shook it this way and then that. "Sis, I hope this is my favorite pair of sneaks that I've been talking about all summer."

"You'll have to open it up and find out."

Trevor tore the paper from the oblong box. "Yeah, Mom and Dad went to some symposium at Duke that had to do with something Mom was working on."

"Oh," Asia said, with disappointment written all over her face.

After a second pause and a quick pull of the lid, a pair of Jordan sneakers fell out of the box. "I love you, Sis!" Trevor hollered, jumping around like he was a Mexican jumping bean. "You sho' hooked a brother up!"

"I aim to please," Asia said, while Afrika looked on.

"Well, Nikki, why don't we watch a movie and then head back to campus?"

"Works for me," Afrika said.

"Dang, I can't get over how much you two look alike," Trevor said, his eyes steadily shifting between Asia and Afrika. "You two look more alike than me and Asia."

"It's not that big of deal, Trevor," Asia said. "Everybody has a twin somewhere in this world. And, Nikki does look like you."

"No way," Trevor said. They laughed.

"Put a movie on, nut head," Asia said. The girls laughed again. "And turn off the lights."

Afrika felt even more at-ease. She settled back in the high-back chair and watched *Friday* with Ice Cube and Chris Tucker for the umpteenth time. Asia slapped her leg when the credits rolled onto the screen a couple of hours later.

"Let's go, girl. You can meet my parents another time."

Before Afrika could respond, the lights flicked on. Almost falling off their seats, three necks twirled around in unison. It was Michael Jackson's *Thriller* movie coming to life.

The fear that had gripped Afrika's body earlier returned. Asia's parents stood in the doorway and gazed at the trio, although their eyes were dedicated to Afrika. After an awkward silence, Asia's mother spoke.

"Happy Birthday, Trevor." His mother moved forward and kissed him.

"Come on, Mom. I'm too old for that."

"You'll always be my baby."

"Yeah, happy birthday, Trevor," Victor Christianson said.

"Thanks, Dad."

Brenda Christianson came and stood next to Afrika. "So, you're the new friend that Asia has been going on and on about."

Offering a warm smile, Afrika shook Brenda's hand. "It's nice to meet you, Mrs. Christianson. I'm Nikki. Asia talks about you both so much," she said, turning to include Victor.

Brenda Christianson smiled. "Her daddy and I are very proud. Well, other than you wearing your hair in a ponytail and being roughly the same height as Asia, I don't think you would pass for twins like Asia says people are saying. Asia is much lighter than you and she has a birthmark on her tummy. Do you have a birth-mark on your tummy? What do you think, Victor?"

"No, I don't have a birthmark," Afrika replied in a hurry. She wasn't sure she liked the way Asia's mother was interrogating her like their daughter was better than her. And she certainly didn't like the way they kept staring at her; especially Asia's father, like she was some kind of alien. Afrika thought about the sixth finger they both had in common but kept it to herself.

"Well, it was nice meeting you, Nikki," Brenda said and began to walk out of the room until she heard her husband speak.

"Nikki?" Asia's father inquired.

"Nikki Bailey. Nikki is my nickname, which I prefer to use. My full name is Afrika Nicole Bailey. People used to tease me when I was younger about my first name and by the time I was in the fifth grade, I had everyone calling me Nikki until I went to high school. Then it was Afrika again."

Brenda and Victor stopped in their tracks. Afrika hadn't noticed their discomfort because Asia started talking.

"Why didn't you tell me Afrika was your first name? It's so like mine. Another coincidence. I don't believe this. We're both named after continents."

"You guys are weird," Trevor said.

"I think it's too cool," Asia added, grabbing Afrika's arm.

Afrika and Asia headed for the door. "It was nice meeting you, Mr. and Mrs. Christianson," Afrika said, shaking their hands.

"It was nice meeting you, too, Nikki…Afrika," Brenda said, cutting an eye at her husband, who seemed to avoid eye contact. "Ah, Afrika, before you and Asia head off to campus, I'd like to ask you a question."

Afrika frowned at the tone of Brenda's voice. The longer she stayed in Asia's house, the more uncomfortable she became. She was sure that it was more than her mother's casual warning. She thought it odd that Mr. Christianson acted as if he had met her for the first time. "Yes, Mrs. Christianson?"

"Did your mother ever attend Central? I had a friend once; in fact we were best friends. I haven't seen her in over nineteen years." Brenda gave Afrika the once over again, and then continued. "Our fathers were both in the Army, and we were stationed in Europe at the same time—Germany, to be exact. Both of our fathers were reassigned to Ft. Bragg, which is where this friend of mine and I ended up. And when it was time to go to college, we went to North Carolina Central University together. But I don't know what happened to her. She vanished from sight at the end of our freshman year, and I never heard from her again. I was crushed for a long while."

Afrika glanced at Victor, who looked away. Something was not making any sense, but there wasn't any time to address it. "Yes, she did. Her name is Mimi."

Both Brenda and Victor gasped at the same time.

"You're Mimi's daughter?" Brenda asked. "Where is she? How can I get in touch with her? I can't believe that her daughter is standing in front of me in my house."

Asia and Trevor's eyes widened. They couldn't believe their ears.

"People said we were inseparable," Brenda continued. "We both said that if we had girls, I would name mine Asia and she'd name hers Afrika because we had travelled to so many places with our parents." Almost as if Brenda was in a trance, she kept going. "I gave her the nickname, Mimi, because she could sing like a bird and would sing up and down the scales like she was giving the performance of her life. Do you remember that, Victor?"

"Yeah, it was a long time ago."

"Look," Brenda said, "I'd like to see Mimi; talk to her. I don't believe it, after all of this time." Brenda paced the room. "Did you say where she was, Afrika?"

"She lives in Durham in a beautiful condo," Asia offered. "I've met her and she's really nice. Now I understand why she was acting strange when I said my name. She probably thought the same thing you did, Mom, but didn't say anything."

"Or was afraid to ask," Brenda said.

"Is there something I should know?" Afrika asked timidly, not sure what kind of response she was going to receive.

"Not at all," Victor said, suddenly wanting to the take charge of the conversation. "Mrs. Christianson and I are merely shocked that, after all these years, a prodigal sister has returned and it took our daughters to bring us together. This is exciting. Trevor, I hope your birthday wasn't upstaged by this turn of events."

"No, Dad, I think it's pretty cool myself. Now you'll always remember my birthday as the day you rediscovered a lost friend."

"No, it will always be the day my son was born," Victor said.

"Listen to Trevor," Asia said. They bumped knuckles. "Happy birthday again, Trev. Nikki and I, no, Afrika and

I are headed back to the dorm. We've got a football game tomorrow. Got to get some sleep."

"It was nice meeting you all," Afrika said for the third time. "Happy birthday, Trevor."

"Be sure to let Mimi know I'd love to hear from her," Brenda reminded Afrika, her voice trailing off.

"I will." The girls headed to the car.

"They really do look like twins," Brenda said under her breath as she peeked from behind the drapes in her oversized living room and watched the girls drive away.

6

Asia and Afrika rode most of the way to campus in silence. Exiting the freeway and stopping at the red light, Asia turned to face Afrika. "Nikki, tonight was freaky."

"Yeah, it was," Afrika said, not bothering to turn in Asia's direction and keeping her voice low. Suddenly, she turned and looked at Asia. To see her was like looking at herself. "So what do you think all of this means?"

"I don't think it means anything more than are parents are old friends. The real question is why did your mom leave without telling anyone or saying goodbye?"

Afrika pondered the question for a moment. The light turned green and Asia drove forward.

"I don't know why my mother chose to leave without telling anyone, but I'm sure she had a good reason. But let's give this up for tonight. My energy is sapped; I need a good night's rest."

"I agree."

Afrika sat back in her seat and closed her eyes. Her mother's warning had fallen on deaf ears, and now she was afraid that she may have opened a door her mother might have wanted to stay shut, although she had no idea why. Afrika pulled out her cell phone and began to text. *Mommy, we need to talk, A.*

THE FANS WERE OUT IN FULL FORCE TO WATCH NORTH CAROLINA Central whip the Fayetteville State University Broncos. Rumor had proven true when Central pulled out of the Central Intercollegiate Athletic Association (CIAA), but the Eagles still enjoyed a non-conference match with their former rival.

The cheerleaders were in the ready position as the band continued to assemble in the bleachers, playing a jazzy number that had booties bouncing and swaying and heads and arms rocking from side to side. Excitement and camaraderie complemented the near seventy-five degree heat and brilliant sun that lit up the afternoon skies. Hotdogs and carbonated drinks kept everyone happy until kick-off.

Afrika kicked her legs and threw her arms in the air. "Do it Eagles!!" she shouted along with the other cheerleaders. She waited for the next command and stood facing the crowd in the stands, waving her hands. Then she spotted him staring at her like she was some kind of science project that he was going to dissect.

She turned away and then looked back and Victor was still staring at her. What was his sudden interest in her? Why was he so quiet last night, acting as if he'd never met her before? It gave her the chills.

Afrika immersed herself in cheering on her team, although in the end, it was a letdown as the Fayetteville State Broncos trounced the Eagles 36-14.

MIMI LOOKED AGAIN AT THE MESSAGE SHE HAD RECEIVED FROM Afrika. Her stomach was in knots. She didn't know what to make of the cryptic message. What if she had learned something about her? Mimi shut her mind down and deleted the thoughts she conjured in her head.

7

E arly Monday morning, Victor hurried to his office and closed the door. Without taking a breath, he turned on his computer and tapped impatiently on his desk until he was prompted to log in. He immediately hit the keyboard, typing in commands while waiting for a response. His brain waves accelerated like someone had pushed the ON button of a blender to high, but slowed only a little as soon as he was logged into the Banner system that gave access to student records and other aspects of the school's internal system.

Victor's fingers raced across the keys and went into search mode. When prompted, he typed in Bailey, Africa.

Curses flew from Victor's mouth when he was unable to bring up Afrika's name. He tried Bailey, Nikki, but without success. He typed in Bailey once more, and then typed in Afr—what he believed to be the first three letters of her name. "Bingo." Victor hit his desk with his hand—a look of success written on his face.

Scrolling down the screen, Afrika's information transformed before his eyes. At last, the information he was seeking stared back at him. He digested it for a minute and then grabbed a pen and a piece of paper and jotted down the address for Setrina Bailey.

"Right here in Durham," Victor said to himself. "Well, we'll see for how long."

Victor stared at the screen a few minutes longer, scrolling backward for no apparent reason. And then he saw Afrika's birthdate—almost two weeks to the day of Asia's.

A frown, then a scowl replaced the smirk on Victor's face. At first it was a mere thought—Asia and Afrika's resemblance to each other so uncanny, their height, the way they wore their hair. But dates say something else. They are markers; place markers for events at a certain time and place. He had to know for sure.

Eight forty-five. It was too early to leave the office without a valid reason. If he could hold himself together until eleven-thirty, maybe his anxiety would decrease. It was going to be a long three hours.

At exactly eleven-thirty, Victor rose from his seat and placed the piece of paper with the address on it in his pocket. Outside of his office sat his secretary, who was obviously gossiping, her voice a hushed whisper that every now and then let out a, "Girl, you're telling a lie." Victor paused momentarily at his secretary's desk and waited for her to finish her personal conversation. Agitated, he rapped his knuckles on her desk. She jumped and the telephone fell from her hands as she finally lifted her head and saw her boss standing in front of her.

"Mr. Christianson, what can I do for you?"

"Sheila, I'm going out for an extended lunch. If I'm not back by one-fifteen, call my one-thirty appointment and reschedule. And remember, you're on company time."

Sheila smirked and batted her eyes. "Okay, Mr. Christianson. I'll see you later."

Victor hurried to his car. Without another thought, he took out the piece of paper in his pocket and keyed the address into his navigation system. He backed the black Mercedes convertible coupe out of its space and barreled out of the parking lot. The voice of the navigation guide irritated him, but the instructions made it an easy ride.

The prospect of seeing Mimi again caused him a bit of anxiety, but the trip was a must and couldn't wait a minute longer. He had long since forgotten the fateful event that had sent Mimi running. Although he didn't know for sure that Afrika was the result of his assault on Mimi, he felt it in every creak of his bones. And he was going to get his answer today. The question was what he was going to do if the information he received was what he hoped it wasn't…that he was Afrika's biological father.

Victor drove through his old neighborhood and others he had frequented while growing up. Memories of the parties, the women, and games of hoops in now empty schoolyards crossed his mind. Sitting at a light, Victor watched a middle-aged sister in three-and-a-half-inch heels get out of a car and head toward a drugstore. He broke his neck to get a good look at her; he was sure that she was one of his exes from way back when. The woman had a booty on her then and she had one on her now. A smile crossed his face at a long ago memory.

It was ten minutes to twelve when the voice of the guide instructed Victor to turn right and then left, slowing down to turn into a complex that he had not heard of. Brand new condos lay beyond the sign that read Willows Bend. Although Victor didn't see any willow trees, Dogwood trees lined the entry way of this isolated community, and beautiful Japanese maples dotted the front yards of each condo.

"You have reached your destination," the voice of the navigator said. "Your route guidance has ended."

Victor had committed the address to memory. When he identified Mimi's residence, Victor drove slowly past it, turned around, and parked across the street in an unmarked space. Nerves gripped his body, and he sat for a few minutes to get it under control. He looked in the mirror, brushed his sideburns, straightened his tie, and got out of the car.

He surveyed the surroundings and walked across the street. Hesitating a moment, he pulled himself together and walked the last few feet to Mimi's door. He rang the doorbell and almost immediately the door flew open.

"Expecting someone?" Victor asked, a smile crossing his lifeless lips.

A gasp, then a hand over the heart. Mimi looked straight into the eyes of a face she had longed to forget.

"Are you going to invite me in?" Victor asked casually, sarcastically, dressing Mimi up and down with his eyes.

All of a sudden Mimi pushed the door, trying to close it before Victor could come all the way in. Luck wasn't on her side. Victor wedged his foot between the door and the frame. Mimi continued to push, but clearly she wasn't as strong as the man who barged his way into her residence.

"What do you want?"

"What do I want, Mimi? Why don't you invite me to sit, and yes, I'd like something cold to drink. I'm on my lunch hour."

Mimi stood with her hands on her hips, glaring at Victor who had already taken a seat. "No one invited you to lunch, so there's no need for you to waste any more of my time."

"Slow down, Mimi. Let's not be so hostile. I came by for a friendly visit."

"How did you find me, Victor?"

"It wasn't hard. I'm the Director of Admissions at NC Central. I'll say, though, you've got a beautiful daughter… Afrika. I like that."

"Don't you go anywhere near my daughter. Do you hear me, Victor? You do and I'll…"

"And you'll do what? Run to Brenda and tell her that you gave it up to me? Time hasn't changed you a bit. You're still feisty as you ever were and you've still got that 'oh help me Lawdy' Coke-bottle figure."

Mimi's finger shot in the air, getting in Victor's face. "Shut up, Victor. Shut the hell up. You're such a liar. Don't you ever talk to me like that again. You have no right barging into my place. In fact, you've already worn out your welcome."

"Mimi, you slay me. You know why I'm here, and I want an answer right here and right now."

"An answer to what?"

"Oh, please, spare me the bull crap. I'm walking across campus calling out to my daughter, but another young lady turns around instead. Damn, she looked just like Asia but a little darker. Same height, about the same weight, hair in a ponytail. It was easy to be mistaken. But I had to ask myself, could this be my daughter? The moment she got closer, in my heart, I realized that she was mine. Right then, I had to find out who her mother was because you weren't the only one."

Slap! Slap!

Grabbing the side of his face, Victor jumped up from his seat. A cold chill enveloped the room, and Mimi moved back as she watched Victor's face turn from light brown to blazing red. Victor gritted his teeth and scowled at Mimi. "I ought to beat the crap out ya now, but that would be too easy. Mark my words though, you're gonna live to regret that little mistake."

Mimi's body stiffened as she continued to watch Victor, whose anger had completely contorted his face. She wasn't sure if he would retaliate, but without a doubt this visit was over. "Please go, Victor," Mimi whispered. "I'll pretend this never happened."

Victor grabbed Mimi by the shoulders and pushed her into a chair nearby. "No, you listen to me. I want you to take your daughter out of Central and move out of town...far away...to where, I don't care. Brenda can never know that Afrika's my daughter."

Mimi knocked Victor's hands away. "I never said she was your daughter. You're making an assumption that you aren't even allowed to make. Now you listen. If you put your hands on me again, I'll have your sorry ass arrested...something I should have done a long time ago."

"You don't scare me, Mimi. Afrika is my daughter. I checked her date of birth. She was born two weeks after Asia. The timing makes perfect sense."

"Perfect sense? Perfect sense because you raped me? And you want me to be silent so Brenda won't know what a bastard she married? I was silent for nineteen years because I didn't want your sins to come between Brenda and me. She and I were friends long before she ever met you. When she came to tell me that she was pregnant and to talk some sense into your irresponsible ass because you weren't hearing it, I should've told her to forget about you. But noooooooooooo, I had to be the mediator. And instead of mediating, I ended up being impregnated against my will by the likes of you. I have no plans to tell anyone, but not for your sorry sake. For Afrika's. I wouldn't want her to know what a pathetic excuse for a man her biological father is and that he's also a…"

"Watch it. Although I don't care what you think, I'm standing here."

"You belong in jail, Victor."

"The statute of limitations has long since run out, Mimi dear. And if anyone is going to jail, it's not going to be me. In fact, I might call my insurance broker this afternoon and increase my policy. Brenda may have to use it, with all the threats you've made on my life. All I want to know is if you're still going to deny that Afrika is my daughter?"

"How many ways do you want me to say it? Yes, Afrika is your daughter! Is that what you want to hear? What you gonna do now, add another notch to your baby-making belt?"

"Don't be so dramatic. I'm not going to do anything. I can't get over how much she looks like Asia. I do make some pretty girls."

"Let me tell you one thing, Victor. Afrika has a father who raised her and helped to mold her into the woman she is today. Not some man without a conscience that forced his way on her mother with some lame excuse about being drunk and upset because he had gotten his fiancée pregnant and wasn't ready to be a daddy. I wasn't ready to be a mother, but if I had been ready, I wouldn't have allowed you the honor of being my baby's daddy. I'm surprised Brenda is still with you."

Victor stood over Mimi. "Just know that it's going to

stay that way; Brenda will always be my wife until death do us part. And for your information, I'll only own up to two children…Asia and Trevor—not Afrika or any other being that has sprouted from my seed."

Mimi stood and moved away from Victor. "So why did you come here today? You're despicable, Victor Christianson. You're a man with no soul. You come to my house unannounced, demanding to know if Afrika is your daughter, but in another breath, write her off with a disclaimer. I want you out of my house now, you sorry son-of-a-bitch." Mimi pointed toward the door. "I don't ever want to see your ugly face again. You don't have to worry about me telling Afrika about the likes of you; you don't exist. You're invisible and always will be."

"Brenda knows you're here in Durham, and she's going to try and contact you."

"What? How?"

"Afrika was at the house with Asia on Friday night. The conversation led from one thing to another. And here I am. Let me take this moment to warn you again about getting out of town. Brenda wants to see you, but that can't happen."

"I have no plans to see Brenda and tell her what kind of person you really are. You have my word on it."

"That's all well and good, Mimi, but I still want you out of town."

"I can't jump up and take Afrika out of school. She's happy here, and the semester just started."

"If you don't do something, I will. Remember, I work in the Admissions Office."

"And…"

"And? You don't want to find out. Well, my lunch hour is over."

Mimi watched as Victor walked out and closed the door behind him, got in his car, and left. She paced around her living room, trying to find a solution for the dilemma she now faced. Standing still, Mimi put her hands on her hips. "This jackass isn't going to run me out of town. No way, Jose."

Without another second thought, Mimi went to the kitchen and retrieved her BlackBerry and prepared a text. *Afrika, Mommy needs to talk to you!*

Mimi pressed the SEND button. Before she was able to lay the phone down, it rang. She didn't recognize the number, but without realizing it, she hit the TALK button. The voice at the other end made her stop in her tracks.

8

"Mimi?" the voice asked.

"Yes, this is Mimi. Who's this?"

"Mimi, is it really you? This is Brenda, your best friend that you did the disappearing act on, just when I needed a hand to hold. Pregnant and all, Victor and I got married. Asia got your number from your daughter; I hope you don't mind that I called."

"Brenda, I...I'm sorry about all those years ago. I didn't mean to leave you by yourself. I had issues of my own that I was going through. Uhh, how are you?"

"I'm fine. Well, to be honest, I was utterly shocked to find out that you had a daughter and that you lived right here in Durham. Why didn't you contact me? Did I do something wrong?"

"No, Brenda, you didn't do anything wrong. I've only been in Durham a month. I'm married also, and my husband, Raphael, is a Colonel in the Army. He just left for Germany, and I moved to Durham to support Afrika while she's in college."

"You can't imagine my surprise when she said her name. Do you remember when we were in high school in Germany and I said if I had a girl I would name her Asia and if you had a girl you would name her Afrika?"

"I remember it as if it were yesterday."

"Mimi, my heart went through my chest when Afrika said who she was. Nineteen years have passed since I've seen you. I didn't know where you were, never heard from you, and I didn't know if you were even alive. Why did you leave so abruptly? Things worked out for me and Victor, but I didn't have my best friend to share it with."

"Like I said Brenda, I had a lot of issues going on that I couldn't talk about. With all you had going on in your life, I didn't think it was fair to burden you with my stuff."

"But that's what best friends are for…at least I believe that to be so. I even tried contacting your mother and father, and they never returned my calls. My mother told me that your parents moved to Missouri…something about taking care of a sick relative."

"Yes, my grandmother, my mother's mother, took ill, and my parents went back to St. Louis to be with her. I don't know if you remember, but St. Louis was my mother's home. Dad is from South Carolina."

"Why don't we get together for lunch? I can't wait to see you and play catch up."

Mimi stammered. The last thing she wanted to do was have a face to face with Brenda. It wasn't that she didn't want to see her—she missed her something awful. But the truth about her disappearance, her leaving Durham so suddenly, was bound to come out, and she couldn't risk it. And then there was Victor, who had already threatened her. She tried to find the words. "I'm really busy unpacking and trying to get this house together. I don't know when I'll be free."

"You've got to take a break sometime. Mimi, I've missed you. What about tomorrow at twelve-thirty?"

"I've really got a lot to do."

"Mimi, it's been a long time and it may be a bit awkward, but I want to see my friend."

Mimi hesitated. "Okay. Tomorrow at twelve-thirty. Where would you like to meet?"

"How about Brasa right off of Highway 70? It has great Brazilian food."

"That's fine. I'll be there." Mimi shut the phone and sat down in one of the chairs. What was she going to do now?

AFRIKA SWUNG HER GYM BAG ACROSS HER SHOULDERS and headed to the gym locker room to get ready for cheerleading practice. She felt good about the test she had taken in English. She couldn't wait to get to practice to tell Asia about Keith, a junior who had walked her to her science class. He was one of the brothers she had met at the frat party on Saturday night.

Just before entering the gym, her cell phone rang. A

smile crossed her face as she hurried to answer the call.

"Hey, Keith."

"Hey, Nikki. What are you doing?"

"I'm at cheerleading practice, but I'll call you as soon as I'm done."

"Okay, sounds good. Maybe we can meet each other later on."

"All right. Bye." Afrika was all nerves and jittery. Keith was a good-looking, tall Alpha brother. Before closing the phone, Afrika saw that her mother had sent her a text.

She opened the text and read her mother's message. Afrika frowned, somewhat alarmed at the tone of it, but she remembered she had sent one of her own and had yet to talk to her mother. Afrika closed the phone and decided she'd contact her mother as soon as practice was over. As soon as she entered the gym, she saw Asia and all else was forgotten.

THE SUN DROPPED BELOW THE HORIZON AND DARKNESS replaced the light. Mimi rushed around the house shutting blinds, checking them twice to make sure no one could see in. She secured the locks back and front, shaking and rechecking them to ensure no one could get in.

Exhausted, Mimi slouched in the nearest chair and heaved her leg over the arm and let it hang. It became a painstaking event, listening for the beep that announced a text or the ringtone reserved for Asia.

Anxious, Mimi picked up the remote and turned the television on in hopes of a distraction as she flipped from one channel to another. However, nothing seemed to capture her attention. Her mind wandered as the day's events wouldn't leave her alone. Victor's face appeared in front of her—she could almost hear him breathing. She fought to be rid of him, but his image wouldn't go away.

She couldn't believe she had struck him dead in the face. A smirk streaked across Mimi's face, gloating in the memory—her one-second victory.

Her face became somber. Something drastic had to be done about the precarious situation she found herself in, although she wasn't sure what it was. The more she thought about Victor, the more defiant Mimi was becoming. Her mind was made up about one thing for sure, and that was Victor wasn't going to run her or Afrika out of Durham. More immediate was her lunch date with Brenda. The timing was all wrong; Mimi wasn't ready to see her yet.

Mimi searched for the time on the DVR. It was seven o'clock, which meant it was one in the morning in Germany and too late at night or early in the morning, depending upon whose perspective it was. She needed to talk to her husband, but she'd give up calling him for the moment.

In the midst of the quiet, the phone rang. Who'd be calling this late? Maybe it was her Mom and Dad calling from St. Louis. Without looking, Mimi sprinted to the

kitchen and picked up the phone before it stopped ringing.
"Hello."

"You should've checked your caller ID," the voice said.

"Who is this?" Mimi asked, confused.

"So this afternoon has already faded from your memory.
I'm calling to remind you that I wasn't paying lip service
to you today. It's not in your best interest to disobey me.
Having lunch with Brenda would be bad for your health."

"Are you through?"

"As long as you understand the message."

"Victor, you don't scare me. Threats are just that—
threats. You can use all the scare tactics you want, but
you won't win. I will not play this game with you. My
advice to you is get your own life in order, and DON'T
CALL HERE AGAIN."

Mimi slammed the phone down and shook un-
controllably. She ignored the phone when it rang a
minute later, and when she didn't answer it and it rang
several more times, she snatched the phone cord out of
the jack. "I'm too blessed to be stressed," she muttered
under her breath, but she was visibly shaken.

Mimi went to her junk drawer, retrieved her journal
and a pen, and then sat down at the kitchen table. She
opened the book and reread her first journal entry,
closed the book and her eyes, and began to pray. She
hadn't been close to God in a long time, and if she
needed Him, now was certainly the time.

When she finished her short prayer, Mimi picked up
her pen and opened the journal to the next available space.

October 6, 2008

A one in a million chance was the odds of me running into Victor or Brenda. I would have never won the lottery with those odds, but somehow fate has a way of making a believer out of me. Who would've thought my worst nightmare, which had been temporarily parked in the furthermost recess of my mind, would descend upon me out of nowhere in the middle of the day when I was minding my own business, oblivious to what the neighbors on either side of me were doing, let alone old friendships that had died hard. Maybe it was my paranoia or maybe I spoke this madness into existence, but now I've got a fight on my hands, one that has put a fight within me that I didn't know existed.

Victor had the audacity to show up on my doorstep today, get in my face, and demand to know if he was Afrika's father. Who in the hell does he think he is? And when he received confirmation from me that Afrika is his child, he had the nerve to tell me that Afrika and I had to leave Durham so that his reputation would stay intact. I'm neither his wife or his concubine. I should have busted his tail a long time ago and explained to Brenda later, but she probably wouldn't have believed me if I told her that her sorry-ass fiancé had raped me.

Brenda wants to meet me, but I can't. Too many years have passed to try and rekindle a relationship that...that I still want. I've thought about Brenda often, wondering whether she married Victor, if she had kids, and what she looked like. Would she have that same award-winning smile that used to melt men's hearts?

Something keeps tugging at me on the inside, telling me to tell Afrika…to tell Brenda before things get out of hand because no amount of talking will repair the damages my silence have rendered.

    Lord, I need Your direction. I need You to show me what I'm to do. I'm prepared to fight Victor, but I need to know the how. Afrika is my primary concern, and I'll let no one hurt her, except over my dead body. She's my baby, my only baby.

    Mimi Bailey

9

Brenda sat in her office and mulled over the thought of seeing Mimi again. It was unfathomable that after all these years she'd reconnected with her best friend. Her thoughts had so many tentacles, like that of a giant squid, wondering and seeking answers to the what, when, and the why Mimi had disappeared without so much as a goodbye. Now, she would be able to ask the questions that plagued her—put an end to the distorted and twisted emotions and thoughts her mind had fabricated. She closed the case file she was working on and checked the clock on her desk. It was eleven-thirty. She'd leave in thirty minutes.

Butterflies fluttered in her stomach. Strange sensations, vibes were trying to take over her psyche. Victor's attitude puzzled her. Brenda didn't understand why he objected to every civil reason for her wanting to see Mimi. Leaning back in her chair, Brenda's eyebrows arched as she contemplated this further and felt the urge to rub her stomach as the butterflies continued to flutter.

Taking a breath, Brenda reached for her purse and pulled out a tube of lipstick. She pulled a makeup compact out of her desk, flipped it opened, and used the mirror as she painted her lips. She smiled at herself, then did a few practice dry runs for the moment she saw Mimi. Her nerves were getting the best of her, the closer it came time for her to leave.

Putting the compact back in the desk, she looked up as the telephone began to ring. The first thought was to ignore it but when she saw Asia's number on the caller ID, she smiled and answered the phone.

"Hey, baby, what do I owe you for this phone call?"

"I was thinking about you and wanted to tell you so. I love you, Mom."

"I love you, too, Asia. Everything going okay?"

"Great."

"What's up with you? You're being secretive. You know a mother always knows. I know...it's a boy."

"Please," Asia said. She giggled.

"I knew it. You'll have to tell me all about this mystery man. Right now I'm getting ready to leave to meet Afrika's mother. I'm excited about seeing Mimi again after all these years."

"That's exciting, Mom. I'll let you go; tell me all about your meeting. Bye."

"Bye, sweetheart."

Brenda clicked off the phone and smiled. "Mimi, I have a thousand questions to ask you."

The phone rang again, and Brenda clicked the TALK button and frowned when she heard her name.

"What is it, Victor?"

"Are you still going forward with your plan to meet Mimi?"

"Yes. Anything else?"

"Why is it so important that you have to see her? She didn't give a damn about you or your feelings when she left you all alone and pregnant nineteen years ago."

"That was then, this is now. I'm ready to move forward and that means seeing Mimi again."

"You're making a mistake," Victor said with an air of authority.

"That's your opinion, Victor. Why do you care?"

"I never told you this, but I never liked Mimi."

"Tell that to the lie detector machine, Victor. In fact, you would've put the moves on her, except she wasn't too crazy about you either."

"Look, Brenda. I don't want to argue with you. Mimi will only disrupt our lives."

"You're acting like this is some kind of competition between you and Mimi. Why are you so paranoid? Mimi cared about me; that's why I sent her to intercede on my behalf after I found out that I was pregnant. You were raging mad, and I wanted you to know that I wouldn't hold you responsible because I didn't want to lose you either. Anyway, that was years ago."

"And we've been happily married for eighteen years. Think about it."

"You have Mimi to thank for us being together."

"Mimi shouldn't have come back here."

"I find your behavior strange, Victor. I don't know what's up with you, but get over it. I'm going to see Mimi."

"And you'll be sorry."

"What do you mean by that?"

"Don't try my patience, Brenda."

Brenda clicked the OFF button on the phone without a goodbye. She brushed down the collar of her St. John gray and white ensemble, picked up her purse, and headed for the door. *Who in the hell does he think he is, telling me whom I can and cannot see?* Brenda slammed the door behind her and headed for the car.

BRENDA PACED HERSELF AS SHE DROVE UP HIGHWAY 70, not wanting to arrive at the restaurant too early but not wanting to be late either. Victor's telephone call continued to interrupt her good feeling, but she managed a smile and shoved the phone call to the back of her mind.

She swiftly moved over in the left-hand lane and prepared to stop at the light. The restaurant was on the other side of the eight-lane divided highway, and her excitement rose as the light changed from red to green. Brenda made a swift U-turn, and began to move to the right so that she could turn into the parking lot a few yards up.

Boom, bam, boom! "Oh my God!" Brenda screamed.

She didn't see...didn't know what hit her. Brenda's head

flew forward and hit the steering wheel, but she held on tight until she lost control and veered into the median and an oncoming car. Whatever hit her was now long gone. Her car was now in an entangled heap of metal on the other side of the road. *Swoosh.* The airbag deployed and Brenda's head bounced between it and the headrest. She touched her finger to her face and swiped at the blood that was oozing from her nose.

Bam, bam, bam! "Lady hang in there!" a voice shouted from outside of Brenda's window. She could feel herself begin to lose consciousness. "Hang in there, lady. We're going to get you out."

Brenda wasn't sure how long it had been between the crash and the moment she heard the sirens. Somehow she managed to unlock the door and when she had come out of her semi-unconscious state, she looked up into the face of a kind gentleman who held her head.

"Ma'am, the ambulance is here to take you to the hospital. Is there anyone I can call for you?" the kind gentleman asked.

"My...my daughter," Brenda managed to say. "She's speed-dial four."

10

It was an easy eighty degrees in the middle of October. Dressed in a colorful pink, purple, and white sleeveless sundress and three-and-a-half-inch white sandals, Afrika crossed the quad in a hurry to get to her two o'clock class. She was hoping to see Keith, who was fast becoming the object of her affection and taking up more time in her already limited schedule. He had met her after cheerleading practice on Monday, and together they had gone to the student union and grabbed a snack.

Just before she entered the building, she heard Asia's voice shouting her name. Afrika turned in Asia's direction, guarding her eyes from the sun. "What's up, Asia?"

"Let me catch my breath."

"This better be good. I only have three minutes before I'm late to class, and I'm never late."

"Girl, you won't guess who asked me for my phone number."

"You're right; I don't have a clue."

"Deon!"

"You mean that fine, juicy lip, I-wish-I-could-squeeze-him-forever Eagles quarterback, Deon?"

"Yes, Nikki. He's the one." Asia and Afrika began to jump around and slap each other's hand.

"I say, go for yours, girl. Maybe you can ask him to meet us on Friday night."

"Been thinking about it ever since he asked me for my number ten minutes ago."

"Didn't know you were giving him the eye."

"The eye and everything else."

The girls laughed.

"I've got to go, Asia. I'll talk to you later."

"Okay, but did you know that our mothers were meeting for lunch today?"

"Really? I can't say that I did."

"You need to talk to your mother more often."

"You're right. I owe her a phone call. We'll talk later, Asia. Gotta run."

Asia smiled as Nikki turned and went into the building. Asia held her hand by her mouth with her thumb and pinky finger sticking out. "Call me."

VICTOR STOOD BACK AMONG THE CLUSTER OF TREES AND WATCHED Asia and Afrika from a distance. They were laughing and seemed to be sharing a best friends' moment. It was only a matter of time, if he didn't take matters into his hands, before one or the other would stumble upon his secret and discover they were more than friends… sisters. But Victor resolved within himself that he'd go to whatever lengths necessary to make sure they never did.

He moved quickly from out of the shadows and headed for his office. It was clear now to Victor that he had to take immediate action to force Mimi's hand.

Victor looked like an ostrich in his gold blazer, white short-sleeved dress shirt, tie of many colors, and black slacks as he high-tailed it back to his office. Sheila, his secretary, was busy on the telephone upon his return, but she looked up when she heard the door slam.

As soon as Victor sat down, he immediately unlocked his com-puter, entered his password, and began to search for Afrika's profile in the student records. Finding her history, he examined several different pages, entered some information, clicked save, sat back, and smiled. The smug look became a nasty laugh and he jumped up from his chair for a premature celebration. He kissed his index and middle finger and tapped the computer screen. "Ms. Afrika Bailey, your tail is out of here. And I've got something for you, Mimi. I've got something for you."

ASIA WENT TO THE LIBRARY, FOUND A STUDY ROOM, PLOPPED HER books and cell phone on the table, and sat down. Only one other person inhabited the room, and she was lost in the pages of her American History text-

book. Asia had an hour before her critical thinking class—
enough time to brush over some notes. This was the
class she enjoyed the most; it pushed her to think in
ways that were well beyond the norm. She hadn't declared
her major yet, but Political Science was definitely an
option.

Her cell phone began to vibrate and do a slow tango
on the table. Asia recognized her mother's number and
immediately answered it, whispering into the phone.

"Hey, Mom. What...Who's this?" Asia asked, a crease
forming across her face, her voice raised. Jerking her
head, Asia jumped up from her chair. "My mother...
what? Accident? Oh my God. What hospital? Thank
you, thank you."

Asia hung up the phone and began to pant, pulling at
her ponytail. "Oh my God, my mother."

The other occupant in the room pulled her head from
the pages of the textbook she was reading and looked at
Asia in alarm. She threw the book down and got up and
went to a tearful Asia, who paced the floor while punching
numbers in her cell phone.

"Are you all right?" the girl asked. "Can I help you?"

For the first time, Asia noticed the other person in the
room. She was tall with even brown skin, and her
braided hair was pulled back from her face and pinned
into some type of ball. She was very attractive but much
older than the average student.

"Thanks, but no thanks. I just found out that my

mother was in an accident, and I need to call my dad."

"Why don't you let me do that for you? You're shaking like a leaf. By the way, my name is Leslie."

"I'm all right. Thanks anyway, Leslie." Asia placed the phone to her ear, but after a minute pressed the END button. She looked up at Leslie. "My dad works on campus; I'll walk over to his office."

"Who's your dad?"

"Mr. Victor Christianson. He's the director of the Admissions Office."

"Oh," Leslie said, her voice trailing. "Dog."

"Thank you for your help."

Leslie stared after Asia as she left the room.

Asia ran toward her father's office, unable to keep her composure. She needed him in the worst way. The man on the phone said that her mother was in an accident and was being taken to the hospital.

With the back of her hand, Asia wiped her face and walked into the lobby of her father's office. Sheila, his secretary, was on the phone when she entered, but raised her hand and waved for Asia to hold on; she'd be with her in a moment. After a minute passed, Asia ignored Sheila and barged into her father's office. Sheila was up in a second, running behind Asia.

Sheila put on the brakes when she saw Mr. Christianson staring at her like she didn't belong. It didn't take a rocket scientist to recognize that the look meant *get the hell out of here.*

"What is it, Asia? Are you all right?"

"No, Daddy, I'm not all right. Mom was in an accident and we need to get to the hospital."

"An accident? Are you sure?"

"Yes," Asia said, somewhat annoyed. "I received a call from someone who was at the scene of the accident and had her cell phone. They're taking Mom to Duke."

Victor got up from his seat. "Let's go."

Victor sat stone faced in his seat, his knuckles wrapped tightly around the steering wheel, navigating his way to the hospital as if the car was on autopilot. Small beads of perspiration glistened on his face...a small droplet settling on his lower lip.

Asia sat and stared straight ahead with earplugs plunged deep into her ears, her iPod offering a temporary distraction. Every now and then she'd steal a glance at her father who had yet to ask for details of her mother's accident.

"We're here," Victor finally said with a strange, confused look on his face.

Without another word, Victor and Asia hopped from the car and walked into the Emergency Room. The waiting room was full and screamed of sickness. People of all ethnicities, sizes, and colors were there for one reason or another. Young kids whined for their mothers to hold them and the drab-colored walls made Asia want to puke.

Victor marched to the information window with Asia right behind him. "I'm looking for my wife, Brenda Christianson. She was in a car accident, and I was told she was brought here."

"Just a minute; let me check," the plump lady with the rosy cheeks said.

The rosy-cheeked lady got up from her chair and shuffled to a triage nurse and said something to her, pointing in Victor and Asia's direction. In the next minute, she shuffled back to the chair.

"Your wife is being seen by the doctor. I believe she's going to be released. Go to window number three, and they'll give you access to where she is being treated."

"You say she's going to be released?" Victor asked, relief in his voice.

"That's what I was told, but the doctor can tell you more. Next."

"Thank you, Lord," Asia said out loud. "I was so worried."

Victor and Asia followed an orderly through the maze in the Emergency Room until he stopped in front of a closed curtain.

The orderly pointed. "Mrs. Christianson is in here."

Victor pulled back the curtain and walked into the area, followed by Asia, and found Brenda sitting up and receiving instructions from the doctor who was attending her. Purple bruises were visible on her face and arms, but there were no other severe lacerations as far as they could tell. Although her face ached, Brenda looked up and offered a faint smile, relaxing the moment the pain became too intense.

"Hi, Mom," Asia said, reaching for Brenda's hand when she extended it. "How do you feel?"

Brenda's eyes searched Victor's and then settled on Asia's. "With a little rest, I'll be like new again. I'm ready to go home."

"You aren't rushing too fast?" were the first words out of Victor's mouth.

"My husband and daughter," Brenda said to the doctor.

Before Brenda said another word, the attending doctor turned around. "Hello, I'm Dr. Thorn. Brenda has sustained a few bumps and bruises, but she'll be all right, considering the banging her car received from all account of things. She needs to take it easy and get plenty of rest—something she could do from home. If she complains of severe headaches or backaches, especially in the first forty-eight hours, she should come back and be reevaluated as soon as possible. She's free to go now."

"Thank you, Dr. Thorn," Brenda said, scooting off the table with Asia's assistance. "Pass me my jacket, Asia, and we can be on our way."

"Thank you, Dr. Thorn, for taking care of my wife. I'll make sure she follows your instructions."

"Good deal, Mr. Christianson." Dr. Thorn took a last look at Brenda and left the room.

"I'll need a rental car," Brenda said to Victor as soon as the doctor's white coat disappeared beyond the curtains that cordoned off her makeshift room.

"You won't need one for awhile. You heard Dr. Thorn; you need rest so you can get better. If you hadn't gone behind my back and tried to see Mimi, this wouldn't have happened," Victor whispered.

"Did you miss your lunch with Nikki's mom today?" Asia asked.

"I was on my way to meet Mimi when I had the accident. It was weird. A car came out of nowhere and hit me in front of the restaurant. It was a hit and run. Mimi doesn't know, and I'm sure she's wondering why I didn't show up. I'll have to give her a call."

"Your mother is hard-headed…running after her past. I bet she thinks I had something to do with her accident."

Anger replaced the placid look on Brenda's face.

"You need to concentrate on getting well," Victor continued, not missing a beat. "You aren't going to be running anywhere anytime soon."

"What's up with you, Dad?" Curiosity clouded Asia's face.

Brenda said, "I'd also like to know, Asia."

"Nothing, nothing. Your mother wants to rekindle a friendship that will do more harm than good. What kind of friend walks out on you without a word, never to be heard of again?"

"Isn't it up to Mom to decide who she does or doesn't want to see?" Asia said, her head cocked like she was the grownup in charge. Victor scowled at her.

"Victor, I don't know what's gotten into you," Brenda butted in. "I'm a bit shaken up, but I walked away from that accident without one broken bone. Thank you, Lord. Now take me home."

"Mom, I'm coming home with you," Asia insisted.

"No, sweetie. You go on back to school. Momma can take care of herself."

12

Mimi didn't care what time it was in Germany, she had to talk to Raphael. She set the few groceries she bought down on the kitchen counter, along with her keys and purse, and let out a sigh. She noticed the light on the answering machine was blinking but hesitated, wondering of it was another irate call from Victor. Something had to be done about his intrusion, and only Raphael could calm her nerves.

Quickly, she put the yogurt, skim milk, apples, lemon, and salmon in the refrigerator. She was dying for the taste of salmon, her favorite. She would broil it after she spoke with her husband.

Closing the refrigerator door, she reached for her purse to get her BlackBerry so she could call Raphael. As soon as she touched the keyboard, the phone rang and a smile danced across her face.

"Hey, Baby, it's about time."

"Hey, Mommy, I know I've been delinquent."

"Delinquent is not the word, but we won't fuss about it now that you've called. How's school going?"

"It's going good. I'm more worried about you. How are you doing?"

"Well, you took long enough to check on me. I've sent you several text messages."

"I apologize. I...I remembered what you said about having more than one friend in my life..."

Mimi took a seat. "Something happened between you and Asia?"

"No, Mommy. We're still cool. I have a new male acquaintance."

"Okay, Afrika Nicole Bailey. Remember what your goal is. You don't need any distractions or stumbling blocks to keep you from reaching that goal."

"No, Mommy. I'm going to be an icon on Wall Street one day. I haven't lost focus. You can bet your bottom dollar on that—Wall Street jargon." Afrika laughed.

"Well, I'm not laughing. I don't want to see anything but A's and B's for grades."

"Not a problem. But I didn't call to talk about me. Asia told me that you were supposed to meet her mother today for lunch. How did it go?"

Quiet ensued. Then Mimi took a breath and exhaled. "I didn't meet her."

"Why? What's going on? You telling me to be careful about getting involved with Asia's family puzzles me. Mommy?"

"I'm a little apprehensive about seeing Brenda again; that's all. I sort of skipped out on her when she may have needed me most years ago, but I had my reasons. I'm afraid that Brenda won't forgive me and I don't think I can endure the thought of it."

"But, Mommy, she wants to see you. You should've seen how her eyes lit up when she realized that you were my mother and that you were living right under her nose. I believe she would've interrogated me all night if I had let her. Now, Asia's father, Mr. Christianson, there's something sinister about him."

"What do you mean?" Mimi asked, holding her heart and her breath.

"It's the way he stares at me, like I've…"

"What do you mean, he stares at you?"

"I'm trying to tell you, Mommy. The first time I saw him on campus, I understood that he might have mistaken me for Asia. However, the next time I saw him, at Asia's house, his eyes…his eyes were spooky. Like they were lasers and he was drilling holes through me. Then the next day at the football game, there he was again with that twisted grin on his face, watching me like he was some kind of stalker."

"Stay away from him, Afrika. You hear me?"

"Yeah, Mommy. You're scaring me."

"I'm not trying to scare you. I never liked him when we were in college. Even then, I couldn't put my finger on it," Mimi lied for Afrika's sake, "but I've always thought he was up to no good. I don't know what Brenda saw in him, but she said she was going to marry that man one day."

"But what has that got to do with him staring at me? And what made you think he was up to no good?"

"I can't explain it, Afrika. If I could, I would. I don't trust him as far as I can see him."

"Well, he gives me the creeps. He's Asia's daddy and all, but you don't have to worry about me; I'm going to stay as far away from him as possible. So why didn't you really want to see Mrs. Christianson?"

"Who said I didn't want to see Brenda? So many questions, Afrika."

"That need answers. Something strange is going on, Mommy, and you opened the can on my curiosity by telling me to be aware of Asia's family."

"Truth be told, Victor, Mr. Christianson, never liked me. I was his wife's best friend, and I believe he thought I was trying to turn Brenda against him."

"Were you?"

"I'll say this. I didn't do a very good job of convincing Brenda to stay clear of Victor. She wanted him. I even think she got...she got..."

"She got what, Mommy?"

"Never mind."

"You want me to act like an adult, but you still treat me like a little girl."

"That's not true, Afrika. Some things are better not said, so let's leave that thought in my head."

"Whatever. So, tell me, Mommy, did you know who Asia's parents were when I brought her by the house?"

Brenda hesitated—thought about how she would answer the question. "Actually no, but I had my suspicions."

"What was it?"

"Her name, since you want to know."

"Asia?"

"Yes. My best friend and I made a pact all those years ago that if we had girls, she would name her daughter Asia and I would name mine Afrika."

"Dang! Asia's mother said the same thing. I don't understand what's going, but it's giving me the jitters. Before I go, I have one last question for you?"

"What's that?" Mimi asked with apprehension in her voice.

"Are the Christiansons why you didn't want me to come to North Carolina?"

13

There wasn't enough air in the universe for all the huffing, puffing, and blowing Mimi was doing when Afrika asked the one question she had never hoped to hear. Good thing Afrika couldn't see her face; she would've never gotten away with the flimsy half-lie she told.

Keeping her secret from Afrika was proving to be a bigger chore for Mimi than she expected. There was always the possibility that coming back to Durham might have repercussions, but the possibility was slim. But in less than a month, she'd been introduced to the daughter of her best friend who looked so much like her own daughter, she'd been confronted by the man whose actions had caused her to leave Durham in the first place, and she'd been contacted by her best friend that she hadn't seen in nineteen years, who was the wife of the man who'd confronted her and the mother of her daughter's new best friend. Damn. Her life was more complicated than it ever was.

It was time to call Raphael. Her husband would have answers. After all, he was a Colonel in the United States

Army and he commanded troops at home and abroad, from Ft. Riley, Kansas to the sandy deserts of Iraq. Mimi punched the first number in on her BlackBerry when she remembered the blinking light on her house phone.

As she suspected, it was from Victor. Mimi had had enough of his antagonism for one day and wasn't about to listen to anymore of his threats taunting her and Afrika to leave Durham. Curiosity wanted her to listen to the message, but peace of mind pressed the delete key. She didn't care what time it was in Europe, she was going to call Raphael.

The voice on the other end of the line was groggy. "Hello, hello."

"Baby, I'm sorry for calling you so late."

"Yeah, it's one in the morning. Mimi, you all right?"

Mimi could hear rustling in the background. "I hope you weren't in a deep sleep. I'm all right."

"Hey, baby, it's me, Raphael. You know I know you."

"Really, I'm fine. I needed to hear your voice."

"My body was down for the count, but I hadn't gone into the zone yet. I do need a good night's sleep, but I'm sitting up now. Busy day. We shipped out twenty-five hundred more troops to Afghanistan."

"I'll be glad when the war is over."

"Afghanistan and Iraq. But you didn't call to talk about that. I've missed you. How's Afrika doing?"

"I've missed you, too. Afrika's doing great."

"Have you changed your mind about coming to

Germany? I can put in for housing right away. As I told you before you made the decision to go to Durham, Afrika was going to be okay."

"No, I need to be here. If something happened to her and I wasn't able to get to her, I would never forgive myself."

"Me either, baby. I guess I saw our baby as all grown up. Afrika has always been very independent and intelligent. She got that from her father."

Mimi was quiet. It was true that Afrika had taken on Raphael's traits and demeanor. A large constituency of Afrika's high school teachers and Raphael's colleagues made a bet that Afrika was destined to follow in her father's footsteps and would probably become the first and only African-American female Commander General in the United States.

"Afrika has been fortunate to have you as a father. Baby, I'm sorry to have disturbed you. Go on back to sleep. I needed to hear your voice."

"I'm awake now. You sure you're all right? I detect a little some-thing in your voice."

"Well, remember me telling you about this guy who harassed me in college?"

"You mean the guy who tried to assault you because you wouldn't give into his advances?"

"Yes, he's the one. As big as Durham is, guess what?"

"Don't tell me you ran into him."

"I did, Raf. It's been a long time since I've seen him, but out of the blue, there he was."

"Did he say anything to you? Did he try anything? I'll be on the first thing smoking back to the U.S."

"No," Mimi lied. "It felt strange seeing him again. He stared at me like I was on display at some museum. It gave me the creeps."

"Listen, Baby. If this guy, for any reason, gives you any cause to feel threatened, get a hold of me right away; I'll be home as fast as I can get there. Nobody messes with my wife. Hopefully, it was only a coincidence that you ran into him."

"I hope it was, too," Mimi said. Raphael meant what he'd said about getting on a plane straightway. There was no way she could tell him that Victor had come to the house, put his hands on her, and threatened her all in one afternoon. It would set him off.

"I'm serious, Baby. If you feel uncomfortable and need me to come home, I wasn't lying when I said I'd be on the next flight out of Frankfurt."

"You know how to make a sister feel safe," she told Raphael, although the nerves that wracked her body said differently. Wasn't the reason she had called him the first place because she was ill-at-ease? She didn't want Raphael to worry, so she played it off.

"So what are you going to do for a brother you woke up in the middle of the morning that has a serious hard-on from listening to his wife tell him about another man looking at her like she was a chocolate sculpture he wanted to eat."

"I didn't say that, Raphael."

"It was close enough 'cuz that turned me on, Baby."

"You're a naughty boy. I'm telling you about some guy from the past who gave me the heebee jeebees when I saw him today, and you've got the nerve to turn it into your own sexual fantasy."

"Baby, I'm glad you're all right, but you know how you do me. Now if you would slide those fine voluptuous hips of yours through the telephone cables, you'd make a brother real happy."

"Now, Colonel, I'm not that kind of girl. What would your troops say?"

"They'd say, 'do it, Colonel. Go on and get your twenty-one gun salute—*boom-boom, boom-boom.*' And you know I'm gonna try."

"Aren't you afraid that you might be reported to your superiors?"

"Sister, I say lay it on me. I'd do fifty push-ups right now, if you were going to set me free. I'm all alone in this dark room, undressing you with my mind, throwing kisses all over your body, feeling every crevice of your being…"

"Well, Colonel, umm…umm, if you don't tell nobody, I for sure won't. There might be something I can do to make your dream come true. Your wish is my command."

"Talk to me."

14

A good night's sleep was all Mimi needed. Making love to her husband over the telephone had erased the tension that had built up in her body. She slept like a baby. But now, as she lay face up on the bed, the desire for her husband returned.

Mimi closed her eyes and let Raphael's sensuous and erotic teasing echo in her brain. She could still feel his breath as he hissed into the phone. Mimi hugged herself, longed for his touch, the feel of his hands and lips all over her body. A small moan left her mouth as she recalled a moment when their lovemaking had been so intense. It was as if Raphael was on an assault mission in the jungle searching for the enemy, the thrill of the hunt pumping his adrenaline. Stalking the enemy with his savage, lustful words spoken only for her ears and she, intoxicated and unable to bear another moment of his grueling attack, found Mimi's hands thrown up in total surrender. She shuddered as the memory made her have her own private earthquake.

Mimi's eyes flew open at the sound of the telephone. Maybe it was Raphael calling, still under the cloud of their early morning tryst. She searched for the phone that had somehow fallen off the bed and found its way to the floor, the caller still intent on being heard. Mimi looked at the time and gasped. It was nine in the morning, and Brenda was the caller.

Her first thought was to not answer. Mimi wasn't in the frame of mind to talk to Brenda. In fact, the call had already spoiled the pleasure she'd derived from her instant replay of the phone sex she had with her husband, and that pissed her off. Maybe she could fall asleep again and recapture the moment, the aura with a couple of new twists and turns, like Taye Diggs did in the TV series, *Daybreak*.

The persistent ringing of the phone caused Mimi's finger to press the TALK button. She sat up, scratched her head before speaking. "Hey, Brenda," Mimi said in a low voice that seemed far away.

"Umm, is this a bad time?" Brenda asked cautiously.

"No, no, I was awake. Didn't sleep well last night but finally found the right spot at about five this morning." Mimi wasn't sure why she lied to Brenda, but it was too early to be confiding in her; especially since they hadn't reestablished their friendship and the culprit for her anxiety was Brenda's husband. The truth was that after Raphael had whipped it on her with his tongue lashing, she had slept like a baby. But Brenda didn't need to know that.

"I only wanted you to know why I was a no-show yesterday and that I was sorry."

Mimi choked on her own spit. She wasn't sure what she was supposed to say since she had also been a no-show. Did this mean that Brenda had chickened out as well? She hesitated and then found what she believed were the right words. "It's all right, Brenda." Mimi frowned, not sure what trap she'd allowed herself to fall into.

"I was in an accident outside of the restaurant. I didn't think about calling you until after I was in the ambulance and on my way to the hospital, but I was in no condition to do so."

"Oh my God, Brenda! Are you all right? What hospital are you in?"

"I'm at home now. I sustained only a few minor bumps and bruises; however, my car is a total wreck. I'm going to pick up a rental car today or tomorrow."

"Well, I'm glad you're all right."

"I still want us to get together, Mimi. How about Friday?"

"Are you sure you'll be well enough to go out on Friday?"

"What is it, Mimi? Why don't you want to see me? We're only going to have a harmless lunch. I'm not going to press you about what happened nineteen years ago. Let's live in the present. That's what counts. I've missed you."

Mimi sighed. Victor's words kept echoing in her head. She was sure he was capable of doing something terrible to her, but it was Afrika she was worried about, and she wasn't about to let stupidity or emotions harm her child.

"Nothing is wrong, Brenda. Let's plan for Friday; same place."

"Okay, I'm fine with that. But please don't back out. I really want to see you."

"Are you all right, Brenda?"

"Yeah, yeah. Other than the small jolt the accident gave me, most times I'm so wrapped up in my work that I don't get to do a lot of me things."

Mimi pondered what Brenda had said. "I'll be there."

"Okay, then it's set. I can't wait to see you."

"Me twice," Mimi said, noting the anxiety in Brenda's voice. "I'm looking forward to it. See you then."

"Great."

BRENDA STARED AT THE PHONE. SHE NEEDED TO TALK WITH HER best friend. She needed to confide in Mimi—to tell her all that had transpired in her life and how miserable she was. It was almost as if it was ordained… Mimi's reentry into her life. Mimi's timing was perfect, even if she was unaware.

Brenda cleared her afternoon schedule as well as for the rest of the week to give herself some time to relax and heal from her ordeal. Maybe she'd go to the spa and pamper herself since it certainly would aid in the healing process. Victor may have thought he had won a small victory by her setback. True, she didn't get to see Mimi, but she was going to keep her new luncheon date a secret. The more Brenda had time to think, the more she wondered if Victor had anything to do with her accident.

Victor was always trying to control her, keep her in line, tell her how to spend her money while he traipsed up and down the Eastern Seaboard and across North Carolina on state money, pretending he was recruiting students when all the while he was sniffing behind other women and bringing his leftovers to her after all was said and done, even though she didn't want any part of him. But they kept up a commanding performance, making appearances here and there like a dutiful couple with ties to the community. But things were going to change.

Brenda picked up her cell phone and called a cab.

15

"Wait up, Nikki!" Keith shouted as he sprinted across the campus lawn to catch up with her.

Clutching her books, Afrika stopped and almost fell when Keith descended upon her.

"Nikki, Nikki. You sure do look hot today, baby," Keith said out of breath, taking a quick peek over his shoulder at Afrika's sculptured buttocks draped in a pair of tight-fitting Dereon jeans and a purple fitted T-shirt with the words *Live, Love, Laugh* embossed on it. He slung his long slender arm around Afrika's neck, pulled her close, and squeezed her tight.

Afrika was loving all the attention that this 5'll", streamlined, chocolate fudge, could've-been-a-basketball-playing hunk was throwing on her. His soft brown eyes danced in his perfect round head and made her melt. But her heart went *ka-thump* as the warm body dressed in a gold linen, buttoned-down blazer along with a pair of black slacks and an artsy gold, black, and eggshell colored tie snuggled next to her. He was fine and set the rest of her body on fire.

Afrika threw her body around and stared him up and

down as if it was the first time she'd laid eyes on him. Her mock smile transformed into an all-out grin, finally parting her lips and then smacking them together, more than happy with her appraisal of the new man in her life.

"Thank you, Keith." She batted her eyelashes. "You don't look bad yourself."

"Well, I've got it like that. The brothers and I have got to do this photo shoot for a billboard sign they're going to hang on Interstate 95. The Alphas are gonna have all the honeys coming to Central. But I've only got eyes for you, girl," Keith said in a hurry. "This photo shoot is about marketing the school. Gotta do my part."

"Hmmph. Tell me anything."

"Nikki, you have nothing to worry about. I'm the luckiest guy on the campus, in the State of North Carolina, across the world...

"All right, all right," Afrika said, holding her hand up for Keith to stop. "I get it."

"So where's your twin?"

"You mean Asia?"

"You know I'm talking about Asia. I swear your mommas must have used the same fertility clinic because you and Asia look so much alike."

"Okay, Keith. This is where I draw the line. Yes, Asia and I have some similarities, but I'm no test tube baby and I'm nobody's twin. And the reference to my momma is out of line and off limits to you. I don't play that when it comes to my mother."

"Whoa, whoa, whoa. Hey, baby, I didn't mean any disrespect. I wasn't trying to talk about nobody's momma. I was only talking about science—how two people with two different sets of parents, with two different sets of genes can have some of the same, almost identical features. My momma used to say that everyone has a twin in this world." Keith took Afrika's head and turned it toward him. "Now, don't I look like your boy, LeBron James?"

"You wish." Afrika's frown turned into a giggle. "You wish you were as tall as LeBron. Now that man is fine." Afrika giggled again.

"I know you aren't saying he's finer than me."

"You are so conceited. But, Boo, you do look better than LeBron."

"I knew it. I knew it."

"Keith, you are so crazy. Look, I've got to get to my class. I don't want to be late."

"What are you doing after class?"

"I've got cheerleading practice."

"After that?"

"I'm not sure. Asia talked about going to some pizza joint."

"Asia needs a man. She's pretty and all, but she doesn't have your personality." Keith pecked Afrika on the lips. "Just because old man Christianson is her daddy, she thinks she's all that."

"Come on, Keith. Be fair. Asia is nothing like her father. She's cool and I like her. And if you like me, you've got to like Asia. Anyway, she's got a man…Deon, the Eagles' quarterback."

"Deon? He'll break her heart. I hear he's been with a lot of women on campus."

"How would you know?" Afrika asked with a frown on her face.

"Stuff like that is no secret. Look, my good friend, Zavion, is probably Asia's type. He's a junior at UNC-Chapel Hill, about six feet, and he plays on UNC's basketball team. I'll talk to him. Maybe we can all get together before the Alpha party on Friday night."

"I don't know if that's a good idea, Keith. Asia is a little high strung, and she may not take too kindly to us interfering in her personal life, and like I said, she's seeing someone."

"True, but it doesn't have to be a date. Look, we don't even have to tell her that Zavion is coming. If everything works out, I'll have Zavion meet us somewhere."

"Whatever. I've got to go. Call me later."

Keith gave Afrika a quick kiss on the lips and took another peek at her behind. Satisfied, he gave her a parting smile. "Okay, babe." Before Afrika was out of sight, Keith took out his cell phone and called Zavion.

TWO DAYS HAD PASSED SINCE VICTOR HAD SHOWN UP ON MIMI's doorstep unannounced. Even the erratic phone calls seemed to cease. She wasn't going to let Victor's threats get her down. Afrika had a right to attend North

Carolina Central University as much as Asia. But it was her talk with Afrika that made Mimi feel much better.

Mimi went to her walk-in closet and pulled out a blue and white Adidas running suit. A run around Lake Johnson would do her some good. It had been a long time since she'd been to the lake, but she remembered they had a nice trail that wrapped around it. Getting into a fitness program was on her list of things to do.

With keys in hand, Mimi did a once around the condo, locked it, and headed for her candy-apple red Lexus that was parked in the garage, a gift from Raphael. Although a little breezy, it was a beautiful October day. The lake was about a forty-minute drive from where she lived in Durham. She couldn't wait to stretch her legs out on the trail and tone those muscles she'd neglected for the past few weeks.

Mimi turned up the volume on her stereo as her favorite CD by Norman Brown played. The love of jazz made Mimi think of the career she might have had if she hadn't been running away from ghosts that she thought might materialize at any time, resurrecting memories she tried to suppress that were now called her secrets.

Lost in the rhythm, Mimi thumped her thumbs on the steering wheel as Norman whaled out one of his ballads. Before she knew it, Mimi was leaving Interstate 40 and exiting onto Gorman Street. She made another quick right onto Tryon Road. In a short tenth of a mile, she arrived at her destination.

Mimi drove around until she found a place she wanted

to park. The temperature had risen slightly, and Mimi opted to take off her jacket and run in her sports bra and running pants. There were more people at the lake than she'd anticipated for a Thursday afternoon. Mothers pushing babies in strollers, students out for an afternoon jog, and business types with suits and tennis shoes hugged the trail. Mimi removed a terrycloth headband from the console of her car and headed toward the trail.

Standing in the grass close to the trail, Mimi spread her legs apart and locked her hands behind her head. She proceeded to loosen up her muscles by doing a few stretches and bends, rocking to one side and then the other, finally lifting her arms one at a time, reaching for the sky. Finished with her upper torso, she did some lunges, stepping back on one leg, moving her body over the forward leg, and bouncing before repeating the same process with the other leg. When she was finished, Mimi shook her body out and headed to the trail to begin her jog.

She was fit for a thirty-seven-year-old woman. Mimi had treated her body right and left the rest for Raphael to tend to. Gliding into her stride, Mimi trotted along the trail, giving herself a power boost every two hundred yards or so.

The lake became a mirror as the sunlit sky splashed its rays upon its surface, reflecting the pine trees that grew nearby and painted a picturesque scene that encompassed the few people who were in paddle boats navigating up and down the lake. A half-hour flew by and then another. Mimi hadn't felt in better shape. Looking at her watch, she decided another half to an hour wouldn't hurt.

Nearing the end of her last stretch she gave her legs a kick. Mimi sprinted like she was practicing for a marathon, but looked as pretty as a thoroughbred on its way to winning the Triple Crown. Her form was great and her muscles taunt. Nearing the last three meters before reaching her car, she slowed to a trot and caught her breath, giving her body time to cool down.

Mimi was in the moment. Her trot became a slow walk. Thrilled with herself for going the distance—a five-mile trek around the lake—she let out a victory scream. With hands on her hips, Mimi blew air from her mouth and nostrils, inhaled, and began to walk toward her car. She stopped cold in her tracks.

She hadn't seen him in nineteen years, but he looked as good as he did then, only now he was a little thicker and older. He was drenched in a layer of medium dark chocolate. He was of medium height, now bald, but she would've recognized him and those slightly bowed legs anywhere. He was what the old women meant when they said he could make a weak woman fall to her knees. If she had stayed in Durham, he would've been her baby's daddy. She wiped the thin coat of sweat that appeared on her face and moved out of her trance as her old love moved in her direction.

16

M imi tried to keep her eyes from devouring his meaty legs that lay exposed beyond the hottest pair of white short shorts she'd seen in a long time. Her eyes continued to travel upward and beyond the hemline of his shorts, relaxing momentarily on the jewel keeper and then up toward the upper torso that was draped in a thin T-shirt, his firm nipples producing a slight indentation, but yet enunciating the healthy pecks that lay underneath. Muscles rippled like an ancient road along his massive arms, for sure the result of lifting weights daily. Then she caught a glimpse of his lips—too inviting to ignore, and when their eyes connected, the smile she tried to hide erupted on her face like a volcano.

"Is that you, Mimi?" the handsome man asked, giving her the once over.

"John...John Carroll, is that you?" Mimi said in response.

They were within a foot of each other, each assessing and reassessing what they had obviously once remembered against what was now in front of them. Then John reached out and hugged her, and Mimi fell into his arms like it was the thing to do.

"Mimi Allen," John said, finally letting go as Mimi moved back. "Where have you been? We were supposed to be building an empire together, making babies, and making all kinds of beautiful music. What happened to you, girl? You look good so I'll assume life's been treating you kind. I can't believe my eyes."

"Hi, John. Wow."

"I know you can say more than that, girl. What have you been doing since you left me at the altar?"

Mimi tapped John playfully on the arm. "I didn't leave you at the altar. We weren't even engaged."

"Girl, you know we said we were going to be together forever. One day you were here, the next, no one could find you. Have you seen Brenda?"

"Not yet. I arrived in town a little over a month ago. My daughter is attending Central, and I moved here to be close to her."

"So what have you been up to?" John made no attempt to be discrete as he looked at Mimi's fingers. "I see you went and got hitched without me."

Mimi folded her arms across her chest and placed her hands under her underarms. "What about you? Are you married?"

"Divorced. Twice. Now answer my questions."

"I'm sorry I didn't tell you that I was leaving. I had some issues I had to contend with, and I had to get away to do it. I eventually went to Hampton U and got my degree, fell in love, got married, and have been moving around the country ever since. My husband is a Colonel in the United States Army."

"Oh, I see. Big dog. Got you a Colonel." John looked around as if expecting to see Mimi's partner trounce on him at any moment. "So where is this Colonel that you married?"

"He's in Germany commanding a brigade. He's been a wonderful husband and father."

"Well, girl, you certainly are a sight for sore eyes. If the Colonel doesn't mind me saying, you've still got it— the full package." John looked at his watch. "Maybe we can have a friendly, platonic lunch sometime."

"I don't think that would hurt. I don't have anything to write your information on, but my car is right over there," Mimi said, pointing in the direction of her car.

"Nice ride. The Colonel can afford it, I'm sure."

"Thank you," Mimi said sweetly, as she and John walked briskly to the car. She fought the urge to touch him, even playfully, as the memory of Raphael's hot phone sex tried to cloud her existing thoughts. There was no doubt in her mind that she loved her husband and she planned to be his wife until death they did part, but Satan had her salivating in the flesh at this sudden reunion of two lost souls.

Mimi opened the door and reached in and got her purse. She knew that John was stalking her booty with his eyes, even though she was covered up completely. He only had to imagine, but as suddenly as thoughts of those times they had been in each other arms were overtaking her, she came to her senses and eased out of the car with a piece of paper and a pencil. She wrote John's number down, and then wrote hers down for him.

He took the piece of paper she offered and looked into her eyes. Mimi saw his eye twinkle and for a half-second thought about giving him a kiss on the lips. She refrained, but she knew he noticed, and because of the intensity of the heat that had formed from them being so close together, John reached out and pulled her to him and kissed her on the lips.

"Mimi, I'm sorry," John said, as they recovered from his assault.

"Uhm, it's okay," Mimi whispered, bringing her lips together, savoring the moment. "Look, I'll call you…to see when you want to go to lunch."

"How about tomorrow? Do you live nearby?"

Mimi wasn't ready to tell anyone where she lived. God knows she'd be in trouble if she let him near her house. A ton of memories came rushing back of the day they had met during her first week in college and the fun they had had and the promises made. The only regret Mimi had was that she had never given him a taste of her forbidden fruit. She was the biggest tease and found herself many times in compromising positions, but she always managed to wiggle her way out of things, because she was saving herself for marriage…that was until Victor Christianson violated her body. She shuddered at the thought, and all of sudden she wanted revenge. "I live in Durham," Mimi heard herself say.

"I have a business meeting in the RTP tomorrow." Mimi wrinkled her nose. "The Research Triangle Park," John reminded her. "You haven't been gone that long. Anyway, I could meet you somewhere—your call. It's a Friday, and all the restaurants might be busy, so if you want to go around two in the afternoon, that would work for me."

"Two sounds good for me, too. I'll let you know the place."

"Well, it's a done deal. I thank the gods for smiling on me today."

"It was nice seeing you again, too, John. I'll see you tomorrow."

Mimi jumped into her car, afraid that if she lingered any longer, another kiss might have been imminent. She had loved John once, and seeing him now only brought memories of love to the surface. Raphael would always be her only true love, and Mimi sat in the car, trying to convince herself that she wasn't cheating on him.

She watched as John disappeared beyond the brush that led to the trail. She grinned in spite of herself, for truly the gods had given her something to smile about. Putting her car in reverse, Mimi moved out of the park and headed for the freeway with thoughts of seeing John again.

"Damn," Mimi said out loud. She had forgotten that

quickly that she'd promised to meet Brenda for lunch tomorrow. Well, she really did have an excuse this time. She'd think of something, and maybe after this second attempt to have lunch with her, Brenda would give up. "Damn."

17

Mimi hummed, whistled, and sang herself home. How she got home otherwise was a mystery. All she remembered was that she had put the car in gear, gotten on the freeway, and now she was pulling into the entrance of her subdivision. She was too old to a let a man that she hadn't seen in nineteen years, but still had it going on, work her nerves like that.

Looking wasn't a sin, but the kiss she had placed on that man's lips or the one he had placed on hers was. After all, she was a married woman—a happily married woman, and no other man would ever take the place of Raphael. Raphael was the provider, the protector, and the only lover for her because he did it so well. They were each other's rock, salvation, the end of all ends.

So why was she thinking about John? He was her first real love, although she never had sex with him. There was no memory to make her stomach feel queasy as it did now. Maybe it was a friendly face in the midst of the warfare she had going on with Victor. Nevertheless, she couldn't wipe the smile off her face as she fantasized about seeing John in his ultra short shorts.

Mimi pulled her car into the attached garage, still humming as she got out. Floating on cloud nine, she retrieved the mail from the mailbox and went into the house. She deposited her things on a chair in the kitchen and immediately went to the junk drawer and removed her journal and began to write.

October 9, 2008

I can't get this silly grin off of my face. Who would have thought that I'd see him again? For the first time since arriving in Durham, I plunged back into my fitness program. I drove to Lake Johnson because I remembered the wonderful walking trails that looped around the lake. After a short warm-up session, I walked, sprinted, ran for five miles. I felt wonderful, and the day couldn't have been more beautiful. And then there he was.

At the end of my run, I headed back to my car. Imagine the shock when I saw this handsome man heading toward me, and as I took a second look, realized it was John, my long lost love, although he was a little older and had added a few pounds. I'm sure it was attributed to age and by all appearances his constant workout at the gym.

He was wearing these cute white shorts, exposing those legs that he used to wrap around me when I would tease him and then refuse to give up the goods. But his whole body made my knees tremble, and when he kissed me on the lips—no tongue, although I would have accepted it, I wanted to melt. I know that if I had gotten any closer to him, felt the bulge in all of his muscles, I would have been done for.

But like most married women, I came to my senses. I don't think Raf would be upset with me for entertaining a fantasy of my brief encounter. He even admitted to me that when I described how Victor was checking me out, it turned him on. And it proved to be the best phone sex we'd ever had.

Maybe I'm feeling a little bit guilty for having these feelings. True, I miss my husband, but John provided a visual to get me through tonight. Help me, Lord. Earth to Mimi.

But I'm going to see John again—to catch up for old time's sake. I really hate to diss Brenda, but it's probably for the best since her crazy, warped husband has warned me to stay away from her. My gut feeling, though, tells me something else is going on in the Christianson household, and I believe Brenda needs a friend. I owe it to her, but I'm going to meet John on Friday. I'm going to see Brenda, but I've got to do this other thing for myself.

Wow, I'm still grinning...smiling. Oops. Dropped my pen, but I'm back. I feel so silly—like I've got this schoolgirl crush on the hottest boy on the football team. He is that, now. But Raf, I love you more.

Mimi Bailey

Mimi closed her journal and sat at the table with the biggest grin painted on her face. She picked up her purse from the chair and pulled out the piece of paper with John's telephone number on it. She fingered the paper, reached for her cell, dialed the first three digits, and hit the END button. What in the hell was she doing?

She had a wonderful life, and her purpose at the moment was to help get Afrika through college.

The BlackBerry clinked on the glass of the kitchen table as it slipped out of Mimi's hand. She picked up her mail and began to sift through it. Advertisement, bill, bill, advertisement and a folded up piece of paper. Mimi unfolded it and dropped it on the table upon reading the cryptic message.

What are you waiting for? I've given you fair warning. Take your daughter and get out of Durham. If you don't take care of it soon, I will take matters into my own hands. And stay away from Brenda.

"You sorry son-of-a-bitch. I'm not going anywhere and you don't scare me," Mimi said out loud. She picked up the piece of paper, wadded it up, and threw it across the room. Two seconds later, she retrieved it and put it in the junk drawer underneath her journal. "This piece of paper is going to convict your ass; I'm going to do something that I should've done a long time ago."

Mimi picked up her BlackBerry and dialed John's number. She needed to confide in someone—she needed to let someone know that Victor had threatened her. John was going to get an earful at lunch and, for the first time, she felt good about sharing her secret.

18

"I'm so glad today is Friday," Afrika said to Asia as they crossed the campus on their way to the W. G. Pearson Cafeteria.

"Me, too," Asia said. "If we didn't have to cheer tomorrow, I could sleep until noon. So what's up with tonight?"

"You said we were going to some pizza joint. I hope you don't mind that I invited Keith along."

"Naw, but that's going to make it a threesome, and I'm the third wheel. Deon has football practice and can't come. Anyway, I get this funny feeling Keith doesn't like me."

"Why would you think that? And for the record, you're never a third wheel. If it makes you feel better, we can pretend that Keith is taking the both of us out."

"It's all right, Nikki. I don't need a man to complete me, even though Deon and I are getting along quite well."

"I wasn't trying to imply you did. I want you to be comfortable with the arrangement because we'll be three friends out for pizza and enjoying each other's company."

"Okay with me."

"Who cares what other people think anyway?" Afrika asked. "We're individuals with independent thinking. We must rise beyond the childishness of high school and act like the adults we're destined to become."

Asia scrunched up her face until her mouth was twisted into some abstract art form. "Did you learn that in Psychology 101 or are you one of those reincarnated beings that have returned to earth to set the Generation X population straight?"

Now it was Afrika's turn to look at Asia in amazement. "Look at us. All this mumbo jumbo because we talked about going out for some pizza—with Keith."

"I know. Silly, huh?" Asia said with a grin.

"Yep. Let's worry about lunch first."

The girls headed into the cafeteria. Afrika pulled out her Eagle card and gave it to the cashier to swipe.

"I'm sorry, your card is declined," the cashier said, handing the card back to Afrika.

"Declined?" Afrika asked. "I used it yesterday. I have a meal plan."

"Well, baby, there's nothing I can do. You need to check with the business office."

"Would you mind trying again?" Afrika pushed. "I don't understand this."

An ugly frown formed on the cashier's face. "Give me the card," the cashier said in a gruff voice. Afrika passed the card to the lady with a glare on her face. "Declined," the cashier said again. "Next."

"Nikki, I'll pay for your lunch. There has to be some explanation. Please swipe it twice," Asia said to the cashier, who still had an ill look on her face.

Afrika rolled her eyes and twisted her foot. She put her card in her backpack and walked with Asia to get her food in silence.

"There's got to be some explanation," Asia said again.

"You're right. But what pisses me off more is how that woman looked at me like I was trying to get in free. I have a meal plan for the whole semester. I've eaten in here every day since I arrived on campus. They're going to fix this today."

"Well, let's go eat now. You can take care of that after lunch."

Mimi primped in the bathroom mirror, finally dabbing her lips with a burnt-orange lipgloss. With her rat-tail comb, she lifted her hair a little in the center, brushed her sides down, and then patted her lips together one last time. Mimi seemed pleased at the reflection in the mirror that smiled back.

She let out a sigh as she walked from the bathroom into her bedroom and took a quick spin in front of the floor-length mirror. Several outfits lay across the bed as Mimi contemplated what to wear. First it was a cute summer dress, and even though it was October, it was still warm outside. But she dismissed it. Then she thought a nice salmon-colored pantsuit would do, but that might have been too much. It was only a casual lunch with an old friend. Finally, Mimi pulled out a cute pumpkin-colored chemise that hit just above the knees—enough to show off a little leg, but not so much that his mind would wander while they were having a heart-to-heart conversation. The scoop of the neck showed enough cleavage to make him want a second helping. Mimi was pleased.

Lunch with John was to be a catch up session about old times, Mimi told herself. Nothing more, nothing less, except she warned him that she had to discuss a personal matter with him that was part of her past. Mimi looked forward to their meeting, although having to break her lunch date with Brenda was more difficult than she had anticipated. Clearly, Brenda was annoyed but mostly pissed off because Mimi had waited until the last half of the last minute to tell her. And Brenda hung up without saying goodbye.

Mimi dismissed her phone call with Brenda and concentrated on her lunch date. She grabbed her purse, locked the door, and went into the garage and got into her car. She eased out slowly, let the garage door down, and looked around. She didn't like the idea that Victor had been lurking around her place sight unseen. Seeing no one, she drove out of the subdivision and headed for Applebee's at Brier Creek.

The restaurant wasn't very crowded as the lunchtime

crowd had come and gone. It was five minutes to two when she arrived, and when she entered, she saw John sitting in a corner, looking dapper in a white woven short-sleeved shirt, his bald head shiny under the light that hung overhead. He waved to her with what looked like a newspaper, anticipating her arrival.

John stood up as Mimi reached the table, kissed her hand, and then sat down after she took her seat.

"A perfect gentleman," Mimi said, and then smiled. "And you smell good, too."

"For a perfect woman," John said, taking snapshots of Mimi with his mind for later viewing. "You look fabulous."

"Thank you."

They made small talk until the waiter arrived. They ordered sweet tea and grilled-chicken salads, and continued their conversation.

"So you were married?" Mimi asked.

"You don't waste time, I see," John said. Mimi smiled. "Twice. You didn't know either one of them. I could never do it right; my mind was always on you and the promises we made to each other."

"John, you're telling a big, fat lie. I probably wasn't gone two minutes before you dismissed me and were on your way to your next conquest."

"No, I beg to differ. It was five minutes." They laughed. "At any rate, I moved on with life. My first marriage was to a girl that I went to high school with. We dated off and on, kept in touch, and when I finished college, I got my first job with a pharmaceutical company, got married, and had a son whose name is Julian. He's attending Xavier…wants to practice medicine."

"Good for him. And what about your second wife?"

"Well, she was my rebound bride. My first wife had an affair with another guy who also went to high school with us. She left me for him. At first, I was devastated. I was truly in love with that woman, Mimi. I thought it would last forever, but apparently I was wrong. So Deborah, my second wife, scooped me up, baggage and all. It was destined for failure. But I'm a better person today. Don't think I'll do the marriage thing again."

Mimi smiled and looked away, letting go of some faraway thought.

"So what about you, Miss Setrine Allen, better known as Mimi, the girl with the golden voice?"

Mimi dropped her head momentarily, then brought it up and smiled. "I'm sorry I wasn't there when you decided to get married. I've often thought how life with you would have been. Don't get me wrong; I do love my life now. After leaving Central, I went to Virginia and finished my degree at Hampton. That's where I met my husband, Raphael. He was an ROTC cadet. We got married in the winter of my sophomore year and I became Mrs. Setrina Bailey. Raphael was commissioned as an Army officer right out of college and immediately, I became a military spouse. We have one daughter, and her name is Afrika."

"Different, pretty," John said. "I like that. So did you ever do any singing? I thought for sure you were going to record on some big record label and give Whitney and Mariah a run for their money."

"I…I thought about it, but my life as an officer's wife was somewhat demanding."

"Hold up. Had your husband not heard your voice? Girl, you know you had some pipes on you. Any man who'd stand in the way of you realizing your dreams is a fool."

"No, it wasn't like that at all. Raphael was behind me, if that's what I had wanted to do. At first, he was a little reluctant, but I had the green light. I was offered a contract with Arista Records…but I turned it down."

"Mimi, were you on drugs? You could've been living large."

"I have everything I need—a wonderful husband and a beautiful daughter. I dote on them."

"That's why I liked you," John said, staring at Mimi as if he'd just discovered who she was. "You were simple but elegant. You didn't need a lot to make you happy. Now, I would've pushed you into that recording contract. And, Mimi, you would've had ten platinum records hanging in the den by now. But this ain't about me.

"So besides being a mother and an officer's wife, what else did you do? What was your degree in?"

"My degree was in elementary education. I taught elementary school for a while, but later, when my husband moved up in the ranks, I stopped working. It was somewhat taboo for an officer's wife to work. You supported him and the wives of his command. I was busy volunteering for this and that, and believe it or not, I rather enjoyed it. Plus, I had Afrika to take care of, and when she went to school, she was involved in everything from A to Z."

"Sounds like a cozy environment."

"It agreed with me," Mimi said and smiled. "And I love my husband."

John seemed to soak in Mimi's words as he went from talkative to quiet. Then he spoke. "So what was it you wanted to talk to me about that couldn't wait?"

Mimi knew John was reacting to her statement about being in love with her husband. Saying it out loud was protection from herself. This man was so handsome, sitting in front of her. It wouldn't take much for her to jump to the side of the table where he sat and rub his head. She pushed back the thought. "Umm…"

"Two grilled chicken salads," the waiter said. "Sorry, I forgot your teas. I'll bring them out right away."

"No problem," John said. Turning to Mimi, "I guess you were saved by the bell. But you're not leaving this restaurant until you tell me what's on your mind."

Mimi looked at John thoughtfully. "Okay."

"Let's eat."

19

They ate their salads in silence, each taking a furtive glance at the other in between sips of iced tea and the next forkful of lettuce leaves. Mimi found John charming and could tell that he was walking the chalk line of their newfound relationship. The cards were already on the table—old friends sharing lunch. She made it known that she was a happily married woman and he wasn't looking for anyone to settle down with for the death do us part.

Mimi relaxed and smiled. On cue, John relaxed, smiled, and put his fork down.

"So tell me, Mimi...uhh...what was so important that we had to meet for lunch today? Not that I'm not enjoying every minute of it."

Alarm rose on Mimi's face and her body tensed. John's body language said one thing, but the tone in his voice said another. She couldn't believe he had the audacity to make her feel as if she had begged him to meet her for lunch.

John caressed Mimi's unoccupied hand. "Chill, Mimi. Did I say something wrong? If looks could kill, I'd already be at the morgue."

Mimi looked at John and then down at her salad. "I hope you don't think I was desperate when I called you last night. I was so taken aback when I ran into you yesterday that I thought it would be great to catch up for old time's sake."

"I'm here, aren't I?"

"It's that cynical tone in your voice that…"

"Mimi, Mimi. Don't mind me. Maybe I'm a little nervous about seeing you after all these years. You're a beautiful woman, got your youth still hanging on you. Truth is, I wish it could've…no need to go there."

"You wish what, John?" Mimi took a sip of her iced tea to cool and calm her nerves.

"I…I wish it was me that married you." John looked away, and then back into Mimi's eyes. He lifted both of her hands and held them. "I can also tell that something is going on with you. I'm pretty discerning of that, although I don't know what it is. I want you to know that I'm here for you, no matter what, if you need someone to talk to. I hope we can always be friends."

"That's so kind of you, John." Mimi pulled her hands back, afraid of the rising tide of lust that was coursing through her body. "We'll always be friends, and I thank you for wanting to be there for me."

"So…are you going to tell me what's bothering you?"

Bring, bring. Mimi picked up her purse, took out her BlackBerry, and looked at the caller ID.

"I know you aren't going to answer that," John mouthed just above a whisper.

"It's my daughter. It must be important if she's calling me in the middle of the day." Mimi hit TALK. "Afrika, what's up, honey?"

"Mommy, I went to eat lunch today, and they said my Eagle card was declined. I've used this card every day since I arrived on this campus, and I can't understand why it won't work today. I went to the card office, and they said some kind of hold has been placed on my account."

"Slow down, Afrika. What do you mean, a hold's been placed against your account? You have a meal plan that I purchased for the whole semester and your tuition has also been paid. This doesn't make sense."

"That's what I'm trying to tell you. Mommy, it was so embarrassing and humiliating. Asia paid for my lunch, but I was so friggin' mad. And those people at the Business Office don't have a caring soul in their bodies."

"Now, don't make rash judgments. There has to be some explanation."

"You weren't there, Mommy. They looked at me like I was some kind of welfare kid sponging off the government or some baby freshman complaining about nothing. I had to point my finger in that girl's face and tell her my parents had paid my tuition and fees in cash and in full."

"That doesn't solve the problem, Afrika. And you know better than that."

"I know, Mommy."

"I hope you weren't disrespectful, Afrika."

"Mommy, I wasn't," Afrika said, her voice raised an octave higher than the moment before. "You would've been mad, too. All that lady did was shrug her shoulders. Pissed me the hell off. I wanted to knock her off the chair she was sitting in."

"I do understand how you feel, baby, and believe me when I say that I'm going to get to the bottom of this. Don't you worry. Do you need any money?"

"No, I have some money left from the allowance you gave me. I'm sorry, Mommy, for my outburst. I just went crazy because it seemed like no one wanted to help."

"You have every right to be upset, baby. Mommy's on the case. Don't you worry about a thing. I'll call you later."

"Love you, Mommy."

"Love you, too, Afrika." Mimi shut the phone off and placed it in her purse.

When she looked up, John was sitting back with his arms crossed and a wicked smile on his face. A tender moment passed between the two. "I loved the way you handled the situation with your daughter."

Mimi grinned. "Afrika is my heart. She's a good girl, good student, and a hard worker. There's nothing I wouldn't do for her. My child has had the best upbringing a parent could give."

Mimi took the opportunity to swipe the top of her blouse with her index and middle fingers, a sign that she was a proud momma and knew it. "John, you've been asking what's on my mind since I arrived at the restaurant."

John sat up and leaned forward, giving Mimi his undivided attention. The waiter stopped by the table and poured refills of iced tea. Mimi took a sip and pursed her lips.

"My daughter called to tell me that her student card that allows her to eat in the dining hall and purchase various things across campus was declined when she tried to get some lunch. I don't know what the problem is but I'm going to get to the bottom of it before this afternoon is over. However, I do have a sneaky suspicion about who may be behind this."

"You really think someone is behind this? It couldn't be some kind of fluke?" John asked with genuine concern in his voice.

"It's not a fluke; it's Victor Christianson."

"Victor Christianson?" John asked, a puzzled look on his face.

"Yes, Victor."

"What makes you think Victor is behind this? I remember him as one of those cocky niggas from the hood that thought he was better than the rest of us. I didn't kick it with him too much. After I pledged Kappa Alpha Psi and he pledged Omega Psi Phi, our circle of friends shifted.

"Brenda, on the other hand, is totally different. I run into her every now and then at some social gathering. I never understood her attraction to Victor. He was a hood rat then, and he's still a hood rat disguised in designer clothing. She deserves much better than Victor. I hear he screwed his way to the admission director's position, and I don't mean with Brenda. He's been stepping out on her for years."

Mimi's eyebrows went up like radar beams as she pondered what John had said. She was going to make it her business to reschedule her lunch date with Brenda.

"John, I don't mean to interrupt, and I don't know why I'm telling you this, but Victor has been harassing me."

"Harassing you, how?"

"He showed up at my house on Monday, threatened me, and…and put his hands on me. This was the first time I'd seen him since I left Durham all those years ago."

"He did what? Did you call the police? What in the hell did he want?"

"I should've called the police but I was afraid to. He told me that I had to take my daughter out of school and leave Durham."

Again, a puzzled look formed on John's face. "I'm sorry, Mimi, but I'm not following you. There must be something I'm missing. Why would Victor tell you to leave town when, as far as I can tell, he's had no contact with you? It doesn't make sense."

"It all began nineteen years ago when I was a freshman."

The countenance on John's face changed again. "What are you talking about, Mimi?" His eyes searched hers.

"Victor raped me."

John sat like a stiff piece of cardboard in his seat, his tongue tied to his lower jaw, afraid to move, although his eyes darted back and forth before finally penetrating Mimi's soul. He recovered from the news, looked away, and then back at Mimi.

"Maybe my ears deceived me, but you didn't just say that Victor raped you?"

"He raped me and I got pregnant. That's why I fled. I couldn't tell anyone; not you and especially not Brenda. You see, she was also pregnant."

"Oh my God! You should've told me anyway."

"I couldn't, John. I was so ashamed."

A scowl crossed John's face. He banged the table with his fist and looked up at Mimi. "I could kill Victor."

"I believe you would've tried to, but at what cost? You might've ended up in jail without the career you're now enjoying."

"Mimi, you were always the voice of reason. But tell me how did Victor know you were here and how did he find out you were pregnant?"

"John, this sounds like a scene out of a made for TV movie, but it's the truth. I had no plans to ever return to Durham. My daughter's the only reason I'm here. It was her desire to come to Central, and while I tried everything I could to discourage her, she prevailed, and I'm here. I hoped and prayed that I wouldn't run into anyone I knew, and that I could remain in the shadows.

"As they say, this is a small world; you ran into me."

"It is. But you don't know the half. My daughter befriended a young lady who happened to be Victor's daughter. Ready for this? They look like twins, except Afrika is a little darker than Asia."

"And they're both named after continents."

"That's only the beginning of their similarities. But what no one knows except you and Victor is that my daughter and her best friend are half-sisters. The girls don't even know."

"Damn, Mimi." John exhaled. "This is reality TV at its best. I feel your pain."

"Anyway," Mimi interjected, "I've got Victor breathing down my neck on one hand and Brenda begging me to have lunch on the other. I've managed to dodge her because I've been trying to protect my secret. Although, if Victor has his way, I'll never see her."

"What are you going to do?"

"Initially, John, I thought about packing my stuff and getting the hell out of Durham. But the more belligerent Victor has gotten, the more determined I am to stay and face him head on. I'm sure he's behind the trouble Afrika is having with her meal card. I need to leave so I can check on it."

"What does your husband say?" John blurted out.

"Raphael? He offered to come home and take matters into his own hands." Mimi didn't tell John that Raphael had no idea that she was raped. What would John say if he knew he was the first person she's shared her secret with?

"Seriously, Mimi, you need to get a restraining order on Victor. I worry that he might try something else."

"While I was at Lake Johnson yesterday, he apparently stopped by my house. He left me one of his little hate messages in my mailbox."

John sighed. It must have been clear to him by now why Mimi had called him so quickly. "Why don't you go and take care of the matter with your daughter, and if you like, I can come by later—to keep you company in the event old dude decides to drop by and give you another warning."

"That won't be necessary, John. I think he has enough sense not to do something crazy."

"He's already begun, Mimi. You believe he's behind your daughter's mishap, and that was to get your attention, but what if he decides to take it to the next level?"

"You're right."

"Of course, I'm right. Look, let me make a couple of calls to let the folks know that I won't be returning to the office today. Then I'm going to go to Central with you. I might have to call on Victor. No ifs, ands, or buts about it."

"John, I don't want you to get involved. I can handle it."

"I'm already involved."

"Ohhhhhhh, woooooooooo." Mimi sighed. She shook

slightly, the weight of her secret, the burden she carried for the last nineteen years finally released. Then her mind wandered—took a second look. Had she done the right thing by confiding in John about something she had been unable to share with her own husband? What if her secret became airborne? What if John unintentionally shared her secret with others? "Gosh," was the lone word that slipped from between Mimi's lips.

"What is it, Mimi?" John asked.

"Nothing."

"Okay, Mimi," John said, as if he could read her mind. "Are you sorry you told me?"

The look in her eyes as they shifted back and forth, gauging the man who sat in front of her, said it all. Mimi dropped her head. "I don't know what possessed me to open up to you like that. I haven't seen you in years, and our first conversation after all this time was a mere ten minutes in passing in a parking lot yesterday."

"Stop, Mimi." John offered his napkin so she could catch the tears that began to form. "Your secret is safe with me. Let's face this demon together."

"Thank you, John."

John waved the waiter over. "As soon as I pay the bill and make these few phone calls, we'll go," he said to Mimi. "No need to go it alone. Big brother has your back." Mimi smiled and John smiled back, winked, and put the phone to his ear. "You're welcome," he mouthed.

20

Mimi walked to the passenger side of John's gray Ford Explorer and hopped in. Only for an instant did she think about having John follow her home so she could drop her car off. Although the idea was tempting, it really wasn't a good idea. She didn't want her new neighbors to think that she was a loose woman entertaining a host of strange men in their quiet neighborhood. It would take two hours tops to complete her mission at NC Central, after which she'd pick up her car and head to her cozy condo, alone.

"All clear," John said, offering Mimi an enthusiastic smile as he shut the lid on his cell phone. "I'm on your clock."

"Thanks for going with me to clear up this matter for Afrika. I appreciate your friendship."

"No need to thank me. I would have done it for you at the drop of a hat."

John put the car in gear and gave Mimi another enthusiastic smile, while running his eyes along the smooth muscles in Mimi's calves.

"Watch it!" Mimi shouted as John mashed the brakes

to keep from hitting a car that was slowly moving in front of him. "Don't make me have to jump out of this car and drive myself."

"No need. The brother ain't gonna let nothing hurt you."

"Yeah, right. Pay attention." They laughed.

"Okay, Mimi, I'm listening. That was a close call. Your legs shouldn't have been looking so good, girl. They are a distraction, you know."

"Then I'll drive myself," Mimi said, attempting to pull open the door handle.

"Okay, sister, close the door. I'm now on my best behavior. From here on out, my eyes are on the traffic in front of me." They laughed again.

"John, I'm glad we got together today. I needed a little laughter."

"Glad to be of service."

They drove in silence for the next twenty minutes, observing the scenery for what it was, while taking quick glances in each other's directions.

"Your colonel is a lucky man," John said, taking a moment to look at Mimi while the light was red.

"He certainly is, but I'm equally as fortunate. Raphael has been very good to me."

"Well," John said changing the subject and moving forward as the light turned green, "we're at our destination. Where to?"

"I want to go to the business office first. John…"

"What, Mimi?"

"John, I need to go by myself. I'm going to call my daughter and have her meet me. I don't think it wise… to…you know…for you to be with me."

"No problem. I'm here if you need me. I may pay Mr. Christianson a visit."

"John, I appreciate you coming with me. I needed your moral support after talking with Afrika. It may make matters worse if you talk to Victor, especially if my theory is right."

"So…you don't want me to…just say hello for old time's sake?"

"John, you're a jewel. I don't want to make any waves for Afrika."

"I thought this was the reason I was accompanying you?"

"Let it go, John. I wasn't thinking straight." Mimi balled her hands into little fists and released them. "I got caught up in…"

"You couldn't resist my charm?" John said, and then chuckled.

"John, you're making this harder than it's supposed to be."

"I got you, Mimi. Handle your business. I'll be around."

"Okay," Mimi said, and took off in the direction of the business office.

John stood at attention with his arms folded and watched as Mimi strolled toward the brick building. Mimi turned around slowly and saw John staring and quickly turned back around and walked as fast as she could. John smiled, unfolded his arms, contemplated something, and began to move forward.

Before John could talk himself out of it, he found himself in the lobby of the Admissions Office. There was very little traffic, and he approached the receptionist with his best smile. The receptionist smiled back.

"Good afternoon," John said, giving the pretty young lady with the bleached blonde hair a quick once over. Her oval face was a smooth caramel with deep, brown eyes that smiled back at John, and her medium-thick lips were inviting. She was very attractive, but getting past her and into Victor Christianson's office was his priority.

"Hello…ahh, ahh," John said as he looked for a nameplate.

"It's Ms. Simpson," the pretty lady said, now showing her pearly whites.

"Ms. Simpson, my name is John Carroll, and I'm an old friend of Mr. Victor Christianson. I was in the neighborhood, and I was hoping to say hello. All I need is a few minutes."

"Let me check with his secretary." Ms. Simpson dialed a number, allowing her roving eyes to keep John in her sight…keeping him under tight scrutiny. "Sheila," she whispered, looking up at John who backed away, "there's a fine brother out front wanting to see your boss. He says he's a friend of Mr. Christianson. Girl, he's so damn good looking, I just want to throw myself at him, and explain later."

"Phyllis, you are so crazy. I'm sure he's not as fine as Victor."

"I don't know what you see in him. Everybody has had him."

"Why don't you let me worry about that? Anyway, he's a last fling before I tie the knot. I'm going to milk Victor for all I can get. I am, however, getting a little sick and tired of his daughter showing up whenever she gets good and ready, demanding his attention. But none of that will matter soon."

"Well, Ms. Sheila, if that's what you want, but you know you're not being fair to the man you claim you're going to spend the rest of your life with. Look, my fine brother seems a little agitated, so would you let me know if the great Mr. Victor Christianson will see him?"

"What's his name?"

"Girl, I forgot that fast. Hold on; let me ask." Phyllis placed one hand over the mouthpiece of the phone. "Sir, may I have your name again, please?"

"John Carroll." He smiled.

"It's John Carroll," Phyllis said to Sheila. "Okay." Phyllis hung up the phone. "Mr. Carroll, Mr. Christianson's secretary will call me in a minute to see if…"

"Saved by the phone," John said, anxious to have his time with Victor.

"Okay, I'll let him know," Phyllis said, hanging up the

phone. "Mr. Christianson will see you, Mr. Carroll. He only has a few minutes."

"That will be fine. Point the way."

John followed Phyllis' instructions and found himself in front of Sheila's desk. Before he was able to introduce himself, the door opened and a smiling Victor came out.

"I'll be damned. What brings you to my neck of the woods after all this time?" Victor asked John, giving him the fist bump. "Come on in."

Sheila recoiled after Victor slammed the door. She picked up the phone and dialed Phyllis. "Girl, I think you're right about this one. I won't be mad if you snatch him for yourself. I'll see if I can get the four-one-one on him."

"Thanks for looking out."

"Gotcha, Phyllis. Will talk with you later."

JOHN FOLLOWED VICTOR INTO HIS OFFICE AND SAT IN the wing-back chair in front of Victor's desk.

"When was the last time we spoke…four, five…six, seven years ago?" Victor asked, as he crossed his legs, leaning back in his chair almost as far as it would go without tipping over.

"It probably has been longer than that. I can't remember."

"So, John, what brings you by? We weren't running partners nor fraternity brothers in college, so I'm rather surprised by your sudden appearance."

"I've been keeping up with you, Victor. You've made a name for yourself here at Central—one of its graduates holding a top spot at their alma mater."

"Well, I'd like to think of it as having reaped the fruits of my very good education. So what have you been up to?"

"I'm doing well. I work in the Research Triangle Park for a drug company. Not much else going on. Now that all prelims are aside, I did come here today to talk with you about something that is weighing heavily on my mind."

Surprise registered on Victor's face. Like a large object in a giant sling, he snapped back into an upright position, waiting to hear what John had to say. He picked up a pencil and began to drum lightly on his desk.

"We have a mutual friend that has some concerns about the treatment of her daughter on this campus," John began.

Victor searched John's face, waiting for the obvious— the name of the student in question.

"Our friend feels that her daughter may be the target of someone's malicious attempt to interrupt her education," John continued. "I hope you can assist me in finding out who the perpetrator might be and put a stop to the madness." John paused a moment to let the information sink in.

"I'm listening," Victor said, the unwelcome sign now posted on his face.

"This student has been harassed in a number of ways, and I come to you as a friend in high places that can move through the system faster than through the regular hierarchy."

Victor looked at John thoughtfully. "Why come to me? The student has a recourse; one being the Counseling Center. Secondly, we are bound by FERPA, which means I'm unable to disclose any information about a student that is enrolled here without that student's permission. The student will have to request intervention. Even the parents must get a release from the student before we can provide them with information."

John licked his lips. "I'm trying to be tactful as I know how."

Victor's stare penetrated John's soul. "Tell me, John, what's this all about? Who is the student in question? Who is this mutual friend we have in common that is concerned about their loved one's well-being? Let them come to me and inquire. So if there's nothing else, I'm afraid this meeting is over." Victor looked at his watch. "I've got another meeting in a few minutes."

"I'm not ready to leave yet."

"This meeting is over." Victor stood up and showed John the door.

"I'm here to serve you notice, Victor. If you as so much go near or call Mimi again, you're going to have to answer to me. *Comprende?*"

"So, you've still got a love jones for an old flame?" Victor snickered. "Look, John, I don't know what Mimi has told you, but it's not true. I haven't seen or heard from Mimi in nineteen years. You should know better than anyone about how she vanished into thin air. Females."

"You can say what you want, Victor, but I've got my eyes on you. Touch Mimi again, and you'll realize that I wasn't spewing out an idol threat." John looked at his watch. "I'm leaving. I've wasted enough of my precious time already."

John walked out of the office without Victor having the opportunity to utter another word. John passed Sheila's desk and gave her wink. Even though she had a phone to her ear, Sheila's smile went from one end of her face to the other.

Inside his office, Victor was fuming. Someone was going to pay.

21

Victor slammed his fist on the desk and flopped down into his chair. Mimi had pushed the envelope. She had been warned, and now she had the audacity to involve someone else in their affairs. What did John know? Had Mimi confided in John that he had fathered Afrika?

Victor picked up the telephone and dialed Mimi's number. It rang without an answer. He slammed the receiver down, pushed back in his chair, got up and exited the office, stopping at Sheila's desk.

"Sheila, I've got to make a quick run off campus. I'm not sure how long I'll be. Clear my schedule for the rest of the afternoon. If anyone should ask, tell them I had a personal matter I had to take care of."

"Will do, Victor."

"Don't ever call me by my first name in public," Victor hissed. "Crazy broad," he said as he walked away.

"Uhm," Sheila retorted under her breath. "We'll see who's crazy."

THE WIND BEGAN TO WHIP, OFFERING A NICE BREEZE. Fallen leaves rattled along the sidewalk along with other debris that wasn't nailed down. Victor brushed back his hair with his hand and moved swiftly toward the parking lot. He stopped abruptly as he caught a glimpse of them out of the corner of his eye. Right in front of him in the parking lot were Mimi and John in an animated conversation.

In an effort not to be seen, Victor moved out of sight, sure that the conversation was about him. Then joining them was Afrika. Mimi seemed to be introducing her to John by the way she was moving her hands. Victor turned and went back to his office; this wasn't the time to confront Mimi, but he would. There was urgency in what he needed to do. His sins of the past were threatening to be exposed, but if he could help it, and he would, this was one secret he was going to keep from Brenda and the rest of the world. Mimi be damned.

A surprised look registered on Sheila's face at Victor's abrupt return. He dismissed her and went into his office, slamming the door behind him. Sheila looked at the closed door with puzzlement in her eyes. She puckered her lips and then picked up the telephone.

"Phyllis," Sheila whispered into the phone.

"Hey, girl, what's up? And why are you whispering?"

"My boss is up to something. He's been acting strange ever since that visitor came in here this afternoon."

"You mean that fine, bald-headed hunk?"

"Yeah, yeah, him. Anyway, Victor has been banging doors and everything else since that guy left. But not only that, he left work to take care of some personal business. It's like he's being secretive about it. In fact, five minutes ago, he said he was going out and to clear his calendar. Then he shows back up two minutes after he left and slams the door."

"Like you don't have secrets. You don't think he's cheating on you, do you?" Phyllis laughed.

"This is not funny, Phyllis. I tell you, something strange is going on with that man. Anyway, how can he cheat on me with his wife?" Sheila and Phyllis laughed. "You know Victor isn't the only one sharing my bed."

"That's what I mean by secrets. When are you going to tell him you're getting married to what's his name?" Phyllis snapped her fingers, trying to remember.

"Jamal Billops."

"And how are you going to manage that? You better hope Mr. Christianson never finds out that someone else has been sleeping in the condo he put the down payment on, and you might as well say he's paying for."

"Who's going to tell him? I don't plan on telling him anything...at least not right away. Not until after Jamal and I are married. We're thinking about getting married soon...like next weekend."

"Shut up, girl. Go on now—you and Jamal. I don't know why you're attracted to that old-ass wannabe player Christianson. Yeah, he still looks good and all, but he's played out, Sheila, and you know he's sticking it to more than you."

"Shut up, Phyllis. I'm using him like he's using me. I like being kept. No strings."

"Uhm hmm. I'm telling you, Sheila, he's still a snake in the grass and you better watch your back. But back to the subject, what makes you suspect he's up to something?"

"I just know Victor is up to something. Call it intuition. It's the way…"

"Sheila, come into my office," Victor said as he stood over Sheila with the phone in her ear.

"May I get your number, please?" Sheila asked into the phone, scribbling down some imaginary numbers.

"Busted, huh?" Phyllis shot back.

"Yes, thank you." Sheila hung up the phone.

Sheila drew in her breath and let out a deep sigh. She followed Victor into his office and stood a few feet from his desk.

"Close the door," Victor said, his face devoid of expression. "Have a seat."

Sheila sat down in the chair in front of Victor's desk. Nerves replaced her usual confident self, and she laced her fingers and looked down into her hand. Her head bobbed up at the sound of Victor's voice.

"So…you think something is going on with me."

"What are you talking about, Mr. Christianson?" Sheila said, worry lines now drawn across her face.

"You know damn well what I'm talking about. Who were you talking to and why were you sharing contrived information about me? Keeping tabs on one's boss could be dangerous."

Her veneer changed...the fear gone. Sheila looked directly into Victor's eyes without batting an eyelash. "I'm not the one keeping secrets. It's very apparent that you're distracted and something has your mind on lock down. Yesterday, I wore a sculptured short dress that grabbed my hips and breasts the way you like it, but you failed to notice."

"I noticed," Victor said snidely.

"See, that's what I mean. Flippant. Downright flippant you've been. It's none of my business anyway what's going on in your life...as long as you don't forget who's been giving you all the good loving you've been blessed to receive the past six months."

"And you've been paid well."

"I'm not your whore, Victor. I'm sure your wife doesn't know that you've dipped into this honey pot and promised me that you'd leave her one day." Sheila smirked, pleased that she seemed to have the upper hand and glad to know that Victor hadn't heard all of her conversation with Phyllis.

Victor fidgeted in his seat and took a good look at Sheila. "I'm not sure whether that was a threat or not, but I'm not worried about you. Newsflash. You'll never be the woman my wife is, Sheila. In fact, you couldn't touch her with the tip of your finger. She could run a hundred circles around you before you blinked once. And, for your information...please hear me well, I'll never leave Brenda."

Sheila jumped from her seat and threw her arm across the large desk and pointed at Victor. But before her tongue was able to catch up with her anger, he caught her by her wrist and squeezed tight.

"You'll do what I tell you to do. And, you're not even that good of a secretary. If you hadn't been able to satisfy me like you do, and you do that well, I'll admit, your ass would've been in the unemployment line a long time ago."

In vain, Sheila tried to pull free of Victor's grasp. "I'm not through," Victor said. "I have an assignment that I want you to complete. If you do it well, there will be a reward."

"And if I refuse?"

"You don't want to suffer the consequence of saying no to me."

Victor pushed Sheila back and released her arm. She rubbed her wrist and stood, watching Victor with a scowl on her face.

"What's the assignment?"

22

S ix o'clock on the dot. Victor touched the remote and watched as the garage door climbed to the ceiling, giving him access to the garage. His mood was sour—unhappy because of the unwelcomed visitor who had the audacity to step to him and hand him some crazy ultimatum.

Victor sauntered into the house, loosened his tie, took off his jacket and neatly hung it on the coat rack that sat off to one side of the foyer. Without making any noise, he moved easily from room to room until he found Brenda in the family room watching television, perched on the end of the white leather couch with Beyonce curled up beside her.

The atmosphere was cool when Brenda turned around and made eye contact with Victor. Even Beyonce sensed tension in the air and plopped up from her resting place, leapt to the floor, and sauntered off out of sight.

"What's for dinner?" Victor asked, a slight chill in his voice.

"It's a free for all tonight," Brenda said, turning back to watch *World News*.

"Ummph," Victor grumbled. "I noticed that a rental car is in the garage. At least you could have run out and got something to eat if you didn't want to cook. It appears you've healed from your injuries."

Brenda swiveled around in her seat so that she faced Victor. "You could've easily brought something home. You walk in here without so much as a how are you feeling, Brenda...is there anything I can do for you, Brenda...and you expect me to be at your beck and call. It would've been nice if during the ten hours you were away from home today that you would've thought to make at least one phone call to show you care about my well-being."

"I do care, Brenda. Today was an exhausting day. I...I had to tackle one problem after another."

"Ten minutes was all I needed from you. You give your concubines more than that."

"Please don't start tonight, Brenda. You're the only one I love and I'll always be here for you and the kids."

"You have a funny way of showing it. But I know you, Victor. Something has got you preoccupied. And I don't understand your obsession with me not seeing Mimi."

"Mimi. So we're back to Mimi again. Wasn't your accident a sign that you should stay away from her?"

"What are you talking about, Victor? Did you have something to do with my accident?" Brenda rose from her seat and moved in front of Victor. "I could've been killed!" she screamed.

"Come on, Brenda. I had nothing to do with your accident. Why would I want to hurt you?"

"Why? Because you didn't want me to meet Mimi? Now you tell me why," she hissed. Brenda folded her arms across her bosom and waited for a reply.

"My God, Brenda, you don't really think that I'm capable of what you're suggesting? You're my wife and the mother of my children. Please give me credit for trying to be the best husband to you for the last nineteen years. You just stuck a knife in my soul, to so blatantly suggest that I could ever hurt you or anyone."

Brenda let her arms drop to her sides and sat down on the couch. "Cut the theatrics, Victor. I don't know what it is, but I've got this vibe that you're up to something... and I believe it has to do with Mimi." There was no way she was going to tell Victor that Mimi had stood her up again.

Victor moved to the couch and sat next to Brenda. "I'm sorry that I haven't been supportive where you and Mimi are concerned. I remember how much her leaving hurt you, and I don't want you to set yourself up for disappointment again; that's all. Mimi wasn't dependable nineteen years ago. What makes you think she's going to be any different?"

"It's not your concern that bothers me but the fact that you told me point blank not to meet her. Seems like that would be a decision I should've made for myself. Maybe I needed answers to why she disappeared."

"I still don't think it's a good idea. You went behind my back and tried to see her after you told me you were going to cancel that luncheon."

Brenda slid off the seat, folded her hands across her chest, and faced Victor. "I don't know what kind of game you're playing, but I don't need your permission to meet my best friend for lunch." She let her hands drop and pointed a finger at him. "Puzzled as I am about your interest in my not seeing Mimi, it will not stop me from seeing her. But don't you dare tell me whom I can and cannot see. I've put up with a lot of mess from you over the years, so now is not the time for you to forget that. You do get my meaning."

"You're still my wife, and I'm still head of this household. Don't you forget that!"

Brenda sneered at Victor. He was hiding something, and whatever it was would eventually come to the light. Oh, his grandstanding meant nothing to her. All it did was prompt her to make every attempt to see Mimi, and she would. Victor didn't scare her. She should have left his sorry behind a long time ago but thought better of it because she didn't want her children to be part of the growing statistics of children living with a single parent. But now curiosity was coursing through her thoughts, and a little research and surveillance was now on the menu.

Exploring other possibilities had also crossed Brenda's mind, and maybe, just maybe after Trevor was in college, she might entertain that desire. Marriage to Victor wasn't a match made in Heaven as people seemed to think, but she had sucked it up because she had fought and won the hand of the handsome prince. Although being a pregnant teenaged girl wasn't on Brenda's list of priorities all those years ago, having the fetus in the womb was the one thing that had secured her place by Victor's side. She was sure it was the reason she doted on Asia like she did.

But times had changed. Her life had changed. Brenda's resilience had made her one of the leading psychologists in the state and probably the country. She was the real force in the Christianson household and could easily sustain life without Victor. Priorities had been rearranged in Brenda's world. And as she glanced back at Victor who was now exiting the kitchen, she mentally dropped his priority number to last place.

Beyonce suddenly bounced into the room. The music on the television set made her bounce from one foot to the other, her tail wagging. A video clip featuring Beyoncé Knowles and a couple of dancers played on television and Beyoncé the cat was moving with the girls as they sang, *all the single ladies, all the single ladies*...the reason Beyoncé the cat got her name.

23

Victor rushed from the house, jumped in his Mercedes, backed out of the garage, and drove away from the subdivision. He barreled down the street as if he had no morale aptitude—a maniac, disobeying the road signs—the law of the land. All of a sudden his right leg flew up and slammed down on the brakes. *Screech*, his tires squealed as he narrowly missed a city bus that pulled away from the curb and into traffic.

His mind was bogged down, clogged with the stress of his ongoing dilemma, a dilemma that Victor was going to alleviate sooner than later. Not once had Victor thought about abandoning his quest to get rid of what he conceived to be the thorns in his side—Mimi and Afrika, but Brenda's insistence upon seeing Mimi left him no option but to nip it in the bud. Mimi, like himself, had no desire to expose her secret, yet having Mimi and her daughter in such close proximity to his family spelled future disaster.

Several traffic lights later, Victor hung a left and forged ahead, making a right turn into Mimi's subdivision. He slowed the car down to a crawl and was about to park his car in an open slot when the door to Mimi's condo flew open and John Carroll appeared on the doorstep.

Victor continued without stopping, circling back to try and assess what was going on. How did John fit into the equation and why was he suddenly interested in Mimi's well-being? After all, wasn't Mimi married? Angry at this sudden turn of events, Victor left the subdivision and headed back into traffic. He picked up his BlackBerry, dialed a number and waited for the caller to pick up.

AFRIKA SAT WITH THE CAR IDLING AS SHE WAITED FOR Asia to put up her cheerleading gear in her room. Finally Asia reappeared and headed toward Afrika's car.

"Girl, I'm starving after that workout," Asia said.

"Well, get in," Afrika said, pulling away from the curb. "My mouth is watering for pizza."

"Where is Keith? I thought he was going with us."

"He's going to meet us there."

"Oh," Asia said, sitting back as she watched the scenery go by. "Why don't we go shopping instead of eating? I want to get another pair of jeans before we go to the frat party. My man will be there."

"Let's do it after we eat. I told Keith we'd be there in fifteen minutes. Don't try to back out now. We won't make you feel like a third wheel."

"Okay, let's do this."

Afrika drove up Fayetteville Street and crossed over

Interstate 95. The mall was ahead on the right, and in a few minutes more they would be at their destination. Afrika navigated her way in the parking lot and found a parking spot not too far away from California Pizza.

The girls exited the car, excitement about seeing Keith consuming Afrika as she walked with a purpose.

"Slow up, Nikki," Asia said, skipping to keep up with her.

Afrika slowed but broke out into a grin when she spotted Keith sitting at a table.

"Who's Keith sitting with?" Asia wanted to know as they approached the table.

Afrika shrugged her shoulders and gave Asia an 'I don't know' look. Keith turned around when he felt the ladies at his back and broke into a grin. He stood up and put his arms around Afrika and introduced her.

"Zavion, this is my girl, Nikki, and her best friend, Asia."

Zavion stood up, taking an extra dose of Asia. "Cool. Nice to meet you." He nodded his head.

Asia looked from Afrika to Keith. Afrika sensed Asia's mood change, but then she saw Asia's eyes travel the length of Zavion who stood tall, in buff medium brown skin, his hair locked in short twists. Zavion seemed to appreciate the mulling over he was getting from the beautiful girl who had yet to say a word. A smile awaited Asia when she finally connected with Zavion's face.

"You a basketball player?" Asia asked, as she continued

to digest the man who stood before her, rocking back and forth like he had stirred up something in her.

"Yeah, I play for UNC. I'm a forward," Zavion answered.

Keith and Afrika seemed to relax as Asia finally sat down next to Zavion.

"Umph. How tall are you?" Asia asked, her inquisitive mind running wild.

"Six-three," Zavion said.

"Are you finished with your interrogation?" Afrika asked Asia, giving her a look.

"Not quite," Asia said. "Go on and order your pizza. Zavion and I are still getting acquainted."

Zavion smiled.

Before long, the foursome were chatting incessantly and eating pizza by the mouthfuls. Time buzzed by.

"Do you still want to go to the store and..." Afrika began before Asia cut her off.

"No, no. I've changed my mind," Asia said. Then she turned toward Zavion, linking her arm through his. "I don't know if Keith bothered to tell you, but there is an Alpha party tonight in Durham. Would you like to tag along?"

Zavion gave Keith a cursory glance, pretending to know nothing. "If you're going to be there, I'm already on my way to the party," Zavion said to Asia.

Asia winked at Afrika. "I say why don't we get out of here and get our party on. Nikki and I are going to the restroom first, but we'll be ready to go when we come out."

"I'll be ready, too," Zavion said, as he watched Asia

work the jeans she was wearing until she and Afrika were out of sight.

"I told you she was high-strung," Keith said.

"Just like I like them. Let me do the worrying; I can handle Asia. But I thought you said she had a boyfriend."

"That's what Nikki told me, but apparently Asia likes what she sees. The girl plays hardball."

"I'm all for playing hardball with Ms. Asia, but I don't want any drama. Asia or no Asia, I plan to still be on the basketball team when they make it to the Final Four next year."

"That's it," Keith said, fist bumping with Zavion. "You've got NBA on the brain."

"My first priority next to graduating from college," Zavion said. "But it wouldn't hurt to bring home a good looking sister to grandma—a possible in my future."

Keith and Zavion laughed.

"Here come the ladies," Keith whispered. "Man up."

The guys followed the ladies out of the restaurant. "We'll follow you," Afrika said to Keith.

"I thought we'd go together," Keith retorted.

"I'll drive," Afrika said, "in case I need to leave folks behind because they aren't ready to go home when I am."

"Who are you talking about?" Asia grinned.

"I haven't a clue," Afrika said, shaking her head.

"I'm ready to party," Keith interjected. "I'll drive around to your car in a second."

"You lead; I'll follow," Afrika said. The girls laughed and got in the car.

"What are you going to do about your quarterback who's going to be at the party tonight?" Afrika asked, shaking her head at Asia.

"Girl, did you see that fine Zavion? Who's worried about Deon?"

"He's the Eagles quarterback, silly."

"And Zavion's going to someday be on an NBA team. I'd rather have a b-baller than a big ole gross football player."

"They both got muscles."

"But Zavion's are all in the right place. I'm ready to find out a little more about this one. Keith isn't so bad after all, if he's got friends like Zavion."

"Let me tell you one thing, Miss Asia. I'm not getting caught up in your mess tonight. And don't forget we've got to cheer tomorrow."

"Have some fun, Nikki. You sure know how to take the buzz out of a high."

"So you're high now?"

"When Zavion slapped those lips around that pizza, I was imagining it was me. His eyes are hazel, like Trevor's. Can you drive any faster?"

"I can't go any faster than Keith is driving. Hold on. You just met the guy."

"Zavion is going to be mine. Mark my words, Nikki." Asia sucked her teeth. "Yeah, I want him."

24

Sheila sat in the back of the Know Bookstore restaurant sipping on a Coke. She looked up as Victor walked toward her, offering up a smile to the man who didn't belong to her but for whom she would walk naked through the city to be with. He wore a green trenchcoat and walked with a purpose.

"You got it?" were the first words out of his mouth.

"As you asked," Sheila said, the smile fading from her face.

"What you having?" the waitress asked, giving Victor one of her best flirtatious smiles.

"Same thing as the young lady," Victor said, pointing at Sheila's drink.

"All right, one Coke coming up. If you want any food, let me know."

"Thanks, but I won't be here that long."

"I thought that since we were out, we could make a night of it," Sheila said, trying to interject a little more pep in her unhappy demeanor.

"Not tonight, Sheila. Some other time. I've got to take care of this matter first."

"One Coke for the gentleman," the waitress said, setting the glass on the table.

Victor slipped the waitress a ten-dollar bill. She smiled and slithered away.

"So, I do you a favor and you toss me out like yesterday's trash."

"Come on, Sheila. It's not like that. Look, I'm sitting here sipping this Coke with you."

"You're not funny, Victor." Sheila sat and stared at him between sips.

"Stop!" Victor said abruptly, wishing he hadn't been so loud. "Put your foot on the floor," he whispered.

"You've never protested before."

"I don't know how many ways I can say this, but tonight is not the time. I've got to go." Victor reached in his pocket and pulled out a twenty-dollar bill. "Get yourself another Coke if you like. I'm out."

"What are you going to do with the gun?"

VICTOR FLEW OUT OF THE BOOKSTORE AND FLED INTO the night. He wasn't sure what he was going to do with the gun. He had bought the small, twenty-two-caliber handgun for Sheila some time ago because she said she needed protection, but now he needed protection from his past. The images he saw in his head made him crazy. He'd never given a thought to killing anyone before and wasn't sure he could do it now, although the voices in his head tossed out commands and implored him to take action immediately to rid himself of the stress that had ravaged his body.

He jumped in his Mercedes and drove around, contemplating his next move. If he killed Mimi, he would be the obvious suspect and Brenda would do the accusing. If something happened to Afrika, he'd still be the suspect because Mimi would do the accusing. Besides, all that he'd work for would go up in smoke because he'd be behind steel bars before the first forty-eight hours passed after committing this premeditated crime. God, he had to stop watching so much television.

Victor felt the gun in the depths of his coat pocket. Perspiration formed on his forehead as he battled with the voices in his head. Maybe he needed to sleep on it... get a clear vision about what he should do. That was it. He'd go home, although he was not up to listening to Brenda's rants about her need to see Mimi.

Mimi, Mimi, Mimi. She bore a daughter, and he was the father. It was so long ago. Surely Brenda would forgive him. Maybe he would tell her that Mimi had forced herself on him, and he had only taken advantage of her because Mimi wanted him to. Yes, that's what he'd tell Brenda. She would forgive him, and embarrassment would send Mimi and Afrika packing. But no, Mimi would tell Brenda that he had raped her....that he had acted like an animal and wouldn't take no for an answer. He couldn't risk it. Could he? No, Mimi had to be eliminated.

The car moved smoothly through the night. Maybe it

wasn't a bad idea to kick it with Sheila tonight, but she probably was in a bad funk because he left her alone nursing her drink. Victor saw an ABC Liquor Store ahead and pulled into the parking lot upon approach. He'd let Jack Daniel's help him out. Yeah, he was a coward, but he was a coward that needed a little help. He dialed Sheila's cell number anyway, and she answered on the first ring.

"Sheila," he whispered. "Sorry for running out on you like that. I was a little uptight, but now I seem to be rational."

"What did you do, Victor? You...you didn't use...you know?"

"No, I didn't use it; at least not yet."

"You need some company?"

"Why don't I meet you at your place?"

"You mean our place?"

"Your place, our place. Yes, our place."

"Come on by, baby. I'm halfway there. Let Momma give you what you need."

"Sheila, I need the works. Don't skimp. And pull out a bottle of Dom Perignon."

"Okay, baby. I'll be waiting. Smooches."

Victor felt the gun in his pocket. He decided against getting a bottle of Jack Daniel's and headed to the other side of town. Sheila would smooth all the ruffled spots on his body and give him the best massage money could buy, allowing him time to come up with a foolproof plan.

25

October 10, 2008

*I had lunch today with John Carroll. It's hard to believe that
he walked back into my life just when I needed someone to
lean on. Listening to him as he talked about his life then and
now made me, for a fleeting moment, wonder what life
would've been like if we had stayed connected. It probably
wouldn't have worked. He did say he was divorced twice.*

*Life with John is not even a question…not even an option.
Raphael is my life, and I will love and cherish that man until
the day I die. I'm not sure how I was so fortunate to meet the
most wonderful man that God created on this earth, but for
all the women out there, I've got him. He's my sunshine and
my rain. He's my everything.*

*Today I shared a bit of myself with John—some of my
thoughts and feelings. However, I had not meant to tell him
about Afrika…about the rape—that Victor is the father of
my child. But it seemed to make sense to do so after I plunged
ahead and told him about Victor coming to my house and
stalking me. I was at peace with it then, but now I'm having
second thoughts and regrets, but it's way too late.*

*What if John tells someone else and they tell someone?
What if Brenda finds out without me telling her first? How
can I tell Brenda after all these years that her husband raped*

me when I tried to intercede on her behalf? She won't believe me because I ran. I ran faster than Raphael's granddaddy did when he tried to dodge a bullet after he was caught in bed with a woman he was putting the moves on who happened to be some other old man's girlfriend. Now that was funny.

John stood up to Victor today on my behalf. He didn't flinch or offer any excuses. I was leery about him talking to Victor about his coming to my house, stalking me, and possibly interfering with Afrika's student account. John went to Victor's office like Rambo, at least that's what he told me. John said that Victor played the role of the ultimate professional in his cocky, 'I'm better than you' voice. However, when John finished telling Victor that he should think long and hard about approaching me again, John said Victor looked like a steam engine that had been rolled over by a Mack truck. Why am I blushing?

I don't trust Victor for one second. He's mean-spirited, and he's going to make an attempt to get at Afrika and me again. I feel it in my bones, and I've got to be ready in case I'm right. First thing tomorrow, I'm going to purchase a gun. Setrina (Mimi) Bailey isn't going to take any more of that man's abuse. Victor has only one time to put his hands on me again.

Whew. I need to put my pen down because my hand is still shaking after writing that last paragraph. But I've got to write this down. I'm not afraid of Victor, and I'm not going to tolerate his crap anymore. I'm going to protect my family, so if I have to spill Victor's blood, so be it. He wouldn't want Raphael to come home and do the deed. That man's been *through Desert Storm, the second war in Iraq, and Afghanistan to protect the United States and the American people, and it wouldn't take much…in fact, if I tell Raphael the whole truth, Victor's guts would already be blown all over Durham in the name of defending his family. Okay, I'm through. Good night.*

Mimi Bailey

Mimi looked at her journal and read over what she had written. The words were raw, but should something happen to her, she wanted the reader to understand that she bared her soul…that her fear was real, and nothing and no one was going to hurt her or her family anymore.

Getting up from the table, Mimi picked up her journal and put it back in its resting place. Her nerves were still on edge and she went to the fridge and pulled out a half-filled bottle of wine. She poured herself a glass and sipped it, letting the liquid roll to the back of her tongue before finally allowing it to slide down her throat.

Savoring the flavor, Mimi's mind began to click. She took another sip of her drink, although she didn't allow it to linger on her tongue as long as the first. She took another sip, put the glass down, and grabbed her Black-Berry.

Mimi leaned on the sink and dialed the numbers fast, as if the call was an emergency. She put the phone to ear and listened while it rang…then she stood up straight as the voice at the other end said, "Hello."

"Brenda, this is Mimi. We need to talk."

Brenda stuttered. "When would you like to get together?"

"As soon as you can get away."

"Well, Victor isn't here right now. I can meet you wherever you like."

"How about my house? I'll give you directions."

"You know Victor has been trying to keep us apart."

"Tonight, you're going to know why."

Silence replaced the voices. Then Brenda spoke. "I'll only need your address."

Mimi gave Brenda her address. "Be careful. I wouldn't want Victor getting wind of this."

"He's probably out with his whore."

It was Mimi's turn to be silent. There was more to Brenda's statement that was left unsaid, and maybe laying her burden on Brenda might not be as hard a chore as she thought.

"I'll see you when you get here. Park in the space marked for visitors."

"I'll see you in a few."

Mimi closed the lid on her cell and stared in space. Backing down was not an option. She had already committed to the deed she had to do. Her hands began to tremble and instead of picking up her glass, she picked up the wine bottle and emptied the contents directly into her mouth.

26

The music was jumping and could be heard down the street. Keith and Afrika parked their cars around the corner from the home that had seen many Alpha parties. Keith caught up with Afrika and led her toward the house, leaving Zavion and Asia alone. They didn't seem too anxious about joining the festivities and slowed to a crawl to get reacquainted.

"I bet all the guys tell you that you're beautiful," Zavion said, lifting Asia's chin to get a better look at her.

"No, not all. You haven't told me that I'm beautiful," Asia said, confidence dripping all over her, narrowing the space between Zavion and her.

"What's the point if you already know it?"

"Really, I'm not stuck on myself. I'm blessed to have reasonably good looks, but I don't go around flaunting it. I'm really down to earth and a lot of fun to be with."

Zavion smiled. "Okay, I can see that you might be down to earth and a lot of fun to be with, but I must be honest and tell you...you are beautiful. I see more than your beauty on the outside. Yes, there's a whole lot more to you, Asia."

"That is deep, Zavion. You're going to make me blush.

You're not like those guys who only want to put their hands all over you." Asia looked away and blushed. "You're a rare breed. Your momma taught you well."

Zavion clammed up and remained quiet.

"Are you okay? I didn't say anything wrong, did I?" Asia asked with concern, stepping back a little.

Zavion sighed. "Naw, you didn't say anything wrong. I was thinking about my mother. She's had it hard all her life. To me, she died when I was eight. My grandmother raised me."

"I didn't mean to upset you."

"You didn't do anything. It's just that my mother died inside from a broken heart. After my dad got killed over some drug deal gone bad, my mother hooked up with some educated dude who bought her nice things from time to time but mainly came around to...to get in bed with her. She got pregnant and had the baby, my younger brother, and after that, dude stop coming around for a while. A couple years after that, my mother gave up on life and nearly died in the streets like my daddy. I think my mother has hooked up with that lowlife again. Most of all, it broke my grand-mother's heart, but she raised my brother and me to be nothing like our parents."

"Where is your brother?"

"He's a senior in high school. He plays basketball, too, and he's pretty good. He's thinking about going to Duke. He's got good grades, and Grandma says that if they pay his way, my brother can go."

"Maybe his father can help pay," Asia said innocently.

Zavion gave Asia a sharp look. "Maybe we should go to the party."

"Okay, what did I just do?" Asia asked.

"It's like this, Asia. I had a rough life. If my brother and I didn't have our grandmother, the streets would've claimed us. We would be a couple of statistics that are recorded in somebody's book in the County Courthouse that nobody gives a damn about. I've actually wiped the images of my mother and father clean out of my mind. My brother never knew his father. He doesn't know if he's alive or dead, and to be truthful, he doesn't even know his name. Grandma saw to that."

"What about his birth certificate?"

"My mother used her married name. My brother has my last name."

"And you're Zavion..."

"Zavion Slater."

"It has a nice ring to it. Zavion Slater. Zavion and Asia Slater."

"You're moving a little too fast, aren't you?"

"Just testing it out to see how it sounds."

Zavion eased up and let out a laugh. "So your criteria for picking a mate will be based on how both names ring together?"

"Yes, sir. That's right. And guess what?"

"What?" Zavion asked, pulling Asia to him.

"Zavion and Asia Slater has the ring."

Zavion laughed again but this time he reached down and kissed Asia. Asia held on tight and put as much into the kiss as Zavion. He was the first to pull away.

"Maybe we should go to that party. People are probably wondering why we've been standing in the middle of the block looking at each other for the last fifteen minutes."

"I don't see anyone looking. You're afraid that one of your brothers might see you? Oh, I don't know if you're even frat."

"I am. I'm an Alpha. That's how I met Keith."

Asia smiled. "An Alpha man and a b-baller. So are you a fresh-man, and is this your first season with the team?"

"No, my third."

"Third?"

"I'm a junior. Grandma told me that I had to graduate before I could join the NBA."

"I'd like to meet your grandmother. She sounds like a jewel."

"She is. Maybe you'll get the chance to meet her some day. Now let's go to the party."

"Okay, Mr. Slater."

27

"Work it, girl. You know you've got the Midas touch."

"Be quiet and enjoy, Big Daddy. I'm going to rub some more oil over your body. Say my name if it feels good to you."

Giant red candles surrounded by a cluster of red and white small and medium-sized candles, lit up the room, emitting an aroma that had Victor in a trance. The room smelled of wild cherries and vanilla mixed with the scent of musk from the oils that Sheila heated and massaged into Victor's naked body. The oil was held in a small vase that sat in a wrought iron holder, kept warm by a small well filled with candlewax that was lit and placed underneath.

A large sculptured mirror hung on one wall of the bedroom, while the rest of the room was furnished with handcrafted antique white furniture trimmed in gold. A king-size bed hugged the middle of the room, a large armoire sat on an opposite wall, and an elongated dresser sat under the enormous mirror. Two high-back winged chairs covered in a yellow silk cloth set in an antique white frame sat to either side of a small fireplace that kept Sheila and her lover, Victor Christianson, warm on cold nights. It was the room of a kept woman because Sheila's salary was barely enough to pay the mortgage.

Victor's arms lay at his sides, his face turned to one side. Eyes closed, Victor moaned as Sheila massaged oil from the top of his shoulders down the well of his back, moving further down until she stopped to give his buttocks a deep tissue massage. Victor moaned again.

"I don't hear you," Sheila whispered.

"Sheila, Sheila, Sheila," Victor whispered.

"Say my name so I can hear you," Sheila shouted.

"Sheilaaaaaaaa. Sheilaaaaaaaa."

"Yeah, Momma is going to make you feel so good. Now turn over and let me finish my work. Oh, oh. You aren't pointing at me because I've been a bad girl, are you?"

"Sheila, come on, baby. Stop talking and get to work. Big Daddy needs your hands to work its magic and whatever else you got up in your bag of tricks. All of my muscles are throbbing. I'll say your name louder if you need me to."

"Raise the roof then, Big Daddy; you and Momma are getting ready to put the fireworks on blast."

"SHEILAAAAAAAAAAAAAAAAA!"

There was a knock at the door followed by the doorbell. Mimi hesitated, took a deep breath, and then walked the few feet to answer it. First she looked through the peephole, in case the face staring back at her was Victor's instead of the person's she was expecting. It was Brenda's face that stared back, and she opened the door.

Brenda still had her youthful good looks. They were both in their late-thirties, but time had been extra good to Brenda. Brenda was covered in a lightweight trench-coat, but from the gold that dipped around her neck and hung from her earlobes, she smelled like success.

"Hello, Brenda," Mimi said, stepping aside to let Brenda pass through.

Once inside, Brenda turned around and looked at Mimi. She tried to open her mouth, and then stifled an onset of tears. "Mimi," was all she said before wrapping her arms around Mimi's neck.

Tears began to fall from Mimi's eyes as she embraced Brenda in return. They stood that way for several moments before Mimi removed her arms. Brenda did likewise. Mimi caught another tear. This wasn't how this get together was supposed to go. Emotions were running too high and threatened to abandon what Mimi needed to say to Brenda.

"Let me take your coat."

Brenda slid out of her coat and handed it to Mimi. Brenda wore an ivory shawl-collar cardigan of light-weight cashmere over a pair of Dereon jeans. Simple but elegant.

"I didn't know these condos existed," Brenda said, as

she followed Brenda into the cozy living area, attempting to ease into the conversation.

"They aren't old at all. In fact, they may be six to seven months old. I bought mine brand new. Make yourself comfortable. Would you like some wine?"

"I would, but I'm still recovering from my accident, and I don't want to do anything to jeopardize my suit when they find the person who hit me."

"Brenda, excuse my insensitivity. I completely forgot you were in an accident. How are you doing? Maybe this is not the right time."

"Mimi, hold it. I'm doing real good. I'm blessed to have come out of that accident without any major trauma to my body. It was a hit and run accident and my car was totaled. They haven't caught the person who did it yet."

"My God, Brenda. I'm glad you're all right."

"I am, but I'm feeling much better because we've finally reconnected. I've missed you so much, and even after the years passed, I didn't stop wondering. I may not have thought of you as often, but every now and then something would come up to trigger a memory. So how are you and what have you been doing since you walked out of my life?"

Mimi sat down and then got up. "Let me get my glass of wine."

"Can't be that bad," Brenda said, a small frown forming on her face.

"No, no. I'm nervous after finally seeing you for the first time in nineteen years."

"I'm still the same Brenda, more or less. You know, Mimi, I thought I'd see your name on somebody's record label and I'd tell everyone that she was my best friend."

Mimi stared at Brenda then looked away. "I'm a terminal disappointment, huh?"

Brenda got up from her seat. "No, you aren't, Mimi. I'm grasping for straws, trying to understand where we went wrong."

"We didn't go wrong, Brenda." Mimi went to Brenda and held her hands. "I've missed you, too. Not a day went by that I didn't think of you. You were my best friend, and I loved you with all my heart. If you don't remember anything else, remember that. Now sit down. I'm going to get that wine."

Brenda sat down, but she was puzzled. She looked around the room and smiled at Mimi's handiwork. She looked in the direction of the marble fireplace and saw what appeared to be a family picture. She started to get up but Mimi returned to the room.

"So why doesn't Victor want me to see you?" Brenda asked forcefully.

Mimi wasn't expecting Brenda's forwardness. She remembered Brenda as more on the timid side. "We'll get to it, but first let me tell you what I've been doing for the last nineteen years. I left Durham and went to Hampton, Virginia."

"Did you continue your education there?"

"Yes, I did, and I met the most wonderful man who happens to be my husband."

"Oh, you're married. Is he working in Durham?"

"No, he's a full bird Colonel in the Army. At the moment, he's overseas getting ready to deploy to Afghanistan."

"What a senseless war."

"Yeah, it's been rough. He's served in Iraq several times."

"So you met this wonderful man and you had a little girl."

Brenda was pushing Mimi's story faster than she wanted it to move. Mimi was planning to tell it a different way, but if there were patches in the story, she would smooth them out later. After all, this was why she called Brenda. To get it all out in the open. No more secrets between them, although it would be on track to hurt others... their daughters' friendship for one.

"Yes, Raphael and I became proud parents of Afrika Nicole Bailey."

"I can't believe you still named your baby Afrika...that you remembered what we said a long time ago."

"I can say the same for you, Brenda. You named your little girl Asia." They laughed.

"Wow, that was a long time ago. So tell me about Raphael. I thought you only had eyes for...for...John... what was his last name, Mimi?"

"John Carroll."

"Oh, John Carroll. You say his name like you've never stopped being friends. I thought that boy was going to die after you left without as much as a goodbye."

"Life is funny, Brenda. I ran into John a few days ago. I went to Lake Johnson to jog, and who should I run into?"

"You're kidding me. Just like that. It's been a while since I've seen John. He's got a bald head now."

"Yeah, but it's becoming." Mimi needed to steer the conversation away from John. Not that she was obsessed with him; it was that he had now become a part of her new story. And again, she wanted to furnish the story in her own time.

"Now, Raphael, he's the love of my life. He's tall, a carbon copy of Vin Diesel, but darker. He has a bald head, too. When I saw him in his ROTC uniform back when we were at Hampton, I realized that I wanted a military man. All that precision built up in one body, saluting and marching to their own frat beat. But we fell in love, and Brenda, I've been in love with him ever since. We complete one another, and my husband feels the same about me."

"I'm happy for you, Mimi. I really am." Brenda looked away and down at her hands that were folded in her lap. She got up and went to the mantel and picked up Brenda's family picture, although it had been taken when Afrika was small. "A beautiful family."

"Thank you," Mimi said.

Brenda put the picture back on the mantel and sat back down in her seat. She looked at Mimi, who was smiling at her. "I wish that I'd listened to you."

"What do you mean?"

"I wish that I had never married Victor. I thought that having his child would endear him to me. Yes, he claims that he loves me and we've had a respectable life together, but he can't keep his thing in his pants. He's like a maggot when he sees a beautiful woman. He's got to get in bed with them, blow on them, and do all kinds of filthy things, and then comes back to me expecting me to be his bitch. You just don't know, Mimi."

"Maybe I do."

Brenda jumped to her feet. "I hate that son-of-a-bitch, Mimi. He's sucked me dry. Yes, I have two wonderful children and I've got my practice, but at what cost? I'm constantly having to bail out his sorry ass because he's indebted himself to his whores and my name happens to be dangling next to his when the creditors come calling. He used to be fine back in the day, but he's a cheap imitation...like a fake Rembrandt. He's so fake that only the old women want him now."

"So why didn't you leave him, Brenda? Why are you still with him if you're so miserable?"

Brenda wiped water from her face. "Because like a fool, I still love him. For some unfathomable reason, I thought I could change him...make him love only me. I have these two children he adores without a doubt and as a couple, we've become limelights in our community. Partially, that's due to Victor, but he didn't get that job as director because he was all of that. No, it was my father who knew the university president and put in a good word for his son-in-law so that he wouldn't look like a college graduate who couldn't find a job and couldn't take care of his family."

"So how long has Victor been a director?"

"For the past fifteen years. Victor got in there and learned the job and is pretty darn good as an administrator. It's all the extra-curricular activities he has under the guise of administrator. I'm sure that Victor is having some tryst with his secretary at this very minute. They say the wife is always last to know, but I'm a psychologist, and not much gets by me. Which brings up my initial question, which is...why does Victor hate you? Why has he forbidden me to see you?"

Mimi's eyes widened. "Forbidden, huh. Brenda you're not going to laugh at the answer; in fact, I'm not sure how you'll respond. I knew this moment would come, and I'm going to lay it all out there because you need to know."

Brenda sat stoically in her seat, almost as if she was afraid to move, for sure afraid of what Mimi was about to say. "You're scaring me, Mimi. I truly wanted us to celebrate our reunion."

"You're going to have to put the reunion on hold. What I'm about to say is going to change our relationship forever. I'm not sure where to begin, but all stories have a beginning, and I'm going to go back nineteen years ago when we were freshmen in college and you had discovered that you were pregnant."

"Maybe I do need a glass of wine, if you don't mind. I'm not sure that I'm going to like what you're going to say to me."

"You won't, but promise you won't throw the wine in my face."

"Maybe I should leave. Maybe today isn't the day I'm supposed to hear what you've got to say."

"Today is the day," Mimi said. "It's time for me to face this thing head on. I'm afraid if I don't, someone will get hurt...maybe killed."

Brenda stood up again and shook her hand at Mimi. "What are you talking about, Mimi?" Tears began to fall from Brenda's eyes. "Tell me right now. Stop stalling and tell me why you ran away...why you didn't have the guts to tell me you were leaving. You were my best friend for God's sake. I needed you. When you left, I had no one...no one. I was left to shoulder the burden of my baby all by myself."

"Listen to you, Brenda. I couldn't stay because I had issues of my own. I couldn't help you because I couldn't help myself. I realized that you needed me, but who was going to be there for me?"

"What are you talking about?" Brenda cried.

"Victor raped me. Now you know. I'll get that glass of wine now."

There was a long pause. Brenda stood stiff in the middle of the room like she had turned into a pillar of salt. "What did you say? Did you say Victor raped you?"

Mimi wasn't sure if she should give Brenda a hug or wait until she had grasped the gravity of what she had heard. "Yes, Brenda, that son-of-a-bitch raped me. I couldn't tell you; I couldn't tell anyone."

"Do you have something stronger than wine?"

"I don't want you going out on me until I've finished my story. I'll be right back."

Brenda flopped back down in the chair while bubbles burst from her nose. Tears rolled down her face like a reservoir had been broken. She wiped her face with the back of her hand and tried to hide her emotions by bringing both hands in front of her face.

"Here's a box of Kleenex and your wine," Mimi said with sad eyes. "We'll both need the box when I'm through."

"When did he rape you?" Brenda asked with accusing eyes.

Mimi looked right through her. "It was the day you asked me to speak to him about his not having to bear the responsibility of your pregnancy, but you wanted to be with him anyway. He was drunk, Brenda, and that sorry son-of-a...I'm sorry. I hate dredging this up. Victor pulled me inside and started talking crazy. I tried to leave but he went crazy. He tore off my clothes and threw me down on the floor. Then...then he pulled down his pants while holding me down on the floor... and it happened.

"When he finished, he let me up and said to me, *now go and tell Brenda that I f'd you.* Brenda, I wanted to run and tell you, but I was so ashamed. I had to run to my room with my clothes all torn up. I prayed that you wouldn't be there when I got there. You weren't, thank God, and I did my best to cover it up until I missed my period the next month. Right then, I couldn't stay there."

"Why didn't you report it to the police?"

"I don't know. In some part because I realized that it would hurt you, and I couldn't risk losing our friendship."

"But you ran away. What's the difference?"

"The difference is that no one knew. I didn't even tell Victor. I called my parents and they came to my rescue. We only had a few weeks until the end of the semester, and no one would question my disappearance until school started again."

"You knew that I would."

"Yes; that was the disheartening part of this."

"So tell me, Mimi. Is Afrika Victor's daughter?"

Mimi sat still and took a sip of her wine. "Yes."

"So why in hell did you come back to Durham after all these years to disrupt me, my family, and your family, for God's sake? Why, Mimi? Why did you come back here?"

"Because my daughter wanted to go to NC Central. I tried to talk her out of it. We were living in Kansas at the time. My husband was about to deploy to Europe, and Afrika wouldn't take no for an answer. I would've gone with my husband, but after Afrika insisted on going to Central and had put the paperwork in herself and got accepted, I had no recourse but to support my child. I thought, just maybe, we could slide into Durham for four years and slide out the way we came, and life would go on as usual. Who would've thought that your daughter and my daughter would become best friends?"

"Just like you and me. Who would've thought it? Now Asia has a half-sister. I remember there was some talk about their similarities when Afrika first came to the house, but now I know why Victor was squirming."

"He didn't know, Brenda. He must've put two and two together; soon after Afrika was at your house, he paid me a visit."

"You mean Victor has been to this house?"

"Yes, he has. He threatened me, put his hands on me, and told me that if Afrika and I didn't leave the city, he was going to make life a living hell for us."

"Weren't you afraid?"

"In the beginning I was, but the more threats he made against me, I resolved to stay and fight. Yes, I thought of taking Afrika out of school, but Victor Christianson wasn't going to make me run anymore."

"Why should I believe your side of the story? What if you were the one who put the moves on Victor? You were talking against him pretty strong. Maybe that was so I'd lose interest and you could have him."

"Brenda, don't do this. I hate Victor with all of my being. It's wrong to hate, and God knows I want to make it to heaven, but if Victor attempts to hurt me and Afrika again, I will kill him."

Brenda clapped her hands. "That was nice. Make Brenda

think that she had nothing to do with Victor coming on to her."

"Brenda, this is the very reason I didn't tell you nineteen years ago. I was afraid you wouldn't believe me. You don't know how many times I wanted to call you and tell you the truth, but I couldn't. I couldn't bear the pain it would cost you. So I kept my secret."

"Only to spit it in my face nineteen years later."

"Believe me when I say, I had no plans of telling you, Brenda. It's only that Victor has been stalking me, causing havoc with Afrika's student records. He threatened me about meeting you for lunch. He's left threatening notes in my mailbox, but this has got to end. That's why I decided to tell you. My husband will be here at the sound of my voice, if I experience any more problems with Victor. And for your information, I told John Carroll all about it. In fact, he confronted Victor this very afternoon. I know this isn't the lunch you had envisioned us having, but I couldn't keep this secret any longer."

"So what are you going to do?"

"I trust that Victor has gotten the message. Brenda, I can't guarantee what might happen if he attempts to bother me again."

"What about the girls...Trevor? When do we tell them?"

"I think that we need to keep that under wraps for now. It's enough that you know, but let's not jerk the children into our mess right now."

Brenda looked at Mimi. "Our mess?"

"Yes, our mess. So what are you going to do?"

"I'm going to divorce Victor; something I should've done a long time ago. Now, I've got to go. I've had enough for one day." Brenda paused as if she suddenly remembered something. "Victor may beat me home. What do I tell him?"

"You want a divorce."

28

"Girl, you aren't ready yet?" Afrika asked, as she closed the door behind her to Asia's dorm room. "We've got to be at the gym in twenty-five minutes."

"I'll be ready. The only thing I need to put on is my tennis shoes and comb my hair," Asia said in a non-committal voice.

"Coach isn't going to tolerate you coming in late."

"Nikki, did you see Deon last night with that skanky ho? He dissed me like he'd never seen me before."

"Well, Ms. Thing, I don't see how you have any room to talk. It sure looked to me like you and Zavion were an item, or are you kissing cousins?"

"Shut up, Nikki. You don't get it. Deon asked me for my phone number and he was talking like he wanted to get with me. I don't like being disrespected."

"I vaguely recall that at the pizza place you denounced Deon because he was a big ole footballer and that your eyes had found a new subject that you were truly digging. Now what's good for the goose is good for the gander. But I'm afraid what Keith said about Deon is true."

"And what is that?"

"That you and your telephone number are merely one of Deon's conquests in his athletic black book."

"For real, did Keith say that, Nikki?"

"Maybe...not quite like that, but he said, in so many words, that on the yard, Deon is not only a killer on the field but off the field, too. I say you're the lucky one, Asia. See, the sister he was with at the party won't be on his arm next week. They've already conquered and divided. But you on the other hand, you've still got Zavion. I like him."

"But what if he turns out to be like Deon? They say all jocks are alike."

"Your statement has some merit, but there's something different about Zavion. I watched him last night at the party. His eyes were only for you. He didn't look at any of those other girls who were trying to throw their stuff at him."

"For real, Nikki?"

"For real. I was looking out."

"Zavion and I had a nice talk before we went to the party. He told me about his life growing up. Mind you, it wasn't very pretty, but because of his grandmother, he wants to succeed. That drew me to him even more than his good looks."

"Girl, it's me, Afrika...Nikki, whatever you want to call me. But I know you. That tall, fine, muscle bound, take-it-to-the hoops b-baller was what drew you to him."

"Yeah, I guess you're right. But he really is a nice guy."

"Well, I'm getting ready to leave your tail. I'm not going to be late for you or anyone else. When we're out there on the field cheering today, flash an extra helping of booty toward Deon. Then diss his ass when you get a chance."

"I feel better already. Tell coach I'll be right there. And, Nikki, thanks for having my back, girl. You're the sister I never had."

"Same at you. I'm out."

MIMI WALKED INTO THE STORE, LOOKING LEFT AND right before she entered. She wasn't sure what kind of gun to get. A small pistol would do. Something to scare the crap out of Victor and maybe a bullet or two to remind him who he was messing with.

The room was full of guns—small, medium, large, rifles, shotguns, you name it. Mimi's lips parted in awe, not sure what she expected but realizing that after all, she was at a gun shop. The wooden walls were lined eight rows deep across the horizontal plane of the shop. It made her dizzy because she had no clue what she wanted and what to ask for.

A stocky, older white gentleman stood behind the counter. She noticed how he sized her up the moment she walked through the door. Her best smile appeared on her face, and the chore of purchasing a gun became painless.

"What can I do for you, Miss?" the proprietor asked.

"I need a small handgun. I live by myself, and I need to feel safe, especially at night."

"Well, you aren't alone, ma'am. You won't believe the number of women who've been in here to purchase a gun or two in the last year. They almost outnumber the men. Let's walk over here and I'll show you something that might fit your needs."

Mimi followed. "What is that with the pearl handle?"

"I can tell you like fashion, even in your weapons," the man said, eyeing Mimi in her short pale yellow brocade jacket that sat on top of a black knit turtleneck and black stretch trousers that hugged her like a glove. "Nice jewelry," he continued, looking at the nuggets and the big rock Raphael had placed on her finger. Mimi let out a small laugh. "That there gun is a twenty-two-caliber Ruger. Cost you about three-hundred fifty dollars. Range is about twenty-five feet."

"I'll take it," Mimi said without hesitation.

"I haven't told you all about it yet. Have you ever fired a gun?"

"No," Mimi said, giving it some thought.

"I can point you in the direction of a good practice range—indoor, outdoor facility. I'll give you the address so you can check it out. May I see some ID?"

Mimi gave him her driver's license and paid with a credit card.

"You won't be able to take the gun with you today.

There's a waiting period. That's the law. But I'm sure that I'll be calling you in no time. In the meantime, check out the practice facility."

"Okay then. Thanks for everything, and I hope to hear from you real soon."

"You will. I hope you won't need the gun before we get clearance."

"We both hope so," Mimi said, grinning. "Bye now."

Mimi walked out of the store and headed for her car. As soon as she settled behind the wheel her cell phone rang. She looked at the number and answered it right away.

"Hey, Brenda, what's up? Did you tell, Victor?"

"He didn't come home last night. Now I've lost the venom I had to confront him."

"The right moment will come. It may not be now. Just don't let on that we've met. You may need to formulate some kind of plan in the event he goes ballistic."

"Maybe you can help me."

"You're the psychologist."

"I know, but I need my best friend's help."

"I'm sorry that I had to lay that in your lap yesterday, Brenda. But I feel better that you and I have no secrets. Why don't we get together on Monday, when Victor goes to work? It's too risky, our being together on the weekend."

"Let me check my calendar. I'll get back with you."

"Sounds good. I'll wait for your return call."

"Thanks, Mimi. Thanks for everything."

"You're welcome, Brenda. Thank you."

Mimi terminated the call. Within seconds she pulled up John Carroll's name from her call log and dialed. She felt good about her immediate accomplishments—sharing her secret with Brenda and having enough nerve to enter a gun shop and purchase one. She collected her thoughts when she heard John's voice on the line.

"Mimi, you all right? Don't tell me that fool had the nerve to contact you again?"

"Nothing like that, John. I'm feeling pretty good right now. I finally talked with Brenda. She knows everything."

"What did she say? How did she react?"

"She wanted to be angry with me for waiting all these years to tell her. She even pointed an accusing finger my way. Those were natural reactions. I didn't expect any more or less. Well, maybe I wasn't quite ready for her to admit that she wanted a divorce from Victor."

"Why wouldn't you? You laid the worst kind of news on her...about her husband no doubt, and that the young lady who befriended her daughter is actually her sister."

"It seems she's been in a miserable marriage for longer than I could even imagine. It was almost as if this was the final nail in the coffin...the one thing she needed, explosive enough to give her the ammunition to walk away. I felt so sorry for her."

"What is she going to do?"

"Ask Victor for a divorce."

"From all I've seen and heard about Victor, that might not be an easy feat. I don't believe he's going to let Brenda walk out of his life. She's the person who's carried him. Sure, he makes good money as a director, but she's the real powerhouse in that family."

"That's true, but I believe Brenda will find a way out. But I've got another surprise."

"Don't make me wait. Maybe that wasn't a good statement, considering our past."

"You're crazy, John. Remember that is our past. Anyway, I purchased a gun."

"For what?"

"Do you really have to ask that question?"

"Yes. Mimi, I hope you aren't going to do anything foolish. Even Victor's sorry ass isn't worth a trip to prison."

"I didn't purchase it so that I can put a cap in Victor's ass. It's more to scare him in the event he decides to continue to harass me. Now if push comes to shove, he just might find himself in the morgue."

"Do you have the gun on you?"

"No, they have to check me out first. I hope to hear something in a few days to a week."

John was silent. "Mimi, think about all you stand to lose going up against Victor—your husband, your daughter, your family, and my friendship."

"Thanks for including yourself in that scenario."

"Mimi, I'm concerned and you're scared. If it means

that I have to spend a few days at your place to make you feel at-ease, I'm there."

"If I need you, I'll call. I've got a couple of more errands to run. Take care."

"You don't like what I'm saying, Mimi, but I'm concerned. I'm only a phone call away." A pause. "Why don't you meet me for lunch after you finish your errands?"

"Thanks, John. I'd better not. I feel guilty taking up all of your time."

"Let me be the judge."

"Besides, I told Afrika I couldn't come see her cheer today because I had so much to do."

"Excuses. Call me when you finish your errands; you make the decision as to where we're going to eat."

"You make it hard to say no, John Carroll."

"I wish I was as on top of things years ago."

"Well, it's a little too late. I'll call you."

"I'll be waiting."

Mimi smiled as she put her BlackBerry in her purse. She was happy John had turned up in her life at a moment she could use a good friend.

Mimi turned on the ignition and sped away from the gun shop. Was she only getting the gun for protection or did she really want to see Victor dead? The gun was not in her possession at the moment. Yet, it was in Victor's best interest to be on his best behavior because she hated him, and nothing at this moment would keep her from blowing that imbecile away if it came to that.

29

Brenda put food in Beyoncé's bowl. Beyoncé was Persian—the outline of her face a dusty brown color that matched the color of her tail, while the rest of her body was white. She stood in full cat stance with her fluffy tail waving in the air, waiting for Brenda to move away so she could take advantage of the food and milk that had been set out for her. Brenda stooped down and rubbed Beyoncé's back. The friendly purr came on cue.

"What's up, Mom?" Trevor asked, dashing into the kitchen. He opened the refrigerator and took out a carton of juice. He got a tumbler and poured juice until the glass was filled.

"What's up with you, Trevor? Looks like you're in a hurry."

"Yeah, I'm going to Central's game. Going to watch Asia and Nikki cheer."

"You mean Afrika?"

"Nikki, Afrika, all the same person."

The mention of Nikki's name made Mimi's reveal rush back to her. She wasn't sure how she felt now that she knew that Nikki...Afrika, was Victor's child as well as that of her best friend. She wanted to accept the situation as Mimi presented it, but the reality of it all made it a bitter pill to swallow. She jumped when the phone rang.

Brenda snatched the phone off the hook before Trevor was able to get it. She looked at the phone as if it was a foreign object and brought it slowly to her ear, sure it was Victor on the other end getting to offer up a string of lies as to why he didn't come home. She sighed and then answered.

"Hello."

"Mrs. Bailey?" said the gentleman on the other end.

"Yes, it is. May I ask who's calling?"

"Yes, this is Sgt. Lewis from the Durham Police Department. We've apprehended a suspect in your hit and run...a twenty-year-old man without a driver's license. We have witnesses that put him at the scene, and he's confessed. I know that you are recovering, and we'll drop by sometime this week and give you all the particulars for filing your insurance claim. We're glad to have him off of the street."

"Thank you for the good news," Brenda said. "Thank you again for calling."

"You're welcome," Sgt. Lewis said and hung up the phone.

Brenda put the phone down and stared off into space.

"Earth to Mother," Trevor hollered.

"I was far away. Good news, though. They found the person in my hit-and-run accident."

"That's good news, Mom. Where is Dad?"

"I don't know," Brenda said matter-of-factly. "He didn't come home last night."

Trevor frowned. "He's still up to his same old stuff."

"What are you talking about, Trevor?"

"Mom, I'm not blind. Please. Everyone knows that your husband ain't a saint."

"Enough. He's also your father."

"Whatever. Don't take up for him, Ma. He's a snake in the grass. I didn't ask to be his son, but I am. I hear what people say about him, and for sure, I see how he treats you when he doesn't think anyone is looking. Please. I thought you would've dumped his ass a long time ago."

"Watch your mouth."

"Mom, you've got to stop covering for him. It's his dirt; let him climb out of the mud all by himself."

"How long have you felt like this, Trevor? You've never said anything. You know that you can talk to me anytime."

"I know, Mom, but what's the use? Look, you want to hang out with me? I was going to hang out with a friend of mine from school, but I can hook up with him later."

"You mean that, Trevor? You don't mind being seen with your mother?"

"Mom, you've still got it going on. You look better than some of those twenty-year-olds."

Brenda grinned. "So I'm still fine, baby?"

"Mom, you're all that and a big bag of chips."

"Okay, let me get my coat. I'm looking forward to hanging out with my son."

"Great." Trevor poured himself another glass of juice and held it in midair when he heard the door that led into the garage open.

"Trevor, what's up, man? Where are you on your way to? Your mother here?"

"You've got a lot of questions for somebody who didn't make it home last night."

"And you better watch your mouth, boy, or you won't be able to talk out of it. Who do you think you are, to talk to me like that? Ain't none of your business where I've been, you got that?"

"Trevor..." Brenda began but stopped short when she saw Victor.

"Where's everyone going?" Victor asked again.

"Trevor and I are going to Central's football game."

"Well, have fun." Victor smirked, giving Trevor a beefy glance. "And Trevor, when you come home, I have some chores I need done."

Trevor sneered. "I've already done my chores."

"Good, but I have some other things I need you to do. Make sure you come home right after the game."

"What's up with you, Victor?" Brenda asked. "No one has seen you since yesterday morning, and now you come home trying to tell everybody what to do."

"I'm talking to Trevor, Brenda. A father and his son. Telling my son to do a little work doesn't have anything to do with you. Taking out the garbage and cleaning his room isn't going to make him a man."

Brenda pushed her hand in Victor's face. "And I guess staying out all night without making a phone call to let me know that you were all right makes you a man? You need to take a bath because you reek of that ho you've been with. Come on, Trevor."

Trevor moved past Victor and followed Brenda into the garage. Victor's gaze burned into Brenda's back.

"Your momma won't be there to take up for you next time," Victor said to the air. "No kid of mine is going to disrespect me."

Hearing the car pull out of the garage, Victor pulled the gun from his coat pocket and laid it on the kitchen counter with a thud. Beyoncé jumped, nearly spilling the remnants of her milk on the floor. Victor traced the pistol with his finger, picked it up, and held it in his hand. He held a pose, holding the gun to the side with his arm outstretched like he had seen on one of the gangster movies he had taken to watching.

"Pow, pow, pow," Victor said out loud. "You didn't listen to me, Mimi, and now you've got to pay the cost. My threats didn't mean much, but this gun sitting upside your temple is going to do the talking. Don't make me use it, bitch."

Victor put the gun back into his pocket and went to his room.

30

It felt good stumping on the grounds of her alma mater. As she and Trevor walked to the football field, Brenda closed her eyes for a moment, remembering a time many years ago when she and Mimi had attended their first football game. She could hear the band playing some jazzy tune that made them sway with the beat and Mimi making up her own lyrics to the song. It was the first time she had heard one of the cute guys she had been admiring ask another who she was, pointing his finger directly at her like she was a prize he'd just won. It was Victor; and she had fallen hard.

Brenda followed Trevor to the stands. The game was already underway, and Central had seven points on the scoreboard. Before she could sit down, Central scored another touchdown, and the fans were up on their feet screaming. The cheerleaders engaged the crowd, chanting loud and stomping their feet, while their bodies twisted and gyrated with the beat of their words. Then Brenda spotted them—Asia and Afrika, her eyes lingering on Afrika much longer, trying to make sense of the news Mimi had dropped in her lap—the news that pierced her heart like she'd been hit with a stun gun. She wondered how many of Victor's features Afrika had. Thank God she was too far away to get a good look.

Brenda and Trevor found seats and stood until the crowd died down. Brenda continued to watch the girls, consumed with their every movement, processing similarities—how they jerked their heads, tossed their hair, and stomped their feet. Even though there were thirteen other girls on the field, Asia and Afrika seemed to do everything in tandem, almost as if Brenda saw them in double vision.

An onset of nausea seemed to rise from nowhere, and the longer Brenda watched the girls, the more nauseated she became. She was oblivious of the Eagle's quarterback who was poised to throw another touchdown pass. All Brenda saw was Asia and Afrika moving in rhythm. While the images of their faces weren't clear, Brenda imagined they looked the same—identical; one light, the other dark.

Brenda needed to distance herself from the crowd. The loud noise made her dizzy and she was having a hard time controlling the emotions that had overtaken her body each time she looked at Afrika. Mimi's revelation affected her more than she realized, clouding her mind also with images of Victor and Mimi together, although the vision wasn't quite as Mimi had described.

Ugh, ugh. Mimi doubled over, holding her throat as she vomited.

"Damn!" a spectator shouted.

"Mom, are you all right?" Trevor asked, standing up to offer assistance.

"Ah, ah, ah," was all that came from Brenda's mouth as she tried to catch her breath.

"Hey, Trev, this your Mom?" a young man asked, gesturing at Trevor.

"Yeah, man; help me get her out of the bleachers. I'm going to take her home."

"No," Brenda managed to say. "You stay and enjoy the game. I'll come back for you. I'll be all right. It must have been something I ate."

"Are you sure, Mom?"

"I'll take you home," the young man said. "I'm borrowing my brother's car."

"Mom, this is my friend from school, Freddie, that I was telling you about."

"Nice to meet you, Freddie. I hope next time it will be under better circumstances."

"No problem. Are you okay, for real?"

"Yeah, I'm all right now. You guys enjoy the game."

"Will you guys sit down or move out of the way so we can see the game?" a rude spectator said.

"We will when my mother is all right!" Trevor hollered back.

Brenda threw Trevor two fingers to let him know she was okay and that she was on her way home.

"Call me if you need me!" Trevor shouted to Brenda.

Brenda shook her head and walked away, not bothering to look at the cheerleaders one last time.

Brenda jumped in the rental car and drove away from the stadium, her mind still conflicted. She let the car window roll down automatically; maybe the small breeze would chase her blues away. Brenda drove in silence, oblivious of the road she travelled. God had to be steering the wheel because she wasn't sure how she made it home in one piece.

After pulling into the garage, Brenda sat in silence, contemplating her next step. Life was complicated enough without having been thrown a Molotov cocktail. She willed the voices in her head to be still—the voices advocating *do unto the one who has done to you before they do it again.*

"Devil, you a lie and the truth ain't in you. Get thee behind me, Satan," Brenda uttered.

Brenda scrambled out of the car and walked into the kitchen. Beyonce, in her catlike stealthy way, entered the room and offered a welcome home. Brenda dropped her keys on the kitchen counter and started for her bedroom but froze when Victor entered the room.

"The game couldn't have been rained out since we haven't had any in weeks. What are you doing back so early? And where is Trevor?"

"I don't feel good. Shouldn't have gone in the first place. Trevor is still at the game."

"You don't listen. Pretending like the accident didn't

do you any harm, even though your car is a mangled mess."

"I was blessed to come out of that accident unscathed, and I don't hurt from the accident."

"So what's wrong with you? You've been in a funky mood much too much lately."

"Move, I'm going to the room to lay down."

"You want me to come with you? Now that we have the house to ourselves, maybe you want to freak with the brother."

"Why would I want to freak with you, Victor?" Brenda said as she left the kitchen heading for the stairs with Victor on her heels.

"Because you're my wife and that's what you signed up for when you said 'I do.' I wouldn't have to go behind these hos in the street if you'd stop holding out. A brother has needs."

Brenda stopped and turned around. "You're disgusting. I don't care if you're my husband; I'm not going to lay behind a ho. There was a time, Victor, that I was truly in love with you...would have gone to the end of the earth for you, but you've breached the contract we made before God and man one time too many. Should've left you a long time ago. It's a miracle I don't have some dreaded disease."

"Don't even think about leaving because you ain't going nowhere. We are a family that stays together."

"At what cost?" Brenda walked into their master bedroom and threw her purse down on the bed. She turned around and stared at Victor. A scowl had replaced the frown that lingered since entering the house. "Victor, I want a divorce."

"Girl, you're talking crazy. So I was out last night. No harm done. Didn't feel like hearing you talk about not being able to see Mimi."

"And why is it you don't want me to see Mimi? And I want the truth...the nineteen-year-old truth."

Victor's eyes widened. "What in the hell are you talking about, Brenda? What do you mean by a nineteen-year-old truth?"

"You shouldn't have to think about it; you know what I mean. Don't look at me like you have amnesia."

"I'm going to ask you one more time, Brenda. What are you talking about?"

"You sorry-ass bastard. You raped my best friend."

Victor rushed for Brenda and grabbed her shoulders. "Who told you that lie? Mimi?"

Tears began to well up in Brenda's eyes. "Take your dirty hands off of me, Victor. You aren't anything but the scum of the earth. Mimi warned me about you. She saw right through you...the kind of person you really were. I made you, Victor. You would be *nothing* without me. My daddy helped you to get that job. Nobody wanted your ass...nobody but me because you were a loser. And I was a fool, but I won't be a fool much longer."

"Go on and get it out of your system. Maybe I had it

coming…not because of Mimi, but because I haven't been the best husband…"

"You arrogant son-of-a-bitch. All the time I thought you were the one for me…the person who dotted my I's and crossed my T's. I wanted to believe in you, Victor; I saw something no one else saw. Yeah, we made some fine babies together, climbed the social ladder, but you couldn't leave those hoes alone. Mr. Victor Christianson had made it to the top and thought that nothing could touch him."

"Shut up, Brenda. Mimi had no right to tell you."

"Do you know what else she told me?"

"It's a lie, whatever it is."

"It's not a lie. Afrika and Asia look so much alike. I have to shake my head now that I recall how you acted when you first saw Afrika at the house. Scared the daylights out of you, didn't she? You thought you'd gotten away with it?"

"I'm not that child's father. Mimi can say what she wants."

"No one had to tell you that Afrika is your child. You did the dirty deed, and now your sins have come to light."

"Mimi has succeeded in twisting your brain."

"Is that why you're fighting like a dog in a cock fight? Afrika isn't some banshee that you want to go away. She's alive and in living color and looks a lot like you."

"Somebody is going to pay for this."

"Who, Victor? Who are you trying to blame for your

misguided deeds this time? As hard as I tried not to believe the words that tumbled out of Mimi's mouth, I realized that they were true. Rumor is, you've got other babies running around the county looking like you. Get out of my face, Victor. I've thrown up enough for today."

Victor turned away and grabbed his coat off the chair. There was a loud thud, followed by a boom, causing both Brenda and Victor to freeze and then look at each other.

Startled, Brenda walked in the direction of the noise. Lying next to Victor's foot on the hardwood floor was a steel-barreled gun. Victor picked it up and looked into the nose.

"A gun, Victor? You brought a loaded gun into this house...our bedroom? What were you planning to do with it? Kill me?"

"Brenda, please be quiet. No one is going to kill anybody."

"Maybe you didn't hear the bang." Brenda looked around the room, stopped, put her hand over her mouth, and began to point. "There's a hole in the wall. And you're going to stand there and tell me that the safety was on the gun and that it accidently came undone."

"Believe what you want. I got the gun for protection."

"Protection from whom? Yourself, Victor? You must think I'm stupid, but I've got your number. My God, what is going on here?"

"Look, I've got to go out."

"Where are you going, Victor? I hope to God you're not going to do anything crazy. Mimi hasn't done anything to you. She should've reported you for rape years ago, but she literally spared your life."

"Shut up, Brenda!" Victor screamed. "I don't want to hear anything else about Mimi! She had no business coming back here! She should've left well enough alone! And you're not going anywhere! You're my wife!"

"Not for long," Brenda retorted, her hands on her hips. "I've had about enough of you as I can stand."

Victor took a long hard look at Brenda and turned the gun over in his hand. "You don't want to make me your enemy. It wouldn't be wholesome for family relations."

"So, I ask you again. Do you plan to kill me?" Brenda asked.

"Don't provoke me, Brenda. I've maintained my composure better than I expected." Victor turned away and put the gun in his pocket.

"Give me the gun, Victor. You're not going anywhere until you give it to me."

"For a psychologist, you don't make much sense. Any sensible person would tell another to move out of my way. Now move out of my way, Brenda."

Victor's voice boomed and Brenda jumped. She watched as Victor hurried out of the room. His feet made pitter patter sounds on the stairs that ran from the top floor to the main floor. And then she heard it. *BAM*. The sound of Victor's anger as he slammed the door, shaking the house like a mini earthquake. Brenda stood a moment and assessed all that had transpired. Then she moved out of her trance, picked up the purse she'd thrown on the bed, and pulled out her cell phone.

Brenda dialed a number. "Answer, Mimi, answer. I've got to warn you."

31

Fuming, Victor drove blindly down the street. He flexed and then relaxed his fingers on his free hand, trying to will the anxiety that coursed through his body to quiet down. He couldn't believe Brenda had dared step to him, slandering his name with accusations that Mimi had put in her head. Brenda had pushed him to the brink, and he couldn't be responsible for what might happen.

Victor wasn't a killer; he was a lover. He loved up on a lot of women, but while he may not have shown it, he loved Brenda. It was his love for her that had kept him from aiming the gun and quieting her down. She kept droning on and on about his indiscretions…how she made him, making him look like the imbecile of the year with no backbone. Why did Brenda want to break up their happy home, a home that he'd cultivated for her and their two children?

Grasping the wheel, Victor sped on until he was finally at the entrance of Mimi's subdivision. He pushed air from his mouth and proceeded ahead; his mind made up on the task he planned to carry out.

He parked the car and jumped from it, looking both ways to see if anyone could ID him. Seeing no one, he marched up to Mimi's door and rang the bell. As he waited, he glided his hand over the bulge in his coat pocket.

Annoyed, Victor rang the bell again, but still no answer. He banged the door with his fist, but still no answer. He put his ear to the door and listened for any signs of movement in the house. Hearing none, he moved away, looking left and right before getting back into his car.

Victor sat a moment, his anger increased twofold. He beat the steering wheel with his hand and rolled his eyes around in his head. Then it came to him. He sat up straight, turned on the ignition, and headed out of the development.

He pushed the car as fast as it would go within the boundary of the law. He took a left and then a right and headed for the interstate. He was pushed for time. He exited the interstate at Fayetteville Street and headed toward North Carolina Central University.

Fayetteville Street and the area surrounding the stadium were littered with automobiles. He was fortunate enough to be at the right place at the right time as someone pulled out of a spot in front of him. Victor patted his trenchcoat and headed for the ticket booth.

"Hi, Mr. Christianson," the pretty brown-skinned girl in the ticket booth said as Victor pushed his money toward her.

"Good afternoon; one adult ticket."

"We're in the fourth quarter. There's no need for you to pay. You've got to get here early next time. I think we're winning."

"Thank you," Victor said, offering a semi-smile to the nice young lady before pushing on. "What's up, dawg?" he said to the school safety officer who stood at the gate.

"Central's kicking some butt. You missed a good game, man. You better hurry on in because this game is about over."

Victor and the guard gave each other a casual fist bump, and Victor moved into the stadium and into the crowd.

"Third down, eight to go with NC Central leading by three points," the announcer said. "NC Central's ball on the thirty-yard line with a minute and half left in the game."

Victor moved toward the bleachers. He spotted the cheerleaders, cheering the crowd on to victory and stopped when he spotted Afrika amongst them. Victor quickly walked up in to the stands without taking his eyes off of Afrika and blended in with the crowd that was now on its feet.

"Fourth down," the announcer said. "Central will go for the first down with a minute left to play."

The crowd yelled at fever pitch as the quarterback received the ball. He handed off the ball to one his linebackers who ran for five yards.

"First down," the announcer called. "The Eagles are in field goal range; forty seconds left on the clock."

The Eagles moved swiftly into a huddle, wanting to capitalize on the play and the momentum they were riding. Adrenaline was running high; the guys wanted this win. Moving out of the huddle, the players reorganized themselves on the field. Snap. The quarterback received the ball and threw a long pass to his running back, who ran for ten yards.

"First down and goal!" shouted the Eagles' announcer. "The Eagles smell victory!"

Victor kept a steady eye on Afrika, noting that Asia was four girls down in the row. He thought she spotted him and moved from what he'd perceived to be her line of sight. The cheerleaders were in a fast chant, waiting for the next play to occur. They stopped and the quarterback threw the ball.

"Touchdown!" the announcer called. "We'll have time for the extra point and kickoff."

The crowd was in an uproar. People were dancing where they stood.

"Eagles are number one! Eagles are number one!"

"The Eagles' kicker, Simon Perry, is ready," the announcer said. "He looks, kicks…and the kick is good for the extra point!"

Victor watched as the cheerleaders were in high velocity, shaking what their mamas had given them, engaging the crowd in a chant. "Eagles are number one! Eagles are number one!"

Defense and the special team unit came onto the field

for the Eagles. Simon Perry swung his foot preparing for the kickoff.

"The Eagles are ready for kickoff," the announcer said with excitement in his voice. "Perry's leg is up. He kicks. You won't believe it. Perry kicked it into the end zone. The opposing team will receive the ball on the twenty-yard line with only three seconds left on the clock."

"Defense! Defense!" the cheerleaders shouted followed by the fans. "Defense! Defense!"

"The opposing team snaps the ball...and...and the game is over. The Eagles have won it, thirty-one to twenty-one."

All mayhem broke loose. Everyone cheered and cried. The Eagles were on target to win their conference. Victor left the fans and the stands to their celebration.

"Hey, Mom. You all right?" Trevor asked.

"Yes and no."

"What's up?"

"I'm scared, Trevor."

"Scared of what, Mom? Speak up. The Eagles are about to win this game and the fans are going crazy."

"Your father has..."

"What about Dad? I can barely hear you."

"Trevor, your dad has a gun. I'm afraid he's going to do something crazy."

Pop, pop, pop!

"What was that?" Trevor asked, talking to Freddie.

"Your father..." Brenda began.

"Mom, I've got to call you back. Something happened. People are taking cover and running out of the stadium. I'll call you back when I find out what's going on."

"Trevorrrrrrrrr!"

Trevor flipped the lid on the phone.

"Come on, let's get out of here," Freddie said to Trevor.

"What happened?"

"I'm not sure, but it looks like a stampede."

"Why is everyone swarming around the cheerleaders?" Trevor asked. "Let's go find out. My sister is down there."

"Okay, let's hurry up. I don't want to be around any longer than I have to."

"You don't want anything to happen to your brother's car."

"Got that right."

Out of nowhere, a siren began to blare. Trevor and Freddie looked up as the ambulance careened in their direction. Police officers were on the scene, pushing back spectators that were drawn to where the cheerleaders stood. Raw emotions and screams could be heard, the closer the young men walked.

A police officer stuck out his hand. "You've got to go back against the fence. You can't come any closer."

"My sister is a cheerleader," Trevor said in a huff. "Is she all right?"

"Who's your sister and what's your name?"

"My sister is Asia Christianson and I'm her brother, Trevor."

"Let me find out. I'll be back in a moment."

Two paramedics rushed to where the cheerleaders were gathered. They knelt down on the ground out of Trevor's view. Within seconds, the paramedics lifted one on the cheerleaders onto the gurney and hurried toward the ambulance. In another few seconds, the siren was switched on and they were on their way.

The police officer returned with Asia close at his heels. Asia was crying and blood stained her uniform.

"Asia, what happened?" Trevor asked, fear in his eyes.

"It was awful, Trevor. Someone tried to kill Nikki. We heard this pop and then Nikki fell to the ground. Blood was running everywhere."

"Did you see who did it?"

"No, there were too many people standing around. I can't believe this has happened to Nikki."

"Has anyone called her mom?"

"I don't know, but I will as soon as I get my cell phone."

"Oh, Asia, this is Freddie. He goes to my school."

"Hey," was all Asia could say. "I want to go home. I can't stay on campus tonight."

"I'm taking Trevor home," Freddie said. "You can ride with us."

"No, the cheerleaders are going to the hospital to be with Nikki. I'll get a ride home later."

"Asia!" someone shouted. "The police want to talk to you!"

"Oh, God. I don't believe this. Who could have done this?"

"They're probably questioning everyone to see if they saw anything," Freddie offered.

"What if the killer is still here?" Asia asked.

"Get your stuff so we can get out of here as soon as we can," Trevor said.

"No, I'm going to the hospital. Nikki is my best friend. Just think, it could've been any one of us."

32

More than twenty minutes had passed since Trevor had hung up on her. Brenda paced the floor, her nerves unending. She'd tried relentlessly to call Victor, but he didn't bother to answer. She prayed to God that he wouldn't do anything stupid.

There wasn't going to be any waiting another minute longer. Brenda picked up her cell and dialed Trevor's number, the phone shaking in her hand. She moved from one foot to the other, anticipating Trevor's voice. She stopped when she heard him say hello.

"Trevor?"

"Yeah, Mom. Are you all right?"

"Why didn't you call me back?"

"Mom, I'm being interviewed by the police?"

"The police?"

"Yeah, Mom. Hold on a second."

Brenda waited until Trevor came back on the line.

"There was a shooting at the game today. That's what happened when we were talking. Nikki was shot."

"Nikki who?"

"Asia's best friend, Nikki."

"You mean Afrika?"

"Nikki...Afrika—yes, Mom. It was horrible. The ambulance took her to the hospital."

"Oh my God. Oh my God. I don't believe this."

"Asia is all messed up."

"Is Asia okay?"

"Yes, Mom. Asia's fine, other than being broken up about Nikki and she has blood all over her cheerleading outfit. She's going to the hospital to be with Nikki."

"Did they catch the person who did it?" Brenda asked, realizing for the first time that Victor had entered her mind as a possible suspect.

"No. That's why they're interviewing everyone who didn't get out of the stadium before the police blocked off the entrances."

"God, this is horrible. What hospital did they take Afrika to? I wonder if her mother has been notified?"

"I don't know where they took her, but if you have Mrs. Bailey's phone number, you may want to call her. Asia said Nikki was unconscious when they took her off the field. The cheerleading coach rode to the hospital with Nikki."

"Okay, Trevor. Thanks for the information. I've got to call Mimi. When are you coming home?"

"When the police finish with us."

"Okay. Hurry home as soon as you can."

"Alright."

Brenda ended the call and dialed Mimi's number. It

went straight to voicemail. "Oh my God; I've got to find Mimi."

"MIMI, YOU LOOK DIVINE," JOHN CARROLL SAID AS HE sat back and watched Mimi approach the table in her short pale yellow brocade jacket, black knit turtleneck, and black stretch trousers.

"Watch what you say to a married woman," Mimi responded, smiling as she sashayed to the table and sat across from John. "I love the atmosphere here."

"So why is the married lady sitting down to lunch with me at her favorite restaurant?" John added with a smile.

"Because you asked and I could use a friend about now."

"Good answer, but you know you started it."

"You're right. How are you doing, John?"

"Great, now that you're here. And if I didn't know better, I would think you're flirting with me."

Mimi blushed and fanned herself with her hand. "Flattery will get you most places." Mimi picked up the menu and began to browse. She looked up to see John staring. "Are you going to eat?"

"I already know what I want."

"I hope you're talking about something on this menu." Mimi chuckled.

"You're funny, Mimi. I meant the menu, but I hope you don't mind if I stare. You look better than any of the desserts on this menu. In fact, they could spice up the walls of this place…take all that old nostalgic stuff down and replace it with your likeness."

Mimi put the menu down. "I'm ready to order."

"So," John began, changing the subject, "all quiet on the front? No more calls or threats from Victor?"

"No. I hope he's gotten the message this time. But it's really too late since Brenda is privy to my secret."

"If she asks Victor for a divorce, you better believe he'll be coming at you with a vengeance."

"Let him. I'll have something for his ass this time."

"Mimi, be careful is all I ask. I had an opportunity to size Victor up. He's no one you want to vex. He's already tried to get at you through Afrika."

"Even more reason for me to have a gun. I want the spinach and shrimp salad. I'm going to call Afrika to see how the game went."

Mimi pulled out her BlackBerry. "I forgot to turn this bad boy back on when I made one of my stops."

"Sometimes it's good to have some peace and quiet if your cell rings all day like mine."

"I know what you mean. Ummm, I've got a few calls from Brenda. Let me call her real quick. It won't take but a minute."

"Don't let that woman spoil our lunch."

"Be good, John. Excuse me; I've got Brenda on the line."

"Mimi?" Brenda asked with a chill to her voice.

"Yeah, Brenda. I'm returning your calls." Mimi laughed.

"I had my phone off, and I just turned it on and saw your number…that you had called.

"So you haven't spoken to anyone?"

"No, Brenda. What's up?"

"There was a shooting today at Central…at the football game."

Mimi looked across the table at John who sat upright with his hands on the table. "And what about the shooting, Brenda? Why are you telling me?"

Brenda began to cry and Mimi couldn't understand a word she said between the crying and the talking.

"Brenda, stop crying and tell me what happened."

"Afrika was shot."

"Did you say Afrika was shot?"

"Yes. She was shot and has been taken to the hospital."

"Oh my God. My baby. Oh my God," Mimi said over and over, trying to catch her breath. "What hospital, Brenda?" Mimi shouted.

"I don't know. Trevor told me the cheerleading coach rode with Afrika in the ambulance."

"I've got to find Afrika. Thank you, Brenda. I'll call you later."

Mimi stood up and covered her face. "My daughter's been shot. I don't know if she's dead or alive."

"What hospital?" John asked, getting up from the table, trying to remain calm for Mimi.

The waitress returned to the table. "Can I get you anything?"

"No," John said. "Sorry, we won't be eating lunch today."

"Mimi, what hospital?" John asked again.

"I don't know," Mimi said through her tears. "I've got the cheerleading coach's number in my cell. I'm calling her now."

"Good."

"Hello, this is Afrika's mother. I understand she's been shot."

"Hello, Mrs. Bailey. I'm with her at Duke Medical Center; you need to come right away. We've been trying to reach you. The doctors say they need to operate."

"I'm on my way."

33

The freeway was crowded with late-afternoon travelers. Mimi sat in silence as John manipulated his way through traffic. The westbound lane seemed to bottleneck the closer it got to the exit for the NC State Wolfpack's stadium. It was too late to try and take a shortcut or maneuver around the city without getting caught up in football game traffic.

"How much longer to the hospital?" Mimi asked impatiently.

"Try and relax, Mimi. I'm doing the best I can, considering the parking lot we seem to have found ourselves in. Don't you worry; I'll have you there in a few."

Mimi didn't say another word. The drive allowed time for her mind to wander...to wonder why her baby had been a target. The answer was not far behind.

"I need that gun," Mimi said out of nowhere. "My gut tells me that Victor is behind this. If something happens to my daughter, I'm going to..."

"Don't say it, Mimi."

"Victor needs to make peace with God; I'm not going to wait for the police to figure this out. I'm going to take that bastard out myself."

"You need to call your husband."

"John, you need to drive this car and get me to my daughter. I'll call Raphael as soon as I've seen Afrika."

John stared straight ahead and didn't open his mouth again until he pulled up beside the Emergency Room at Duke. Mimi didn't wait for the car to come to a complete stop before she was out of the car and into the ER.

Frantic, Mimi approached the window of the intake processor. "Excuse me, my daughter was brought into the hospital by ambulance an hour or so ago. I'm her mother and I need to see..."

"Ma'am," a woman in a pink and purple print smock waved, "follow me. You are here for..."

"Afrika Bailey."

"Right this way."

"Mrs. Bailey."

Mimi stopped and turned in the direction of the person who called her name. There was Asia, her eyes as red as tomatoes. Several police officers were in the room, continuing their investigation, trying to get answers...anything that would lead to the shooter.

"Hi, Asia," was all Mimi could say, fighting back the tears. "Thanks for being here."

"Hello, Mrs. Bailey, I'm Miss Deavers, the cheerleading coach. We're all so sorry about what happened to Nikki. It is incomprehensible."

"Thank you, Miss Deavers. I appreciate you being with Nikki when she was taken to the hospital. The one time my phone was off..."

"Don't worry about it. We've been praying that Nikki will be fine."

Asia went to Mimi and hugged her; the other cheerleaders rose and followed suit. They all began to cry and console each other. Mimi moved away first.

A police officer stepped in front of the girls. "Are you Ms. Bailey's mother?"

"Yes, sir, I am. Right now I have to see about Afrika; the nurse is waiting on me."

"Ma'am, I'm Officer Stokes. I'll need to ask you some questions when you get a moment. I understand you need to be with your daughter."

"Thank you, Officer Stokes. I'll be happy to answer any questions later." Mimi turned to the others. "Thanks, Asia; Miss Deavers."

"Tell Nikki I love her," Asia said, echoed by the others, tears continuing to flow from their faces.

"I will," Mimi said and turned to leave. Just as she did, she caught a glimpse of John. She nodded in recognition and he found a seat and waited.

The nurse escorted Mimi behind the Emergency Room doors, through a long hallway and a large room of makeshift smaller ones, separated by walls made of heavy muslin hung by metal rings that slid along metal bars. Finally the nurse stopped beside a bed, whose curtain had not been drawn as a team of doctors stood around, prepping the patient for surgery.

"Are you this young lady's mother?" a doctor asked upon seeing the nurse and the woman behind her.

Mimi held her chest and willed herself to move closer. Her nerves were on edge, and it felt as if a spear was piercing her heart. She moved closer still until she saw Afrika with IVs running from her arm to a pole. Her eyes were closed; she seemed so peaceful.

"Yes, this is my daughter, Afrika."

"Ma'am, I'm Dr. Daniels. We need to get your daughter to surgery as soon as possible. We're waiting for clearance to take her to the operating room. She's suffered a bullet wound in her back; she's fortunate to be alive. She's lost a lot of blood."

"Oh my, God." Mimi blew air from her mouth. "Thank you, doctor. Please save my baby."

"We'll do everything in our power. It may be a tough road, but for a Saturday afternoon, you've got a good team of doctors on call."

A phone rang.

"Let's move her to the OR," Dr. Daniels said.

The team pushed the gurney out of the room to an elevator, on their way to the surgery room, as Mimi stood helplessly by.

A gentle rub made Mimi look up. "I'll take you to the waiting room," the nurse said. "Is there anyone in the ER waiting room that you'd like to have go up with you?"

Finding her composure, Mimi shook her head. "Yes. My daughter's fellow cheerleaders and a friend of mine are in the lobby. I could use their comfort about now."

"Let's go and get them."

"I need to make a phone call first; then we can get them."

34

Mimi walked back into the Emergency Room waiting room on her way out of the building. She saw the girls look her way, and she lifted a finger and mouthed that she'd be back. John got up from his seat and followed Mimi outside.

"John, I need to do this by myself. I'm going to call Raphael. I need to talk to him alone."

"If you need me, I'll be inside," John said.

"Thanks."

Mimi watched John reenter the hospital and then dialed Raphael's number.

"Hello."

"Raf, this is Mimi."

"Hey, baby? How are you doing?"

Mimi hesitated trying to get it together. "Not well. Someone shot Afrika this afternoon..."

"Mimi, did I hear you correctly? Someone shot Afrika? How?"

"Yeah, Raf. Afrika was cheerleading at the football game. Some-one shot her, and now she's in surgery."

"Jesus. Don't let nothing happen to my little girl. Is she going to be all right?"

"She was hit in the back; lost a lot of blood. The doctor said he'll do all that he can to save her."

"How in the hell did this happen to our little girl, Mimi? Have the police found the shooter? Somebody's going to pay. Our baby is just beginning her life."

"I know, Raf. We don't have any answers yet. I've been beating myself up about letting her come to North Carolina. Only if I had been more forceful and put my foot down."

"Mimi, you couldn't control what happened today. Look, let me get off the phone. I'll be home on the first flight out. How are you holding up?"

"As best as I can under the circumstances. I've got to go now. Please come home as fast as you can get here, baby."

"As soon as I get the paperwork done, I'll be there. I love you, Mimi. Afrika is going to be all right."

"I want to believe that so badly. And I love you, too. Please hurry; I need you."

"I hope to see you tomorrow."

"Okay."

Mimi ended the call and held the phone to her heart. She let the river of tears flow—an image of Afrika lying on the bed lifeless so vivid. She thanked God for this private moment...a moment where she could sift through the rubble of her broken heart to try and discern what this was all about without answering everyone's questions.

It was to be short-lived. She looked up as she heard someone calling her name. It was Brenda.

"Mimi, how's Afrika?" Brenda asked upon approach.

"She's in surgery. A bullet is lodged in her back."

"Oh, my God. Mimi, I'm so sorry." Brenda went to Mimi and hugged her. Mimi hugged her back.

"Let's go in. The nurse is waiting to take me to the surgical waiting room. I had to call my husband to tell him about Afrika. Brenda..."

"Yeah, Mimi, what is it?"

"Do you think...do you think Victor did it?"

Brenda's ashen face gave away her thoughts.

"Why do you ask? Victor is many things, but he wouldn't do anything as ludicrous as try to hurt Afrika."

Sadness took on a different meaning. Mimi felt sorry for Brenda. Although she was a successful psychologist, Brenda allowed Victor to control her life...impair her vision of the road she had mapped out for her life. Mimi remembered how she and Brenda would have sleepovers when they were teenagers and their fathers were stationed together in Germany and how they said they would conquer the world—Mimi as a successful singer and Brenda a renowned researcher who was going to find a cure for cancer. Neither had followed their dream; both had been double-crossed...betrayed by a man—the same man, who had taken from them without any apology.

"This isn't the time," Mimi conceded. "Let me go in and check on Afrika."

"Okay, I'll go with you."

They began to walk toward the entrance into the ER

when the door opened. Brenda looked at Mimi and then back to John.

"John Carroll, is that you?" Brenda asked. "I haven't seen you in awhile. What are you doing at Duke?"

John looked from Mimi to Brenda and smiled. "I heard that Mimi's daughter had been in some kind of accident, and I came to see if there was anything I could do."

"Uhm, hmm," Brenda said under her breath, smiling for the first time.

Mimi smiled and blinked her eye at John. "Thank you, John. I need to go to the waiting room. You all come with me."

ALL WAS QUIET WHEN VICTOR FINALLY ARRIVED HOME. He moved quietly through the house but jumped when Beyoncé sauntered into the hallway, seemingly from out of nowhere.

"Damn cat. You need to get a freaking job, walking around the house like you own the damn joint. Get out of here."

Beyoncé ignored the snide remarks from the man of the house. She went to her litter box and did her business.

Believing he was by himself, Victor pulled off his trenchcoat and plopped down on the leather couch in the family room. He picked up the remote and turned on the television. The scene that played out in front of him was lost on Victor as a blank stare covered his face, his mind consumed with the events of the day.

Several minutes passed without any signs of life. Reaching for his coat, Victor pulled the gun out of his pocket. He turned it over in his hand and sat it in his lap, the weight of the world now on his shoulders. Without warning, Victor dozed off. Fifteen minutes passed.

A noise broke the silence in the house and woke Victor from his mini-nap. He scrambled to hide the gun under his coat and looked up to see Trevor staring at him as he walked down the stairs.

"What's up, Trevor? Just getting home from the game? Where's your mother?"

A deep frown clouded Trevor's face. "I was up in my room. Mom wasn't here when I got home."

"How was the game?"

"The game? It's what happened after the game."

"What happened after the game?"

"Asia's best friend was shot?"

"Who, Afrika?"

"Yeah. The police wouldn't let anyone out of the stadium...at least the ones that didn't get out before the police were on the scene. They questioned everyone. Asia went to be with Afrika at the hospital."

"That's terrible. I hope she'll be all right."

Trevor sat at the opposite end of the couch. He glanced at the television. "Tyler Perry is making bank with *The House of Payne*."

"What?"

"The show on television."

"Oh," Victor said.

"Dad, may I ask you a question?"

"What is it, son?"

"Was that a gun I saw on your lap?"

35

Curtis Payne was going through his nightly tirade, yelling at C.J. and his kids, threatening to put them out of his house. Aunt Ella, as usual, saved the day, admonishing Curtis to be nice to his nephew before God strikes him dead. And Curtis doesn't hesitate to remind Ella that C.J.'s crackhead wife had burned down their house, and if C.J. had paid a little more attention to what was going on in his home, he and his eating him-out-of house-and-home kids wouldn't be in his house at all.

Trevor picked up the remote and switched channels and stopped abruptly at a news bulletin.

"There was a shooting today on the campus of North Carolina Central University," the newscaster said.

Trevor sat up. "This is it!" he shouted.

"A young woman, one of the North Carolina Central Eagles cheerleaders, was hit by a stray bullet that was fired as the crowd began to leave the stadium at the end of the game. The young woman, identified as Afrika Nicole Bailey, was taken to Duke University Medical Center. We have yet to get a full report from the doctors on the severity of Ms. Bailey's injuries; however, we were able to find out that she was whisked away to surgery upon the arrival of Ms. Bailey's mother, Mrs. Setrina Bailey.

"Police have yet to apprehend anyone at this time for this senseless shooting. Officers interviewed a number of persons who were in the area at the time of the shooting after blocking entrances off and onto the campus. However, no leads have been obtained. There is some question as to the response time of the police officers; especially since the shooter is believed to have been among the fans that attended the football game. At this time, the subject is still at large.

"I'm Charlotte Wilson, reporting to you live for WTVD News. We will bring you up-to-date news on this breaking news story as soon as it becomes available."

"Dang," Trevor said to no one. "What animal would do such a thing?"

Victor flinched. "Whoever did it should have both arms cut off."

"I say the perpetrator should have to stand in front of a firing squad so they can feel the agony of being gunned down just before the executioners fire their weapons. What did Afrika do to deserve this?"

Victor felt a chill run through his body. He wanted to get as far away from Trevor as possible. Hearing Trevor talk that way made him extremely uncomfortable. The deed had been done, and now he felt like crap. He didn't want to kill Afrika; he simply wanted Mimi to go away. He pulled out of his trance as Trevor continued to drone on about the punishment he should receive.

"For real, I hope they catch the son-of-a-gun real soon and put him away for life...in solitary confinement without food and water."

"You have strong feelings about this."

"Yeah, it happens every day, but I've never known anyone it has happened to. I really like Afrika. So...what are you doing with a gun, Dad?" Trevor said, changing the subject.

Trevor managed to invade his comfort zone again. "Trevor, what if I told you that I got it for protection... for us...the family?"

"If that's the case, why were you trying to hide it? It doesn't make a whole lot of sense to me since no one has tried to break into our house."

"Well, this is in the event that someone gets the urge to. Have you picked up a newspaper lately, Trevor? Crime is all around us. We've got to protect ourselves from the elements."

"Whatever."

"You need to grow up, boy. Your mother has been so over-protective of you and your sister all of your lives. Out in the real world, beyond the high school you attend, are people from all walks of life, with their own agendas, many looking to get ahead in life, some aspiring to do great things, and some with criminal intent and malice in their hearts. With the economy in the shape it's in, even those in high places with the seven and eight figure salaries are committing high-collar crimes to save themselves and their families. We can't be too careful."

"What does all of that have to do with you having a gun?"

"Look, Trevor. You are too trusting."

"You've never talked about having a gun in the house before. Can't blame me for asking."

"Where's your mother?"

"I told you, she wasn't here when I got home. Maybe she went to the hospital to see about Afrika; especially since Asia and her other cheerleading buddies went there."

Victor mulled over what Trevor had said. Trevor was his alibi. There was no way to connect him to the shooting...or even to the gun. Thank God for this moment with Trevor. He was safe for now.

THE WAITING ROOM WAS FULL—CHEERLEADERS, MIMI, Brenda and John. Mimi paced back and forth, the soles of her shoes making black marks on the tile. Brenda and John watched Mimi...watched her anguish as the seconds, minutes, and the hours flew by.

"You want some coffee?" John asked.

Mimi shook her head and began another trek back and forth across the room. There hadn't been any word from anyone about how the surgery was going. Mimi stopped as her BlackBerry rang. She looked at the caller ID.

"Hey, baby," she said, moving over to a corner of the room for privacy.

"How is the surgery going?" Raphael asked.

"No word yet. My nerves are on edge and I have the onset of a headache."

"Believe, baby. You are the one who tells me all the time about prayer. I've been praying to the rafters, and I know God heard my big mouth."

"You are so strong, baby. I'm not going to be able to get through this without you."

"Well, I'll be there before you know it. I'm catching an early morning hop to New Jersey. The closest I can get to Durham is Fort Bragg. Don't worry about picking me up; I'll catch a taxi if I have to."

"That's good news. I can't wait to see you."

"Look, hold on and be strong for Afrika. She's going to be all right. I can feel it. Gotta run."

"Okay, Raf. I'll see you when you get here."

"I'll come directly to the hospital."

"Okay, baby. See you tomorrow."

Mimi ended the call and relaxed a brief moment. She saw Brenda walk her way. Seeing her brought the reality of what had occurred back to the forefront of her mind. Mimi couldn't shake the thought that Victor may have had something to do with Afrika being shot. She pushed it from her immediate thoughts as Brenda approached and patted her on the back.

"You okay?" Brenda asked.

"Yeah. That was Raphael. He'll be here tomorrow."

"Mimi, I need to talk to you."

"Can it wait, Brenda? I'm so distraught over Afrika getting shot, I can't think straight."

"All right, but you asked me a question earlier... whether I thought that Victor might be capable of doing this heinous crime."

"I was grasping at straws, Brenda. I wanted someone to blame... As you said, Victor may be a lot of things, but he wouldn't stoop this low. I can't believe he would lift a finger to shoot my baby."

"Mimi, Victor has a gun."

"He what, Brenda?" Mimi said loud enough for the whole room to hear. Her eyes began to bulge from their sockets.

"I saw it today with my own eyes," Brenda continued. "I didn't even know Victor owned one. I was upset about what you'd told me that he'd done to you when we were in college. I'd gone earlier to the game with Trevor but I couldn't stay because every time I looked at Afrika, I thought of you and Victor together."

"Brenda, I'm sorry..."

"Mimi, listen. I left the game early and confronted Victor. Then I told him that I wanted a divorce. A heated argument ensued and when he picked up his coat to leave, a gun fell out of his pocket. And it went off. What if he was trying to kill me?"

"Look, Brenda. We've got to tell this to the police. Do you know where Victor is?"

"He took off. I don't know where he went, but I pray that he didn't do this thing...that he didn't shoot Afrika."

Mimi began to hyperventilate. "Oh my, God. This is too much. If you don't tell the police, I'm going to tell them."

Brenda grabbed Mimi's hands. "Mimi, let's wait until Afrika gets out of surgery. Victor is my husband and I want to believe he didn't do this."

"Brenda, you don't have a daughter lying in the operating room teetering between life and death. If Victor is the one who did this, he needs to be picked up off the street so that he can't hurt anyone else."

"Ladies," John said, as he looked from Mimi to Brenda. No one saw him approach. "What's going on?"

Brenda's eyes pleaded with Mimi but Mimi looked away.

"John, please find the police," Mimi said. "I have some information that may help them apprehend the person who shot Afrika."

"What information?" Then John looked from Mimi to Brenda. "I'll get the police."

"Why couldn't you wait, Mimi? I don't know if Victor did it. I'm only speculating that it's a possibility because he has a gun. Asia is over there with her fellow cheerleaders. I don't want her to become upset."

"I'm sorry, Brenda. But my daughter is laying in there...my only child. You've got to understand that."

Tears rolled down Brenda's cheeks. She left Mimi and found a corner of her own.

Mimi went to Brenda and rubbed her back. "Thank you for parting with that piece of information. If nothing else, it will help us get to the bottom of this and rule Victor out if he hasn't done anything."

Brenda said nothing.

Brisk footsteps made everyone look up. John led the way followed by two plainclothes detectives. John stopped in front of Mimi.

"Ma'am, Mrs. Bailey, I'm Officer Rathmusen. I understand you're in receipt of some information that may help us apprehend the person or persons who may have shot your daughter."

"It's a long shot, sir..." Mimi looked over at Brenda and turned away. "I believe it may be someone I know. I don't have any concrete evidence that this person was even at the game, but I've been threatened and stalked by this person in the last week, and it may have led to this. It's a starting point; and if he didn't do it, this will be a sure way to find out."

"Maybe you should start from the beginning," Officer Rathmusen said.

Mimi shared her bizarre story with the police, even the event nineteen years ago. She took several glances in Brenda's direction as John stood over her, trying to calm her spirit. Officer Rathmusen stopped writing and looked at Mimi.

"Why didn't you report this?"

"What would anyone have done?" Mimi asked. "I hoped

that this would all go away, and I could go on with my life."

"What is this person's name?" Officer Rathmusen asked. "You have yet to say."

Mimi looked over at Brenda once again. "It's Victor Christianson. His wife is sitting over there." Mimi pointed. Officer Rathmusen had a puzzled look on his face.

"We're best friends."

36

Restless, Victor got up from the couch and began to pace the room. Fear replaced the inner confidence he had exuded earlier in the day when he left home with a gun in his pocket to do bodily harm. It was like coming off of a high and the realization of what he'd done suddenly hit him full force. Victor stood still as the voice floated through his brain—*you're a fool. Your secret was already exposed. You didn't have to kill.*

But Victor hadn't killed anyone. Thank God for that. He needed some fresh air to sort out the mess he'd made. He put on his trenchcoat and touched his pocket to make sure the gun was still there. He needed to get rid of it.

"Trevor, I'm going out for a while." Victor looked at his watch. "It's getting late, going on seven o'clock. Tell your mother whenever she comes in, I'll be back soon."

"Yeah," Trevor said from the kitchen. "You taking your gun?"

Victor walked into the kitchen where Trevor was stuffing his face full of microwave pizza. "You aren't to mention that gun again. Your mother would be hysterical if she knew I had it."

Trevor looked at Victor thoughtfully. "So why do you have one?"

"Boy, eat your pizza."

Victor slipped through the door that led into the garage and was on his way.

WITH REMOTE HELD STRAIGHT OUT, TREVOR SURFED the channels with one hand and stuffed pizza into his mouth with the other. He finally had the house to himself, and he lay across the couch with his sneakers on like he was king of the castle. Even Beyoncé gave him a disapproving look when she strolled into the room.

A knock at the front door startled Trevor. It was faint, but he heard it. He put the small amount of pizza that remained in his hand on the pizza box and got up to answer the door. Two medium-build, tall-to-medium height gentlemen in business suits, one black and one white, stood at the door. They sized Trevor up.

"May I speak with Mr. Victor Christianson, please," the black man said, flashing his badge and hastily putting it away.

"I didn't see your badge," Trevor said. "Can't be too careful."

The man was not amused. He flipped it out again.

"Detective Ernest Marshall," Trevor said with a smirk on his face. "And you are…"

"Detective Bryan Samuels," the other detective said, flashing his badge.

Detective Marshall snapped the lid shut with a thud in an attempt to irritate Trevor.

"Well, you just missed him."

"Do you know where he went?" Detective Marshall asked.

"I don't know. He said he would be back later on. He's only been gone fifteen minutes."

The two detectives looked between each other. "Do you mind if we sit and wait for him?" Detective Samuels asked.

"Yes, I mind. My parents don't allow me to have company when they aren't here."

"Smart boy," Marshall whispered under his breath. "All right, kid. Let your dad know we came by to speak with him. I'm Marshall and my partner's name is Samuels."

"I saw your badges and I remembered your names. May I tell him why you wanted to speak to him?"

"No, just tell him we need to speak to him soon," Samuels said. "Thank you and good evening."

Trevor watched the detectives retreat to their car. Wheels began to turn in his head. Did the detectives' appearance have something to do with the gun Victor had on him? Trevor went back into the kitchen and picked up his cell from the table. He dialed his mother's number, but there was no answer.

Victor found his way to Sheila's—the condo he had provided for their occasional sexual rendezvous. He needed to expend some energy...have some rough and playful sex to send the tension that racked his body to the other side of the globe. He climbed the stairs and lay on the doorbell when the master key refused to give him entrance.

"Sheila!" Victor shouted, and then quieted when Sheila came to the door.

"Why is the freaking key not working in the door?"

"Victor, you can't just walk up in here anytime you get good and ready. A girl has to protect herself, and anyway, there's some kind of crazy running around. You heard what happened at Central today?"

"Yeah, I did. Now are you going to let me in? I don't understand why I'm still standing on the porch of my condo."

"Victor, tonight isn't a good time. I'm feeling a little under the weather."

Victor pushed the door in and stood in front of Sheila. He slammed the door shut and followed Sheila into the living room that reminded one of an African paradise. The walls were painted tangerine with curtains made of a Kente cloth in colors of black, white, tangerine and lime. African masks and wood carvings littered the room tastefully, and throughout the room were yellow, orange and green candles in various sizes in specially picked candle-holders.

"So what are you doing with this lacy number on, barely covering your ass and titties? I know you don't have anyone else up in my house."

Sheila's voice shook. "No, Victor, there's no one here.

I don't feel so well. I might have a touch of the flu. I was preparing to lie down right before you showed up at the door."

Breathing hard, Victor swooped down on Sheila and grabbed her by the shoulders. He began to kiss her neck. "I need you, Sheila. God, you smell good."

"Uhh, Victor." Sheila stood afraid to move.

Victor took off his coat and threw it on the arm of the overstuffed green chair that sat next to the plush green sofa. He pulled Sheila to him and eased her on the sofa and began to kiss her passionately on the lips and all over her neck, intoxicated with her scent. He slipped his fingers under her bra strap and pulled it down, exposing her breasts; her nipples extended at attention. He kissed them like a hungry man who had been deprived of food, savoring the taste to the very last drop. Then Victor lifted himself to get a better look. He knelt over Sheila and kissed her stomach, sliding his hands over her, exploring every nook and cranny, feeling her smooth and supple skin before finally lifting the sides of her panties so he could continue his pleasure.

Sheila placed her hands on top of Victor's. "I don't feel good, Victor. My stomach is rumbling and if I don't get up, I might throw up." Sheila grabbed her stomach. "I've got to go to the bathroom."

Victor looked at her. "Damn, girl, I was almost there. Now, I've got to find some other way to get rid of this hard-on. You arouse me to no end, Sheila, with that fine body of yours."

"I've got to go to the bathroom."

Victor rolled his body to the side and let Sheila up as she fled to the bathroom. On her way in, she reached for her cell phone. Once in the bathroom, she sent a text and heaved a sigh of relief when she received a reply. She made an awful noise like she was throwing up, flushed the toilet, washed her hands, and went back to the living room to face Victor.

"Baby, let's call it a night," Sheila said, using every bit of tact to get rid of him.

"I know you don't feel good. Why don't you let me lie with you for a while? I won't try anything."

Sheila sighed. "Victor, all I want to do is go to sleep."

"Just a few minutes," Victor begged.

Victor laced his arms around Sheila's belly as he held her close, bunched up on the sofa. Sheila's face was twisted in a nasty scowl. She lay like a limp doll in Victor's arms, but sat up at the abrupt ringing of the phone.

Victor pulled out his BlackBerry and saw that Trevor was calling. He started to ignore it but pushed the green icon and spoke into the phone. "What is it, Trevor?"

"Dad, some guys…detectives, came to the house looking for you."

Victor pushed Sheila aside and brought both feet to the floor. "What did they want?"

"They wanted to talk to you. They wouldn't say what it was about. They asked if they could sit until you returned, but I told them no."

"Good. Did you get their names? Maybe I'll try and contact them."

"The black dude's name was Ernest Marshall and the white dude's name was Bryan Samuels."

"Thanks."

Victor ended the call. "Look, Sheila. I've got to run. My son called. Some old friends of mine got into town and are trying to catch up with me. Another day. I hope you feel better."

"You do care."

"Yeah." Victor paused, reached in his pocket, and pulled out the gun. "Look, you can put this away. I don't need it. I've changed my mind about what I was going to do with it."

Sheila looked at him strange. "A few days ago you acted like your world was about to cave in and you had to teach somebody a lesson. Give it here; I'll put it away. Thanks for understanding, Victor. I'm going to crawl in bed as soon as I close the door."

"Yeah." He reached down and kissed Sheila lightly on the lips. "I'm out."

37

"We interrupt this program for a breaking news story," the announcer said.

Trevor pulled his feet off the coffee table and sat up straight on the leather couch.

"Good evening. We have an update on the breaking news story we brought to you earlier this evening. There has been a new lead in the shooting of student Afrika Nicole Bailey this afternoon on the campus of North Carolina Central University. Ms. Bailey, who is a cheerleader at NC Central, was preparing to leave the stadium after the Eagles' win today. As the crowd dispersed, a shot rang out and a stray bullet hit Ms. Bailey in the back, narrowly missing her heart. We understand that Ms. Bailey is now in recovery after a four-and-a-half-hour surgery at Duke University Medical Center.

"An unlikely source provided information that has led this investigation to someone of possible interest along with a possible motive. The local sheriff's office has declined to provide the media with the identity of this person of special interest at this time.

"Tune into WTVD eleven o'clock news for more of

this story. I'm Charlotte Wilson, reporting to you live for WTVD News."

"I wonder who the person of interest is?" Trevor said out loud to no one. He picked up his cell phone and dialed.

"Hey, Trevor," Brenda said in a low voice.

"Hey, Mom. I hear Afrika is in recovery."

"Yes, they've stabilized her, but she's a long way from being out of the woods. Poor Mimi."

"Mom, the news reporter said a few minutes ago that they have a lead as to who may have shot Afrika."

Silence. Then Brenda spoke. "What did they say exactly?"

"That a source tipped the police off but they're not saying who it is."

"I pray that whomever did this will turn themselves in."

"Mom..."

"What is it, Trevor?"

"Some detectives came to the house looking for Dad. Said they needed to talk to him. They missed him by fifteen minutes, and that was about two hours ago. Dad told me to tell you he'd be back shortly."

"Does your dad know that these detectives came by?"

"Yes. I finally caught up with him on his cell phone."

"Thanks for sharing with me. Only your father can tell us what that's all about. I'll be home soon. I didn't want Mimi to be alone."

"Is Asia coming with you?"

"No, she and the other girls went back to the dorm.

The cheerleading coach is going to stay with them for the rest of the weekend. The university is probably more secure than it has ever been. Let me get off of the phone; Mimi is calling me."

"Okay, Mom. I'll see you later."

Brenda walked to where Mimi and John were sitting.

"Have they found Victor?" Mimi asked.

"Not yet," Brenda said with tears in her eyes. "Not yet."

"My baby is lying in that room helpless. Why did this have to happen to her?" Mimi wailed. "Why, God? Why my baby?"

"She's going to be all right, Mimi," John said assuredly, as he rubbed her back. "I'll be back. I'm going to get you and Brenda some coffee."

"Okay," was all Mimi could say.

When John was out of earshot, Brenda sat next to Mimi and rubbed her arm. "That was Trevor on the phone. He said that detectives had been to the house looking for Victor, but he wasn't home. Maybe we can get some answers soon."

Through her tears, Mimi faced Brenda. "Thank you, friend. I know it was difficult for you to give up Victor's name like that. I'd do it for you. But if Victor did do this...tried to kill Afrika, he has to be punished."

Brenda looked away, not wanting Mimi to see the tears that were falling for her family. Yes, it was somewhat dysfunctional, but it was a home—four people cohabitating under the same roof. It was a proud moment when Asia had graduated from high school and then set foot on a college campus, preparing for life beyond Victor and her. Now there wasn't any sunshine, only dark clouds, and she wanted to see the sun again.

"You're right, Mimi. That's why I had to tell you."

38

Haze clouded the afternoon sky, but there was a sign that the sun would break through at any moment. Mimi pulled back from the window and crossed over to where Afrika lay sleeping and brushed her hair with her hand. Like a person examining a beautiful piece of art, Mimi moved from Afrika's hair and gently rubbed the hand that held the needle that supported the IV drip—the tube running from the needle to the clear plastic bag that contained an assortment of medicines.

Drip, drip, drip, drip. Mimi watched the IV as if it contained healing power. Afrika looked like a sleeping princess in the small steel-framed bed, lying on her side. Mimi wanted to scoop Afrika up and place her in her old room that was bright, alive, and painted in bold pink and red colors; full of posters of her favorite actor and singing groups; filled with her teen drama books that had become real popular; filled to capacity with over-stuffed pink and red pillows that matched her comforter... to get her away from the pain the hospital represented. Dr. Daniels said the surgery was successful, but Afrika was still in a critical zone. The bullet deflected off a bone in the vertebrae and that most likely kept it from going into her heart. The possibility of infection or pneumonia could set in, but Afrika was young and otherwise healthy, and the doctors counted on that scenario to help in her fight for survival.

Mimi walked to the chair that sat next to the wall, got on her knees, and began to pray. She prayed for a miracle. She prayed that God would make her daughter well. She prayed for Brenda who'd been with her through the night but had finally conceded to go home at Mimi's urging so that she could get some rest. Brenda was afraid to go home, but it was where she needed to be. Mimi thanked God for reuniting her friendship with John who had been a great support during the past week. Finally, she prayed for her husband, Raphael, that he would have safe passage to her and Afrika and that she would see him soon.

She felt something. Mimi flinched and realized she'd fallen asleep while on her knees. She turned and looked up into familiar eyes with Dr. Daniels standing directly behind. His rugged good looks, still dressed in his Army dress greens, were a sight for sore eyes. Mimi's surprise turned to joy as she got up from her knees and fell into Raphael's waiting arms, nearly knocking him down along with his suitcase. He looked worn but Mimi knew the smile was all for her. She planted kisses on his lips.

"Hey, baby," Raphael said, pointing his eyes in the direction of the doctor standing behind him. "Fell asleep on your knees, huh?"

"I was not only praying for Afrika but for this moment. Thank God you're here."

"Why don't I give you a few minutes to catch up and then come back?" Dr. Daniels said.

"No, no," Raphael said. "We need you. You're going to help our daughter get well. We'll move out of the way."

Everyone managed a light laugh.

Dr. Daniels went to Afrika's bedside after lifting her chart from its holder at the foot of the bed. He sat on the edge of the bed and lifted Afrika's eyelids. She began to stir. A smile crossed Dr. Daniels face as Afrika tried to focus, opening one eyelid at a time.

"Hello, Afrika," Dr. Daniels said.

Mimi and Raphael rushed to Afrika's bedside. Smiles of joy and happiness pushed to the north and south of their faces.

"Hey, baby," Mimi said, as she and Raphael stood on the other side of the bed.

"Hey, sweetie," Raphael said and gave her a big wink.

Afrika looked at everyone and tried to smile. She was groggy but managed to say, "Hey."

Dr. Daniels checked Afrika's vitals again and took a look at her wound site. Mimi turned her head; she couldn't stand to see the place where the savage assault had taken place.

"We took out a nine millimeter bullet from her back that was lodged in her vertebrae. Our hope is that she's only temporarily paralyzed," Dr. Daniels said, turning around to look at a frightened Mimi.

Mimi's hands went to her face. "Does that mean she won't be able to walk again?" Mimi asked with alarm in her voice.

"We hope that isn't the case, Mrs. Bailey. As I told you last evening, we're fortunate that the bone was the shield that kept the bullet from hitting her internal organs. She wouldn't be with us now."

"I'm hungry," Afrika whispered.

All attention was directed back to Afrika. Mimi smiled but internally she was a broken down mess.

"We're going to see if we can't get you some food now," Dr. Daniels said. "You slept right through breakfast and lunch."

"Mommy, Daddy," Afrika said, her voice hardly audible. Afrika tried to lift her arm. "It hurts."

Raphael sat down on the bed as Dr. Daniels got up. He gave Afrika a kiss on the cheek. "Don't worry about trying to do everything all at once."

Afrika smiled.

That's what Mimi loved about Raf. He could make you laugh when you were sad. He could turn a total disaster into a thing of beauty. Yes, she loved this man. She was glad he was home.

"Mommy."

"Yes, baby, I'm here." Mimi leaned down and kissed Afrika on the other cheek. "My baby's going to be all right."

"I will when I get some food."

They laughed.

"Someone should be up with some food for Afrika in a few minutes," Dr. Daniels said. "I think they were about to make the evening rounds anyway. I'll be back before I leave the hospital to check on her."

"Thanks, Dr. Daniels," Mimi said.

Mimi and Raphael joined hands and rubbed Afrika's face with their free hand.

"Tell me what happened," Afrika whispered. "I was getting my things to leave the stadium and now I'm all bandaged up in a hospital."

"It's a long story, Afrika," Mimi said. "A stray bullet hit you in the back. The police haven't apprehended anyone yet, but I'm sure they'll catch someone soon."

"But why...oohhhh...me," Afrika managed to say.

"Enough talking," Raphael said. "Lie still for awhile. You need to rest."

"Okay. I'm a little tired."

"We aren't going anywhere," Mimi said.

Afrika lay still and, within a few minutes, dozed off to sleep. Mimi and Raf left the room and stood in front of the door.

"I'm going to get the son-of-a-bitch who did this. They've been walking around free a minute too damned long."

"We all feel that way, baby, but you've got to calm down."

Raphael paced the floor. "Did you see my baby in there,

Mimi? The doctor said she may be paralyzed. For how long…two weeks, two months, two years? I can't stand idly by knowing that some human animal who guns down innocent children is loose on the streets. Lord give me strength."

"The police have a person of interest they'd like to find and interview."

"A person of interest? Who is it? They should've caught the son-of-a-gun by now. I've watched grown men gunned down in the heat of war, but an innocent child? In a crowd? My God, Mimi, what has this world come to?"

"I know, Raf. I'm scared, too. Let's go back in the room. Everyone is looking at us."

"Let them look. Their daughter isn't lying up in ICU. Ours is, and I need to vent."

Mimi pushed open the door and dragged Raphael into the room. Afrika was still sleep. Mimi placed her arms around Raphael and gave him a big sloppy kiss.

"I needed that, girl." He pulled Mimi to him and kissed her back, locking his fingers and holding her around her head. "You're the brave one, baby. That's for being in place for our daughter. If you had come to Germany with me, who would've been here to take charge? My girl, Mimi."

Raphael sat in the chair next to the wall and motioned for Mimi to sit on his lap. "I'm sorry, baby, for expressing my feelings like that, but I hate the son-of-a-bitch that

did this. All I want is to get to this person first and ask
why before I punch his or her lights out."

"I love you, Raf."

"I love you, too, Mimi." Raf turned Mimi's head so he
could kiss her again. "So who's this person of interest
the police are trying to find?"

39

The door to the room pushed open. Raphael stared at the bald-headed man who moved forward like he knew he was in the right place.

Mimi jumped off of Raf's lap and stood between her husband and John. "John," Mimi said with a smile, extending her hand to shake his. "John, this is my husband, Raphael. Raphael, this is John, an old college friend."

Raphael stood and looked at John with amusement. He noticed how Mimi lit up when he walked through the room, like there was some chemistry going on. He shook John's hand.

"Nice to meet you," Raphael finally said.

"Well, look, I just came by to see how Afrika was doing...how you were holding up, Mimi."

"Thanks, John. I'm much better now that Raphael is here."

"Old college friends. John...John...I don't remember Mimi mentioning your name."

John darted his eyes at Mimi and abruptly turned away. "It was a long time ago."

"So you just happened to run into each other in the hospital?"

"Raf, what are you doing?" Mimi asked, perplexed.

"Pulling a security check. You've forgotten how you told me that you like bald-headed men who..."

"Raf, enough. I know you're aren't jealous," Mimi said.

"No, I'm not jealous. Can't be too careful. Stray men walking into my daughter's room. You aren't the stalker?"

"What?" John asked. He scrunched his eyebrows in confusion. "Look, I came by to check on your wife and daughter. Truth of the matter, we did run into each other a few days ago." Raf lifted his eyebrow. "I was out for a jog and ran into an old schoolmate," John continued. "Life happens, man. You need to lighten up."

"Is that so?" Raf said. "I don't know if Mimi told you, but I was on my way to a war zone. This wasn't my first but third time. Excuse me if I seem uptight because I am. My little girl is lying helpless in that bed and they haven't found the son-of-a-bitch who's done this. Let's start over. Nice to meet you, John."

John took Raphael's hand with some reluctance. "Nice to meet you, too. Glad to see you're doing better, Mimi. I'll check on you all later. If there's anything I can get you, Raphael, let me know. Maybe we can go and get some suds—get your mind off things."

"Now that's the second nicest thing I've heard today. I'll take you up on that offer, but later."

"All right. Will see you later." And John was gone.

"And who the hell was that, Mimi?"

"I told you. An old college friend."

"Uhm, hmm."

"Remember, we're here for Afrika."

BRENDA TURNED OVER AND LOOKED AT THE CLOCK. IT was one in the afternoon. She'd overslept; the morning had disappeared, and as much as she'd wanted to go the house of the Lord today, it was past too late. With arms outstretched, she yawned, closed her eyes, returned to her fetal position, and pulled the comforter up high. She stuck her arms underneath her stomach and began to doze off.

Within a few minutes, Brenda's eyes popped open. She released one of her arms from underneath her and felt for the place that was usually occupied by her husband. The sheets were cold and hadn't been parted, an obvious sign that Victor had not come home or had chosen to sleep somewhere else in the house.

Brenda willed herself to sit up. Her eyes and ears met a silent, still room—no evidence that anyone had been there other than herself in the last eight hours. Brenda wasn't sure what to make of it, but her mind started spinning and every conceivable negative thought she had about Victor raced to the forefront.

She pulled back the covers and placed her feet on the floor. Brenda felt gloomy like the day outside. Her thoughts turned to Mimi and Afrika...praying that Afrika would recover and Mimi wouldn't hold her accountable if indeed this was the work of Victor. Then Brenda's subconscious went to rewind as she replayed Mimi's story about Victor raping her over and over. Mimi's words marinated in her soul, and Brenda couldn't let go…and then the visual.

Jumping up from the bed, Brenda balled her fists. "Why, Jesus? Why is this happening to me? God, I want to believe Mimi, and in my heart of hearts I know she's telling the truth. But Victor is my husband… and…and, he wouldn't have done that to me…hurt me that way."

Brenda sighed. The place was too quiet for her. She put on her robe and went in search of Victor. Surely he was in another room.

Brenda went from room to room but no Victor. She opened the door to Trevor's bedroom. There was evidence Trevor had slept in his bed, but he was not there now.

"Trevor!" Brenda yelled.

"Down here, Mom!" Trevor yelled back.

"Is your dad down there?"

"Do you mean, did Dad come home?"

"Don't be a smart mouth, Trevor."

"Haven't seen him."

"Thank you."

Brenda retreated to her bedroom. Before she could close the door, the doorbell rang.

"Get that, Trevor!"

"Yeah, yeah!"

Trevor went to the door and opened it. He stared into

the faces of the detectives who had graced their presence on the Christiansons' doorstep yesterday.

"May I help you?" Trevor asked, his head cocked to the side.

"Detective Samuels and Detective Marshall," Marshall said. They flipped their badges.

"I know who you are."

"I'm glad we made an impression," Detective Samuels said. "Son, is your dad here? We need to talk with him."

"Nope; he didn't come home last night. Haven't seen him since yesterday."

"Is your mother here? We would like to talk to her."

Trevor stared at the detectives. "Wait here. Let me see if she's up."

Detective Samuels bunched up his lips and rolled his eyes at Detective Marshall. "All right, we'll wait here," Detective Samuels said.

Trevor closed the door and hollered for Brenda. "Mom, those two detectives I was telling you about are standing on our front porch. They want to talk to you."

"I'm not dressed. Tell them I just woke up."

"Okay."

Trevor opened the door as the two detectives chatted away. They stopped and turned around at the sound of the door opening.

"My mother just woke up and she's not dressed," Trevor said.

"We'll wait," Marshall said, taking the lead. "We've got all day."

"Come in."

The detectives followed Trevor into the foyer and looked around. Trevor led them into the family room and offered them a seat.

"We'll stand," Detective Samuels said as Beyonce tiptoed into the room and made an appearance, stopping to check out the two gentlemen who dared to invade her space. Uninterested, Beyonce turned around and walked out of the room.

"Cute cat," Samuels said.

"I'll be right back," Trevor said.

Trevor took two steps at a time and hurried to his mother's bedroom. He knocked at the closed door. Brenda peeked out.

"What is it, Trevor?"

"The two detectives? They're in the family room. Said they aren't going away until they speak to you."

"Jesus," Brenda hissed. "I'll be down in a few minutes."

Trevor returned to the family room where Samuels and Marshall were engaged in a lively discussion. Upon Trevor's entrance, they clammed up and waited. Trevor sat down and the detectives decided to do so as well.

Marshall sat on the edge of his seat. "So, son…"

"My name is Trevor."

"All right, Trevor, is it normal for your father to stay away from home for long periods of time?"

"No!" Brenda's voice boomed as she made her way into the room dressed in a pair of denim jeans and a white cotton tee but void of makeup.

Detective Marshall rose from his seat and looked Brenda over, touched the back of his pen to his face as if he was contemplating something, looked over at Samuels, and then back at Brenda. "So, Mrs. Christianson, do you know where your husband is?"

"He must have risen early and stopped by the university to do some work."

Detective Marshall motioned to Samuels. Samuels rose from his seat and walked outside. He was gone for no more than four minutes and reappeared. Brenda began to fidget in her seat. "Is it customary for him to go in to work on a Sunday?"

Brenda said nothing.

"We'll have someone check the university to see if we can locate Mr. Christianson," Marshall said, looking Brenda square in the face.

Detective Marshall made Brenda nervous. He continued to stare at her, as if using one of the tactics he'd learn at the academy or wherever he had received his training to break her down. Too many police dramas. She needed some romance in her life.

Detective Marshall pulled her out of her daydream. "Mrs. Christianson, you indicated to the officers at the hospital that your husband is in possession of a gun and you were concerned about his state of mind...that you were afraid he might do something...in your words 'stupid.' What prompted you to say that?"

Trevor shot a quick glance at Brenda and looked away. Brenda stole a glance in Trevor's direction and then into the face of Detective Marshall who waited for her answer.

"I asked my husband for a divorce and he became visibly upset. He was angry and decided to leave the house. When he picked up his coat, a gun dropped out."

Trevor shot Brenda another quick look.

"Do you know why he would be carrying a gun in his pocket and was there a particular reason that led to your announcement at that time?"

Sweat dotted Brenda's hairline. She balked at Marshall's line of questioning, hoping it wouldn't cause her to reveal more than she was ready for Trevor to hear. She stared at Trevor as he sat stoically in his seat, as if gnawing on the bits and pieces of information that flowed from her mouth. She was not ready to reveal the contents of Mimi's secret, so Brenda searched hard for an answer.

"Victor...Mr. Christianson and I have been somewhat estranged in our marriage for some time. I can't say what actually caused the moment, but a petty argument led to a bigger one, and I had had enough."

Marshall rapped his pad on his knuckles. He glanced at Samuels and back at Brenda.

"If Mr. Christianson should come home, please let him know that we need to speak to him right away," Marshall said.

"I'll let him know," Brenda said matter-of-factly.

Detectives Marshall and Samuels moved toward the

door. Samuels turned around. "Have a good day. It would cause grave consequences to you if you harbored a fugitive."

Brenda looked at Samuels without a word. Then they were gone.

"A divorce, Mom?" Trevor asked. "When were you going to tell me...Asia?"

"It happened after I came home from the game. And then Afrika was shot."

"You think Dad did it, don't you? But why Afrika?"

"I hope not, Trevor." That's all Brenda would say.

"He doesn't deserve you, Mom. You can do better by yourself."

Brenda stared at Trevor. "You think so?"

PARKED DOWN THE STREET IN A COMPANY CAR, VICTOR watched the detectives as they retreated from his house, surveyed the surroundings, and finally got in their car and drove away. He slid down in his seat to avoid being seen when they passed. He was grateful for the Sunday gathering at the house a few doors from his own and the basketball game that allowed him to park and be incognito for a little while. There was no way he could return home; he was sure the house was being watched. He pulled off an hour later when the basketball game came to an end.

40

"Girl, have you heard any more about the shooting on Saturday? I still can't get a grasp that some lunatic out of the crowd shot one of our cheerleaders."

"Phyllis, it's crazy," Sheila said. "The cops have been buzzin' around here like vultures like we're supposed to know who tried to kill that student. They look like ants at a picnic crawling everywhere, looking for I don't know what."

"What is Victor saying?"

"Victor? Girl, I haven't seen him all morning. It's ten o'clock; he's usually here by now. Must be running late. He and his wife must be on the outs because he keeps stopping by."

"Sheila, I don't know when you're going to tell Victor about you and Jamal getting married because he's not going to be too happy about some other dude up in the place he pays for. You're not only going to be on the street; he might just fire your ass."

"I haven't thought it through yet. Phyllis, girl, Victor stopped by Saturday night, and he was some kind of weird. Wanted to be all up in my business...throwing himself all over me—forceful like. I couldn't roll with him because Jamal was due to come over at any minute."

"What did you do?"

"I faked like I wasn't feeling well, but he insisted on laying there with me. I would've been up the creek if I hadn't gotten an opportunity to text Jamal and tell him to hold off for a while."

"If you're not careful, you're going to be hanging by the neck in Victor's leather noose," Phyllis said. "I don't know what it is about that man you want because I don't trust him."

"Victor was my ticket out of the dump where I used to live. Once you give in and begin reaping the benefits, it's hard to say no. Victor can sex me as good as any twenty-something, but my heart belongs to Jamal. I have a man who loves me for me, and I can't wait until Jamal and I are married this weekend at the Justice of the Peace. We applied for the license and did our blood work last week. I should receive the results of my test today."

"That's cool...you and Jamal are getting married. It's about time you made a respectable woman of yourself. When are you going to tell Victor?"

"I really have done a lot of soul searching about my life, Phyllis, and it's thanks to you that I'm choosing to fly right. Jamal has been my man for a long time. We have what you call an open relationship, and yes, he knows all about Victor," Sheila lied. "We talked into the wee hours of the night last week about where we were going with our lives and decided right then and there that we would get married. I don't need all the fanfare that comes with having a wedding; Jamal and I decided that the time was now to settle down and live our lives as husband and wife. I've made up my mind that I'm going to tell Victor about Jamal when he comes in."

"Wow, you've thought this all out. If you need a witness, call me. Sister got your back."

"Thanks, Phyllis. I appreciate it. Let me go; the police have returned."

"All right. Love you, Sheila."

"Love you back."

"Yes, may I help you?" Sheila asked, putting down the telephone.

"Yes, I'm Detective Marshall, looking for Mr. Victor Christianson." Detective Marshall flashed his badge.

"He hasn't come in yet," Sheila replied.

"What time will he be in today?"

"I expect him any time. He hasn't called, so I assume he's running behind schedule. Is there something I can help you with?"

"It's urgent that I speak to him," Detective Marshall said, peering into the empty office with the door marked DIRECTOR. In the meantime, I'm going to confiscate his computer."

Sheila followed him with her eyes, getting up from her desk to see what he actually planned to do in Victor's office. "Does this have something to do with the shooting on Saturday?"

Marshall looked at Sheila. He smiled. Sheila looked at

Marshall for the first time. He might be a catch for Phyllis. He was tall, medium build, had dimples on both sides of his face, a little on the old side, but Phyllis seemed to like older men. Sheila made a mental note to remind herself to call Phyllis—that was until she saw what appeared to be a wedding band wrapped around his ring finger.

"Yes, it does," Marshall said. "I was hoping Mr. Christianson could give me some information about the victim in his capacity as Director of Admissions."

"There are others in the office who could assist you, sir. Also, you may want to speak with our Vice Chancellor for Student Affairs. I'm not sure you have authority to take Mr. Christianson's computer."

"My badge says I have every authority. Thank you, Miss..."

"Sheila Atkins and the future Mrs. Sheila Billops." Sheila smiled. "Detective Marshall, do you have a business card on you so I can have Mr. Christianson call you?" Sheila winked.

Detective Marshall gave Sheila a quick once over. He pulled his business card from his holder and placed it in Sheila's hand. "Miss Atkins soon to be Mrs. Billops, can you tell me if Mr. Christianson has been acting strange in the past week or so?"

Sheila gave Marshall her serious look and pretended to ponder the question. She didn't relish the position she now found herself in. She folded her hands together and let out a sigh.

"Well?" Marshall asked, his patience getting thin.

"Now that I think about it, he kept leaving the office like he was on some secret mission. He was clearly agitated about something, but I have no earthly idea what it could've been. A couple of times he slammed the door..."

"Was slamming the door uncharacteristic of Mr. Christianson?"

"Well, yes. He is pretty mild-mannered."

"Ms. Atkins, someone let it slip that you and Mr. Christianson might have..." Marshall coughed. "...might have been something other than boss and subordinate."

"And what are you implying by that, Detective Marshall?" Sheila asked, the smile on her face evaporating.

"Just what you interpreted it to mean. However, if I need to spell it out for you...you and Mr. Christianson are having an affair. I wonder if your future husband, Mr. Billops, knows you're leading a double life," Marshall stated sarcastically.

"Mr. Billops is my concern, not yours." Sheila began to tap her toe on the floor and her nostrils began to flare. Suddenly, Detective Marshall no longer looked so good to her.

"When was the last time you saw Mr. Christianson?"

Sheila turned away and began to tap her fingers on her desk. "I don't remember exactly. I'm sure it was on Friday at work."

"Such a small thing to remember; especially since Friday was only two days ago. Did you see him over the weekend, perhaps at the football game?"

"No," Sheila answered fast. "I didn't even go to the game. I was home all day."

Marshall wrinkled his face and gave Sheila a look that said she was lying. "I'll let you simmer on that some more, Ms. Atkins, but as soon as Mr. Christianson comes in, please have him call me."

Sheila stared straight into Marshall's eyes. "I'll do just that," Sheila said flatly. She watched as Marshall walked out of the office, and then grabbed the phone to call Phyllis, but not before she canvassed the room to see if she could identify her Judas.

SHEILA PUT THE PHONE IN ITS CRADLE AND PONDERED Detective Marshall's questions. It was becoming clearer by the moment that Victor was connected somehow to the shooting on Saturday. Then she thought about the gun Victor had conveniently dropped off at her house, almost immediately after the incident on campus, but unless asked, she was going to stay out of the spotlight, keep her mouth shut, and let the police handle their business. If the police investigation should lead them to the piece of hardware she had conveniently stored away in her house not realizing that it might have been connected to their investigation of Victor, she'd be more than happy to turn it over—but not a minute sooner.

41

Raphael's naked body lay face down on the bed like a log on the slate-blue satin sheets as Mimi brought in a cup of hot coffee and a plate of buttered toast for him. His legs were spread apart—one up, the other down, with his massive arms circling his head. Mimi knew he was at a good place in his sleep and hated to wake him, but she smiled at the sight of him as she recalled their night of passion.

Mimi set the tray on the dresser and picked up the cup of coffee to drink herself. She took a sip and turned her head at the sound of Raf's body shifting on top of the sheets. Aroused, he opened his eyes and smiled when he saw Mimi.

"Girl," he said in low raspy voice. "You drained all of my energy. Where am I going to get enough energy to see my daughter today? Mimi, you put a hurting on me." Raphael let out a breath. "I'm willing to do it all over again, baby. Why don't you take off those clothes and come back to bed. You are some kind of good."

Mimi smiled. "I love pleasing you, Raphael; you give back and know the meaning of pleasuring your woman. I felt guilty though."

Raphael sat up on his elbows. "Guilty how, baby? I was making love to my woman...my wife."

Mimi put the cup down. "And it was all that, but I couldn't help thinking about Afrika in that room all alone."

"She has police protection now, and as soon as I get up and get dressed, we're heading for the hospital."

"Okay, baby, but..." Mimi's cell phone rang, cutting her off. "Hold on a minute, Raf."

"Is that the hospital?"

Mimi waved no. "Hello," she said.

"Mrs. Bailey, your gun permit has been approved. You can come down any time today and pick up your gun."

"Thank you very much," Mimi said and ended the phone call.

"Was it the hospital or was it John?"

"Neither, Raf. It was the school. Afrika was having problems with her meal card, and the business office called to say that everything was straightened out," she lied. "Look, take your time getting ready. I need to run to the store to pick up some toiletries for Afrika before we go to the hospital; I'll be right back. I'll fix you some more coffee and toast."

"Are you all right, Mimi? You seem in a fog all of a sudden."

"It's the whole Afrika thing, Raf. Receiving that call reminded me of this whole ordeal with Afrika—the shooting, I mean." Mimi looked at Raf. "We have to talk."

"Okay," Raf said, getting up from the bed in his birthday

suit. He threw his arms over his head and let out a great big yawn.

"Take your shower and get some clothes on, buddy."

"I will since I can't get you to play soldier with me. As my POW, I'd treat you real good, so much so you'd beg not to be rescued. Total surrender."

"You think I'm that easy, huh?"

"Girl, you love what I give you."

"I do indeed, but right now the only thing on my brain is our child."

"Don't worry about the coffee. I'll drink what you left on the dresser."

"I'll be right back."

Raphael watched Mimi leave the room with a perplexed look on his face.

Mimi jumped in her car, backed out of the garage, and headed out of the subdivision. She could feel the adrenaline coursing through her veins. In the next half-hour, Mimi would have protection from the man that she despised, although not sure what she was going to do with it. If Victor was indeed the perpetrator, the police was on his trail, but if she saw him first, she was going to shoot him in cold blood.

"God, please remove the bad thoughts that are roaming around in my mind. Take the hate from my heart, Lord. Your commandment says, *Thou shall not kill*. Afrika is still alive, and You have allowed this blessing. Thank You, Lord. Thank You. I won't forget."

Mimi drove as fast as the law would allow but slowed down as she turned down the street to the gun shop. She found a park directly in front of the place, turned off the ignition, and sat a moment, contemplating what she was going to do when she picked up the gun. She didn't want to seem anxious...only another female trying to protect herself from the mean streets of the city.

Exhaling, Mimi got out of the car and went inside. The store owner remembered her with a smile. Mimi palmed the gun in her hand and took the information about the location of the shooting range should she need practice. Not lingering, Mimi quickly left the place and got in her car.

The gun was housed in its own wooden box. She took the box out of the bag and sat it in her lap before opening it up. She lifted the gun from its bed and examined it like it was a new Prada bag. She brushed her hand over the steel barrel and Victor's image zoomed in front of her. "You'll never mess with me again." Mimi put the gun away and headed home.

Turning into the subdivision, Mimi abruptly turned around. She'd forgotten to go to the supermarket and pick up some sundry items for Afrika—deodorant, lotion, toothpaste, and a toothbrush. She flew to the store and was in and out in ten minutes. Upon arriving home, Mimi placed the gun under her seat until she could find a more permanent place to hide it. Good thing; Raf was standing at the door when she opened the door to the garage.

42

Raphael got in the passenger side of the car. He watched Mimi with renewed interest. Somehow, she seemed different, but he couldn't quite put his finger on it.

"You want me to drive, baby?" Raphael asked.

"No, sweetie. I'm already comfortable and I would have to bark directions to the hospital."

"You look good driving this Lexus."

"How else would I look? Let's change the subject; Afrika is our priority."

"Don't you think I know that, Mimi? She's never left my mind. I prayed to God that He wouldn't let anything happen to her...that she would have her life back the way it was the moment that SOB's bullet hit her."

Mimi smiled. "I believe that, too, Raf. She's going to make it; she's resilient. She's got to get over these hurdles first."

"You're right." Raphael paused. "Do you want to talk now?"

Mimi seemed nervous and put her foot on the gas.

"Slow down, Mimi. If now isn't the right time, we'll talk later."

"Let's wait until we get home this evening. I can't have a serious talk with all of these crazy, cell phone talking drivers whipping around me."

"Okay." Raphael stared straight ahead in silence until they reached the hospital.

There was a still coolness between Raphael and Mimi, but Raf wasn't going to let that spoil his visit with his favorite girl. He waved to the nurses at the station and gave the black officer sitting outside of Afrika's door a fist bump. Raphael followed Mimi into Afrika's room.

Raphael stopped short when he saw the two young men and young lady sitting on the side of the bed talking to Afrika. However, it was the young lady that caught him off-guard. It was as if Afrika had an out-of-body experience in front of him. The young lady, about Afrika's age, was a split image of Afrika; except that her skin was two shades lighter. She even wore her hair in a pony-tail like his daughter—pulled to the top of her head with a Scrunchie around it. He stared, not sure of who he was looking at.

"Daddy," Afrika said with a little more volume in her voice, her thin blue and white hospital blanket pulled up high as if she was cold. "This is my best friend, Asia, my friend, Keith, and Asia's friend, Zavion."

Raphael nodded to the two young men but was locked in on Asia. After a moment, he looked from Afrika to Mimi to Asia. "Asia, what a pretty name. So nice to meet you."

"Nice to meet you, too, Mr. Bailey," Asia said with a smile. She turned toward Mimi. "Hello, Mrs. Bailey."

"Hello, Asia. Hello, Keith and Zavion. Looks like Miss Afrika is coming along well." Mimi stooped over and gave Afrika a kiss on the cheek.

"I feel much better, Mommy. I wish I could go home. What's wrong, Daddy? You look like you've seen a ghost. Look at him, Mommy."

"I know what it is," Asia chimed in. "Your father can't get over the fact that we resemble each other. Don't worry, Colonel Bailey, everyone does the same thing. Even our birthdays are in the same month."

Raphael retreated...didn't say a word. He chewed on the words of this young lady. So obvious was his shock, but more than anything, Mimi had never mentioned Afrika's best friend. Was Mimi hiding something from him? Raphael finally smiled.

Raphael noticed Mimi's irritation and her convenient silence. Before Raphael could approach Mimi, the door to the room opened again. A well put together woman in a smart black pantsuit about Mimi's age rushed through the door. She looked from Mimi to Raphael, finally realizing that Raphael had to be Mimi's husband. There was no smile on her face.

"Hi, I'm Brenda," she said to Raphael, extending her hand to greet him.

"Brenda Christianson, this is my husband, Raphael. He finally made it."

"Nice to finally meet you, Brenda," Raphael said. "I've heard a lot of nice things about you."

"Nice to meet you, too, Raphael," Brenda said. "Mimi and I go a long way back. We were best friends."

"Brenda is also Asia's mother," Mimi interjected.

"I do see the resemblance," Raphael said, looking from Brenda to Asia and then to Mimi. "I'm sorry if I look perplexed. Although Mimi talked about you, I didn't know you were best friends."

Brenda smiled. "It's easily understood. We've been estranged for many years. We lost touch and everyone moved on with their lives."

"I guess so," Raphael said, still sensing something else. Mimi avoided his gaze but he could tell she seemed pissed off. He loved that woman, but he had an eerie feeling...like something wasn't right and he had been caught in a dragnet.

Raphael smothered the urge to comment on how much Brenda's daughter looked so much like Afrika. No matter how much Raphael tried to toss it to the back of his head, the thought of it kept rumbling through his brain, itching to be addressed. It would be a conversation for Mimi and him later that evening.

Niceties were set aside and Brenda lightly touched Mimi's arm, urging her with a slight movement of her head to go outside. Raphael didn't miss a beat; that eerie feeling squeezed his brain...his need to know what was going on.

"I'll be right back, Raf. Brenda needs to talk to me."

"Okay," Raf said as he watched the two women exit the room. He went to the edge of Afrika's bed and listened as Asia babbled on about some boys they had met. And then she said something that struck Raphael as odd—pricked his ears, made him pay close attention.

"Trevor called me today. Said my mom and dad have been acting strange. Police were even at the house."

"Why?" Afrika asked.

"It could be domestic. Trevor said he heard my mother tell the detective that she asked Daddy for a divorce."

Afrika tried to sit up. "I'm so sorry, Asia," she whispered.

"They've been having problems for a while," Asia went on, "but it seemed to get worse after you came over that day. My mom wanted to contact your mom, but Trevor heard Dad tell my mom later that he didn't want her to. Strange, huh?"

"Yeah," Afrika said. Letting that little tidbit settle in her mind, she asked the one question Raphael had thought of. "But why would the police come to your house?"

"Trevor said that after Mom told Dad that she wanted a divorce, they started arguing and my dad picked up his coat to leave and a gun fell out of the pocket. What if he was going to try and use it on my mother?"

"So your mother called the cops?"

"It's kind of vague to me."

"I don't mean any harm, Asia, but your dad scares me. I caught him staring at me when we cheered at our first football game. I felt weird, and I called and told my mom."

Raphael didn't hear anything else. He turned his head toward the door the ladies had exited and wondered if their conversation had anything to do with what Asia and Afrika were talking about.

Raphael put on his thinking cap. He'd barely been home twenty-four hours but something was wrong with all the scenarios floating around him. Mimi's obvious awkwardness when John showed up and her nervousness upon him seeing Asia in the room to Brenda's need to see Mimi in private right away didn't add up. And why didn't Mimi tell him about the man staring at Afrika? Maybe that's what she had tried to tell him the night that she called, Raphael thought back.

In the military, Raphael was paid to think—to provide strategies to fight wars on foreign soil in a place they called the war room. He was in the war room, and if he had to draw a map, the pieces to the puzzle centered around his wife, her so-called best friend, Brenda, Afrika, and Brenda's husband—the one with the gun. The gun. The gun that might have been used to shoot Afrika, but why? That was what Raphael was going to find out. He needed to find Asia's father. He needed to solicit someone's help. He could use a beer or two.

"Baby cakes, Daddy's got to leave for a little while. You seem to be in good hands with Asia by your side," Raphael said. He went to the side of the bed and kissed Afrika. "I'll be back in a while."

"Okay, Daddy. Don't stay away too long."

"All right, baby."

Raphael exited Afrika's hospital room and saw Mimi consoling Brenda outside the glass doors to the ICU unit. Brenda seemed to be crying and wiped her face as Raphael approached.

"Where are you going?" Mimi inquired, surprised by Raphael's look of departure.

"I need to get some air; I'm uptight, I guess. I thought about taking John up on his offer to get some beers. Do you have his number?"

Mimi looked Raphael squarely in the eye. Raphael knew she wondered why he had the sudden desire to meet with John.

"I feel useless. I need to find my daughter's shooter."

Brenda and Mimi looked at each with fear in their eyes.

"What's wrong? Do you know who the shooter is?"

"No, Raf," Mimi said a little too fast. "The police are doing all they can to find the person who did this awful thing to Afrika. I know how you are, Raf, but you're going to have to let the police do their work. I need you to be calm for Afrika and let law enforcement handle it."

Raf looked at Mimi, the love of his life. She was shielding him from something; he could feel it in his bones. When it was time, he would deal with it. "John's number?"

Mimi pulled out her cell and pulled up John's number. Raf looked at her. His black book was empty. There had to be a good explanation why John's number was in Mimi's black book, if they had indeed just run into each other.

He punched the numbers Mimi had given him into his phone. "Thanks. I'll be back in a while."

Mimi sighed and watched her husband disappear behind the elevator door.

43

Raphael entered the hospital lobby, dialed John Carroll's number, and waited for him to answer.

"Hello," said the gruff voice.

"John Carroll?"

"Who wants to know?"

"John, this is Raphael; Mimi's husband."

Raphael heard John groan. There was a long pause before John spoke again.

"How did you get my number?"

"Mimi gave it to me. I need to get some air and I remembered your offer to go for some beers. I'm at that moment."

John hesitated and then cleared his throat. "I'm busy right now. Maybe some other time."

"I understand, man, but I do need to talk. My daughter is in the hospital, and the person who did this is still at-large. My hands are tied, and I need a friendly male ear to sound off my frustrations."

"I can take a break. Where are you?"

"I'm at the hospital."

"I'll pick you up in thirty minutes."

"I'll be waiting in the lobby."

JOHN PULLED IN FRONT OF THE HOSPITAL AND DIALED Raphael at the number that was recorded in his phone. His first impression of Raphael was that he was full of himself because he was a high-ranking officer in the military. He carried his stripes on his shoulders and John was his stepstool. John was surprised to receive Raphael's phone call.

John watched the tall, rugged man in a pair of khakis pants, a blue and yellow polo shirt, and a short tan London Fog jacket approach his Ford Explorer. Raphael's eyes were well hidden behind a pair of Giorgio Armani sunglasses, but John knew he was being inspected by the Colonel by the way he rotated his face as he looked at his SUV and then at him as he peered inside the open window.

Raphael opened the door to the vehicle not giving a second thought that it might be someone other than John in it.

"John, my man," Raphael said as if he and John had been old friends. He jumped in and extended his hand.

John hesitated and decided to put what unspoken differences they had aside, at least for the moment. "Good afternoon, Colonel."

"Raphael will do just fine. John, I need to go someplace where I can think and sort this whole matter out. You got me?"

John put the car in gear and headed away from the hospital. "I think I do."

"Look, we got off on the wrong foot. Didn't mean to scrutinize you the way I did. I'm overprotective of Mimi. She's my life...my world; she's been through a lot."

John shot Raphael a look. Mimi made it seem that life with Raphael was a fairy tale dream come true—the handsome prince and the beautiful princess. Maybe Raphael was alluding to the present stress Mimi was under with Afrika being shot. He sat back and listened. "It's cool; no hard feelings," John said matter-of-factly.

Raphael was silent for the next few minutes and looked straight ahead. John checked him from the corner of his eye to see if he was still breathing.

"This place is very progressive," Raphael finally said, as they rode through Raleigh and finally into the North Hills shopping area.

"Luxury condos—I'm sure they cost a cool million with the nice restaurants and luxury hotels serving as its welcome mat. The recession isn't hurting everyone."

"I can see that."

"How about the Fox and Hound Pub for some cold brews?"

"I'm game."

John led the way into the restaurant with its twenty-eight television screens serving as borders along the wall and a tournament size pool table that made John itch to rack 'em and hit 'em. Whatever was on Raphael's mind was temporarily thwarted by the scantily-clothed barmaid whose triple D's were tipping over her top like the foam in the beer mug she was handing to a customer, John noticed. They were shown to their seats, took off their jackets, ordered two mugs of beer and wings, and listened to the chatter that surrounded them.

"So what's on your mind?" John asked, getting to the point.

"Frustrated, man. My daughter is lying in a hospital bed because some crazy lunatic that belongs behind bars shot her for no reason, and all I can do is stand by helpless. If I had an ounce of a clue, I'd be out on the street now looking for that coward to put him out of his misery."

John leaned his body forward, his elbows on the table and his hands cupped together as if he was getting ready to let Raphael in on an important secret. Then he let his hands drop and rapped the table with his fingers, pausing a moment to formulate his words. "I know you're used to being the man in control, but let the police handle their business." John paused again, but decided to go for it. "Mimi and Afrika are going to need you."

Raphael looked at John and stewed on the information for a minute. "Yeah, I guess you're right. But I'm angry, man. I left my family behind, believing they were going to be fine on American soil. I was going overseas to fight a war, but damn, I never thought the war would be on the college campus where my daughter had chosen to go to school. And I wasn't even there to protect her." Raphael slapped the table.

"We can't always protect the ones we love. I'm going to tell you something that might get me into a lot of trouble, but you need to know."

"What is it?" Raphael asked, his eyebrows raised and giving John his full attention.

"Mimi purchased a gun."

Raphael's eyes penetrated John's until John looked away. "My wife purchased a gun...and she didn't tell me?" Raphael finally asked and then paused to think. "For what reason would she purchase a gun? Tell me, John; you seem to have all the answers."

"Look, Raphael; it's not like you think."

"What's not like I think? You're doing all the talking and you sure as hell know a lot more than I do."

"Let me start from the beginning. Mimi was my girl-friend in college."

"Oh hell. You must be on the missing pages in Mimi's scrapbook."

"Excuse me. Two beers and hot wings," the waitress interrupted.

"Thank you," John said, lacing his hand around one of the mugs and thanking God for the small interruption. The talk with Raphael had gotten twisted—John had violated Mimi's trust, but now he had to go for it because Raphael was staring at him with iron eyes, and John could see the muscles in Raphael's face contract as he processed what John said. Even the muscles under Raphael's shirt were flexed. John took a sip of his beer to calm his nerves, but the other beer sat on the table untouched.

"You've been stalking her?" Raphael asked, his mouth clinched and grinding his teeth.

"Stalking her? No," John said. Then it came to him; he believed that he understood what Raphael was making reference to.

"Mimi called me one night and told me that she saw this guy who used to harass her in college. When you came into the room yesterday and Mimi said you were old college friends, I assumed it was you that she had referred to."

"No, she wasn't talking about me."

"Well, if it wasn't you she was talking about, then who?"

Why had he tried to be the negotiator? John had opened Pandora's box, and there was no way he could lie about what he knew because he wouldn't be able to keep the facts straight. John looked at Raphael and decided he would skirt as far away from Mimi's secret as possible. It wasn't his to tell and he'd already given up too much information.

Raphael picked up his beer and drank half without stopping, the foam making a visible moustache when he came up for air. "You going to tell me, man?" Raphael asked.

"Victor Christianson."

John watched Raphael as he seemed to roll the name over in his head—like it was a name he'd heard before but couldn't remember where. "Christianson?" Raphael asked.

John didn't try and connect the dots for Raphael. Instead, he picked up a hot wing and began to munch on it.

Snap, snap went Raphael's fingers as John continued to tear at the meat. "Mimi's best friend…Christianson… that's it." Raphael continued to marinate on a possible connection…the wheels turning ever so slowly in his head.

Licking sauce from his fingers, John dove in and picked up another wing and began to gnaw on it. Somewhere between *breaking news story* and *Victor Christianson*, John snapped his head backward and faced the wall of television screens along with the two dozen other patrons, his eyes glued on the image of Victor. The newscaster was in the middle of her teleprompter scripted dialogue when John caught up with the commentary that linked it to the picture.

"If you have any information on the whereabouts of Victor Christianson, please call CRIMESTOPPERS at the number posted at the bottom of your screen. Again, Victor Christianson, Director of Admissions at North Carolina Central University, is being sought as the key suspect in the shooting on the campus of NCCU of student Afrika Nicole Bailey, that occurred at the end of NCCU's Saturday afternoon football game. Again, this was not a random shooting. This is Charlotte Wilson reporting to you live from Raleigh for WTVD Eyewitness News."

The chill rolled the numbness off of the room as the patrons slowly returned to their private conversations at their individual booths, at the pool table where a pool stick was now raised in preparation to hit an eight ball in a side pocket, and at the bar where the bartender, who had temporarily closed the lid on the beer tap because she was entrenched in the story, was back to the business of serving beer. The chill had rolled off of everyone except Raphael, the victim's father, who sat in utter silence...in shock, baffled by what he'd heard.

Raphael looked straight at John who was stuffing yet another wing into his mouth. "Why would he want to shoot Afrika?"

John finally put the remnant of the chicken wing down on the plate when he saw the anger in Raphael's eyes. "It had to be a random act of violence, man. Hopefully, they'll catch his ass soon."

"I'm ready to go back to the hospital," Raphael said without expression. "I need some answers.

John scrambled for his coat, pulled out a twenty and some ones from his wallet, and laid them on the table. "I got this man; let's go."

The air was thick in the car as silence lay between John and Raphael. John moved to turn on the radio, but a large hand waved him off. Traffic moved along well, and John pushed his SUV as fast as it would go without exceeding the speed limit. This was not his battle; this was Mimi's husband, and she needed to do the explaining.

All this Victor stuff had unearthed more than John really knew.

John's anxiety seemed to evaporate as he approached the hospital. He couldn't wait to get rid of his passenger. As he pulled to the curb, John kept his foot on the brake as Raphael got out. "If you need me again, holler."

"Aren't you coming in?" Raphael asked.

44

John's immediate thought was to distance himself from the explosion he anticipated was about to happen. He was a grown man and had no plans to jump at Raphael's bark. He wasn't one of Raphael's soldiers who saluted every time he walked past. He was the Colonel's wife's friend who, against his better judgment, had come to the rescue in the time of crisis, although he would've rather been somewhere else.

Letting his thoughts roll through his brain, John allowed his subconscious to take a right turn into the parking garage of the hospital. He rubbed his head, sighed, and caught his breathe as he moved forward toward unchartered waters.

When John entered the lobby of the hospital, he was surprised to see Raphael standing inside almost as if he knew that John would show up rather than be AWOL—absence without leave. They walked and then rode the elevator to ICU without uttering a word, tension mounting the closer they got to Afrika's room.

There was no warmth or smile when Raphael pushed the door open. Once inside, Raphael's eyes zoomed straight for Mimi, like a target he'd locked on during combat.

She was talking to Brenda, while Asia chatted with Afrika about who knows what. It was obvious they hadn't seen or heard the broadcast about Victor.

"Excuse me," Raphael said to Brenda, "do you mind if I speak to Mimi?"

"Of course not," Brenda said, a little taken aback by the gruffness in his tone.

"What is it, Raf?" Mimi asked, looking from him to John.

Raphael looked at the girls who stopped their chatter and looked directly at him. He wanted to blurt out what he'd just witnessed on a television screen that was viewed by hundreds of thousands of people, but thought better of it. The girls need not be witnesses to what he wanted to ask Mimi.

"Mimi, sweetheart, let's go outside a minute. I need to talk to you."

Everyone looked from one to the other, wondering what was so important that Raphael couldn't say it in front of everyone. Brenda glanced at John, who turned away without offering any further explanation.

"What's going on, John?" Afrika finally asked. "Why is Daddy so upset? Wasn't he with you?"

"Only your dad can answer that question, Afrika. Maybe you should ask him when he returns to the room."

"John," Brenda interjected, "what's going on? You know something that you're not telling us."

John threw his hands up. "I'm out of here. Tell Mimi to call me if she needs me."

RAPHAEL AND MIMI STOOD IN THE HALLWAY OUTSIDE of the double doors to ICU and out of earshot of the women who manned the nurses' station.

"What is it, Raf?" Mimi barked before Raphael had a chance to get a word out. She was thinking the worst since he and John had some time together. "What's so important that you needed to drag me from our daughter's room?"

"Victor Christianson is what's the matter."

"Vic…" she began and cut short as John breezed by without a word.

"John," both Mimi and Raphael said simultaneously.

John stopped in his tracks, turned around, and looked at the couple that seemed to be pleading with their eyes.

"You're not leaving?" Raf asked before Mimi had an opportunity to do so.

"Yes, if you don't need me. I need to head back to the office and wrap up a few things."

"Tell Mimi what we saw on television today," Raphael said, holding up John's pending exit from the hospital.

"What did you see, John?" Mimi said with a puzzled look on her face.

John looked at Raphael and then back at Mimi. "They named Victor Christianson as the suspect in your daughter's shooting."

Mimi cupped her hand over her mouth. "Oh my God."

"His picture was also splashed on the screen for everyone to see," John offered, looking at Raphael. "Satisfied?"

"John tells me that Victor's the person who's been stalking you. Is that correct?" Raphael asked.

Mimi let out a long sigh. "Yes, Raf, Victor is the person who was stalking me."

"But why? And how is it that John knows all about this and I don't? I'm your husband, damn it. We aren't supposed to keep secrets from each other. We've always been a team, Mimi."

"Maybe Mimi felt comfortable sharing that with me," John put in.

"You're the ex-boyfriend; I'm the husband," Raphael reminded John.

"True as it may be, I was here for her when she needed me...not on the other side of the world."

"Let me tell you something, John Carroll. I work hard for my family and my country...to keep your ass safe from harm, but that doesn't mean you're supposed to be all up on my wife while I do so."

"I've had about enough of your—" John began.

Mimi threw her arms up in the air. "Stop it, both of you." Mimi stood in front of Raphael and held his hands. "Baby, we've got to talk. I realize that all of this is upsetting, but now is not the time for you to take it out on John. I ran into him in the park and I kind of poured my heart out to him. Nothing more. Our daughter needs our attention. We're fortunate that her life was spared, and the person we should be upset with is Victor."

"Hell, if I had a gun, I'd shoot his brains out now," Raphael said.

"Raphael, please listen. You're talking irrationally. What is there to gain by taking someone's life?"

"I'd like to know your take on that, Mimi, since John tells me you purchased a gun. What were you going to do with it?"

Mimi fell silent and looked at John in disgust. What else had he told Raphael? Does Raphael know about the rape? "I bought the gun for protection...in the event Victor tried anything crazy."

"Look, I'm going to leave." John tried to beg out. "This conversation is between the two of you."

"No, I believe you're part of the reason we're having this conversation," Mimi said without a smile. "If—"

"What's wrong with Brenda?" John cut in, pointing at Brenda, who had surfaced from Afrika's room. Mimi and Raphael turned around to see Brenda frantically pacing outside the room. "I think she's looking for you. I hope nothing is wrong with Afrika."

The trio pushed through the double doors to ICU and headed for Afrika's room. Brenda held her heart while tears dripped from her face. Brenda pulled them into the room.

"What's wrong, Brenda?" Mimi whispered as the trio huddled together. Then she turned when she heard Afrika crying. Raphael was at her bedside before Mimi.

"What's wrong, baby girl?" Raphael asked.

Tears covered Afrika's face. Then Mimi heard more muffled cries. She looked at the window where Asia stood looking out. Brenda hurried to where Asia was standing and took her in her arms. Asia buried her face in her mother's breast and continued to cry.

"Why did Daddy do it? Why did he shoot Afrika? Tell me it's a lie, Mom," Asia moaned.

Afrika looked into the faces of her mother and father, wet tears staining her face. She tried to stop but the water kept coming. "Why me? I didn't do anything to him."

"Baby girl, you don't have to worry about him trying anything again. Daddy is here, and your mother and I aren't going to leave your side," Raphael said.

Mimi stroked Afrika's face and reached down and kissed her. "Like your father said, we aren't going to leave you. We'll be here every minute."

"But why, Mommy? Why did he shoot me?"

Mimi looked from Afrika to Raphael, who also wanted answers. "I'm not sure why," Mimi lied.

"I've never liked him, Daddy," Afrika said to Raphael. "He was always watching me like I had some kind of disease. Mommy warned me not to get too friendly with Asia's family."

Asia unlocked herself from her mother's embrace and walked to Afrika's bed. "Your mother warned you about staying away from us?" Asia snapped, the tears free-flowing down her cheeks. She looked at Mimi. "What are you trying to insinuate?" Asia turned back to Afrika and placed the tips of both hands on her chest. "You come to my house, pretending to be my friend, when all the while you were afraid that my father was going to do something to you? My father is the Director of Admissions at a prestigious Historically Black University.

You're a peon to him. Why would he give you the time of day?"

Afrika stared at Asia, both parents flanked on either side of her.

"Because your father is Afrika's father," Brenda blurted out, looking at no one.

The room was deathly silent. Five pairs of eyes had Brenda on lock down. An occasional beep on the monitor that read Afrika's vitals and several rapid exhales from one of the six people in the room was the only sound that could be heard.

Asia looked from her mother to Afrika. "Oh my God! Oh my God!" Asia yelled, holding her chest as the words settled in.

"He raped Afrika's mother," Brenda continued her litany, "and instead of calling the police, Mimi left town. But when you brought Afrika home Asia and your father found out that Mimi was her mother, I believe your father was afraid that what he'd done so long ago was going to come into the light. I believe he was trying to get rid of his secret. Now let's go; we've distressed these people enough for one day."

"I don't believe you, Mother!" Asia began to shout. "You're lying!" Tears cascaded down her cheeks.

Afrika stared in disbelief. She was unable to move her body, but the words had penetrated to her core. Everyone continued to stare at Brenda without uttering a word.

"So Nikki is my sister?" Asia asked.

45

Mimi, Raphael, and Afrika watched in silence as Brenda quickly ushered Asia out of the room, followed by John. The silence in the room was cold and piercing like a Chicago winter with a chill factor of fifteen below zero. The silence was so cold and bitter you could cut it with a knife and serve it on a platter.

Mimi and Raphael sat there, and Afrika lay as still as a mummy in her hospital bed, numb from the news that had taken everyone's breath away. There were no parting words for the family who left the room in haste and not one of the three persons who remained in the room was willing to break the ice. *Beep. Beep. Beep.*

Raphael was the first to move away from Afrika's bedside. He walked to the window where Asia stood earlier, careful not to look in Mimi's direction. Tears slid down his face as he recalled Brenda's abrupt and painful statement of who Afrika's biological father was. In his heart, he had known that Mimi was with child when he met her. He remembered the day they had met and how eagerly she had gone to bed with him...on that first date.

But he wanted to believe that Afrika was his, although she looked to be full-term when Mimi said she was premature.

He looked back at mother and daughter. They had yet to acknowledge the bitter news. Raphael turned back to look out of the window, allowing his mind to wander. Now he understood why Mimi was so reluctant to let Afrika come to North Carolina. Her secret was a ticking time bomb. Just like Victor, Mimi was afraid of what would happen should her secret be exposed. But Raphael loved Afrika as his own and always would. It was Mimi's deception, deceit, and betrayal that he was having a hard time swallowing.

Their lives were magical and wonderful for all of their marriage. And even though a child was part of Mimi and Raphael's wedding package, they loved and nurtured Afrika with all they had to give. There wasn't anything Raphael wouldn't do for his family; they were his top priority, *next to loving God*, as Mimi would often say.

Raphael remembered the day Afrika was born. It was a cold winter night in December and he and Mimi were already on Christmas break from school. Mimi and Raphael were living together in a one-room, second-floor apartment to save money in preparation for their pending marriage that was to take place on Christmas Day.

Settled in for the night, Mimi began to twist and turn because she was uncomfortable and then the moment of truth—her water broke. Little Afrika decided to come early in Raphael's estimation, and they braved the cold and headed for the hospital.

Lamaze classes didn't work as Raphael couldn't remember a cotton-pickin' thing he was supposed to in order to help Mimi through delivery. But there was nothing but admiration and joy in his heart when the doctor pulled the eight-pound, two-ounce baby girl from Mimi's womb, gave her to the nurse who patted her softly, and then the wails that woke up the hospital ward. Although covered in afterbirth, Raphael counted the fingers on each of the two hands and the toes on each of two small feet. She was pale in color, but Mimi told him later that by looking at the baby's ear, you could tell what color she was going to be.

Raphael grinned as if Afrika had come from inside of his being. He followed the nurses as they cleaned her up and brought her back to Mimi for her to hold and behold. It was a beautiful family portrait that would stick in Raphael's mind forever, and whatever question he may have had about his daughter's parentage, it was lost forever in the recesses of his mind. This was his and Mimi's child. And when Mimi said she wanted to name her Afrika, he agreed without question. He was a proud father.

"Daddy?" Afrika called out.

Startled, Raphael turned around and went to Afrika's bedside. "What is it, baby girl?"

"Daddy, I don't care what Asia's mother said, you are my dad, my only dad. I love you, not that monster who was on television."

Raphael hugged her. "You will always be my daughter. No one can take you away from me. I love you, Afrika."

"I love you, too, Daddy."

Mimi sat on the other side. Raphael knew she was hurting, but so was Afrika. If the news was true, she shouldn't have had to hear it the way she did.

"Your mother loves you, too, Afrika."

"But why didn't she tell me...why did I have to find out like this?" Afrika cried.

"Your mother went through a terrible ordeal a long time ago. She was probably afraid and ashamed to tell anyone," Raphael said.

"How do you know how I felt, huh?" Mimi lashed out. "You weren't there. You didn't feel Victor's grubby hands pull me down and tear my clothes off."

"Okay, Mimi. You're right, I don't know how you felt or what you went through, but Afrika doesn't need to hear the details."

Mimi closed her mouth and looked at her daughter who somehow thought it was her fault. They say the truth shall set you free, but all it had done was make her life miserable. If only Afrika hadn't wanted to come to North Carolina, she could've taken her secret to the grave or could she? Mimi looked up when she heard Afrika call her.

"Mommy, I'm not mad at you. I'm hurt because you kept your secret from me and pretended you wanted nothing to do with Asia's mother when all the time you were trying to protect…protect me."

"Yes, protect you, Afrika," Mimi said. Mimi looked at Raphael. "Baby, I'm so sorry that I deceived you, betrayed your love. And although you won't believe this, the moment I saw you and you spoke to me, I knew you were my soulmate. Don't ask me how I knew; I just did."

Raphael smiled, but didn't go to Mimi. He gave Afrika a kiss on her cheek and looked across at Mimi. "Let me have the key, Mimi. I need some air."

Mimi went to her purse and pulled out the key to the car. "Raf, please promise me you won't do anything stupid."

"I can't promise you anything." Raphael took the keys and proceeded to leave the room. He turned back and looked at Afrika. "I'll be back, baby girl."

46

Anxious to read the results of her blood work, Sheila dropped her purse and the other mail she'd retrieved from her mailbox onto the couch and turned on the television. Sitting on the arm of the couch, a broad smile lit her face as she raced to open the sealed envelope, a step closer to marrying her man.

Sheila held the piece of paper tight in her hands. Her eyes began to bulge as she scanned the contents, little that they were. Like a slow tremor, her hands began to shake and her mouth opened up as if someone found the magic button that exposed a hidden door. Tears fell from her eyes before she ever made a sound—and then it was only the sound of paper being shredded into tiny little pieces.

Whimpering, Sheila finally moved from the place that had her paralyzed for more than a few moments and went in search of the gun that Victor had so conveniently returned to her. It was his mistake because he had placed a death sentence on her and she was going to return the favor.

"HIV positive?" Sheila wailed, as she finally retrieved

the gun from the back of her clothes closet where she'd hidden it after Victor had given it back to her. "How can I get married now?" Sheila shouted as she continued on her rant. "I've waited all my life to find the one man I truly want to spend the rest of my life with, and now I've got to tell him that I'm HIV positive...that I could possibly get AIDS."

Sheila twirled the gun around and around in her hand. She kicked off her pumps and rocked back and forth on the heels of her feet, blowing air out of her mouth at two-second intervals. She looked like a deranged woman on the verge of a breakdown, ready for a showdown with either the law or the white-coat doctors who'd come ready to put her in a straight jacket.

She stood with her legs spread apart, wielding the gun in the air, with black mascara running down her face. The large sculptured mirror that hung on the wall in her room captured the moment. Catching a glimpse of herself, Sheila passed the gun from one hand to the other, took off the black and white houndstooth light wool jacket that complemented her sleeveless black shift, and picked up the gun again.

"When the police come to cart me off to jail, my hands will be up in total surrender!" Sheila shouted to no one, continuing to point the gun at the ceiling. "I'm getting ready to commit a crime that will have all of Durham talking for days. I'm going to riddle his body with so many bullets, he'll wish he'd never put his nasty infected penis in my body. But what will he care? He'll be dead meat."

Poised to shoot, Sheila abruptly dropped her hands at the sound of the knock on the door. "Oh, Victor, if that's you, you'd better get your running shoes on. I'm going to shoot your ass dead on the front porch. You'll never infect another person again."

With a tear-stained face, Sheila marched the few feet to the door, her arm out ready to shoot. She didn't ask who it was because the surprise was going to be on the visitor standing on the other side of the door. Sheila took her time unlocking the door, all dramatic like she was rehearsing for a gut-wrenching scene in a play. She put on her evil face, slowly turned the knob, and snatched the door open, her finger steady on the trigger. Shock, then anger, registered on her face as she began to swing the gun.

"Fool, what's wrong with you?" Phyllis shouted, snatching the gun from Sheila's hand and pushing her into the interior of the house. "Are you some kind of crazy? You could have killed me."

"But I didn't."

"Who were you trying to kill?" Phyllis asked, dropping the gun on the coffee table.

"You don't want to know!" Sheila hollered.

"Look at you," Phyllis went on, dropping her purse on Sheila's couch. "You look like a snot-nosed kid that's been smoking crack. All right, I'm here. What's going on with you?"

"Get out, Phyllis. I'm not in the mood to talk to you or anyone else." Sheila plopped down in one of her green chairs.

"Well, something has got you like this. You were all bells and whistles when you left work today. Did Jamal threaten to cancel the wedding?"

"Shut up, shut up! You don't know nothing."

"Calm down, sweetie. I was messing with you. This is serious. Do you want to talk about it?"

Tears began to fall again as Sheila searched for the piece of paper with the bad news. Then she remembered; the piece of paper was now in tiny pieces. Not able to accept the verdict the paper rendered, she had torn it up as if the disease would go away.

Sheila sniffed and Phyllis walked over and sat next to her on the arm of the chair. "What is it, sweetie? What's got you wanting to kill somebody?"

Sheila's face looked like black marble fudge. Every time she wiped at her face, the water from her tears and the mascara would mix and form a new pattern. Sheila tried to hold her head up and look at Phyllis, but she couldn't. She began to cry profusely, until her body began to shake.

Phyllis got on her knees in front of Sheila and grabbed both of her arms. "Tell me what it is, Sheila, so I can help you."

"I...I...I'm HIV positive."

Phyllis dropped Sheila's hands and jerked back as if

she had been bitten by the disease. "Did you say HIV positive?" she asked, getting to her feet.

"Yes, Phyllis. I'm HIV positive."

"Jamal did this to you?"

"No, it wasn't Jamal."

"How do you know it wasn't Jamal?

"Because we've always used protection."

"Surely the great Victor Christianson didn't give it to you."

"Why do you believe Victor didn't give it to me? Just because he lives in a fine home on the other side of town, drives the latest model car, and has a little money in his pocket? He is in no way somebody's millionaire, but I'll tell you what he is. He's a ho; a bona fide ho…and don't say it; I'll save you the trouble. I deserved what I got for sleeping with him."

Phyllis looked at Sheila with downcast eyes. "What are you going to do?"

"I don't know, Phyllis. How can I get married to Jamal with this death sentence hanging around my neck? This weekend I'm supposed to experience the happiest day of my life. Now, I have nothing to look forward to."

"Maybe you can explain it to Jamal. If he loves you, he'll understand."

"It's not that easy, Phyllis. I feel like my body is a booby trap—a time bomb ready to go off. It's easy if you get a little cold with the sniffle and sneezes. You go to the drugstore, pick up some cold medicine, and in a few days you're all right. Not so with HIV. Death is what I have to look forward to. I'll have to take some expensive drugs that I may not be able to afford and sit around and wonder how long and when will it become full-blown AIDS. I can't live like this."

"They are making remarkable progress with AIDS research. You've got a fighting chance, Sheila."

They both turned when they heard the door rattle. Without a second thought, Sheila jumped up and scooped the gun off the coffee table. Victor walked into the room in a starched pair of jeans, white shirt, and a blue linen blazer. He was startled to see Phyllis.

Sheila held out the gun, her nostrils flaring.

"Don't do it, Sheila," Phyllis begged. "Don't do it."

"What's up with her?" Victor asked Phyllis. "That virus you had has gone to your head."

"You've got that right, Victor Christianson. I have a virus but it hasn't gone to my head." Sheila walked closer to Victor, who began to back up.

"Phyllis, what's wrong with this crazy bitch? I bought her a nice house to stay in, fixed her up with diamonds and pearls, and I can't come in my own house?"

"You asshole, don't talk like I'm invisible. I'm standing right here, right in front of you. But you won't for long because I'm going to sentence you to death like you've done to me."

"What in the hell are you talking about?" Victor roared, with a scowl on his face.

"I'm talking about being HIV positive, you imbecile. I'm talking about my future not being so bright because I might get AIDS. You stand in my face with that cocky look on your face, but that—"

"HIV?" Victor shouted. "You stupid wench." And before anyone could blink, Victor tried to reach for the gun.

"Don't do it, Sheila!" Phyllis shouted.

Sheila pulled the trigger. "You animal, you scum of the earth. You don't deserve to live!" Sheila screamed. Her eyes narrowed as the water from the tears clouded her vision.

Another shot rang out and Victor grabbed at his left arm, his eyes wild with fright and his face pinched by the sudden graze of the bullet. "I'm going to kill you, bitch. You tore my good jacket." And he lunged.

Phyllis cowered on her knees in a corner of the room, using her hands as a shield as Sheila pulled the trigger again.

Pop, pop, pop. Victor danced to the tune as he dodged the bullets that rained down on him.

"Didn't you hear me, you sorry, no good for nothing ho? You've already killed me. I have HIV. I'm going to die. And to think, I was going to get married this weekend to the love of my life."

Crouching behind the wall that led into the foyer, Victor suddenly reappeared, stood wild eyed, and stared at Sheila. "Married?"

"Yes, married. I was going to marry the love of my life

this weekend. Had I not gotten the blood test, who knows when I would've found out about the HIV?"

"Married? And where were you going to live? Hell, how do you know it wasn't that other nigger that got you infected?"

"I know, and you need to get tested. I wonder what your wife will say when I tell her?"

"You—"

Pop, pop! Either Sheila was a bad shot or Victor had nine lives. Victor danced and ducked, but seemed to dodge the bullets Sheila hurled. Sheila marched forward, until she had Victor cornered. *Pop!*

"Damn, woman." Victor grabbed his left arm again, but only for a second as he pulled the door open and stumbled outside.

"Call the po po!" Sheila shouted after Victor as she watched him stagger to the street. "Be glad that the coroner isn't picking up your ass." Sheila slammed the door. "Dog blood all over my wall. HIV blood. Damn."

Sheila dropped the gun on the floor and looked around. The warmth that made the house so beautiful was gone. The candles, the soothing colors of the room, the posh furniture couldn't heal the wound that had been made. Sheila crossed her arms over her bosom and walked slowly through the living room, then stopped in her tracks as if she was paralyzed.

"Phyllis, you all right?"

Phyllis' mouth was clamped shut. Her eyes were those

of a scared child who'd seen a horrible crime. She looked as if someone had pasted her against the wall with some strong adhesive. Shock, that's what it was.

Sheila held her belly and began to laugh. "Phyllis, girl, are you all right? You look like a scared rabbit stuck on the wall."

"I peed on myself—in my brand new suit. Paid a little money for it, too, but not so it could smell like pee."

Sheila fell on the couch and laughed to her heart's content. "Get up off the floor. And you're going to clean my carpet before you leave."

"Did you kill Victor?"

"Hell naw; he's still alive."

47

Raphael walked briskly away from the hospital and jumped in the Lexus. His mind was heavy…heavy with Mimi's betrayal, heavy with the dark thought of finding Victor Christianson who'd come blasting into his life without notice, although, unbeknownst to him, Victor was a thread in his life dating back nineteen years ago.

The sun was almost set—the moment right before total darkness. Dark clouds began to form in the sky, kind of like the mood Raphael was in. His mood was thick, unpredictable, although the clouds' movements seemed to be swift and sure. Raphael drove blindly through the streets without any direction, without any formal plan, and without any idea of how to begin. He wasn't sure where he was as he'd only been in Durham a little over forty-eight hours, but if he needed it, the car was equipped with GPS. Clearing his head was paramount because he needed to think things over.

Mimi's legs were a little shorter than Raphael's and the seat needed adjusting. He reached for the lever to move the seat back, and when he did, a portion of a wooden box peered from under the seat. Raphael reached down with one hand while keeping his eyes on the road and pulled the box up. Sitting the box on the seat, Raphael unlatched the lock that kept the box closed. Upon opening it, his medium brown eyes became large brown saucers.

Honk, honk, honk. "Damn," Raphael said, steering the car quickly to the right to avoid a collision with the car to the left of him. "Whew, that was close."

Raphael picked up the gun and sat it carefully in his lap, making sure not to call attention to him. He drove until he saw a grocery store and pulled into the parking lot to further examine the gun.

Mimi had good taste—a twenty-two Ruger with a pearl handle. Whomever she planned to pop, she was going to do it in style. And Raphael had an idea who it was—Victor Christianson. Well, he had the gun now, and all he had to do was find Victor before the police did. How he was going to accomplish that, he wasn't sure, although he knew that one part of his plan was solved.

Raphael thought about driving to NC Central's campus, but it was too late in the day. It was six-thirty and everyone would be gone. He drove on aimlessly through downtown Durham that would have been scenic if darkness hadn't approached, but then he saw the sign that gave him an idea.

He turned onto Pettigrew Street and headed for the Greyhound Station. Luck was on Raphael's side, and he eased into the parking space made just for Mimi's car. He jumped from the car and ran inside and found a phone book. Flipping the pages with his finger, Raphael found a listing for Victor Christianson in Chapel Hill.

Taking an ink pen from his jacket, Raphael recorded the address on the back of a piece of advertisement that he scrounged from inside the terminal. Satisfied, he returned to the car and entered the address in the GPS. It was about a thirty-minute ride, but he was up for it, not sure what he was going to do when he got there.

Raphael turned on the radio to distract his attention from what he might be on the verge of doing. He drove down the interstate, rolling around in his subconscious what he would do if this or that scenario presented itself, ignoring Mimi's phone calls that were coming every five minutes.

The exit for Chapel Hill loomed in the distance, and guided by the friendly voice of the navigator, Raphael left the interstate and travelled where directed. Even under the cloak of darkness, it wasn't hard to tell that the neighborhood was affluent and that if he were to settle in North Carolina, this would be the kind of neighborhood where he'd set up domicile.

Raphael slowed then made a left turn onto a long winding road. He crawled down the street until the guide announced that he was at his destination. Lights out, Raphael got out of the car and walked up the circular driveway. Halfway up he jumped, startled by the flood of lights that were triggered by the motion sensor as he passed by.

Pressing his way forward, Raphael descended the few steps to the porch, looked around, and rang the doorbell. Perspiration formed around his hairline as he waited for someone to answer the door.

Someone peered through the peephole. His body tense, Raphael continued to wait patiently. Finally the door opened and Brenda stared back at him, still wearing the black pantsuit she had on at the hospital.

"Raphael?" Brenda said coolly. "What are you doing here? Has something happened to Afrika?"

"No, to your last question," Raphael replied. "Look, may I come in?"

"Where is Mimi? Is she with you?"

"No, Mimi isn't with me."

Brenda hesitated and looked at Raphael with a different set of eyes. "Raphael, I don't think this is a good idea— you coming to my home. I don't know what's on your agenda, but now is not the time. I'm sorry about Afrika, and after this afternoon's reveal, I'm not up for any conversation."

"Just for a minute. That's all I need," Raphael insisted.

Brenda sighed, looked at Raphael with a question mark on her face, and pulled the door open. "Only for a moment." She moved aside and let Raphael come in.

Raphael walked inside and followed Brenda to the family room by way of the foyer. He wasn't sure why he was there, but maybe, just maybe he hoped to find Victor holed up in a corner. The gun was still in the car, and if Victor was in the house, the only thing Raphael could do was have words with him. He jerked his body when Beyonce rubbed up against his leg as she came out of no-where and jumped on the sofa, ready to protect the woman of the house should it be necessary.

Raphael's eyes roamed as he took in the splendor of the Christiansons' home that was picture-perfect and immaculate. He sensed Brenda's agitation, and turned his attention to her before his minute was up.

"Does Mimi know you're here?" Brenda asked before Raphael had a chance to state his case. She continued to stand with a demure look on her face without extending Raphael an offer to sit, although they were in the family room.

"No."

"So why are you here?"

"I thought…"

"You thought you'd find Victor here?" Brenda finished Raphael's sentence. "He's not here, and I've not seen him. And what were you planning to do if he was? Kill him?" Brenda's eyes dropped to Raphael's body, searching with her eyes.

Raphael threw his hands in the air with Brenda following his every move. *I'm suspect*, Raphael thought; *she thinks I might have a weapon.* "Brenda, I don't know what I thought. Yes, maybe I thought I would find your husband here and maybe get him to go to the police so he could own up to what he'd done to Afrika."

"How do you think you could've done that when the police haven't been successful in doing so? But if you want to know the truth, Raphael, I believe Victor is holed up in some rat hole with one of his hoes. He has many." Brenda's face relaxed. She sat down on the sofa next to where Beyonce was perched and directed Raphael with her hand to sit in the chair opposite of where she sat.

"Victor has a reputation in this town. I hear the rumors. Even before Mimi told me what Victor had done to her all those years ago, I was only two steps from walking out the door. I shouldn't have married Victor; Mimi warned me about his womanizing years ago, but I just had to have him. I thought I was in love. Victor was a good-looking man and he wanted me, only I wasn't the only one he wanted. The marriage was good for a time—the best part was the birth of my babies, Asia and Trevor. I can't say exactly when, but things began to fall apart...sour, but he wouldn't let me go."

"Why is that?"

"Because Victor had a good thing with me. He wouldn't have made it as far as he did if my family hadn't intervened. Everyone knows that Victor is spoiled rotten to the core, and it's my practice that has given us the lifestyle we've become accustomed to. But I would have traded the lifestyle for real happiness in a New York second. I do believe Victor did...no, he does love me, although the womanizing part of him is so seeped into his soul, he can't give it up—like a smoker who has to have his nicotine."

"I'm glad we had this conversation, Brenda. I was an angry man when I came here tonight; still am if I'm truthful about it. And you guessed right, I wanted to do bodily harm. Like Mimi said, our daughter is going to live, although she may be paralyzed. I feel rather foolish, sitting in your house with contempt in my heart. I hope you can forgive me for barging in like this."

For the first time since Raphael entered the house, Brenda smiled. "Mimi is fortunate to have you in her life."

"She is the love of my life. And although every day hasn't been a bowl of cherries, I will tell you that even though I heard some very disheartening truths today, I love Mimi as much as I did the first day I met her— maybe even more. To hear that Afrika wasn't my biological child hurt me to the core and I wanted someone to pay."

"We'll get through this."

"Thanks, Brenda. I'm in real trouble. This is Mimi now. She's been calling me for the last two hours. I better answer this call before I don't have a place to sleep tonight."

"You best."

"Hey, Mimi," Raphael said in a low voice of surrender.

He listened while she chewed him out, talking about how he just up and left, not answering her phone calls, acting like everything was all her fault, and how he needed to man-up and be the father and husband he was supposed to be. And if he was going to continue to act the way he'd been doing for the last couple of days, he should have stayed his behind in Germany.

"You're perfectly right, baby," Raphael conceded. "I'm at Brenda's." There was a long pause—no instant reply. "I thought I'd find Victor here, but he's nowhere to be found. I'm leaving now and will be at the hospital in an hour." Still no answer.

"I love you." The line went dead on the other end.

Raphael looked at Brenda and curled up his lips. "I better go. Mimi isn't too happy with me right now, and my daughter probably isn't either. One thing you said, Brenda, is true. We will get through this. I'll see myself out." Raphael got up and headed for the door but turned around and looked at Brenda still sitting on the couch. "Thank you."

"WE HEARD EVERYTHING," ASIA SAID AS SHE AND Trevor appeared in the room and sat on the couch next to Brenda. Asia picked up Beyoncé and put her in her lap. "You all right, Mom?" Asia asked, laying her head on Brenda's shoulder.

"So…it's true. Afrika is our sister," Trevor said half-heartedly.

"One at a time," Brenda said, holding up her right hand. "Yes to both."

RAPHAEL WALKED BRISKLY TO THE CAR, ANXIOUS TO GET as far away as possible from his embarrassment. He clicked the remote, hopped in, and started the ignition. Before pulling away from the curb, Raphael pulled out his cell to call Mimi.

"Drive and don't turn around," said the voice in the darkness.

Raphael's body stiffened as the cold piece of metal touched the back of his neck. Out of the corner of his eyes, Raphael searched for Mimi's gun that he had sat on the floor, but he couldn't see the wooden box in his peripheral vision.

"If you're looking for your gun, it's stroking the back of your neck. You are some stupid nigger not to lock your car door and leave a gun almost within plain sight. You don't think rich people steal?"

Raphael remained quiet and let the person sitting in his back seat talk.

"So blood, what were you doing in my house talking to my wife?"

Fear tangled in Raphael's throat. He had come looking for Victor, but Victor had found him and had his weapon pointed at the back of his head. Then he reached for his head as the butt of the gun hit the nape of his neck. "What did you do that for?" Raphael asked.

Victor grabbed Raphael by the neck. "So you do talk. Now I'm going to ask you one more time. What were you doing in my house?"

"Looking for you!"

"Looking for me? Who in the hell are you, that you'd be looking for me?"

"I'm Mimi's husband."

Victor let go of Raphael's neck. There was an icy chill in the car. A minute passed without a word being said. Without warning, Victor's voice pierced the silence, erupting in a guttural laugh.

Raphael felt the gun again but this time next to his ear.

"Drive."

48

Mimi was angrier now than she'd been when Victor first set foot at her front door. She couldn't believe Raphael had walked off, took her car, and left her to deal with the aftermath of Brenda's announcement earlier that afternoon. She felt bad for Afrika...that she had to hear the raw truth of her birth while lying in a hospital bed because of a bullet wound to the back inflicted by the biological father she'd just learned about. It was a shame in more ways than one, but Mimi never expected Brenda to blurt out the reality of that truth in front of everyone it was going to hurt.

Maybe she deserved Raphael's wrath. In her heart, Mimi knew he was hurting because she hadn't been truthful about her pregnancy...that she was already pregnant when she met him. A terrifying thought came to Mimi. *What if Raf thought she'd married him because her baby needed a father and that it would make her respectable? Well, was that the truth?* Mimi looked back at Afrika, who lay staring at the ceiling. No, she loved him. God sent her an angel, and his name was Raphael Bailey.

"Mommy," Afrika said, softly causing Mimi to catch

her throat with her hand, bracing for Afrika's question. "Mommy, let's talk about it."

"Is that what you really want to do, baby? All I want is for you to get well."

"I have two wounds now, Mommy. I can't get well unless you help me to mend my broken heart. It's strange how a bullet darn near got me in the heart, but then it's true when they say words can cut you with a knife."

Mimi watched Afrika, as she lay on her side, so vulnerable and so wise. "Mommy had a terrible secret that she felt needed to be buried alive, never to surface. I was ashamed of what happened because the repercussions would hurt so many people."

"But, Mommy, you were raped by that vile man. You should've reported him; he should've been in jail."

"Baby, if I was as confident about myself then as I am now, I might've done that. But I was afraid...afraid that Brenda wouldn't understand and that she'd say it was my fault. After all, she was my best friend."

"Well, she wouldn't be my best friend if she knew me as well as you two say you knew each other and then wouldn't believe you. That's crazy."

"It's easy to say, Afrika, but you weren't in my shoes."

"I know that Grandma and Granddad supported you. They've been so supportive of me all my life."

Mimi closed her eyes. "That they were. I...I had even thought of aborting the baby." Everything was still. Mimi opened her eyes and saw tears streaming down Afrika's cheek. Mimi brushed Afrika's face. "But I didn't, baby, thanks to your grandparents. And I'm so glad I listened to them. You wouldn't have been in my life. So I went to school in Hampton because I didn't want the pregnancy to hamper me from getting my education. Hmph, and to think my first day there, I met your father."

Afrika wiped the tears from her eyes. She looked at Mimi thoughtfully. "Mommy, did you love Daddy?"

"Yes, sweetie. I know it seems suspect, considering I met your Daddy with you in my stomach and he was none the wiser...at least I believe so, but I fell hard for that man, and not out of obligation either. I loved Raphael Bailey almost from the moment I met him, and he still has my heart. Afrika, he's been so good to me, and I thank the Lord every day for placing him in my life."

Mimi wiped away her own tears. She couldn't help but notice how Afrika's countenance changed...that warmth had replaced the pain.

"Mommy, I'm so glad. Daddy will be glad to hear that, too. And so that you know, I love him with all of my heart. I may have Victor Christianson's DNA, but he's no part of me."

"It's going to be okay, baby. Why don't you try and get some rest and let this other stuff go for a while. It's still you, me, and Daddy."

"Mommy, I'm going to transfer to Hampton. I'm sorry for not listening to you."

"It's all right, baby. I believe God was telling me that

it was time to come clean, to purge my soul, repent, and get it straight...not just with you and your dad..." Mimi pointed her finger upward, "...but Him, too. I've betrayed a lot of people, but God knows my heart."

"Okay, Mommy." Mimi smiled for the first time today.

OVER AN HOUR PASSED SINCE RAPHAEL HAD CALLED. Mimi looked at her watch and then at Afrika, who was now fast asleep. Where could he be? She had made up in her mind to spend the night in Afrika's room, but she needed a friendly voice to talk to, she needed her husband, she need to make things right with him.

Mimi picked up her cell and dialed his cell phone. It rang and rang without an answer. Puzzled, she tried the number again without any results. Mimi sighed. She didn't like the fact that he was at Brenda's house. Why would he go there? Surely not to get back at her.

Mimi dialed Brenda's number.

"Hi, Mimi," Brenda answered. "Raphael get back okay?"

"He's not there?"

"No, he left right after he spoke to you. That was about an hour and a half ago."

"I've tried calling him, but he hasn't answered his phone. He was angry when he left the hospital, but this is out of character for Raf. This worries me."

"The last words he uttered before leaving here was that he had to go and that you were angry with him. But,

Mimi, that man loves you with all of his heart and soul. He told me as much. Yes, my announcement wasn't the best way to handle things, but Raphael was looking forward to getting back to his wife."

"Question?"

"What is it, Mimi?"

"Why did Raphael come to your house?"

"Girl, I know you're not jealous of the man who only has eyes for you. He was hoping to find Victor. Give Victor a piece of his mind. He was mad enough to kill Victor if he'd actually run into him."

The ladies laughed. "Raphael would put a hurting on Victor if he did. Well, I'll wait a few minutes longer. It just worries me that he hasn't called to say he was held up or whatever."

"I'm sure that man of yours is fine. How's Afrika?"

"She's sleep. How are Asia and Trevor?"

"They're in denial. They're hurting deep to their core. I tried to keep it inside, Mimi, but I couldn't. Maybe it was selfish; I've hurt our children and Raphael, but I couldn't stand to let Victor off the hook."

"I wished I'd been as brave as you nineteen years ago."

"You did what you thought was best at the time, Mimi. Don't beat yourself up about it."

"You're talking like a psychologist, Brenda."

"That's what I get paid to do. Love you."

"Love you back."

49

Raphael drove where instructed with the barrel of the gun still aimed at his head. Nothing more was said between the two men; only the occasional giving of directions by Victor. The night hid the beauty of day, but Raphael knew there was no beauty, day or night, in and on the streets they now travelled as evidenced by all the brothers hanging out on the street corners, their cigarette clad fingers raised high in the air, giving their take on the hood's daily news.

"Make a right here," Victor barked.

It was a small incline, and Raphael pushed down on the accelerator so he could beat the train he could see barreling down in the distance, although the crossing gate had yet to come down. Sailing over the tracks, the car bounced a couple of times, jerking Victor in the back seat.

"What in the hell were you trying to do, fool?" Victor yelled. "Get us killed?"

"I'm driving like you told me to do," Raphael retorted.

"Don't get smart or you'll never see Mimi again. I don't understand, but I guess I don't have to. You aren't even Mimi's type."

"And what type is that?"

"Protecting your woman. Hmph. Maybe I had you pegged wrong."

Raphael kept his eyes on the road, although secretly recording his location.

"Okay, pull over in front of that house," Victor said, pointing the gun at a run-down wooden-frame house. "I can't let you drive off; you can pinpoint my location. I'm going to pick up someone and you're going to be our getaway driver."

"I've got to get to the hospital. If I don't show up soon, Mimi is going to have the police looking for me."

"Then maybe I'm going to have to eradicate you from the face of the earth."

"The police will be looking for my car."

"Oh, I've got another plan. Now get out of the car... slowly. Place both hands in front of you, and put the keys in your right hand and hold them out so I can get them."

Raphael got out of the car as instructed and quickly surveyed his surroundings. The block ended several houses down. There was a Laundromat on the opposite corner and he couldn't see much else. He held the keys in his right hand and waited for Victor to take them from him.

With gun in his right hand, Victor walked up to where Raphael stood.

"Drop the keys in my hand," Victor demanded.

Raphael hesitated but saw the gun pointing at him.

He held on a second longer, but Victor moved closer and snatched them out of his hand.

Pow. Raphael saw the moment to change the course of his fate. He knocked the gun out of Victor's hand, kicked him in the groin, and pushed him to the ground. Raphael took off running, but knew he had to get farther than the Laundromat. Too many people's lives would be at risk, so he kept running.

Raphael believed he heard footsteps following him and he ran faster still. There was a moment of silence, but still he ran on. He dodged between houses, trying to find a safe haven from the devil. Catching his breath, he peeked from behind the safety of the house and crept to the front to see if the coast was clear.

"Whatcha doing sneaking behind my house?" said the husky voice that belonged to a dark-skinned, heavy set, middle-aged woman who held a piece of plywood in the air. Pink foam hair rollers covered her head, and she wore a pink and orange house-dress that came to her knees that was zipped down far enough to see her ample helping of breasts. And on her feet were a pair of white, off-brand tennis shoes, no socks, with the shoelaces untied. "I'll take this board and smash your face in."

Eyes bulging, Raphael jumped and held his hands up. His voice was stuck somewhere in his throat. "Uhh, uhh, Miss...uhh..."

"I said whatcha doing here?"

"Miss..."

"Shirley, my name is Shirley."

Raphael put his finger to his lips. "Shhhh."

"Don't shush me. You're the one that don't belong here."

"Shirley, I'm not here to do you any harm," Raphael whispered. Then he pointed toward the house. "Can we go in there for a minute?"

"Fool, is you crazy? Don't you see this board I'm fixin' to drop across your head?"

"I'm in trouble...not with the law," Raphael continued whispering. "Please, I need your help."

Shirley sized him up. "It's going to cost you. And don't try nothing."

Raphael fumbled in his pants for his wallet. He pulled out two twenties and gave them to Shirley.

"I guess so, but I'm going to keep this board aimed at your face."

Raphael followed Shirley into her small kitchen. Fried chicken, rice and gravy were on the stove. Three small children, two girls and one boy, whose ages ranged from three to ten sat at a small round table in the small kitchen. The children were dressed in dingy white underclothes with pigtails flying at half mast on the two girls, and the boy's hair was wild about his head as if Shirley had just taken his cornrows down. Rice and gravy were half in their plates and half on the table, as the children nibbled and played in their food.

"Want some dinner...I didn't get your name?"

"Raf. No."

"Raf? What kind of name is that?" Shirley asked, putting down the plywood. "Look, mister, I don't care what your name is, but you need to do what you've got to do and be gone before my boyfriend gets home. He's at work now."

"I need to make a phone call, Shirley, and I promise I'll be out of your hair soon after that."

Tired of the talk, Raphael walked to the front of the house—Shirley following right behind him. The living room was the color of egg yolk after it had been hard-boiled and it was smaller than his office at work. There was a brown Kankelon couch with a patchwork quilt thrown over it to hide the springs that pushed from it, and a matching chair sat off to the side. Metal TV trays covered in brown and orange fall leaves on an eggshell-colored background served as coffee and end tables. Children's toys were littered throughout the room; however, the one luxury Shirley and her man afforded themselves was a thirty-two-inch plasma TV.

Raphael navigated through the toys on the floor to the window and peeked out of the blinds. "What street is this and what city are we in?"

"You are in trouble. Now look, I can't have no cops coming up in here. I'm doing you a favor, but if it has to do with the cops, you've got to G-O, go."

"Do you have a car?"

"No car, but my boyfriend does. I take public trans-portation."

"Okay, okay. Where are we?"

"You're in Durham, baby." Shirley turned on the television. "Missy, Sissy, and Baby Boy, ya'll come on into the living room so me and this gentleman here can talk in the kitchen."

Gravy and gummy rice stained their undershirts, but the motley group tumbled into the living room and began to play with their toys. "Okay, Raf, let's go in the kitchen. You've got to get going. You're wasting time."

Raphael dialed Mimi and thanked God when he heard her frantic voice on the other end of the line.

"Where are you, Raphael?" Mimi shouted into the phone.

"Calm down, baby. You won't believe the night I've had. Victor had me at gunpoint; I just escaped."

"What? Oh my God! Are you all right? Where are you? Where is Victor now?"

"Oh, my Lord!" Shirley hollered.

"Who was that, Raf?" Mimi wanted to know.

"This kind lady let me find refuge in her house. Victor was behind me, but I think I managed to dodge him. I've got to get out of here, baby."

"You've got the car."

"The car is another story. When I went to Brenda's house, I left the car unlocked. Victor must have been watching the house and saw me go inside. He was hiding in the backseat of the car when I got in. He pulled a gun on me...your gun..."

"Oh, God!" Mimi said. "Baby, did he hurt you?"

"No, but he made me drive to some neighborhood in Durham. And I had to leave the car after I knocked him down; it was the only way I was able to get away from him. Baby, you've got to help me get away from here. I can't risk walking in this neighborhood because Victor may still be out there looking for me."

"You can't stay here all night," Shirley said in the background.

Raphael fished for his wallet and threw her another twenty.

"I'll see what we can work out," Shirley said.

"Baby, I'll call John," Mimi said on the other end of the line. "He'll help us. Give me the address so we can find you."

"Shirley, what's your address?"

"Who wants to know?"

"My wife, so she can get me out of here before your boyfriend comes home."

"Okay, okay. It's 555...hold on a minute. Missy, Sissy, and Baby Boy, shut that noise up in there. I can't hear myself think. Okay, let's try this again. It's 555 Dunbar Street."

Raphael repeated Shirley's address to Mimi. "Hold on, baby. I think I hear sirens."

In two giant steps, Raphael moved to the window in the living room, waddled through the children's toys, and pulled back a corner of the blinds. Red and blue lights streaked by, sitting on top of three or four patrol cars whose sirens pierced the night.

"Let me have a look," Shirley said. "Lawd, here comes a fire truck. Must be bad."

Raphael drew the cell phone to his mouth. "Something has happened, Mimi. I saw several patrol cars and a fire truck pass by. If I had just stayed my behind at the hospital, I wouldn't be in this predicament."

"It's water under the bridge now. I'll call you back once I find John."

"Hurry." Raphael hung up the phone.

"She better make it fast," Shirley said. "My boyfriend will be home soon."

"You ain't getting any more money, Shirley."

50

Mimi ended her phone call with Raphael and breathed a sigh of relief, although she shook her head in disbelief. It was hard to fathom that her coming back to Durham had caused so much hurt and pain. Hindsight was twenty-twenty.

She walked back into Afrika's room to check on her; she was still asleep. The room was quiet and still; the only movement came from the monitor that recorded Afrika's vitals. Mimi leaned over the bed and pulled the thin spread up to her shoulders. She patted Afrika's head and said a prayer. Mimi thanked God for her family, specifically that Afrika was going to be all right and that Raphael was safe.

Taking one last look, Mimi slipped from the room and dialed John's number. The night nurse gave her a smile and went back to her paperwork that was spread out on her desk. Mimi walked down the hallway and prayed that John would answer his cell. Just as she was about to hang up, she heard John's groggy voice.

"Hel-lo," John said almost in a whisper.

"John, this is Mimi. I need your help."

"What is it, Mimi?" John asked, his voice more alert, no doubt sensing the stress in Mimi's voice.

"It's late, but I need a real big favor. Raphael is in trouble. He was kidnapped by Victor at gunpoint tonight, but he was able to escape."

"How in the world did Victor kidnap Raphael?"

"I don't know the whole sordid story, but I do know that my husband is hiding out in some woman's house who, thank God, happened to be in the right place at the right time when Raf was trying to get away from Victor. I have to go get him and bring him home. I have an address."

"Your husband is high-maintenance, Mimi, if I may say so. Ever since he rolled into town, it's been one thing or another. He's got some serious issues."

"Say what you will about Raphael, but he's a good, kind, caring, decent man. Some of what he's going through is my fault, but right now John, my priority is getting my husband out of harm's way."

"Where's your car?"

"That's part of the long story. Raphael was in it when Victor surprised him."

"Damn."

"You're right. Can you help?"

"Look, Mimi. This might be too dangerous for you. Afrika is going to need at least one parent at her disposal. It may take less time if I just go and get him."

"John, pick me up. I'm going with you. End of conversation."

"I'll be there in twenty or thirty minutes."

"Hurry, I'll be waiting."

CHAOS MET JOHN AND MIMI AS THEY CRUISED DOWN the street, looking for the address Raphael had given them. Not wanting to bring attention to themselves by driving into a neighborhood that was notorious for drugs, John chose to drive his beat up Nissan, which didn't have GPS. Several groups of people walked in their direction as if they had come out of a revival meeting, talking amongst themselves and rehashing a poignant point the minister made that had them in a tranquil mood; although the hour was nearly one in the morning.

"An awful lot of folks out in the hood at this time of night," John said, driving slowly.

"Raphael said something about police cars and a fire truck passing by while he was talking with me."

"Umm, must have been some fire."

"There it is, John," Mimi said, pointing to a weather-beaten A-frame wood house.

"Raphael must've been some kind of scared to stop off here. Go ahead and call and let him know we're out here, in case Victor is still lurking around. He might be watching from that crowd in front us."

"You're right."

Mimi took out her cell phone and dialed Raphael who picked up on the first ring.

"Baby, we're parked outside but not in front of the house," Mimi said. "John is driving a dark blue Nissan. When we see you, he'll blink the headlights two times. We're taking precautions in the event Victor is somewhere nearby. Do you know what all the commotion is about?"

"No. Shirley, the lady who lives here, went to the corner to see if she could find out. I've got to wait until she gets back because she left her three little kids in here."

"Well, we can't wait forever. We're putting our behinds on the line being over here."

"I know, baby. But what was I going to say after the lady let me hide from the enemy?"

"I see someone heading this way. They look like they're in a hurry," Mimi said, excited.

"Hold on, let me peek out of the window." Raphael held a corner of the blind but couldn't see anyone. "Mimi, I didn't see anyone."

"Whoever it was went between the house…"

"They found a dead man near the railroad tracks on the next street over," Shirley said upon entering the house, huffing and puffing. "People down at the corner there whispering, talking about they heard some shots. Look, I don't know if you're hooked up with that man, but you got to go. Can't have no criminals in my house; even though you seem like a nice man. Don't worry about me; I won't say a word. I can promise you that."

"All right, I'll leave now. But I had nothing to do with anybody getting shot, Shirley. I was the one being pursued."

"Whatever, mister, it's time. Don't look like my man coming home tonight, but you can't stay here no more."

"Well, thank you for your hospitality," Raphael said as he shook Shirley's hand and high-tailed it out of the door.

"You can always come back on a better day!" Shirley hollered. "I can throws down in the kitchen and the bedroom, too. You know the address." Then Shirley shut the door.

Raphael picked up the phone and could hear Mimi laughing. "It's not a laughing matter, Mimi. I'm coming out to the sidewalk." Raphael clicked the phone off and inched his way from the side of the house to the sidewalk. Looking left, he could see people milling about, and to the right he saw the headlights blink—one, two. Risking everything, he ran like his pants were on fire.

Reaching the car, Raphael jumped in and John pulled away from the curb, making a U-turn.

"Let's get the hell out of here. Someone was killed tonight."

51

Daybreak ushered in a beautiful sunrise. Brenda lay face up in bed, her eyes focused on the oak ceiling fan that looked like a gigantic upside down palm in the middle of nowhere. Her mind raced and then drifted in a thousand directions as the events of yesterday descended upon her like an instant replay.

Her heart ached for Asia and Trevor having to hear that the father they adored—at least for most of their lives—had been unfaithful and had fathered Asia's best friend, Afrika...their sister. Brenda wasn't sure what would become of the friendship, but by all accounts, it was now strained. And her brain moved to the next stop.

The gall of Mimi's husband, showing up on her doorstep in an attempt to try and find Victor. Who in the world did he think he was...the President of the United States? Did he really think he was going to come into her home, Victor's home, and do bodily harm? He had some nerve, but Brenda also admired him because he had the backbone to stand up and confront the enemy...to protect his family in the face of conflict.

It was time to rise and Brenda sat up, bringing her

legs over the side of the bed. In a circular motion, she rolled her head to one side and then the other, finally stretching her arms upwards. Then she stiffened, her neck locked into place with her ears pointed in the direction she believed the slow sing-song melody flowed. There it was again, but Brenda, now alert, recognized the tone of her doorbell.

"Trevor, are you up?" she called. There was no answer. Of course, he was up and gone to school. Although Asia had spent the night, she had probably left for campus, too. There was no need to call out to her. The doorbell rang once more.

Brenda looked back at the clock. It was eight thirty-one. Who in the world would be ringing her doorbell this early? Maybe Victor decided it was time to show his face, but she'd be damned if she was going to the door and let him in. He still had a key; however, the only way Victor would get through the door, even with a key, was if he crawled on all fours and begged.

There was silence. Brenda realized the doorbell had stopped ringing, but she heard voices. She sprung from the bed, grabbed the pink satin robe that lay at the foot of her bed, and tiptoed to the door. Asia was still here, but Brenda couldn't hear the conversation that was taking place downstairs.

" N o o o o o o o o o o N o o o o o o o o o o o o o o o ! Noooooooooooooooooooooooo! Oh my God. Mother!"

Brenda wrapped her arms around her chest and began

to shake. The blood-curdling scream paralyzed her and kept her from responding.

"Mother!" Asia screamed.

From the safety of her room, Brenda listened to Asia's screams. Dread and panic constricted her throat as images began to run rampant through her brain. Asia's screams could only mean bad news and the thought of what was at the core petrified Brenda.

Heavy footsteps pounded the stairs. "Motherrrrrrr!" Asia shouted again.

As if her strength returned with a quickness, Brenda jerked the door open. "What is all that screaming about?" Brenda inquired, afraid to look into Asia's face, fearing the words that might fall from her mouth.

Wet from crying, Asia stood in front of her mother's bedroom door. She looked like a zombie who had awakened from a drug-overdosed stupor. Then Asia began to whimper and reached for Brenda. "Daddy... Daddy's dead," Asia finally said, placing her hand over her pounding heart in an effort to calm down.

All Brenda could do was stare with glazed eyes. Without saying a word, her tear ducts filled and coursed over her lids and dropped wherever they fell, like the rushing waters of Niagara Falls. Brenda grabbed Asia and pulled her into her bosom, holding her in a tight embrace as if that would cause the hurt and pain to go away.

"Hello," said the voice from below.

Brenda pulled back and looked into Asia's eyes, pleading

with her silently…that the information she just delivered was all a mistake.

"Police officers," Asia whimpered, "they want to talk with you. I'll stay here until you come back."

Wracked with pain, Brenda looked at her daughter and then turned and walked slowly down the stairs. Her soul was ripped apart, and now she had to face the men who would confirm everything Asia had said.

Now at the bottom of the stairs, Brenda continued her slow walk through the foyer and to the large double doors that stood ajar. Stone-faced, she pulled her robe tightly around her and faced the two officers that looked about as unhappy to be on her front porch as she was to see them. She waved them into the foyer, closed the door, and listened.

"Mrs. Christianson?" the officer asked.

"Yes." She didn't recognize the two officers.

"I'm Officer Lacy and this is Officer Carter. Umm, I guess you're already aware that we're the bearers of not-so-good news."

Brenda was in a daze, looking well beyond where the officers stood.

"What happened? What happened to Victor?" she finally asked in a low monotone voice, directing her question at Lacy.

"Ma'am, a couple on their way home from church found Mr. Christianson bleeding and non-responsive near a set of railroad tracks in east Durham. He was probably already dead. Someone shot him, and when EMS arrived, he was pronounced dead. Looks as if he may have been dumped at that location."

Brenda cringed and hunched up her shoulders. A sudden chill rolled through her like an unexpected avalanche that made her tighten her grip on her body. A dull sadness shone in her eyes, but the tears refused to drop anymore.

"Thank you, Officer Lacy."

"We're sorry for your loss, ma'am. The body…uh, uh Mr. Christianson's body, was taken to Duke University Medical Center. If you need anything, please let us know."

With downcast eyes, Brenda held the door open as the officers left. She watched as they retreated and ambled down the walkway, got in their patrol car, and drove away. *Dead!* It wasn't possible that Victor had departed this life without her getting her last say. Good and bad memories joined together as she fought back tears sifting through the last twenty years of her and Victor's life.

Brenda closed the door and sighed. She shook her head. "It can't be true; he's still alive. No, he isn't dead."

"Mother?"

Brenda walked through the foyer and stood at the base of the stairs and stared up at Asia. "He's dead, Asia. Your father is dead."

Asia stood at the top of the stairs, rocking back and forth. "I hate Nikki."

52

Sheila stumbled into her office and plopped down at her desk anchored by the weight of the devastating news that found its way into her mailbox on yesterday. Unable to rid herself of the funk that engulfed her like a cyclone that swooped her up into its inner core, she continued to sit, unmoved by the ringing of the phone or the voices of her co-workers who drifted past, offering a word of salutation. They were invisible to her, as the dread of her ill-fated disease ate at her like cancer.

She pulled her head from the sand and looked up as the noise from the object landing on the counter disturbed her daydream. Fresh spring flowers—lilies, iris, carnations in purples, pinks, and bright yellow—stuck in a beautiful vase full of water met her eyes as a middle-aged, white gentleman dressed in a khaki short-sleeved shirt, his hair parted and slicked to the side, stood behind them.

"I'm looking for a Sheila Atkins," the delivery man said, his hand still clutched around the neck of the vase, poised to pick it up in the event there was a need to do so in order that he might take them to their rightful owner.

"I'm Sheila," she said half-heartedly. "I wonder who sent me flowers?" she asked absently, reaching for the card that was stuck on the plastic pitchfork in the midst of the beautiful arrangement.

"They must be from someone special," the delivery-man said. Taking a look at Sheila, he continued, "And I can see why."

Sheila offered the gentleman a smile—her first for the day, however, after plucking the card and reading Jamal's name, tears jumped from her eyes. How was she going to tell Jamal about the curse that had been placed on her?

"Sheila, girl, I know you're not just letting the phone ring," Phyllis said as she strolled up to Sheila's desk. "Has Victor shown up yet?"

"If he knows what's good for his dog ass, he'd do better to never show up here again. Anyway, the feds took all of his electronic equipment; I believe he's in worse trouble with them than he is with me."

"Don't let him off the hook. Sheila, you should have seen you in action yesterday. Crazy girl gone wild. You were waving that gun at Victor like it was going to be his last day on earth. It would've been great if he could've gotten a few bullets in his behind, but you had him going, girl."

"It's kind of funny, now that I sit back and think about it. You know what, Phyllis? I'm so glad I didn't kill him. As mad as I was and how intent I had been on seeing his sorry ass suffer, I couldn't do it."

"You need that condo paid for another month or two before he throws you and Jamal out." Phyllis laughed out loud.

"Phyllis, it had nothing to do with Victor paying for anything. Shoot, I'm not sure Jamal and I will even get married now that I've been sentenced with..." Sheila looked around to see if anyone was listening and then whispered, "With HIV." She sighed. "I'm not in love with Victor; in fact, I don't want another thing from him. My life has been shortened, and I'd rather spend what time I have left on this earth fighting this disease than sitting in a jail cell, while Victor eats dirt."

"That's the spirit, girl. You've got a fighting chance to win this thing, Sheila. There are medicines that can prolong your life. Look at Magic Johnson. He found out he was HIV positive in 1991; it's been almost seventeen years and the man is still alive and has built an empire since then."

Sheila smiled. "Thanks for the pep talk, Phyllis. I can always count on you to turn my negative self into a positive one."

"Hey, did you guys here about Christianson?" Phil Murray, one of the admissions counselors asked, walking toward Sheila's desk.

"What about Christianson?" Phyllis asked.

"What happened, Phil?" Sheila asked, her face full of worry.

"He's dead," Phil said.

"No!" Sheila shouted, bringing her hands to her face.

"Somebody hosed his body with bullets," Phil continued. "They found him late last night near some railroad tracks in Durham."

Sheila and Phyllis stood still, panic striking their bodies. Neither of the ladies moved, until Sheila began to shake her head.

"Dead? I don't believe it," Sheila stammered. "Anyway, how do you know?"

"It was announced on the radio."

Phyllis put the tips of her fingers in her mouth and began to gnaw on her fingernails. Sheila found her seat and plopped in it for the second time that morning. Only seconds ago, she and Phyllis had talked about Victor and what he deserved for what he'd done to her, but never had she considered their venting would turn out to be the real thing.

Scared eyes looked from Phyllis to Phil. "Are you absolutely sure?" Sheila wanted to know. "How did it happen? When did he die?"

"Calm down, Sheila," Phil said. "I know you're upset. Everyone knows that you and Mr. Christianson have a connection."

Phyllis grinned and turned her head away, trying to control the laughter that threatened to push its way outward, but it wasn't funny to Sheila. The affair she had with Victor was kept under tight wraps or so she thought. The only person who knew anything about her tryst was Phyllis. Sheila's eyes narrowed.

"I don't know what you're talking about," Sheila barked, her eyes bulging from their sockets.

"It's okay, Sheila. The only folks you need to worry about having your story is the *National Inquirer*; they do pay good money for a tidbit."

Laughter erupted from Phyllis but she quieted when Sheila gave her the evil look.

"Dead," Sheila said again as if the idea was foreign and absurd, dismissing Phil's innuendo. Hell, hadn't she fired a few shots at Victor less than twenty-four hours ago? But he ran from the house and Phil said he was found by some railroad tracks in Durham, which meant he was found somewhere other than at her place. Sheila breathed a sigh of relief, but she couldn't shake the coldness that ran through her body. The news made her shiver.

53

October 14, 2008

Hell's gate has burst wide open. I don't know if my scribble can articulate the week's events in as colorful a prose as it played out. My worst fears have been realized, but I feel that I may be responsible.

I don't even know where to begin. My mind is knotted up in so many places that even as I write, my thinking isn't clear. The one thing I can safely jot down is that my daughter, Afrika, will be all right, although we're not sure if her paralysis is temporary or permanent.

My loving and adoring husband came home from Germany to be with me during Afrika's illness. I believe Iraq and Afghanistan have twisted his mind. While Raphael will stop at nothing to take care of his family and keep us safe, his irrational behavior has been upsetting. He's like a lie detector analyzing pulses scoring those things in the negative that are questionable to him because they don't sit right in his mind's eye.

Poor John was dissected from head to toe when he came to visit Afrika at the hospital. Instead of Raf taking John's visit as it was, Raf acted as if I was trying to hide something from him…that I might have been attempting to renew a relationship with John.

Let me hold that thought a moment and think about what I just wrote. I may be the one writing more into this and may be blaming my husband falsely. Because truth be told, I was probably using John as a crutch, and yes, it was good to have someone near to help me go through this ordeal with Victor, even if he was an old flame that stirred up some emotions and caused an inner turmoil. But if the tables were turned, I don't think I'd be too receptive of an old flame of Raphael's coming into my daughter's hospital room.

Confusion, that's what this is. This Victor crap…this secret that has been so destructive. I can't believe I went and blurted it out to Brenda. I didn't do it to hurt her; she had to know because Victor has been ruthless in his efforts to get rid of Afrika and me. My baby was almost killed, but by the grace of God, she's still alive. But all of these events have made one confession after another burst at the seams. Lord, I didn't want Raphael to find out that he wasn't Afrika's biological father the way he did. Of course, if I could have kept the secret forever, I would have taken it to my grave.

I guess Brenda owed me…blurted the truth for all of God's children to hear, crashing down on the ears of the innocent who are now broken and hurt. Damn. Now Raf hates me, hates Victor and what my deception has caused him, although he hasn't come out and said it to my face. Instead he's acting out because his heart has been bruised, betrayed. But I know that man still loves me because he wouldn't have taken my car and went looking for Victor half-cocked. He's a warrior, Army All You Can Be, a take-no-prisoners kind of man. And I believe Victor would have been a dead man if Raf had found him.

However, the truth is Victor snared him first. I have to give it to Victor. His survival skills almost measure up to Raf's. But I hope the police find that sorry-ass gutless wonder soon and get him off the street so he can't cause any more pain. He could have killed my husband tonight.

Thank God Raf got away from Victor. I had to call on faithful John to help me get my husband out of harm's way. I love them both—John, who will always be dear to my heart because he was the first man that I thought that I could absolutely marry, and Raphael, the man I love unconditionally and will go the ends of the earth for...my absolute soul mate.

I'm going to close now. I think I hear Raf moving around upstairs. It's eight-thirty in the morning. I couldn't sleep. I've been up since six, pondering the mess that I'm in. Didn't even go back to the hospital last night because we were a mess after picking up Raf from that woman's house in the middle of nowhere. God help me; help us.

Mimi Bailey

Hearing footsteps on the stairs, Mimi rushed from the chair she was sitting in and threw the journal in the drawer. She went to the stove and picked up the black tea kettle that matched the other appliances in the kitchen just as Raphael entered.

"Want some coffee?" Mimi asked in a sweet, soft voice.

Raphael paused and roamed the length of her as she stood in her soft pink thick cotton robe that covered a thin, white cotton gown and Mimi's best assets. "Instant coffee; I'd love some. I see you weren't able to sleep this morning."

"No," Mimi said in a slow breath. "I'm...I'm so overwhelmed with all that has happened in the last few days."

Raphael took a seat at the black marble table. He waited while Mimi placed the coffee crystals in the cup, add the hot water, stirred it, and brought it to him. He gently clutched her hand as she put the coffee down. "Why don't you sit down so we can talk about it?"

Mimi swallowed, not wanting Raf to see her anxiety... her fear. Yes, all that led up to Afrika's brush with death was now out in the open. What more was there to discuss? But she knew this moment would come, but she hadn't wished it to come so soon. She had yet to explain to Raphael that she was pregnant with Afrika when she met him, but how would she be able to explain that she didn't pawn her baby off on him? Was it love at first sight, probably not, but it was close because she felt something the moment she laid eyes on him. And yes, she saw an opportunity in Raphael Bailey to legitimize her unborn child.

Grabbing her own cup, Mimi fixed a cup of coffee and sat opposite Raf. She looked into his brown eyes for a hint of hatred, animosity, but seeing none, she dropped her eyes. She looked up again when he called her name.

"Mimi, thanks for saving my ass last night."

"You're my husband. I would do anything for you."

Raphael looked away and then back at Mimi. He reached over and put a hand over one of hers. "You may not believe this, but I fell for you the first time I saw you. I said to myself, now that's a Black princess. You seemed different from the other girls...not fast...not slow, and you weren't wearing your top down to your navel. But maybe I understand it all now...now that I know that you were with child.

"But having said all of that, the odd thing was that you slept with me on that first day I met you...without protection. Was it all an elaborate scheme to punish...I'm sorry, to find a father for your child?"

Mimi pulled her hand back and stared at Raphael. His words cut deep and hurt more than she could have imagined. However his words brought the truth to the light, although she would never in her wildest dreams utter them out loud. But Mimi had also felt something for Raf. He was kind and gentle, not just a gorgeous face along with a jaw-dropping body who could articulate words that beckoned her to lay her mother's teaching aside and crawl into bed with the first man who barked. She and Raf had talked most of the afternoon, and she learned that he was a college student who had plans for his life, that he wasn't going to waste it in the streets, he was going to be an officer in the Army and lead soldiers to battle and beyond. Those were the things he had shared with her that afternoon, and Mimi knew this was a man she could love. And so the decision was easily made when Raphael asked her to go to his room.

Mimi took a sip, put her coffee cup on the table and sighed. "It tears at my heart that we're at this crossroad." Mimi slid her hand over Raf's and squeezed it. "You are my life, and I love you with all of my heart. You are my man and I'm your girl, and that will never change.

"Although I'm guilty of entrapment or presenting myself falsely, I can truthfully say that I was smitten the first time I saw you. It wasn't that you were the finest brother on that campus and you gave me your eye, you represented yourself well. I don't know if you remember what we talked about that afternoon; I do. You spoke of how you were going to be a leader of men—that you were joining the ranks of the Army and you were going to be somebody. That turned me on, Raphael. And while my conscious decision to make love to you that same day may have bordered on deceit, by nightfall, I realized that I wanted you. Yes, I wanted you. You had demonstrated to me how a woman should be treated, even in the throes of lust. I'm sure you just didn't fall in love with me all of a sudden.

"I thought about you night and day, and the more time we spent together, I knew you were the one for me. I'm sure you're saying that I had run out of time and I had begun to show. Maybe that was part of it, but the truth is I had fallen in love with you. Yes, my baby had a father when you asked me to marry you and I agreed, but even to this day, you *are* Afrika's only father. Victor's name was forever erased from my mind...that is, until Afrika insisted on going to college at NCCU."

"Why didn't you tell me, Mimi? Don't you think I would have understood?"

"I wasn't taking any chances, Raf. After being with you those few months, I couldn't believe that God had sent me a good man. You don't understand the terrifying experience I endured with Victor. It was traumatic. I was violated. I didn't feel safe with anyone until I met you."

"What about John? He was the man of your dreams. You couldn't wait to look him up once you got here."

"That's not fair, Raf. Like we told you, I ran into John when I was out jogging. I haven't seen or talked to John in over nineteen years. I'm sure that you won't believe this, but John and I never had sex."

Raphael cleared his throat. "You're right, I don't believe you; especially since I've caught him looking at your booty on a couple of occasions."

"Raf, all men look at my booty. Didn't you?"

"But you gave me yours."

"But I didn't give John any...ever."

John tapped the coffee cup on the table.

"Don't scratch my table, man. You'll have to cough up fifteen hundred dollars to replace that marble."

"Fifteen what? For this table, Mimi?"

"Yes, because my husband deserves a fine place to sit and talk to his wife."

"Even if she's betrayed him?"

"Raphael, I'm sorry. I didn't mean to hurt you and..."

Brrng, brrng, brrng. Mimi reached for her BlackBerry. She looked at Raphael. "It's Brenda."

Mimi pressed the TALK button and said hello as Raphael took another sip of coffee and looked on. "What?"

Raphael put his cup down and cocked his head and waited for Mimi to say something else.

"Victor...Victor is dead?" Raphael's eyes became wide with fear while Mimi jumped up from the table, almost knocking over her cup of coffee. Her free hand grabbed the side of her head and then covered her mouth for only a second. "Oh my God. How? Are you all right? Hold on, Brenda; let me tell Raphael."

Mimi placed her hand over the speaker and turned to Raf, who was now standing next to her. "Did you hear that? Victor is dead...he was murdered. It happened last night or early this morning."

"I heard. Did Brenda say how and where it happened? Jesus, I was with him last night. Your car, Mimi."

"Oh my God. Let me get Brenda off the line. Turn on the TV to see what they're saying about it on the news."

"Okay."

Mimi uncovered the speaker. "Brenda, Raf and I are both so sorry. If there's anything we can do, please let us know."

"Mimi, I need you. I don't want to be alone."

Mimi looked at the phone and across the table at Raphael. "Sure, Brenda. Let me put some clothes on and I'll come right over."

"Hurry," Brenda said and hung up the phone.

Mimi ended the call and looked at Raf. "Jesus. Brenda wants me to come over. I'm not sure that I'm up to that, Raf. I've never even been to her house, and now that Victor is dead, I certainly have qualms about going there. It would be like walking in the valley of the shadow of death."

"What do you mean, Mimi?"

"It would be like walking into Victor's inner sanctum—the place where he came at the end of the day to rest his sorry ass. You said Victor was alive when you got away."

"I told you, I knocked the gun out of his hand, kicked him, and pushed him to the ground. After that, I took off running, Mimi, and that fool was very much alive. When I darted between Shirley's house and the neighbor's, I could hear someone running behind me—like they were following me. It may not have been Victor at all, but who else could it have been? All I know is he was not dead and he has your gun."

"We've got to remain calm, Raf. Who else do you think would have killed him?"

"You knew him; I didn't." Raphael turned to the small flat-screen that was mounted on the wall between two sets of oak cabinets. "Quiet, the local news is on. Let's see if they say anything about Victor."

"Around ten-thirty last evening, the body of Victor Christianson, Director of Admissions at North Carolina Central University, was found dead near a set of railroad tracks in Durham by a couple coming from a late-night worship service. Upon receiving a tip, Victor Christianson became a person of interest in the shooting of one of NCCU's cheerleaders, Afrika Bailey, that occurred after a football game last Saturday. Mr. Christianson failed to report to work this week, giving further cause for the police to suspect that he may have been linked to the shooting of Miss Bailey.

Raphael turned the volume down and turned to Mimi. "Do you want me to go with you to Brenda's?"

"No, baby. Let me go alone. I'll drop you at the hospital to check on Afrika before I go. Brenda needs a sister-girlfriend to talk to."

54

Brenda ended her phone call, tied the belt to her robe around her waist, and paced the floor as a nervous Asia rocked back and forth in one of the high-back chairs in her mother's bedroom. Tears shed earlier were now dry on Brenda's face and only thoughts of moving forward and getting on with her life consumed her. But in order to move forward, she had to close the lid on Victor and all of his garbage—his unfaithfulness, disloyalty, betrayal, and all of his countless other indiscretions. It was a shame that it was going to cost close to ten thousand dollars to shove all of it into the ground.

The realization of Victor's death hit her hard. It was so un-expected—a bad ending to a movie that started out so full of promise. And even as Brenda contemplated leaving him, knowing that she couldn't say goodbye on her own terms made it hurt much worse. And the first person she called was Mimi, her best friend, who always had a knack for soothing her disappointments.

As if she suddenly realized Asia was in the room, Brenda stopped pacing and looked at her daughter, who sat coiled up in the chair as if she was laced up in a straitjacket ready for the crazy house, her feet tucked underneath her body and her arms wrapped securely around her waist, wearing her red and pink cotton pajamas with the white hearts on them. Brenda went to Asia and knelt down on the floor in front of her, brushing her disheveled hair that looked like tumbleweed on a Texas plain away from her face, and brushed her cheeks as well with the back of her hand.

"Hey, baby," Brenda said in a soft voice, "It's going to be all right."

Asia glanced at Brenda, turned away and then looked back at her again. "It's going to be all right for whom, Mother? You? You hated Daddy. Trevor told me that you all have been arguing and that you were going to leave Daddy. I can't believe this is happening. I can't believe all the lies and secrets you've kept from Trevor and me and then…and then to find out that Nikki is my sister."

"Don't make this about you, Asia, because it isn't. I hate to speak ill of the dead, but your daddy was no saint by any stretch of the imagination. He was a whore."

"Shut up, Mother. My god, he's dead for heaven's sake."

"Heaven? Surely, your father will not be going there."

Asia unwrapped herself from her cocoon and prepared to leave the room. She stopped under the doorway and turned slightly to look at her mother. "It's your fault Daddy is dead. I blame you."

Brenda's hand began to fly. "Young lady, don't sass me;

it doesn't become you. All of my life, I've done nothing but protect you and Trevor from your father's deceitfulness and the mockery he made of our marriage. I'm the one people painted as a fool because I stayed with your father when all the world knew that the great Victor Christianson was bedding and laying seed with all the women in Durham."

"Mother, that's disgusting,"

"Yes, the hell it is."

Asia rolled her eyes at her mother. "You're jealous of Daddy's success."

"Listen here, Asia. You can try and disrespect me if you want, but his success was due to me. He was nothing on his own."

"Why are you talking about him like that, Mother? I don't understand you."

"Go sit down," Brenda said, pointing to the chair Asia had vacated, "and I'm going to explain it so there will be no questions left in your mind."

Asia stood still for a moment as if contemplating what Brenda had said. Then she turned completely around and plopped into the chair, placing her feet underneath her again. She stared at Brenda as if to say, *the clock is ticking. Talk.*

Brenda went and sat on the side of her bed, fluffed one of the decorative pillows with her hand, and looked at Asia. "You know that both your father and I loved you and Trevor unconditionally. That's what parents are supposed to do. You are our children. And in loving you, our job is to protect you from the elements by providing a roof over your head, food to eat, clothes on your back, and anything else to sustain life. And because we could afford to do so, we gave you more. In protecting you, it's also our job to keep you safe from the predators in the world—drugs, alcohol, and child molesters. In doing so, it may mean we have to protect you from family members or situations that may be detrimental to family survival— I'm sure you get what I mean."

"Yeah, since you're talking to me like I'm a ten-year-old."

Brenda looked at Asia and then dropped her eyes. "This is a sensitive issue for me, Asia. I can treat you as the adult you purport to be, but I'll break it on down for you if I need to."

Asia looked up at her mother and smiled. "I'm sorry, Mom. This thing with Daddy…his dying…Nikki…it's so overwhelming. This kind of stuff happens in other people's family, not ours. I…I can't believe it's happening to my family."

Brenda got up and rushed to Asia's side. Asia stood up and fell into her mother's embrace.

"We will get through this, baby," Brenda said, rubbing her fingers through Asia's hair. "We will get through this."

Then all of a sudden, Asia pulled away. She looked into her mother's eyes. "Who do you think killed Daddy?"

"That's the very question I asked myself, Asia. I don't

know how many enemies your father has out there, but he's done some questionable things in the past week. I have to tell you that I'm almost sure he tried to kill your friend. If I hadn't seen the gun with my own eyes that day, I might not have believed it. The bullet hole in the wall from where the gun went off last week is proof positive that something wasn't right."

"What? Daddy fired a gun in the house?"

"He was mad at something, and the way he tore out of here with that gun in his pocket at least an hour before Afrika was shot only leads me to believe the worst; especially since Mimi had only shared her dark secret the night before."

"Did you ever love Daddy?"

"Asia, I've always loved your father. Maybe too much. There are times when I've wondered where my life would've been if I hadn't fallen for Victor Christianson; especially knowing even as far back before we were married that he couldn't love just one woman and that it might be the death of me. But I had to have him. I was the one who came out on top. Despite all of his other conquests, Brenda won the trophy…He chose me to be his wife."

Brenda hugged Asia tight. "The greatest gift Victor gave me though was you and Trevor. You don't know how proud you both have made me."

Asia returned the hug and squeezed Brenda tight. "I love you, Mom. You're right; we'll get through this. I've never said this to you before, but here goes. I want to be just like you."

"Asia, you are a smart, beautiful young lady who will aspire to do great things. You will make your own mark in the world and will do it well. Know that your proud mother will always be near, cheering you on. Now go and get out of your pajamas. We have a full day ahead. Oh my goodness. Have you called Trevor?"

Asia sighed. "No, but we've got to tell him."

"Mimi's coming by. Maybe I'll get her to go to the school with me."

"I don't want her to come over here."

"Asia!"

"If she and Nikki hadn't come to Durham, Daddy would be alive."

"It isn't her fault. The old adage about your sins will find you out...it was your father's time. Mimi didn't even want to come to Durham; however, by denying Nikki to go to the school of her choice, she may have had to explain a harsh reality, and Mimi was trying to protect her. Your father has done some awful things, and if he hadn't been trying to cover it up, he might not be lying in the morgue at Duke."

"God, Mother, you say that like Daddy didn't exist in your life. I remember so many good times and I can't stand to hear you talk about him like that."

"All right, let's not talk about Victor in a negative light."

Asia sighed. "I'm not ready to see Nikki's mother. I'll go with you to tell Trevor. Nikki needs her mother at the hospital. We can handle it."

Brenda smiled. "Okay, baby. I'll call Mimi and tell her not to come. I needed a friend, and she was the first person I called."

"There will be time for that, but you've got me now. I'll help you call the relatives before word hits the street and they find out that way."

"We may not be able to stop it. I'm sure it's already on TV blast. This may sound crazy, but it was time for a family reunion."

"Mother, stop." Then Asia began to laugh. "You can't help it, I know."

"It sounds rather absurd, but in the midst of this tragedy, I need some good ole down-home country family loving."

Asia rolled her eyes into her head at her mother's suggestion. "If that's what you want."

"That's what I need."

"I think you need a hot shower and a massage."

"I need that, too."

very two feet in nice even rows, two metal desks sat
pushed together so that each occupant faced each
other. At each occupant's backside, a three-foot
aisle separated the next row of desks. Unlike the even
neat rows, the desks were cluttered full of case files and
police reports for cases not yet gone cold.

Detective Ernest Marshall picked up the cup of hot
coffee from his desk, blew softly on it, took a sip, and
sifted through his notes with his free hand, muttering
something to his partner, Samuels, about how Victor
Christianson, the suspect in a case they were working
on, had eluded their dragnets for days. However, a
single bullet from someone's gun had put him out of his
misery before they had a chance to get a foothold on the
case. He shook his head at the thought of all the legwork
he and Samuels had put in for someone to find their
perp dead, stretched out near a set of railroad tracks.
For sure, the case wasn't closed.

Looking into the folder, it hit Marshall. The case
was not closed because Victor Christianson had found
himself at the end of killer's handgun, and the evidence

already collected was only part of a larger picture. Christianson may have shot Afrika Bailey and the real truth might go with him to his grave, but given Victor's societal rap sheet, this case might get real ugly.

"Samuels," Marshall called out, taking another sip of coffee, "we've got ourselves a mess on our hands with this Victor Christianson murder."

"Yeah, Christianson had a long list of folks who are probably happy with his early demise," Detective Bryan Samuels replied.

"That's what I mean. The Afrika Bailey shooting was just the tip of the iceberg in this case. Christianson was up to his ears in alligators—hiding behind some nasty mess."

"Why do you say that?" Samuels asked, peeking his head over the top of the day's *News and Observer*.

"Only a hunch and my great intuition. I can't get Brenda Christianson's demeanor out of my mind when she spoke about her relationship with her husband."

"What was that?"

"What was that...are you listening, Samuels? Put the paper down so I can see your face. Isn't that why they placed our desks this way...so we could bounce ideas with our partners?"

Detective Samuels put the paper down on the desk, loosened his burgundy tie, pulled his body straight up in his chair, cocked his head, and stared at Detective Marshall. "So, what did she say?"

"Remember when she told us that she asked her husband for a divorce and he became visibly upset. She said he became angry and decided to leave the house and when he picked up his coat, a gun dropped out and it fired. She could be our prime suspect. We need the murder weapon."

"I don't think it was Christianson's wife. What about his secretary? What was her name?"

"Sheila...something—I don't remember right off hand."

"Sheila...yeah, that was it," Samuels said, filling in a word on the crossword puzzle he had started. "Sheila Atkins."

Yes, that's it, Sheila Atkins soon-to-be Mrs. Sheila Billops. She was trying to flirt with me until I told her that her coworkers said she and Christianson were an item. Also, she was hiding something because her demeanor immediately changed when I let her in on her little secret. If she doesn't have a motive, I'm sure she knows a lot more about Christianson's wheeling and dealing than I initially gave her credit. She deserves a follow-up visit.

"The computer we took from Christianson's office didn't yield a lot, except that he seemed to be consumed with Afrika Bailey," Marshall continued. "He had logged on to her records almost every day up to the day she was shot. I would most likely conclude that Ms. Bailey was his target, and with all that Mrs. Bailey told us, the puzzle pieces seem to fit."

"I still say the mother, Setrine Bailey, wanted Christianson put away bad. She had a real hatred for the man."

"You blame her?" Marshall took a sip of his coffee and put it down. "Coffee got cold that quick."

"No, I can't say that I do. She told Rathmusen at the hospital that Christianson stalked her, came to her house, and threatened her—told her to leave town or else."

"But look, Samuels, if she was willing to tell that to Rathmusen, why would she go out and kill Christianson? For sure, she'd realize that we'd be after her before the clock struck another second after we found out Victor was dead. She's divulged a lot of information to us, which could ultimately place her as the number one suspect on our most wanted list."

"True, however, you hit on my point. If she believes that we wouldn't point the finger at her because there is no earthly way we'd believe she did it since she's been so forthcoming with all this information, guess what?"

"What?"

"She would kill that sucker in a heartbeat and leave it to us to figure it out."

"I don't think she'd be that stupid."

"Umph."

"Marshall, Samuels," a close, cropped curly head, dark-skinned Idris Elba look-alike called out, as he entered the two detectives' space.

Marshall nearly spilled his coffee while Samuels laughed, not realizing the intruder was that close on him without being heard. "What is it, Smith?" Marshall asked, annoyed.

"Got what is believed to be the murder weapon," Detective Chad Smith replied in his robot voice.

"What murder weapon?" Samuels asked, making Smith spell it out. "And I don't have all day."

"The Christianson murder," Smith replied. "Twenty-two-caliber. It's registered to a Setrine Bailey. It was picked up from the gun shop the day of the murder."

"What? Where is it, now?" Marshall asked.

"Ballistics," Smith said.

"I can't see the mother of that shooting victim...ah, ah, Afrika Bailey, killing the man, although she had every reason to want to see him behind the jailhouse," Marshall said, with a small hint of irritation in his voice. "What perplexes me is that she purchases a gun that she picks up on the day of the murder but has done everything she knows to arm us with the kind of information we needed to pick up Christianson to do something as stupid as murder the dude."

"Maybe we were taking too long, and she got tired of waiting. Had to do the job herself."

"Yeah, that's a reasonable explanation, Samuels, but I don't think she did it, I don't care what you think. She was praising God that her daughter was going to live."

"Well, the gun definitely belonged to a woman," Smith said, not wanting to be upstaged.

"Now how did you deduce that, Smith?" Samuels asked.

"Would a man buy a gun with a pearl handle?"

"You gotta point there, kid," Marshall plugged in.

"Watch who you callin' kid. I might not be ten seconds from claiming my retirement check like you old fogies, but I'm not your kid."

"Forty-three ain't old," Marshall said. "I can still make women whisper my name."

"That's why you had that welt on your face yesterday?" Samuels cracked. He began to laugh and Smith joined him, doubled over in laughter at the sight of Marshall. "Margie slapped the smile off your face the other night during one of your hot, erotic dream episodes."

Marshall jumped up from his seat. "Shut the hell up, Samuels. You wouldn't know what to do with a woman if you had one. If you must know, that welt was the remnant of good sex—rough and tumble good sex."

Samuels looked at Smith and Smith looked back at Samuels. They grabbed their sides and burst out in laughter, causing the other detectives in the room to stop what they were doing and cash in on the comedy act. Marshall looked at all of them, grabbed his jacket, swung it over his shoulder and began to move away from his desk. He stopped at the end of the row and looked back at Samuels.

"Don't forget, we have a dead man lying in the morgue. Call me when they ID the prints on the gun." Marshall turned and walked away, the laughter trailing behind him.

56

Mother and daughter held hands as they entered Duke Medical Center, prepared to identify the remains of their loved one. They were met by Dr. Bluefield, the Emergency Room chief who took them to the morgue to view the body, which they identified to be that of Victor Christianson. Full of emotion at the sight of her father, Asia left the room in a hurry and headed for the nearest bathroom. Finding an empty stall, she cried until her tears were spent.

"The remains will be taken to the coroner's office for autopsy," Dr. Bluefield said to Brenda.

"Do you have to do that?" Brenda asked, tears rolling down her cheeks.

"It's procedure, ma'am. This is a homicide case, but it's apparent to us that he died of a bullet wound to his heart."

Brenda grabbed her chest and began to hyperventilate. "Oh my God, oh my God," Brenda said over and over.

"I'll walk you back to the ER, and we'll have a counselor to come and talk with you in the family room," Mrs. Christianson. "Someone will be along any minute. You may want to find your daughter first."

Brenda nodded her head at Dr. Bluefield without saying a word. She took one last look at Victor lying on the steel bed. She closed her eyes and clasped her hands over her face and broke down.

The walls of the hospital seemed to close in as Brenda and Asia walked in silence back to the entrance to get as far away from the hospital's sterile environment and the knowledge that Victor's remains were temporarily housed there. They walked past a number of people who didn't have the foggiest idea about the pain they were in because those people were attending to their own agenda, which may have included their own kind of pain. Brenda heaved a sigh of relief when she saw the light shining through the glass of the double doors. Escape was near.

As Brenda and Asia reached the turnstile, they had to wait until they were able to enter. But neither had recognized the two people already in the turnstile until they met face to face.

Mimi jerked back as did Raphael who was right behind her, surprised to see Brenda and Asia waiting to exit the hospital. "Brenda," Mimi mouthed softly, taking her hands and pulling her into a warm embrace. "I'm sorry about your loss."

Brenda's smile was weak. "Thanks, Mimi," she whispered in her ear. They released each other and it was Raphael's turn to give Brenda a hug.

"If there's anything we can do, let us know," Raphael said. "We're on our way to see Afrika."

Asia ignored Mimi and Raphael and went through the turnstile and waited outside for Brenda.

"It's going to take Asia a while to sift through her pain," Brenda offered. "Don't take offense; it's been hard on her—her father being killed and finding out about you and Victor, Mimi," Brenda lowered her eyes, "and that Afrika is her sister."

Mimi offered a half-smile but didn't look at Raphael, who stood by expressionless. "We understand. We've got to check on Afrika. I'll stop by later and bring you a dish."

"Thanks, Mimi," Brenda said. She watched as Mimi and Raphael strolled out of sight. Then she turned and saw Asia standing outside with a scowl on her face. "Victor didn't deserve to die," Brenda mouthed to herself, "but what goes around comes around." She walked through the turnstile to a waiting Asia.

57

"Has anyone seen Marshall?" one of the detectives in the row shouted. "I've got a phone call for him! The person at the end of the line says it's important!"

"I'll take it," Samuels said. "Marshall went out to get some air."

"Okay, line two!" the detective shouted.

Samuels picked up the phone and tapped into line two. "Hello, this is Detective Samuels."

"I told the other cop I wanted to speak to Detective Marshall. If you aren't Detective Marshall, I don't want to speak to you."

"Ma'am…"

"My name is Miss Ellen Pomeroy."

"Miss Pomeroy, Detective Marshall is my partner, and he's out of the office at the moment. Anything you want to say to him you can say to me."

"I don't like this one bit…but if you're the only somebody I can talk to, I guess you're it. Are you sure you're Detective Marshall's partner?"

"Ma'am, I'd swear on the Bible if I wasn't a religious man, but you can rest assured that I will take good notes and get the message to Detective Marshall."

"Good. You have a pen and pencil? You better be ready to write. See, the feller that they found dead near some railroad tracks in Durham…"

"Yes, what about him?" Samuels asked with renewed interest.

"I'm getting to it. Don't push me. Anyways, I've seen that feller over at the condos where I live. My wonderful grandson who's on one of those NBA basketball teams put me up in this nice place, and I ain't got nothing to do but watch the soaps and look out my window."

"Uh-huh," Samuels said under his breath, hoping Miss Pomeroy would hurry and get on with her story.

"Anyways, that feller came around here a lot last week, but on yesterday, there was a big fight between him and the girl he sees over here."

"Miss Pomeroy, are you sure it's the same man? Was it Victor Christianson?"

"Sho I'm sure. They had his picture covering the whole television screen. I was mad because I was trying to solve the puzzle on *Wheel of Fortune*. I had the answer, but them rude TV announcers cut into my program and started talkin' about the man that got murdered. Anyways, getting back to the story, I hear what I think is gunshots and a few minutes later the man comes staggering down the stairs holding onto his arm, shouting obscenities at the girlfriend. I mean to tell you, he had a filthy mouth, but hers weren't no better."

"Do you know the name of the woman you call…his girlfriend?"

"Yes, I do. She's really nice, though. Helped me a time or two with my groceries. Took them all the way into my condo and put them up for me, too. I hate to squeal on her."

"But you already have, Miss Pomeroy, by calling in with the information about the man who was killed. We need to speak with this woman; she may be a lead in our case."

"Well, I hope she isn't in too much trouble because that Christianson feller was most definitely alive when he left her place; although she kept shouting that she should've killed him like he killed her. Now, I didn't understand it because as I said, both of them were good and alive. Anyways, her name is Sheila Atkins."

"Oh, Ms. Sheila Atkins," Samuels said, wishing he hadn't been so demonstrative upon recognizing Sheila's name.

"Did I say something wrong?" Miss Pomeroy asked.

"No, Miss Pomeroy, you have been most helpful. I will need your telephone number in the event Detective Marshall needs to follow-up and talk with you further. Would that be okay?"

"Oh, yes. My number is 555-1520."

Miss Pomeroy had warmed to Samuels and figured he'd ask his next question. "Miss Pomeroy, if we need for you to testify in a court of law to what you just told me, would you be willing to do that?"

"Testify…in court…like they do on *Perry Mason*? Why sho, honey. Just tell me what day to be there. Give me enough time, though, so I can get my grandson to buy me a new dress. I want to look real pretty when the judge tells me to 'Answer the question, Miss Pomeroy.'"

"Again, you've been very helpful, Miss Pomeroy. We will call you if we need to speak with you further. Have a good day."

"You too, young feller. Don't leave out anything when you tell Detective Marshall."

"I'll make sure I tell him the story exactly as you told it to me," Samuels said with a grin on his face.

"All right. I'm through. I've done my civic duty for today."

"Goodbye, Miss Pomeroy."

Samuels set the phone down, put his feet up on his desk, and reflected on the phone call from Miss Pomeroy. It certainly could be a lead in the case, although Christianson was very much alive at the time of the incident Miss Pomeroy spoke about. But it might certainly be a key in the Afrika Bailey shooting. "Uhm," Samuels hummed to himself.

"Uhm…what's that all about?" Marshall asked, coming up behind Samuels. He placed his jacket on the back of his chair and sat down. Samuels remained cool, kept his feet on top of his desk until Marshall stared him down, and then removed them.

"Got an interesting call a moment ago. And you won't believe what about."

"Shoot. Give me the four-one-one," Marshall said.

Samuels gave Marshall the low down just as Miss Pomeroy had told it to him. Marshall's eyebrows shot up to his forehead when Samuels got to the part about Sheila and Christianson having a fight at her condo and that gunshots were heard.

"Get your coat. We're going to the campus to interview the lovely Ms. Sheila Atkins. I'm anxious to see how much flirting she's going to do this time."

Samuels laughed. "She was a looker."

"She ain't the kind of woman that's gonna look at a white boy; especially you. Even if she did, you wouldn't get to first base. I can tell Ms. Sheila Atkins the future Ms. Sheila Billops is a feisty one. Back in the day, we'd call her a brick house with nothing but fire and desire."

"How did you get that welt on your face, Marshall?" Samuels began to laugh again.

"Shut the hell up, Samuels," Marshall billowed. "It's none of your business."

Before Samuels could shoot off another word, Detective Chad Smith bounced into the corridor where Marshall and Samuels stood.

"What is it, Smith?" Marshall asked.

"Ballistics ID'd the prints on the gun found near Christianson's body."

"Well, don't just stand there; tell us who they belong to," Samuels pushed.

Smith's nostrils flared and he gave Samuels a *don't work my nerve today* look. "There may have been several people who handled the gun. Christianson's prints were definitely on it. Ballistics was able to get an ID of a fingertip that didn't belong to Christianson but did belong to Raphael Bailey."

"Who's Raphael Bailey?" Samuels asked.

"The father of the kid…the cheerleader that got shot," Marshall offered. "Smith said earlier that the Bailey woman picked the gun up on the day of the murder. Could be…she showed it to her husband, which would explain his fingerprint on the gun but it doesn't explain how Victor Christianson's fingerprints got on it."

"Yeah, his prints were all over the gun like he had a good grip on it," Smith continued. "Only thing, the fingerprints were smudged by something—maybe someone was trying to conceal their prints."

"A third person," Marshall said. "Thanks, Smith. We're on our way to question another person of interest who I believe is in-directly linked to this case, and then we're going to make a visit to see the Baileys."

"Here's the address for Mrs. Bailey," Smith said, handing the paper with the information on it to Marshall. "I'll keep you posted if anything else comes up."

"Do that," Samuels said, getting in the last word.

58

Butterflies flitted about Sheila's empty stomach, causing it to rumble every two minutes. Police were scattered throughout her section, collecting what they called possible evidence and interviewing members of the administration. They had yet to ask her any more questions, but she was grateful. It might have been that what she offered to the black and white detectives earlier had been enough.

Unable to concentrate on her work, Sheila got up to go use the bathroom but was happy to see Phyllis as she rounded the corner. With the back side of her hand, Phyllis shooed Sheila back to her seat as if she had been sent to deliver a secret message for Sheila's ears only.

"What's up?" Sheila asked, her nerves getting the best of her. "I can't think with all this extra activity going on around here."

"Girl, they're questioning everybody about Victor's behavior in the last few weeks. Hmph, I've got nothing to say because I don't know anything. Not a thing to tell."

"I keep thinking about what happened at the house. What if he died from one of the bullets I clipped him with?"

"Sheila, you're going to worry yourself to death. Victor would have been laying on the sidewalk if you had inflicted any bodily harm on him. If I recall, your beautiful walls have now become bullet art." Phyllis let out a small laugh.

"Phyllis, it's not funny at all. My stomach is all in knots from worry."

"Girl, you have nothing to be worried about. The police have to find the murder weapon, and once they do, you'll be home free."

"Easy for you to say. I was the one playing the mad-woman, acting like I was Jessica James and the outlaws."

"Sheila, you are too funny."

"Phyllis, I'm not laughing. What if the bullet I hit Victor with killed him?"

"If that's the case, how is it that they found him on the other side of Durham?"

"Phyllis, I don't know. Somehow I feel partially responsible for Victor's demise."

"Listen up, Sheila, you are still carrying the HIV virus and Victor doesn't get off because his slimy ass is dead in somebody's morgue. His time was coming, but I don't believe you were the one that brought that monster to his end."

"You're right."

"I know I am. So chin up and stop pouting like some-body stole your knock-off Prada bag. Guess what? You don't have to move out of your condo."

"Phyllis, you know you ain't right."

"I got you to smile, didn't I?"

"Yeah, but only for a second. Don't turn around."

"What is it, Sheila?" Phyllis asked, twisting her body so she could see what had interrupted Sheila's developing good mood.

"I told you not to turn around."

"Look, girl, got to go. Ring me later."

Sheila watched as Phyllis sashayed away from her desk and Detectives Marshall and Samuels approached her desk. She noticed how Marshall eyed her, outlining her body with his eyes. He wasn't her type, even if she were to put out an APB on Match.com for a man to wine and dine her. She'd only given him a sideways glance because some of his handsome was still there and he typified the kind of man Phyllis would fall for.

Sheila pushed her nervousness to the center of her stomach and extended a hand. "So you two gentlemen are back. What can I do for you this time?"

"You seem very confident in yourself, Ms. Sheila Atkins soon to be Mrs. Sheila Billops," Marshall said, studying her body language closely.

Sheila dropped her head back in surprise. "Scared of you. Your memory serves you well."

"That it does, Ms. Atkins. I remember asking you about the last time you saw Victor Christianson, too. Do you remember what your response was?"

There was a pause and Sheila exhaled, sizing Marshall up while straying only a second to peek at Samuels who appeared uninterested. She tried to put a finger on the angle Marshall was coming from, but whatever it was, she could smell the trap.

"Since you're all-knowing, why don't you tell me what I said?" was Sheila's response.

Marshall smiled. "I like you."

Sheila looked between him and Samuels without breaking a crack on her face. Her nerves were unraveling and whatever they had come for, she wanted them to get to it and be on their way.

"How may I help you detectives?" Sheila asked again.

This time Samuels spoke up. "In the event you are unaware, your boss, Victor Christianson was found murdered last night." Sheila nodded. "We received a call today about an argument that transpired between you and the deceased, Victor Christianson, on yesterday that had gunfire to go with it."

A lump formed in Sheila's throat and she swallowed hard. "An argument between me and Victor Christianson? He didn't come to work yesterday," Sheila hastily said.

"Who said it was at work, Mrs. Atkins?" Samuels said, stepping up to the side of her desk and sucking up the air between them.

Sheila sighed. "Damn, damn, damn, damn." Tears began to form in her eyes and she grabbed her face before she could make a puddle on the desk. "I didn't kill Victor Christianson. Yes, I saw him yesterday evening when he stopped by my house."

"So why don't you tell us what happened," Marshall

said, pulling up a chair that sat off to the side of Sheila's desk. "We've got plenty of time."

Sheila dropped her head and wiped the water that kept streaming down her face. "It all started when I received a letter in the mail from the health department. The letter contained the results of my blood work. Jamal and I were supposed to get married this weekend.

"When I opened the letter and read the contents, I thought someone had blown my brains out at close range. There on the piece of paper in black and white were the words 'HIV positive.'"

Marshall stiffened in his seat and Samuels took a step backward.

"I was livid, mad, pissed off, angry…because I understood too well what the words meant," Sheila continued. "It was like telling a cancer patient they had only two weeks to live. It was a death sentence and there was only one person who could be responsible."

"How can you be sure?" Marshall asked with a straight face and without sympathy in his words.

"Because, detective, Victor was the only person I'd been with for the last five years, except for Jamal. And contrary to what you might believe, I'm not a promiscuous woman."

"I'm sure you were aware that Mr. Christianson was a married man."

"I was, however that doesn't make me promiscuous."

Marshall rolled his eyes in Samuels' direction. Samuels shrugged his shoulders slightly and spoke up.

"Why couldn't this Jamal guy have given you ahh… the sentence of death, as you call it?"

"Because he and I used protection," Sheila said, not happy with this line of questioning.

"That's strange to me," Samuels countered. "You and Christianson didn't use protection, but Jamal comes along, and you use protection. Makes no sense to me. What makes him better than Christianson?"

"Because," Sheila began with clenched teeth, then tried to soften it a little, "Victor wanted sex in the natural. He didn't like rub…I mean prophylactics. And, of course, I went along with it because he set me up in my condo and who was I to complain? Yes, I enjoyed it, too. Now, Jamal was someone I met six months ago, and while things started out innocent enough, we fell in love."

"So you had a sugar daddy you strung along and a real man that you were going to marry until you received the bad news, news so bad you wanted to hurt the person who had done this horrible deed that the letter indicated to you," Marshall cut in.

"You want to know the truth, detectives?" Sheila jumped up from her seat and Samuels jumped back, not sure what Sheila was about to do. She wagged her finger at them and made Marshall get up from his seat. "Hell yeah, I wanted to kill Victor. He deserved the same sentence he gave me—death. I was angry because I finally found someone who loved me for me and we were going to be married. And then I received this letter stating I was HIV positive and to notify my sexual partners.

Partners? Hell, Victor was the only person I was having casual sex with on the regular without protection. I wonder if his wife knows?"

"Someone should tell her," Marshall said, staring straight into Sheila's soul.

"I don't deserve to die. I'm a good person. I'm a good worker—check my performance appraisals." Sheila huffed and sighed. "I didn't kill him. I have a witness."

"Witness?" Samuels asked.

"Yes, my co-worker, Phyllis…the girl who walked out as you all were coming in," Sheila said in a daze. "She was at my house when Victor stopped by and she witnessed the whole thing. Yes, I fired some shots at Victor, but that was the first time I had ever fired a gun. Check my house; I'm sure the bullets are still lodged in the walls."

Sheila stopped and then sat down in her chair. She looked like she was thinking. Then she looked at the two detectives who were looking anxiously at her. "I did hit his arm or elbow. Victor screamed like a flying monkey, and that's when he decided to take his ass out of my house. He started cursing at me, and do you know what he was worried about? You won't believe it."

"Try us," Marshall said, sitting back down in the seat he had vacated.

"The asshole was mad because I made a hole in his designer jacket. Can you believe that?"

Samuels began to laugh and so did Marshall. Sheila looked at them and hunched her shoulders. "He did. And he called me a bunch of dirty names."

"I understand you called him a bunch back," Samuels said, still laughing.

"Nosey Miss Pomeroy tell you that? I know it was her; she has nothing else to do but get in people's business. But she got the story right."

"She likes you a lot," Samuels said. "In fact, she didn't want you to get into any trouble."

"She means well," Sheila said. "Her grandson put her in a nice condo and left her there. I don't think she has many visitors."

"Where's the gun you used to shoot Christianson?" Marshall asked.

"At my house."

Marshall looked at Samuels and then said, "Ms. Atkins, I believe you're telling the truth, but we need to see the gun and the bullet holes at your house."

"I'm ready to get this over with; let's go," Sheila said.

"It's long from being over, Miss Atkins," Samuels said. "We're just getting started. One thing may lead to another. We need to talk to your co-worker."

Panick was stricken on Sheila's face. "I don't want to get her into any trouble."

"She's a witness and we have to ask her a few questions. We need to see if she remembers the story as you did. It's all part of our preliminary investigation," Samuels said.

Marshall and Samuels did not move from their respective places. "We need to talk to this Phyllis now," Marshall said to Sheila.

"I'll call her."

59

Phyllis' story jibed with Sheila's. Not much was gained from her interview that would incriminate either her or Sheila in Victor's death. Obtaining Sheila's gun would help to rule her out completely, but then there was the gun found near the scene of the crime and registered to Setrina Bailey that disturbed Marshall more.

Detectives Marshall and Samuels trailed Sheila to her condo. The area south of North Carolina Central University and across Interstate 40 had become a thriving community in the past five years. Small corporate offices, a large mall considered to be one of North Carolina's premier shopping and dining places, the spattering of medium to luxury condos and not to mention the proximity to the Research Triangle Park and the Raleigh/Durham Airport sprung up from out of nowhere and made the area an allure for people newly coming to the area.

"Fifteen, twenty minutes at the max," Marshall said as they turned into the entrance to the condos where Sheila lived. "Nice place and I'm sure she couldn't afford it on her salary."

"She's someone's sugar baby all right," Samuels put in.

They followed Sheila until she pulled her car into a small garage, and by the point of her finger, pulled into a space marked VISITORS. Marshall and Samuels got out of their vehicle and followed close behind Sheila, taking in the landscape and its manicured vegetation that smelled of money.

"That must be Miss Pomeroy's place," Samuels pointed. "Can't miss much at the Atkins' condo from her vantage point."

"Got that right!" Marshall hollered back over his shoulder, as he paused to get some air as he climbed the stairs.

Sheila opened the front door and ushered the detectives inside.

"You can sit, if you like. Don't be scared. I've got lemonade if you want something to drink," Sheila offered.

Marshall rolled his eyes and looked at Samuels. "I'll pass," Marshall said.

"Me, too," Samuels chimed in.

Sheila turned to look at them. "It's not because I'm HIV positive, is it?"

"No," both Marshall and Samuels said simultaneously. They looked at each other and smiled when Sheila turned her back.

"I'll be back with the gun," Sheila said.

"We aren't going anywhere," Marshall said as he moved from where he stood to the wall in front of him. Just as Sheila had so colorfully told them, what looked to be four bullet holes dotted the wall in an abstract way, almost as if it was the intention of the person who put them there.

Marshall reached in his pocket and pulled out a pocketknife and a plastic baggie and began to dig into the wall. Samuels walked over to the wall to see what Marshall was doing. One, two bullets were uncovered, and Marshall dropped them into the baggie. Before he was able to excavate any more, both Marshall and Samuels turned in the direction of the shrill voice.

"Hey!" Sheila screamed. "What in the hell are you doing?"

"Saving your ass from the gas chamber," Marshall mumbled. Samuels snickered.

"I heard that and it's not funny. You're going to have to pay for enlarging that hole in the wall," Sheila said, swinging the gun at the trigger on her middle finger.

A frown formed on Marshall's face. "Ms. Atkins soon to be Ms. Billops, the wall was already in need of repair when we entered your dwelling. Why don't you let me have the gun before you shoot any more holes in the wall."

"Suit yourself," Sheila said.

Sashaying to where Samuels stood, Sheila reluctantly dropped the gun into the plastic bag Samuels held open. The weight of the gun made the plastic bag sag, causing Samuels to almost drop it. With a smirk on her face, she watched as Samuels recovered from his clumsiness. "And you call yourself a detective?"

Marshall laughed and patted Samuels on the back. "Stay close, Ms. Atkins," Marshall said, trying to control his laughter. "We appreciate your cooperation, and you will be hearing from us again. Now, let me get the rest of the bullets out of the wall so we can analyze them and the gun and clear your name, if indeed that's the case."

Sheila looked in the detectives' direction, but it was almost as if she was staring straight through them. And almost as if she'd reconciled in her mind what had her in a daze, she looked at them with pointed eyes. "I didn't kill Victor. I should have but I didn't… I couldn't. It wasn't in me, although I wanted him to feel the pain that I was feeling after receiving that notice in the mail." And from out of nowhere, she burst into tears. "Why me, Lord? Why me?"

AFRIKA WAS SOUND ASLEEP WHEN MIMI AND RAPHAEL entered her room. They stood on either side of the bed and hovered over her, allowing somber faces to turn into a smile. As if on cue, Afrika began to stir, stretching her arm slowly upward. Then she opened her eyes, blinking and batting her eyelids until recognition set in. Mimi was the first to reach over and kiss her on the forehead, followed by Raphael.

"Mommy, Daddy, where have you been? Mommy, I waited for you to come back, but you never did."

Mimi's eyes shifted to Raphael and back to Afrika. "I had

every intention of returning to the hospital," Mimi said, "but your father needed me in a worse way last evening."

"Why, what happened?"

"Nothing for you to worry your pretty little head over," Raphael chimed in. "We want you to focus on full recovery."

"How can I accomplish that when I'm worried about you guys?"

"Why would you be worried about us?" Mimi asked.

Afrika wasn't sure how to respond. She licked her dry lips and focused on the blank screen on the television set that was perched high up on a brace in a corner of the room. Her voice was soft when she finally opened her mouth to reply. "Are you and Daddy mad at each other?" Afrika made herself say.

Raphael leaned against the wall and glanced at Mimi. He kept his mouth shut, probably in anticipation of Mimi's answer.

"No, baby, we're not mad at each other. Your father and I have discussed things…" Mimi looked at Raf, who dropped his head. "We love each other and we love you. You will always be our baby." Mimi paused, not exactly happy with her choice of a word. "We're going to be fine; we only want you to get well."

"Is that true, Daddy?"

Afrika caught Raphael off-guard. He looked at her, came over and sat on the bed, offered her a smile, and kissed her on her forehead. "Your mother is right. You'll always be our baby, and…we'll always be a family." He picked up Afrika's hand and squeezed it. "I love you, baby girl."

"I love you, too, Daddy." Afrika turned toward her mother. "I love you, Mommy." Mimi smiled. "I've got something to tell you."

Mimi and Raf looked at each other, alarm written on their faces. "What is it, Afrika?" Raphael asked.

"Stop frowning; it's good news." Afrika smiled as her mother and father's countenance changed. "I wiggled my toes today."

"Thank You, Jesus!" Mimi hollered. Tears of joy immediately ran down her face.

"Thank You for answering our prayer," Raphael mumbled, clasping his hands together as if he was about to pray. "Thank You."

A faint knock at the door caused the trio to turn their heads toward the sound like a precision drill team. Raphael got up to answer the knock just as the two detectives pushed the door in. Tears of joy were interrupted.

"Detectives Marshall and Samuels," Marshall said as the two flipped out their badges for the obviously surprised Raphael.

"Okay," Raphael said apprehensively.

Marshall and Samuels moved further into the room and nodded in Mimi's direction. "Mr. and Mrs. Bailey?" Marshall asked.

"Yes," Raphael said, his lone word short and blunt.

The detectives looked at Afrika, covered by the thin white and blue bedspread whose eyes were transfixed on them, waiting to hear like her parents the cause for the interruption.

"We need for the both of you to come to police head-quarters with us and answer some questions," Samuels said to Mimi and Raphael.

Raphael looked at the pair with suspicion. "What is this about?"

"If you have to ask, Mr. Bailey…"

"Daddy, what is he talking about?" Afrika asked, trying to sit up and digest what was taking place.

Mimi watched Raphael as he contemplated what to say. They hadn't told Afrika yet about Victor, but the time had come. She held Afrika's hand, wanting to shield her from all the pain she'd experienced in the past week, but the truth was the light—it was what it was—and there was no way of getting around it. She believed Raf had nothing to do with Victor's murder, and she would stand behind him no matter what.

"Mr. Christianson, Asia's father, was found dead late last night according to the news," Raphael said. He looked up and saw the detectives analyzing him, no doubt checking his body language, what he had said and how he had told Afrika that Victor was dead.

"Dead? How? First I get shot, and then I find out that…" Afrika paused. She looked at the two detectives, who were watching her.

"What did you find out, Ms. Bailey?" Marshall asked in a calm, reassuring voice.

Mimi and Raphael stood still. Afrika searched for support from her parents, and then turned back to face Detective Marshall. She closed her eyes and let out a long breath. "I found out that Mr. Christianson is my biological father."

Marshall and Samuels looked at each in amazement at the new bit of information they had been thrown. "When did you find this out, Ms. Bailey?" Samuels asked.

"Yesterday."

"Yesterday as in yesterday morning, afternoon, early evening?" Marshall pushed.

"Okay, detective," Raf cut in. "She said she found out yesterday. My daughter is ill; please be a little more sensitive to that fact. "

"It's routine, Mr. Bailey. "

Afrika sighed again. She didn't even look Detective Samuels in the eyes. She pushed the answer from her mouth to be rid of it. "Yesterday morning."

"Thank you for being so cooperative," Samuels said.

"Mr. and Mrs. Bailey," Marshall began, "if you go with us now, maybe we can have you back with your daughter before long."

The moment Mimi dreaded had come to pass. Deep in the back of her mind, she knew the police would be knocking at their door. There was the matter of her car and her gun. Both were still missing. Even after reporting it stolen, somehow she knew it might be tied into Victor's death. She and Raphael had stayed awake most of the night talking about it.

Raphael kissed Afrika on the forehead and whispered something to her. Mimi did likewise, and they followed the detectives out of the room.

60

Family and friends converged on the Christianson household bearing casserole dishes and large tin pans filled with fried chicken, honey-baked ham, collard greens, corn, macaroni and cheese, and dinner rolls. Brenda's two sisters, Mabel and Tracey, worked the kitchen like it was their domain—as if the stainless steel chef's kitchen had been installed for their exclusive use. They heated food and dished it out—limiting folks to the amount of food they could put on their Styrofoam plates to shooing the small children who took to running in the house absent of their parents' immediate attention.

Someone said something funny, and Brenda laughed along with the rest of them, as a group sat in the family room reminiscing. Brenda loved family gatherings, and although the occasion was a sad one, the chit and chatter down memory lane was good for her nerves. The last few weeks were laden with one bad situation after another, even though Brenda's heartache had lasted most of her adult years. For a moment her mind wandered as she recaptured the few precious moments with Victor when their lives seemed to be grand and unstoppable. But the moment was short-lived as she recounted Mimi's subtle announcement…that Victor had raped her nineteen years ago and her daughter's best friend was her sister.

The doorbell rang and a new face emerged. Brenda noticed that the sullenness that had become a part of Asia's demeanor had evaporated…vanished into thin air. The young man, Asia's new interest, had come by to lift her spirits and take her mind off the tragedy for a moment. He was tall and handsome, and while Brenda had met him only briefly in Afrika's hospital room, anyone who could make Asia smile was a welcome sight.

Trevor was another matter. He was withdrawn and stayed out of sight. Having to go to Trevor's high school and deliver the terrible news to him was the most painful moment for Brenda aside from hearing the news herself. There weren't any tears, but Trevor seemed to be mad at the world, retreating from everyone. He didn't want to talk about the events of Victor's death, and Brenda kept the television off so they didn't have to be reminded. But she had wondered if the police were close to finding Victor's killer.

"I brought you a plate of food," Mabel said to Brenda, handing her the plate. "You need to eat something."

Brenda looked at the plate and smiled. "Thanks, Sis. I'm not hungry, but I'll eat it because you fixed it."

"You better because if you had refused, Tracey and I were going to gang up on you and make you eat. I was going to hold you down and Tracey was going to pry your mouth open and shove the food in."

That made everyone laugh, and Brenda lightened up and tasted the macaroni and cheese. "Umm, good. Somebody put their foot in this mac and cheese," Brenda said.

"I did!" Cousin Cora hollered.

At that announcement, everyone got up and fled to the kitchen to get seconds. Brenda looked around and smiled. Her family was there. Victor's mother, father, and siblings hadn't come by. She'd spoken to her mother-in-law, and they chose to mourn privately…at least initially. They'd come by tomorrow to help with the arrangements.

Brenda looked at her watch. It was seven o'clock and already pitch-black outside. Daylight savings time was over—the sun was well over the horizon a few minutes after five. Brenda gazed often at the door, hoping that Mimi would come. As people paraded in and out, her hopes dwindled. She understood that Mimi might be with Afrika…sharing the bad news that her biological father was now a casualty. And to think, all of this might have been avoided if Mimi had never returned to Durham.

"Mother," Asia said, placing her arms around Brenda's neck and giving her a kiss.

This caught Brenda by surprise, given Asia's mood. But she realized that the young man standing next to her was the reason for Asia's newfound attitude.

"We're going outside for awhile. Do you remember Zavion?" Asia asked. "You met him at the hospital."

"Yes, but it was for only a brief moment. Thank you for coming by, Zavion."

"Thanks for having me, Mrs. Bailey. I wanted to come and support Asia."

"I'm glad you did. This is the first time she's had a smile on her first since this morning."

Asia kissed her mother again on the forehead, and Brenda watched as they walked outside and closed the door behind them. Now if only someone would come and lift Trevor's spirits.

All of a sudden there was a hushed silence in the house. Brenda heard someone say *oh my goodness* and one of her sisters admonishing the group to keep it low. Brenda picked up her unfinished plate on the coffee table, got up, and marched into the kitchen area where the majority of the folks were hanging out. She noticed that someone had turned on the flat-screen television that was embedded in one wall of the kitchen.

"What's going on?" Brenda asked as she watched the puzzled looks on the faces of those standing around her long granite table.

"The police have brought in a husband and wife for questioning in Victor's murder," Mabel said, not wanting to upset Brenda, who stood and stared. "The newscaster said they were persons of interest…"

"Well, who were they?" Brenda asked Mabel, as everyone stared in their direction.

"Your best friend, Mimi, and her husband," Mabel said and turned to put a piece of chicken on one of her small niece's plate.

Mabel and Tracey were on either side of Brenda, ready

to hold her up if needed. Brenda swallowed hard. Brenda's eyes pleaded for the truth. "Mimi? I don't believe it. I don't believe she would do it. Yes, she hated Victor, but not to the point that she'd commit murder. What else did they say?"

"Nothing, but I'm sure there will be more on the late-night news," Tracey said reassuringly. "Why don't you go and lay down."

"No, I need to talk to Mimi myself."

"Don't do this, Brenda," Mabel pleaded. "Let the police handle it. If Mimi didn't do it, the police will be the ones to find out." Mabel turned to the others. "Turn that TV off."

When Brenda looked up, Trevor was standing in the kitchen doorway, shaking. "Trevor, are you all right?" Brenda went to him and hugged him. "Baby, I'm sorry about your father."

Trevor looked at Brenda and the rest of the group whose attention was now on him. Even Asia and Zavion had come back inside and were standing behind Trevor, trying to assess what was going on.

"Trev, you okay?" Asia asked as well.

"Mom, they didn't kill Daddy," Trevor said.

"What are you talking about, Trevor?" Brenda asked with apprehension in her tone.

"She didn't do it. He didn't do it." Trevor seemed lost in a fog.

"Who didn't do it?" Asia cut in.

"Afrika's mother and father. I saw the whole thing."

"Slow your roll, Trevor," Brenda said, not understanding where Trevor was coming from. "You're obviously upset and not rational at the moment. I know you've been internalizing what's happened with your daddy—"

Tears erupted from Trevor's eyes, unable to hold them back any longer. He could barely speak. "A red Lexus drove up and stopped in front of my friend's house. A man got out of the car and Daddy was holding a gun to his head." Trevor wept but willed himself to go on. "The man kicked the gun away and knocked Dad to the ground, but the man ran away. Then…" Trevor looked up into Brenda's eyes, the tears streaming down his face. "Then…" Trevor looked away and tried to begin again. "Then Dad got up, picked up the gun, and chased the man. I guess Dad didn't catch up with him because he came back and busted into my friend's house, shouting obscenities at my friend's mother. He didn't even notice that I was there, standing on the porch, watching the whole thing go down.

"I didn't want to admit to my friend that I knew who Dad was so I didn't say anything. But we could hear everything that was going on inside the house. Dad and my friend's mother were cursing at each other, and then… and then Dad said she had given him AIDS."

Brenda, Mabel, Tracey, Asia, and everyone gasped at Trevor's words.

"What in the hell are you talking about, Trevor?" Aunt Mabel asked.

"You're lying, Trevor," Asia accused.

Trevor ignored Asia. His tears had eased up. "Dad accused the lady of giving him AIDS. He said another lady friend of his told him that she had HIV and had gotten it from him, which meant that Dad had gotten it from my friend's mother. My friend's mother slapped Dad, and he slapped her back. And that's when my friend ran into the house, pulled a lamp off of a table, and hit Dad in the back. Dad was about to pull the trigger when he saw me."

"You've got to report this to the police," Brenda said.

"He didn't kill Dad. He was alive. But I bet you can't guess what my friend said next."

Brenda looked perplexed. "What did he say?"

"My friend asked me why Dad was staring at me. I don't know where I got the courage to admit that he was my father. My friend looked at me like he didn't believe me. Then my friend asked how Dad could be my father when he was *his* father."

Everyone continued to stare at Trevor while the countenance on Brenda's face changed. Anger replaced concern and her fingers begin to curl along with the knot in her throat.

"That sorry-ass bastard got what he deserved," Brenda growled. "Let his momma take care of his funeral. For all I care, they can take his body and burn it up because he's going to burn up in hell anyway. Made a damn fool out of me." Then as if she had digested the words, Brenda began to scream and the tears fell along with it. "AIDS? My God, don't tell me…don't tell me…ah, ah, ah."

Brenda collapsed. Mabel and Tracey fell right beside her, fanning and asking folks to move back. Asia came and stood over her mother, pulling her hair and holding onto Zavion.

Zavion gave Trevor a strange look. He moved away from Asia and stood in front of Trevor. "Trevor, what is your friend's name?"

Trevor gave him a puzzled look. "His name is Freddie."

"Freddie Slater?" Zavion asked.

"Oh, no," Asia said out loud. "Tell me it ain't so."

"I wouldn't have that bastard for a father," Zavion said as he turned and looked at the shock on the faces of Asia's family members without offering any apologies. He looked at Asia and shook his head. "I'm sorry, Asia, but I didn't realize the man who's abused my mother for years was your father. Forgive me, but I can't stay. I've got to go see about my mother."

Asia stood as still as a statue. Her face was ashen like she'd seen a ghost. She watched as the door closed behind Zavion.

The room was numb with all that transpired. There was no movement, only silence until Trevor walked over and stood where Brenda now sat after recovering from her fainting spell, her sisters still fanning.

"Mom," Trevor began, as he choked on his words, "I hope you don't hold it against me, but I killed him."

61

If ever Mimi believed in miracles, she truly believed in them now. God had granted her family one of the greatest miracles she could've asked for. Afrika regained feeling in her lower extremities. She could wiggle her toes and move her legs, although she needed the aid of a walker to walk because her muscles were weak from days of lying in the bed.

Mimi and Raphael waited for her to return from the pool where her physical therapy was being conducted. It was a load off of their shoulders—the second in a matter of days.

"Mimi, if this is what putting your trust in the Lord is all about, I'm His," Raphael said.

Mimi couldn't hide the joy and the smile that took up half of her face. "God is so good. I can't begin to under-stand how bleak life looked when they told us at the police station that my gun was the weapon that killed Victor and that my car was used to transport him to where he was dumped...that the car had human blood all over the back seat." The smile faded and Mimi held Raphael's hand.

"If I hadn't been so pigheaded and gone out to Brenda's house that night, Victor might still be alive."

"But he kidnapped you, Raf. He's the one who took my gun and put it to your head and made you drive out to that woman's house."

"That's true, Mimi, but if I hadn't gone, we wouldn't have been involved. I put my family's life in jeopardy— you and Afrika are my whole world. I can honestly tell you that I was afraid...afraid that I was going to be locked up in that jail because the evidence was mounting against me."

"If I hadn't purchased that gun, there wouldn't have been a weapon."

"Don't beat yourself up, Mimi. If it wasn't your gun, it would've been something else. Victor was poison, and he was trying to get rid of it and everything that threatened him."

Mimi held her head down. She squeezed Raphael's hand tight and looked at the clock on the wall. "It's one o'clock. Victor's funeral should be over. I'm really sorry that I couldn't be there for Brenda. Too much bacteria has set in to ever heal the wounds of our lives. Even more, I hate that Asia blames Afrika for something that's not her fault. You didn't see them together, Raf. They were inseparable."

"Hopefully, time will heal."

"Maybe it will. Raf, I don't want to stay here. I've got to get as far away from Durham as possible. Too many memories, too many scars."

"What if Afrika wants to finish her education here?"

"Let's ask her," Mimi said as Afrika was being wheeled into the room.

"Ask me what, Daddy?"

"Afrika was a champion today," the nurse interjected, not realizing a family conversation was being had. She helped Afrika into bed and pulled the blanket over her. "She moved those legs in the water like a giant tadpole and she was able to walk with the walker about fifty yards, although I know it was a little painful and slow. But we're on the move."

"That is great," Mimi said, giving Afrika a great big hug, followed by Raphael.

"I want to thank the hospital personnel for all they've done for Afrika," Raphael said, stopping to give the nurse a hug. "We appreciate you so much."

"Afrika has the will to get better. We're only trying to help her capitalize on it. It's going to take some time, but I expect to see a full recovery. Well, I've got to move to my next patient."

"Thank you again," both Mimi and Raphael said.

"Ask me what, Mommy? You promised no more secrets."

Raphael took one of Afrika's hands. "Your mother wants to leave Durham as soon as you're able to get out of here. I know you're in the middle of your first semester at Central, and I'm sure you want to at least complete the year."

Afrika looked at her mother and father in thought. "Laying up in the bed has given me a lot of time to think about it. Too much has happened, and I don't think I could bear to live here another day without the constant memory of all that has happened. And anyway, I lost my best friend. It hurt the way Asia looked at me the moment she found out we were...we were sisters. I was flabbergasted like she was...I couldn't believe my ears." Afrika looked at Mimi and Raf. "I didn't ask to be Victor's daughter; I have a father."

"I'm sorry for how I acted," came the familiar voice from the doorway.

Mimi and Raphael spun around, while Afrika sat straight up and stared at their visitors. Coming through the doorway were Brenda and Asia. They wore identical black two-piece Ralph Lauren suits with French cuffs in satin crème accentuated by a small crystal rock that served as buttons.

"We're coming from the cemetery," Brenda said. "Asia wanted to stop and see Afrika on the way home."

"Thank you," Afrika said. "God has granted me another miracle."

"Another miracle?" Asia asked.

"Yes, I got the feeling back in my legs. I'm no longer paralyzed, although I'm not able to walk well without a walker. I got in the pool today, and the nurse said I'm on my way to recovery."

Asia walked to Afrika's bedside as Raphael moved aside. She sat on the side of the bed and rubbed Afrika's arm. "I don't want you to go anywhere. I've never had a sister...and one that's a best friend. Afrika, I freaked out when my mother was saying all of those things about Daddy...things I didn't believe to be true, and then to find out that you were my sister and how it happened... I couldn't take it.

"You won't believe this. Zavion's brother is also our brother."

"What?" Afrika hollered. "Is Zavion our brother, too?"

"Lucky for me, Zavion is not." Asia looked in Brenda's direction. "It seems that Zavion's mother was one of Daddy's conquests, and Zavion's brother, Freddie, is the result. It's hard to talk about it. But Zavion couldn't handle it. We haven't spoken to each other since Trevor broke the news to us about shooting Daddy."

"I'm so sorry, Asia," Afrika said.

"You don't have to be. I know it's wrong to speak ill of the dead; especially if they're your loved one, but if you live by the sword, you die by the sword. That's what the preacher said today. And from that moment, I knew I wanted to give my life to Jesus. I can't endure any more heartache and pain. So I'm asking you, sister, please stay at Central. I'd be lonely without you."

The uneasiness in the room lightened. Glances were passed throughout the room.

"If that's what you want to do, baby girl," Raphael said, "your mother and I are behind you."

Mimi smiled. "If that's what you want to do Afrika, I'm behind you as well."

Afrika sighed. "I had already made up my mind to leave."

"I know," Asia said. "I heard you when Mom and I came

through the door. Please don't let all that has happened drive you away."

"Like it did your mother," Brenda put in. "If she'd only told me all those years ago what I know now, I wouldn't have married Victor."

"But you wouldn't have had me or Trevor." Asia smiled.

"You're right," Brenda said. She turned to Mimi. "I'd like for you to stay in town, also. It would make me happy to become reacquainted with my best friend."

Mimi smiled. "That sounds nice. I'll have to give it some thought and talk it over with my other best friend." Mimi smiled at Raphael, her rock. "He's been everything to me, Brenda. I've been blessed."

"Well, you and Raphael talk. I'm praying that you'll have a change of heart and decide to stay in Durham. Mimi, we're like sisters, you and me; we've got a lot of history. The only thing I've got to figure out is how to save my son.

"Now, we better get back to our family. Mabel and Tracey are holding it down. They didn't want to go back to the church for repast. They are doing it up in the kitchen. Why don't you and Raphael stop by later on?"

"We'll be there," Raphael said.

Once again, all heads turned toward the door as it opened.

"Is this a family reunion?" John asked. "Just came to check on you all. I haven't seen you since that…that night, and after reading in the paper that you weren't in trouble, I thought I'd pay you a visit."

"Oh, I see," Raphael began. "Mimi, if you and I had been on lock down, behind prison bars, John here wasn't going to have anything to do with us."

"Man, you know it wasn't like that. I was letting you have your space. Too much going on for me to digest."

Everyone laughed. "It's all right, John," Mimi said. "You were there when it counted."

Raphael went to John and gave him a brother's handshake. "Yeah, John, thanks for being there for us. I know we got off on a rocky start, but you're all right."

Raphael and John bumped fists.

"Well, I'm going to go," Brenda said again. "Mimi, I'll see you and Raphael later. John, if you'd like to come by the house, you're welcome."

"Thanks, Brenda," John said. Then he reached out and gave her the biggest hug.

"If you want to go now, I'll stay with Afrika," Asia said. "We've got a lot of catching up to do."

Mimi looked up at the ceiling. "God, You are so good. I thank You for this day. And if Miss Afrika is all right, I guess we can go, Raf. John, you can ride with us. We're in a rental."

Raphael put his arm around Mimi. "After you, Brenda."

Afrika and Asia watched as their parents held each other and walked out of the room.

Asia laid her head on Afrika's shoulder. "Yes, God, You are good."

Afrika pointed her finger to the sky. "Yes, You are."

62

There was coldness and hardness in this new place called home. Trevor sat on the edge of the thin mattress collecting his thoughts, trying to figure out when he'd been driven to the edge to do the vile thing he had done. He knew the why, but when had his mind—the uncaring part of it—taken over and grabbed his conscience? His body jerked as he recalled the feel of the metal in his hand that ushered forth death when his mind had willed him to pull the trigger and fire.

Trevor's eyes roamed and scanned his surroundings that contained half of a bed he was used to sleeping in, a small latrine where privacy was at a premium, and a face bowl that would hold just enough water to splash on his face or in the words of his sister, Asia, take a hooker bath. No posters of the singers Beyonce and Rihanna adorned the walls nor were there pictures of LeBron and Kobe shooting hoops, Trevor's favorite pastime. Yes, he should be somewhere shooting hoops with his boys. College, he could forget it; no school was going to enroll a student who had been proclaimed a hardened criminal.

A shadow appeared on the floor in front of Trevor, reminding him that he was indeed in prison. He looked toward the neatly spaced bars that prevented him from enjoying his freedom. Blocking the small amount of light that penetrated his cell was a rough-looking character who flaunted several gold teeth in the front of his mouth and whose thin hair was twisted in what seemed like a million micro braids. The inmate grinned at Trevor, sizing him up as he gripped the bars of the cell.

"Yo blood, my name is Hammer. Heard you laid your daddy out."

"What's it to you?" Trevor said, the lines flat on his face.

"I need a young brother like you who ain't scared to take out the competition."

"I did what I had to do. I didn't like what I did, I'm not proud of what I did, but I'm not apologizing for it either."

"So you and your old man weren't down."

"That's between me, his soul, and the Lord."

"You got a lot of an…i…mosity, yeah, animosity clogging that mean heart of yours. I sure could use a mean spirit like you."

"I hated him, okay? Didn't deserve to live the way he treated my mother. Now leave me the hell alone."

"Deep, my brother. But let me give you a word of caution. You're in my house now, and I'm the daddy. Dudes here play by my rules. *Comprende?*"

"I'm not scared of you," Trevor said, still sitting on the cot. "Yeah, I took my daddy out, and I'll take you out, too, if you mess with me."

Hammer slid his hands slowly down the length of the bars. "It's your first day, so I'll pardon you this time. Remember this if you don't remember anything else. You may come from money on the outside but in here there's no position and no protection. I'm going to rob you of your soul until you get down on your knees and beg for my attention. Young blood, welcome to Central Prison."

Trevor watched as Hammer walked away, his swagger tight even though he wore an ugly orange jumpsuit. He felt the full breath of his words and he was afraid. Trevor lay back on the cot and cried for the first time since his father had died.

63

Loneliness was a bitter pill to swallow. Although the whole office had gone to Victor's funeral, Sheila felt alone, felt as if she was being judged. She watched as different ones looked in her direction, whispered among themselves like she was the cause of Victor's demise, or maybe it was her paranoia. Even Phyllis remained somewhat at a distance, not handing out the love and support she thought she deserved.

She didn't have to tell Jamal about her disease. The *News and Observer* announced it to the world. Even the fact that she was exonerated in Victor's death and in the shooting of Afrika Bailey, although the gun was definitely involved, the news was buried on page three of the local section of the paper. But oh her name, and that of several other mistresses of Mr. Victor Christianson, were on page one for all to see. But hers carried an extra caveat—*who announced she was HIV positive and Victor Christianson was the carrier.*

Sheila fingered the obituary. She opened it up half-expecting to see her name as one of his surviving family members. She chuckled at the thought, then threw the program down and got up to change her clothes. If nothing else, she looked good in her red Ralph Lauren suit, a last and final gift from the great Victor. Sheila chuckled again as she recalled how she looked down at him in disdain, laid out as if he really was somebody's somebody. "Ho."

Walking toward her bedroom, Sheila suddenly stopped and turned around. She crossed the length of her living room and stopped in front of the wall of shame. She ran her fingers over the holes that held the bullets that luckily didn't claim Victor's life. She remembered how he danced and dodged bullets, how he looked at her with that shocked expression on his face when she told him she was HIV positive, and the moment he cried because she had put a bullet hole in his jacket. Sheila laughed.

The doorbell rang. Sheila's eyes were wide with wonder. Who could it be? She hadn't even been invited to lunch with the others after Victor's service.

The doorbell rang again. Slowly, she moved toward the door almost afraid to answer, afraid that there would be more bad news. She looked through the peephole and her eyes widened.

With some apprehension, she opened the door and there stood Jamal. He was dressed in a black and white tweed jacket, a white shirt, and black slacks. In his hand, he held a beautiful bouquet of flowers and wore a warm smile on his face.

"For the lady of the house," Jamal said, handing the flowers to Sheila. "May I come in?"

"Sure. Yes, please come in."

"How are you doing?" Jamal asked.

Nerves were getting the best of Sheila. Her hand began to shake and Jamal rescued the flowers before she dropped them. "Excuse me, Jamal. It hasn't been a good day."

"Look, get a vase to put these flowers in."

Without a word, Sheila went into the kitchen and found a vase. Jamal followed her and once Sheila poured water into the vase, he set the flowers in it. He took Sheila's face in his hands and turned her around to face him.

"I've been doing a lot of thinking. I'll assume you found it hard to tell me you were HIV positive, but I knew before the papers published it."

Sheila's eyes grew large and tears began to fall.

"I waited for you to tell me, but when you didn't, my subconscious tried to tell me you weren't the woman for me. You are every woman, Sheila. You may have had your issues, but I found something in you that all the Victor Christiansons in the world didn't see. You have a heart and you do know how to love.

"When I found out you were in a relationship with this married man, I was ready to throw you to the wolves, but my heart wouldn't let me."

"When...when did you find out?" Sheila asked, her eyes searching his for a clue.

"I did a background check, and that's all I'm going to say."

"A background check? You didn't trust me?"

"No need to get upset. It served its purpose. You see, I was in love once a long time ago, and if I had known what I knew on our wedding day, I wouldn't have married her. I can't say that I was happy with this report either, but I knew there was more to you than what was written in that investigative report. What I'd like to know is do you still love me?"

"Jamal, the question is do you love me…after all you've discovered…HIV and all?"

Jamal looked at Sheila as if he was searching her soul. "Most brothers would kick you to the curb in a heartbeat, but I'm not most brothers—I'm not even the average brother." Sheila smiled. "I fell in love with you, and my love for you was real," Jamal continued. "I found it hard to just walk away…at least without talking with you. You are love, Sheila, and I want to help you through your situation. So, I've come here today to ask you a very pointed question."

Sheila was choked up and brushed tears from her eyes. "What is it?"

"Let's fly to Vegas tonight and get married." Jamal pulled back the lapel on his jacket and took an envelope out of his pocket. "See, I already have the plane tickets because I knew you were going to say yes."

"Oh my God," Sheila cried and she grabbed her face

and then hugged Jamal. "Vegas? To be married? I'm going to be Mrs. Sheila Billops? *Yes!* Yes, Jamal, I still want to be your wife. Let me pack a bag."

Jamal smiled, pulled Sheila to him, and kissed her greedily. Then he pulled away, holding her face in his hands. "No need to pack. I had a personal shopper pick up all of your favorite things and put them in a cute Louis Vuitton travel bag for you. It's already in the car."

Sheila gasped. "Are you for real? Jamal, I love you. I've waited for this day all my life."

"It's not going to always be peaches and cream, but I'll always love you and will forever be by your side."

"I can't ask for anything better than that."

"Well, let's go, the future Mrs. Billops. And while you're at it, you can throw that obituary in the trash."

"It's done."

ABOUT THE AUTHOR

Suzetta Perkins is the author of *Behind the Veil; A Love So Deep; EX-Terminator: Life After Marriage; Déjà Vu, Nothing Stays the Same* and a contributing author of *My Soul to His Spirit.* A native of Oakland, California, Suzetta resides in Fayetteville, North Carolina. Suzetta is the co-founder and president of the Sistahs Book Club and Secretary of the University at Fayetteville State University. She is a member of New Visions Writing Group in Raleigh, North Carolina, and a mentor for aspiring writers. Visit www.suzettaperkins.com, www.myspace.com/authorsue, www.facebook.com/suzetta.perkins, and email nubianqe2@aol.com.